TEN THOUSAND SKIES ABOVE YOU

Also by Claudia Gray

EVERNIGHT

STARGAZER

HOURGLASS

AFTERLIFE

BALTHAZAR

FATEFUL

SPELLCASTER

STEADFAST

SORCERESS

A THOUSAND PIECES OF YOU

A MILLION WORLDS WITH YOU

TEN THOUSAND SKIES ABOVE YOU

—A FIREBIRD NOVEL—

CLAUDIA GRAY

HarperTeen is an imprint of HarperCollins Publishers.

Ten Thousand Skies Above You

For information address HarperCollins Children's Books, a division of HarperCollins Publishers, 195 Broadway, New York, NY 10007.
www.epicreads.com

Library of Congress Cataloging-in-Publication Data
Gray, Claudia.
Ten thousand skies above you / Claudia Gray. — First edition.
pages cm
Sequel to: A thousand pieces of you.
Summary: As eighteen-year-old Marguerite struggles to get to the heart of the corrupt company that almost killed her father, she tries to save the boy she loves, whose soul is scattered in various dimensions.
ISBN 978-0-06-227900-2
[1. Space and time—Fiction. 2. Adventure and adventurers—Fiction. 3. Love—Fiction. 4. Science fiction.] I. Title.
PZ7.G77625Tj 2015 2014047816
[Fic]—dc23 CIP
AC

Typography by Torborg Davern

19 20 PC/LSCH 10 9 8 7 6 5 4
❖
First paperback edition, 2016

1

THE FIRST TIME I TRAVELED TO ANOTHER DIMENSION, I intended to take a life. Now I'm trying to save one.

But I can't do that unless I save myself. At the moment, I'm running through the winding streets of a near-medieval Rome, trying not to get burned at the stake.

Welcome to the nonstop fun of traveling through alternate universes.

"She is the sorcerers' daughter!" someone from the mob shouts. "She bears the tools of their witchcraft!" Her voice echoes off the cobblestones, just like the jeers from the crowd around her. A few of them hold burning torches, the better to chase me through the night.

My parents are scientists, not sorcerers. In this universe, looks like nobody knows the difference.

What I'm carrying in the pockets of my robe or cloak or whatever you'd call this shapeless red thing—it's not witchcraft. It's a spyglass, a.k.a. a primitive handheld telescope. This six-inch-long gadget looks like a prop for steampunk cosplay: tortoiseshell sides, brass fittings, lenses ground by hand. But this might just be the tool that brings this dimension out of the Dark Ages—assuming it doesn't get my entire family killed first.

Panting, I dodge around every corner I come to, paying no attention to where I'm going. It's not like I have any idea where I am anyway. When I leap into one of my other selves—the other Marguerites, who live in these parallel dimensions—I don't get to access their memories. Some of their knowledge and ability carries over, but those are only the deeper, no-longer-wholly-conscious things. Knowing where the hell I am in this version of Rome? No such luck.

All I know is that I have to get away. Finding the Castel Sant'Angelo—and Paul, who should be there—well, that has to wait until I'm safe.

Of course, I could escape this dimension at any moment, thanks to the heavy weight on a chain around my neck. To anyone in this dimension, and virtually anyone in ours, it would look like nothing more than a large, fairly elaborate locket—if they even noticed it, which they probably wouldn't.

This isn't any old necklace. This doesn't belong in their reality. This is the Firebird.

The Firebird—the one and only device that allows human consciousness to travel through alternate dimensions. The invention of my mother, Dr. Sophia Kovalenka, with the help of my father, Dr. Henry Caine. The thing that can instantly transport my mind out of this universe completely and send me back to my own body, my own home, and safety. Even as I run through an alternate Rome in an ankle-length woolen dress and cloak, my stiff boots sliding against the rain-wet cobblestones on the road, I keep the Firebird clutched in one hand; if I lose this thing, I'm screwed.

But I won't go. I can't leave this dimension until I do what I came here to do.

I must save Paul Markov.

A couple more twists and turns through dark alleyways, and I finally manage to lose the mob. Although I can still hear murmuring and shouting in the distance, I have a moment to catch my breath. The frantic thumping of my heart begins to slow. My back is to a wall the color of terra-cotta; the only illumination comes from a few lanterns and candles visible through windows that have no glass. And, of course, the stars. I look upward, momentarily dazzled by how many more stars you can see in a sky unclouded by artificial light.

The view around me could have been taken from any one of a hundred early Italian paintings I've studied. This is a world without electricity, where only fire shows the way after dark. A cart pulled by a donkey rattles along in the distance, stacked high with bags of something, probably grain. Forget Wi-Fi, tablet computers, or airplanes—here, even steam engines are centuries away. It's not that I've traveled back in time, though; the Firebirds don't do that. But some dimensions develop faster, some slower. I've already been to futuristic worlds where everyone communicates by hologram and travels by hovership. It was only a matter of time before I reached one where the Renaissance is still in full swing.

Not that this is exactly the same as our Renaissance: The clothing looks more like tenth or eleventh century to me, and yet the telescope my parents have invented didn't come into being in our world until long after that. Also, somehow, there doesn't seem to be any old-fashioned gender roles in place, or any gender roles at all. The priest who condemned me to the mob was a woman. I'll cheer for equality later.

The man I spoke to told me I could find Paolo Markov of Russia at the Castel Sant'Angelo. I imagine Paul chained in a castle dungeon, being beaten or even tortured, and I want to cry.

This is no time for tears. Paul needs me. Crying can happen later.

And once I've handled everything else, I'll deal with Wyatt Conley.

The angry buzz of the crowd has faded. Where do I go now? I'm surrounded by dark, twisting alleys and a jumble of buildings filled with people I can't trust. They said the Castel Sant'Angelo was to the west, but which way is west? Without the sun in the sky for me to judge by, I can't guess what direction to go in. Still, I have to begin somewhere. One more deep breath, and I start toward a narrow street that leads down a seemingly quiet road—

—then gasp as a hand closes over my shoulder.

"Not that way," a woman whispers. A noblewoman, I realize, her face all but hidden under her blue velvet cloak. "They may gather near the Pantheon."

I don't know what that is, but if the mob is going to be there, I'll head in another direction. "Thanks."

(The above conversation? Not verbatim. Both my new friend and I are speaking what I have to assume is either late-stage Latin or early Italian. I don't know what it is exactly, but thanks to the deeply ingrained knowledge of this world's Marguerite, I speak it.)

"Your parents are leading us to wisdom," the noblewoman says gently. "The others fear what they do not understand."

She steps forward, just enough for some of the dim lighting to illuminate her face—thick golden hair, strong square jaw—and it's all I can do not to gape at her.

We've met before.

Her name is Romola. If I ever knew her last name, I've forgotten it. I encountered her in the very first alternate universe I ever visited: a futuristic London where she was the daughter of a duchess. Spoiled, rich, high on drugs, and drunk on champagne—Romola dragged me from nightclub to nightclub while I drank as much as she did. I was exhausted, afraid, and heartsick; it was only two days after the police told my family that my father had died. Dad turned out to be fine—well, if "fine" includes "kidnapped into an alternate dimension." But I didn't know that at the time. So those surreal, sick, miserable hours with Romola loom larger in my mind than they should. It seems like I knew her forever, not just for one weird day.

I shouldn't be surprised to see her again. We've learned that people usually cross paths in many dimensions—that no matter how different the worlds may be, fate draws us together.

"Are you well?" Romola puts one hand to my forehead, like my mom did when I was little. "You seem dazed. No one could blame you, after what they've put you through."

"I'm fine. Really." I pull myself together for the rest of my escape. "I need to get to the Castel Sant'Angelo. Which way should I go?"

Romola gives me directions. Most of the landmarks she names are unknown to me (Via Flaminia?), but she points along the road. I thank her and wave as I start running again.

At home, I think I could run a few miles without getting winded. This Marguerite doesn't seem to get as much exercise. A stitch makes my gut clench; my breaths are coming too fast. Despite the cool air of early April, sweat slicks my skin. These thick woolen clothes feel as if they're loaded with weights. And my boots—let's just say shoemaking technology is a whole lot better at home. The blisters already swell at my heel and toes.

But I have to reach Paul as fast as I can. He could be in terrible danger—

Or he could be fine. Maybe he's one of the castle guards. He could even be a prince! You'll probably interrupt him at a banquet or something.

How long has he been here? We tried not to panic when

he hadn't returned to our dimension after twenty-four hours; after forty-eight hours, we all knew something was wrong. We got really afraid when we searched for him in the Triadverse and realized he'd left but hadn't come back home. Mom and Theo outdid themselves, coming up with a way to trace Paul's next leap, which was into this dimension.

Paul had no reason to come here. If he'd found what he was looking for—the cure for Theo—he would have come straight home. That was how we knew he'd been kidnapped. I haven't been able to sleep since.

Just get him back. We'll figure the rest out later—how to save Theo, how to defeat Triad. That can all wait until you bring Paul home.

I know the Castel Sant'Angelo as soon as I see it: an enormous stone structure at the top of a hill, lit by blazing torches. The firelight reveals the dull black gleam of cannons jutting from slots in the masonry. As I walk up, I see that the palace guards wear outfits simultaneously hilarious and intimidating: full striped breeches, brilliant yellow coats with puffy sleeves, metal breastplates and helmets, and swords that look like they could run through a human being in an instant. Although the soldiers come to attention as I step closer, obviously a winded teenage girl isn't their idea of a threat.

What if Paul's a prisoner here? I have no idea how the guards are going to react, but there's only one way to find out. A couple of deep breaths, and then I say as firmly as I can manage, "I've come to speak to Paul Markov of Russia."

The guards look at each other and say nothing. Crap. Should I have called him Paolo, the Italian version of the name? Or Pavel, the Russian version? Or maybe he is a prisoner—or he isn't actually here at all—

"Follow me," says one of the guards. "You can wait in the usual room."

The usual room? I have to stifle a smile as I follow them to a small, stone-walled chamber. Of course Paul and I know each other in this world too.

Always, we find each other.

In my world, Paul is one of my parents' research assistants as he works on his doctorate at Berkeley. For the first year and a half I knew him, I mostly thought he was strange: silent, awkward, too big for any room he was in. When he did speak, he was blunt. Most of the time he didn't speak at all. But as time went on, I began to realize that his bluntness wasn't him being rude or unkind—that instead it was a rough kind of honesty, sometimes hard to hear but always true. His awkwardness was only shyness, Paul's belief that he had never fit in anywhere and never would. And the way he hung around my parents' house wasn't because he had no life and nowhere else to go. It was because nobody had ever accepted him before. He'd never been around a family who cared about each other, never had a real friend before he met my parents' other assistant, Theo.

And he had never fallen in love before he knew me. He just didn't know how to say it.

I've visited a few dozen dimensions by now. Paul and I

have known each other in most of them; in many, we're already together. Fate and mathematics bring us to each other time after time. Paul's doctoral thesis presents a series of equations that prove destiny is real . . . but I don't need the math to convince me. I've seen it for myself so many times, beginning in a Russia where the tsars never fell.

For a moment I think of Lieutenant Markov, the Paul I knew there, and my throat tightens. But that's when a figure in a dark cloak appears in the stone archway of the room.

Paul steps forward, looking at me so sadly that I ache for him without even knowing why. "You know you should not have come," he says softly.

"I had to."

Bluffing your way through alternate dimensions can sometimes be tricky. When in doubt, remain silent as long as you can, and let the natives do the talking.

And right now I'm only speaking to this world's Paul. A few cues tip me off to the differences—subtle things anyone else might miss, like the way he walks, or his ease in this medieval chamber. My Paul's consciousness—his soul—must be within this body, but semiconscious, unable to act, unable to think, hardly even able to remember. For the time being, he's forgotten himself. That's what happens to most people when they travel through the dimensions: they become absorbed into their other selves, unable to escape, or even think that they should escape.

It's like a fairy tale in reverse. The prince is the one asleep in a glass coffin. I'm the one who'll awaken him.

If only a kiss would work.

Paul steps closer to me, and the flickering lanterns paint his face in golden light. He's a big man, almost intimidatingly so—six foot two and broad-shouldered. This version isn't as powerfully muscled, or maybe I just can't tell beneath the black robes he wears.

Wait. Are these *priest's robes*?

"I have prayed and prayed," Paul whispers. His gray eyes search mine, and I wish I didn't recognize how lost he looks. How alone. "Surely I cannot abandon the vows I made to God. And yet if he did not want me to marry as other men do—to feel desire, and love—why would he have brought me to you?"

Even without knowing any more of the story, this is enough to make me melt. This world's Marguerite must be as in love with him as he is with her, or else they wouldn't have had this conversation before. That makes it okay for me to say, "We're brought together by a power greater than either of us. Something bigger than our own world."

It's not just a romantic saying; it's scientific fact.

Paul breathes out heavily like a man struggling. I wonder what his life has been like here—born in Russia, surely. Back in the Middle Ages, lots of children were more or less given to the church when they were small, so they had no real choice about whether to enter the priesthood or convent or whatever; if Paul's already taken vows one month after his twentieth birthday, that must be what happened to him. Perhaps he traveled to Rome to serve the pope. Then he met the inventors' daughter, and everything changed.

I hope this world's Paul and Marguerite will get their chance to be together. At any other time, I'd be tempted to stay here longer and help if I could. For now, though, nothing matters as much as rescuing my Paul and bringing him home.

"Paul?" I step closer to him. The firelight catches the faint reddish tint in his pale brown hair. "Come here."

"We shouldn't," he says, like a man who desperately wishes we would.

"Not for that. It's all right." I lift my eyes to his and smile as gently as I can. "Trust me."

At that Paul straightens, nods, and closes the distance between us. It would be so easy to hold him, for him to put his arms around me—

—but instead, when my hand brushes against his chest, I feel metal under the cloth. I reach beneath the collar of his robes and pull out his Firebird.

He still has it? I'd brought a second one with me, believing Conley would have stolen Paul's. Maybe it's broken. That would explain a lot.

Paul stares at the necklace he just discovered hanging against his chest. To him it must have seemed to appear by magic. Obviously he can't imagine what I'm up to, but he remains silent, trusting me completely. That makes it a little harder to manipulate the Firebird controls into the combination for a reminder. Because reminders *hurt*.

Paul shouts in pain and jerks backward. But this is the part where my Paul wakes up inside him, when we're together again and we can go back home.

Except that the reminder doesn't work.

"Why did you do that?" Father Paul lifts the Firebird and frowns. "What manner of device hangs around my neck?"

He doesn't know. He really has no idea. Nothing like this has ever happened before. How could a reminder just . . . not work?

I run one hand through my curly hair, thinking fast. "It's my parents' latest invention. It wasn't supposed to hurt you—probably it's broken. Here, let me have it."

Paul hands it back, still trusting me, but now wary of the Firebird itself. I don't blame him. If only I were another science geek instead of the artist in the family, because then maybe I could fix this on my own. As it is, I might have to go home without Paul. Even though I know I could come back for him, maybe in only a few minutes, I can't bear the thought of losing him again.

You're the scientific wonder of the twenty-first century! I think as I look down at the Firebird. *How can you go dead on me now?* Maybe Conley broke it. But why bother breaking the Firebird when he could have stolen it for his own use?

The Firebird hasn't gone dead. It isn't broken. Every control reads normal. Yet when I double-check, I see that the Firebird is showing a reading I've never seen before.

Another man steps into the room, and my eyes go wide.

"Allow me to interpret it for you," he says with a smirk. "That's what splintering looks like."

His red robes look as if they belong in this strange medieval world, but his face is familiar. Too familiar.

Fate and mathematics don't only bring you back to the people you love. They can also bring you to the people you hate.

In this world, they brought me back to Wyatt Conley.

2

WHO IS WYATT CONLEY, AND WHY IS HE SUCH A SON OF A bitch?

My parents explained the situation pretty well the day after I brought my father back home from our first adventure through the dimensions. That night we'd all been crying and happy and too freaked out to even think; then, once we woke up, we couldn't stop talking about our adventures—everything we'd seen and done. Everyone we'd been.

That morning, it turned out, the physics faculty was holding a departmental meeting. Mom said that was as good a place to begin explaining as any, so my parents, Paul, Theo, and I headed to the university. As usual, I felt out of place as we walked through the hallways of the physics building. It's like you can almost *smell* the math.

All of us went in together, interrupting the meeting in progress. All the science professors seated around the long oval table sat upright and stared.

"Forgive our lateness," my mother said. Even in her faded cardigan and mom jeans, she was immediately the person in charge. Mom has this effect on people. "I need to raise an urgent issue not on the agenda, namely Triad Corporation's role in funding research into the Firebird device."

"As in, they shouldn't have one anymore," Theo chimed in. "We need to be independent from them, *now*."

Dad stepped forward. "Triad has brought agents from another dimension into our own. These agents have been spying on us and attempting to direct and control our progress with the Firebirds. Their CEO, Wyatt Conley himself, is deeply involved in this—orchestrating it, even—in both worlds. To this end, he altered my daughter Marguerite's dimensional resonance so that she can travel more effectively than anyone else in this world."

Mom's eyes flashed with anger as she cut in. "The procedure only works once in a dimension. By choosing our daughter, putting her in this dangerous position, Conley thought he could control us."

"Conley also hoped to blackmail Marguerite into working for him, operating as his spy in countless dimensions. That's why I was kidnapped into an alternate universe in the first place," Dad said.

A silence followed. Everyone in the room just kept staring at us, this sea of huge eyes behind thick glasses. I wondered, *Do they think my parents have finally lost their minds?* The events Mom and Dad had just talked about sounded pretty fantastical, but every physicist in this department (and probably the world) knew that my parents were on the verge of a breakthrough—that dimensional travel was going to become a reality.

Then Theo held up his hands in the time-out signal. "Uh, we probably ought to back this up. Turns out the Firebirds work! Dimensional travel is possible! I guess technically Dr. Caine went first, then Paul, and then Marguerite—but the point is, we've tested the devices. The Firebird is a success. Yeah, we should've led with that."

"Not that," Paul said, expression grim.

I realized what he was getting at, and my eyes went wide. *Uh-oh.*

Paul stepped forward and said, as formally as if he were defending his dissertation, "We should have first informed you that Dr. Caine is alive."

"Oh!" Dad said, as Mom put her hand to her mouth. "Right! Thought that was sort of obvious—but ought to have gone over it anyway. I'm not dead! Body not lost at sea or in the river, wherever it was supposed to be. I'd been kidnapped into another dimension instead. Left out that important detail, didn't we?"

"Also, most of you will have heard that I killed Dr. Caine, when in fact I was framed for the crime. I am not guilty," Paul continued. Then, with a glance at my dad, he finished, "Obviously."

"Because I'm alive." Dad clapped his hands together, amused and embarrassed at the same time. "Of course. No wonder you're all startled, since to you it's like I just rose from the grave! Can't say I blame you. We ought to have phoned a few people when I got back last night, but we got a bit carried away there, with the reunion and all. But no, I'm not dead. I'm absolutely fine. Never better." The professors in front of us remained still, and I realized several of them were pale with shock. My father broke the awkward silence. "So, how are all of you? Ah, Terry! Changed your hair, I see. Looking good."

That was when someone fainted.

Believe it or not, that has to count as a positive reaction. For years, the scientific community wrote off my parents as lunatics; a lot of people would like to do that again. Their colleagues finally accepted that cross-dimensional travel might be possible—but spies from other worlds? Wyatt Conley, inventor and entrepreneur, the mastermind behind a mysterious plot? Triad makes the most advanced personal electronics in the world, and sells them in stores you can find in any shopping center. Their cheery ads and emerald-green signs don't seem like they'd belong to the front company for a James Bond–esque supervillain. And what was Conley supposed to have done to me? "Changed" me? "Blackmailed" me? Why would a powerful billionaire ever need to blackmail an average eighteen-year-old girl?

Or so the thinking goes.

After the paramedics revived Professor Xavier, my parents, Theo, and Paul had to answer questions from the physics faculty for almost three hours. The president of the university has pleaded with Mom and Dad not to issue any public statements about the Firebird project for the time being. So far they've agreed, even though reporters have kept calling, and their questions have become more pointed, suggesting the public mood has shifted from breathless anticipation to doubt. Wyatt Conley hasn't made any public statements either. As far as anyone in the general public knows, he's still going about his usual routine, a thirty-year-old CEO who wears jeans instead of stuffy suits. His boyish face grins from beneath his curly auburn hair on the covers of business magazines. He even agreed to continue providing funding for my parents' research going forward—or so he told the dean, who passed this info along to us probably hoping we'd decide we were just being paranoid jerks about the guy.

The other side of Conley lies just beneath that glossy surface.

Not long after that meeting with the physics department, we got our first visit from the general counsel of Triad Corporation.

Her name was Sumiko Takahara. If Wyatt Conley ran a global business while wearing blue jeans, it was because he had people like this behind him—armored with business suits and legalese. Ms. Takahara stood in our house as if she couldn't believe she'd been sent on an errand this pedestrian; no doubt she spent more time suing megacorporations than talking to academics seated around a table that had been painted in rainbow swirls by me and Josie when we were little kids. Despite this, her professional demeanor never faltered.

"The folders before you represent Mr. Conley's best offer," she said. Her gray business suit had a slight glimmer to it, like the skin of a shark. "You'll find paperwork regarding several Swiss bank accounts, one for each of you. The amounts of money within—"

"Would stun a maharaja," Theo finished for her, then whistled, like, *wow*. Paul shot him a look, and Theo shrugged. "It's true."

Ms. Takahara seemed encouraged. "If Miss Caine will accept Triad's offer of employment, I'm instructed to turn these accounts over to you, effective immediately."

My mother handed her folder back unopened. "In other words, this is the price Wyatt Conley has set on our daughter," she said. "His offer is declined."

The chill in Mom's voice would've cooled Siberia in winter. To Ms. Takahara's credit, she wasn't fazed. Instead, she looked at me. "The offer is Miss Caine's to accept or refuse."

I slid my folder across the table, back to the lawyer. "Then tell Mr. Conley that Miss Caine refuses."

Finally Ms. Takahara hesitated. She couldn't have seen many people turn down that kind of money. "Is that all you have to say in reply?"

I thought it over. "You can also tell Conley to bite me."

So that's how *that* conference ended.

Ms. Takahara brought the next offer directly to my parents at the university, supposedly for them to pass along to me. But Conley was trying to bribe them with something they'd value far more than money—this time, he promised information.

"All the research from the Triadverse's Firebird project," my mother said that night as we stood in line for pizza at the Cheese Board Collective. "He promised he would share everything they'd learned so far. Experimental data, theoretical work, every bit of it."

That research had won the Triadverse version of my mother a Nobel Prize. "What did you guys say?

"Honestly, the nerve of the man. The Triadverse is only a few years ahead of us. We'll catch up." In her calm, precise voice, my mother added, "Therefore we told Conley to stuff it."

I wanted to laugh, but I couldn't help thinking that Conley had baited his hook more intelligently this time. For my parents, new knowledge would be the greatest temptation of all. "Are you sure? You guys would learn a lot."

"Marguerite, we never considered it for an instant." Mom pulled my arms around her so that I was hugging her from behind. Her hands squeezed mine. "It wouldn't matter if Wyatt Conley offered us the theory of everything, with cold fusion as the cherry on top. Nothing matters more than you girls. And there's not one piece of information more important than our love for you."

I embraced her more tightly, and didn't worry about Conley any more that evening.

Conley, however, was not done worrying about us. Nearly

six weeks ago, he sent Ms. Takahara back to us. This time, she didn't bother smiling.

"Mr. Conley has improved his offer," she began.

"You said his last offer was his 'best offer,'" Paul pointed out.

"He has reconsidered, and encourages you to do the same. I've been instructed not to accept any final answer from you today." Ms. Takahara didn't make eye contact with anyone at the rainbow table; if she had, she'd have seen her "final answer" written all over our faces. Instead, she continued, "Take your time. Look this over, and discuss it among yourselves. For the time being, Mr. Conley intends to allow you to conduct your research in peace. He asks that you show him the same courtesy. To clarify, he requests that you refrain from traveling to the dimension corresponding to the coordinates in the document before you, henceforth referred to as the Triadverse. Not only would this violate his request, but he warns that the consequences could also be dangerous."

"Dangerous in scientific terms?" Paul asked. "Or is Conley merely threatening us?"

"I don't pass along *threats*," Ms. Takahara huffed. Probably she thought she was telling the truth. Conley might have told her about dimensional travel, but there was no way he'd explained the full story. "Instead I have shared an extraordinarily generous offer from Triad Corporation. Consider it at your leisure. When Mr. Conley is ready to hear your answer, I'll be back in touch."

After she left, Mom, Dad, Paul, and Theo got into a long, intense discussion about what Conley might do after he finally realized I'd never agree to work for him.

"After the carrot comes the stick," Dad said. They got to work then on superior tracking technology for the Firebirds, so that if Conley tried kidnapping any of us into another dimension again, we could find that person easily, tracing their jumps through the universes no matter how long or complicated the trail might become. Paul and Theo's pet project was working up a way of monitoring Conley's cross-dimensional activity; the day might come, Paul said, when we'd need to report Conley to the authorities.

"What authorities?" I asked. Pretty sure the local cops don't have the power to arrest people in other dimensions. "The FBI? Interpol?"

"Jurisdiction is unclear," Paul admitted. His hand closed over mine, warm and reassuring. "But if he threatens you, we'll do whatever it takes to keep you safe."

I hugged him then, though at that point I felt safe enough. And Conley's "terms" were easy enough. It's not as though I was in some huge hurry to go back to the Triadverse, to revisit the Theo who deceived us all.

(Or the Londonverse, where my other self drank too much, partly to kill the memory of Mom, Dad, and Josie dying in a horrible accident. Or the Oceanverse, which was actually a pretty cool place, but where I am probably criminally liable for wrecking a submarine. The Russiaverse—where I was the Grand Duchess Margarita, and Lieutenant Paul Markov was my personal guard and secret love—that world, I would return to. I haven't, though. Going there again would mean revisiting that Paul's death.)

But Conley knew something we didn't. He knew we'd be compelled to return to the Triadverse soon, that we'd break the truce no matter what.

He knew what was about to happen to Theo.

3

"YOU TRICKED US," I SAY TO CONLEY AS THE THREE OF US stand together in this stone room, in an Italian castle a world away. Paul looks from Wyatt Conley to me in confusion. "Saying you'd let us 'think it over'—"

"I did, didn't I? You had weeks." Conley straightens the red robes he wears as if he's proud of them. "Then Paul Markov came to my dimension, even though you were warned it would be dangerous. He's paying the price. It's as simple as that."

My dimension, he said. That means this is the Triadverse Conley I'm dealing with. Not that it makes much difference; the two Conleys work together, forming a conspiracy of one.

"Cardinal Conley—I don't understand." This world's Paul looks hopelessly bewildered, and no wonder. "What law have I broken?"

Conley smiles, all grace and benevolence. "This is between

me and your lady fair, Father Paul. You can speak with her later. At the moment, she and I need to have a private conversation."

Paul steps between us. It's more obvious than ever how much taller he is than Conley, how much stronger. "You can't blame her for my weakness. I alone am responsible."

Is he amazing in every universe? I place one hand on Paul's back, a small touch meant to say *thank you*.

However, Conley remains in faux-kindly mode. "She won't be punished. More than that, I hear her parents have been condemned for their studies by some of the local priests. Tonight I shall tell Her Holiness to officially declare them under her protection. You see? All will be well. Now go."

When Paul hesitates anyway, I murmur, "It's all right. I'll talk to you soon. Con . . . the cardinal and I don't have much to say to each other."

At last Paul turns to go, with one last look at me filled with such longing that my heart turns over. No sooner has he walked out, however, than Conley starts to laugh. "Oh, Marguerite. You and I have *so much* to say."

"What did you do to him?" I demand. "I tracked Paul here from your universe. I gave him a reminder, and the Firebird seems like it worked—"

"Inconvenient, isn't it? The way most people forget themselves between dimensions. You don't appreciate your gift."

That's how it is for virtually everyone who travels through the multiverse. Without constant reminders, they quickly become silent, passive witnesses as those dimensions' selves take over again. For Mom and Dad's purposes, this doesn't matter; the travelers remember everything they experienced through their "other selves" in each world. As long as you have your Firebird to remind you, you can still get back home and analyze what you learned.

But as I discovered on my first voyage, there are serious flaws in this procedure. For instance, you can lose a Firebird. It can be broken or stolen. And if you haven't got your Firebird to remind you of yourself, then you'll remain in that alternate dimension, within that other self—unconscious, paralyzed, and trapped—forever.

That's why it would help to have a "perfect traveler," someone who always remembered who she was, who remained in control no matter what.

So Triad turned me into one.

I still don't exactly understand what it was that was done to me. The device Triad loaned us seemed like any other piece of scientific equipment, and all I felt when the conversion happened was a moment of dizziness. Paul and my parents have explained it to me a dozen times, but it's the kind of explanation you need a graduate degree in physics to fully understand.

All I know is that I can go to any dimension and remain in total control. Where to go, who to see, what to do: It's entirely up to me. I also know that you can create only one traveler like me in any given universe. (Apparently, creating more than one exception to the laws of physics can seriously destabilize reality.)

But I still don't understand why Wyatt Conley makes such a big deal out of it. "Other people can travel through dimensions! Okay, so, it's more of a hassle. It doesn't matter. You'll use Nightthief on anyone—you proved that much. And you can travel as well as I can, so you can run your own creepy errands! So why do you keep after me?"

"Important work is coming." Conley's smile fades. "Tricky work, some of it in universes I can't reach. Triad needs you on our side, and soon. Be fair—I tried gentler persuasion, didn't I? If you work with me, you'll be rewarded beyond your wildest dreams. But it looks as though more extreme measures are necessary to get you on board."

"Like kidnapping Paul into this dimension, just like you did my dad?"

To my surprise, Conley shakes his head. The flickering orange light of the torches casts eerie shadows on his face. "Not exactly. This time, I've given you a challenge."

"You mean, because the reminder didn't work." How was Conley able to prevent my Paul from waking up? The Firebird seems to be functioning normally, except for this strange, unique reading I don't understand.

Conley walks to the arched window and looks out, though in a world without electricity the view isn't much to speak of. Moonlight paints the city dimly, a sprawl of buildings beneath the high hill of the castle. He says, "I told you already, but I suspect you were too upset to listen."

"Told me what?"

He turns back to me, once again cocky as he leans against

the stone wall, arms folded across his chest. "Haven't your parents discovered the danger yet? The possibility of splintering?"

My parents have never said word one about "splintering," unless they were talking about literal splinters to be removed with tweezers. I open my mouth to tell Conley to stop playing games—

—before realizing my parents *did* talk about this. They didn't have a name for it yet, but they'd glimpsed the danger. But we'd had no idea how close that danger really was.

Did that conversation happen only five nights ago? It feels like long, hard years have passed since then.

"We ought to have recognized the potential before," my mother said, talking about what I now know is called splintering. "Consciousness is energy. Energy consists of packets of quanta. It stands to reason that those packets could become . . . disassociated."

"Fragmented," Paul said, his mood black. "The danger—"

"Is remote," my father cut in. The three of them were seated around the rainbow table, piles of paper and a glowing laptop evidence that they were hard at work, even after dinner on a weekend.

Normally, Theo would have been working alongside them, but it was my turn to do the dishes, and he'd volunteered to help. Still, he couldn't resist weighing in. "Are you sure of that, Henry?"

"Incredibly sure. The odds against it are staggering. You'd

almost have to do it on purpose, not that anyone's likely to try such a damn fool thing." Dad began typing on the laptop with such gusto that I knew he was trying to find something similarly unlikely to compare it to.

"Great," Theo muttered as he dried the salad spoons. "Like the Firebirds needed to get any more dangerous."

I tried to reason with him. "You're like one of those people who's more scared of flying than driving, even though you're way more likely to die in a car."

"Yeah, but if I'm in my 1981 Pontiac, at least I'm going out in style," he said, and I laughed.

Paul, from his place at the far side of the great room with my parents, shot me a look—not jealous, but hopeful. He wants things back to normal with Theo. That has always meant laughter.

The two of them have always been such good friends. They seem to have so little in common besides their interest in physics: Paul in his plain secondhand clothes, clueless about pop culture, while Theo wears fedoras and Mumford & Sons T-shirts. Yet they're both young for doctoral students: Theo is twenty-two, and Paul just turned twenty. They both believed in Mom and Dad's Firebird project when few others did. And they became a part of our weird little family. During that time—while everyone was involved with rewriting the laws of the natural universe as we knew them—emotions got confused.

("We ought to have expected it," my mother said the first time I talked to my parents about all this. "Isolating individuals for long periods of time, away from any other likely romantic partners, particularly at this highly active stage of sexual development—strong emotional bonds were all but inevitable."

"We don't care about each other only because we spent so much time together!" I protested.

"Of course not, sweetheart." Dad patted my hand. "Still, you have to admit it *helped*.")

Both Paul and Theo fell in love with me. I fell in love with Paul.

It's not that I don't care about Theo; I do, deeply. I'd be lying if I said I hadn't been attracted to him sometimes. For a brief time—when Paul had been framed for my father's murder, and I was sick with grief and betrayal—I wondered whether Theo wasn't the one for me after all.

But Paul and I came back to each other. And Theo was left on the outside looking in. Even though all three of us know nobody did anything wrong in this scenario, both Paul and I haven't been able to help feeling awkward when Theo sees us together.

That night, however, I could almost believe nothing had changed. Our house in the Berkeley Hills looked exactly the same, with houseplants in every corner and on every shelf; the hallway black with chalkboard paint and thickly covered with equations; the rainbow table exactly where it should be; and stacks of books nearly as high as the furniture around us. Paul's plain backpack and Theo's battered messenger bag were nestled by the door along with my denim jacket and

Mom's bike helmet. The guys still practically live with us, like most of my parents' grad assistants over the years.

Yet Paul and Theo have always been different from all the rest. Closer to us, more important. I knew that even before they finished assembling the first Firebird.

"Thought Josie was going to get here tonight," Theo said. "Wasn't she coming in from San Diego?"

"No, she said the surfing was too great today to pass up." I squirted a little more dishwashing liquid into the sink. My rubber gloves were bright pink; Theo doesn't bother with them, so suds covered his wet hands. The bubbles smelled like lemons. "She'll fly in tomorrow."

Theo shook his head. "If the waves are that good, I'm surprised she's coming at all. Not like Josie to pass up a chance to surf."

"After what happened to Dad, or what we thought happened to Dad . . ." I didn't have to finish the sentence; the look Theo gave me told me he got it. My family has always been tight-knit, but now that the world's turned against us—and we know what it would mean to lose each other—it's like we can't be close enough. With a smile I said, "So that's her spring break. What about yours? Doing anything fun?"

"I learned my lesson," he said. Last year Theo dragged Paul to Vegas. Paul got thrown out of Caesar's Palace for counting cards, because he didn't understand that casinos consider "mastering probability theory" the same thing as "cheating." He got to keep his winnings, but apparently he had to spend all that cash buying back Theo's muscle car, which he'd wagered on a losing round of baccarat. They came home better friends than ever, but Paul said he didn't see the point of spring break.

Theo would always see the point of a party. But no matter how casual he acted about hanging around here, he wanted to stay close too.

Still, there are other ways to travel. . . .

I had meant to ask this for a while, but that night I finally felt comfortable enough with Theo to speak. "When are you going to take a trip of your own? See some other dimensions for yourself?"

He was quiet as he placed another plate in the dishwasher. Finally he said, "I don't know that I ever will."

"Not ever?" During the past two years, Theo had been more psyched than anyone else at the thought of seeing new worlds.

He turned to me, and I'm not sure I've ever seen his expression so serious. "I've seen what it's like from the other side, Marguerite. That part isn't as much fun."

Last fall and winter, whenever we talked to Theo, whenever he persuaded us to do something—we weren't talking to *our* Theo. It was his body, but the consciousness inside belonged to the Theo Beck from another universe—acting as Conley's ally and his spy. That Theo was the one who arranged my father's kidnapping and framed Paul for his murder. The one who turned me into Conley's ideal "perfect traveler," then persuaded me to take my first voyages with the Firebird.

The one I clung to after I thought my dad was dead—the one I kissed in another dimension, and at my weakest moment nearly slept with—and the one Theo blames for destroying whatever the two of us might have had.

Theo's wrong about that. For me it was always Paul; it could never have been anyone else. But the other Theo's shadow hangs heavy between us.

"I still crave it sometimes, you know." Theo stared out the kitchen window into the darkness beyond. "The Nightthief."

Nightthief is the one and only way to cheat the rules of traveling between universes. It's a drug—emerald-green, injectable, invented in the Triadverse—that allows a dimensional traveler to maintain control. See, a traveler on Nightthief remains as much in control as I am. But the drug has certain serious drawbacks. One, it's addictive and can cause seizures. Two, Nightthief can be made out of what we'd consider common household chemicals—but if you're in a universe where those aren't common, you won't be able to supply yourself. (While consciousness can travel through dimensions easily, it's very, very hard for physical matter to travel. So forget bringing any Nightthief with you.) Three, the drug wears off after a day or so, which means if you don't have more on hand, you're screwed.

When the other Theo took ours over, he took that drug for months on end. My Theo—the one who stood beside me that night, our elbows brushing—he had to go through the withdrawal. Worse, he had to live with the memories of another Theo using his body to endanger and betray us all.

"It's not always like that," I said quietly. "Paul and I take care of our other selves. We try to live their lives, as much as we can. We'd never make them do anything they wouldn't want to do on their own."

Though at least once, in the Russiaverse, I might have stepped over the line.

"Not judging you guys. I know it's different, the way you and Paul handle the journeys. It's just—" Theo went very still. "I've seen who I am as a traveler. I justified some of the worst stuff you could ever do to anybody, because I told myself I was 'protecting' you. Really I was delivering you straight into Conley's hands."

"Hey. Nobody got hurt." I nearly touched his shoulder before I remembered I was wearing wet rubber gloves.

He shook his head, and his smile was hard. "No thanks to me. Come on. I helped them kidnap Henry." Theo gestured toward my father, who at this point might as well be Theo's adoptive dad too. "I framed my best friend for murder. And I dragged you off on an extremely dangerous trip, just to prove Wyatt Conley could use you after all."

"*You* didn't do any of that!"

"A version of me did. You've said a hundred times—every one of our other selves out there is the same in some important way. We have the same framework or essence or soul, whatever you want to call it." Theo leaned against the refrigerator and sighed. "Listen to me. When a physicist starts talking about souls, we are officially off the map."

"I don't think it's silly or crazy—talking about souls." I never did, really, but after these journeys began, I learned how real they are, how much they mean.

Theo shrugged. "The point is, we've all seen the danger. Apparently, when I get a little bit of power, it goes to my head. Never, ever would I want to turn into a guy who could do *anything* like what that other Theo did to all of you. So I think it's better if I stay on the sidelines."

Although I wanted to reassure him, I couldn't. I've come to believe that there really is something that flows through every version of us, one common identity that outweighs our different situations in the various worlds. The ruthlessness and self-delusion of that other Theo—they have to be a part of this Theo, too, don't they?

When our eyes met, I knew he could tell what I was thinking. Theo cast down his dark eyes with shame for things he never even chose to do.

The shadow that had haunted us these past three months fell between us again. He turned back to the dishes, attacking them with new vigor; I took my place at his side just like before. Neither of us spoke, because there was nothing more to say.

Afterward, Theo buried himself in his work, taking his laptop onto the back deck. "I need some quiet," he said, and my parents had the good grace not to ask why. Paul walked him out, though, and it took all my self-control not to eavesdrop on their conversation.

As soon as the door to the deck was closed, Mom blithely said, "Is Paul staying over?"

"Mom."

"I'm not prying." She took her seat at the rainbow table again, ready to get back to work. "I simply need to know what I ought to plan for breakfast."

Our living room might as well be an unofficial university dorm. When grad students work that closely with my parents, they practically move in.

But Mom wasn't asking whether she should grab blankets for the couch.

Most parents would be freaked out even thinking about their teenage kids having sex. Mine haven't got around to the freaking-out stage yet, because they are *so completely thrilled* Paul and I are together.

(Back in January, during that first conversation with my parents about my new relationship with Paul, Mom—prompted by absolutely nothing I'd said, by the way—made a suggestion. "You'll need a method of birth control. We'll have to review efficacy rates for condoms, birth control pills, hormonal inserts—"

"Oh, my God." My face had to have turned carnelian red. "That's—we're not—it isn't an issue yet."

Which was not addressing what happened in the Russiaverse, but that's between me and Paul. And another Marguerite, a few dimensions away.

"Will be eventually," Dad said smoothly. "You and

Paul are young, you're healthy, obviously attracted to each other—it's only a matter of time. And you don't want to fall pregnant this early in life, do you?"

Mom brightened as she looked at Dad. "Though the genetic combination—their various talents and potential—think of it, Henry. Were they to reproduce, our grandchild would be extraordinary."

"Wouldn't she? Or he?" Dad leaned back on the sofa, where they were relaxing and I was staring in disbelief. "The two of you should have a baby together, by all means. Just not now."

"Whoa. Slow down." I held up my hands, like I could physically stop them from this whole line of thought. They didn't listen.

"Pregnancy and child rearing would seriously interrupt your art studies, and Paul's defense of his dissertation, at least in the immediate future," Mom mused. I think if I'd handed her a calendar, she would have started counting off months until the ideal conception date.

Dad took her hand. "You know, Sophie, we could help out. Even be primary caretakers while Marguerite and Paul finished their education. We always wanted another little one around. So the kids might as well get started." My mother beamed at him, like this was the best idea ever.

When I could speak again, I said, "You guys—you're—you two are the *worst role models ever.*"

"We are, aren't we?" Mom's smile became so wicked that I finally realized they'd been putting me on—mostly.

I balled up one of Josie's discarded T-shirts and threw it at them, which made them laugh. Much later that night, as my mother and I sat out on the back deck, she finally spoke to me more seriously. "You know how much your father and I like Paul. No—how much we love him."

I nodded. We were side by side on the wooden steps that led down into our small, nearly vertical scrap of a backyard. The light around us was provided by the strings of tropical-fish lights Josie had put up a long time ago. "This isn't going to mess things up between everyone, is it?"

Mom put her arm around me. "Marguerite, as dear as Paul is to me, you are my daughter and always my priority. If you and Paul have problems, or break up, I'm on your side. Even if you're in the wrong! You know you come first."

Which was really sweet, but not what I'd been asking. Splitting up with Paul—that wasn't ever going to happen. Really I was worrying about Theo.

She continued, "We are all very much a part of each other's lives, and our work. To some extent that will always be true. No matter what happens between you and Paul in the future, that connection will remain." Her fingers combed through my hair, just as curly-ratty as hers. "Lifelong relationships are complicated. It's a great deal for a new romance to carry."

"I know," I said. But I'd already realized Paul and I were meant to be. Destined, in a real, literal, provable sense. You can't fight destiny, and I didn't even want to try.)

Paul hasn't slept over at my house since we got together

in this world. Partly that's because we feel hyperobserved, partly out of consideration for Theo's feelings, but mostly because we're taking this slow. Making sure the moment is right.

In the Russiaverse, we rushed it and then some.

That night when they discovered the risk of splintering, Dad returned to the great room just when Paul came in from the deck. As he took my hand, Paul said to my parents, "Do you want to run the numbers again?"

Mom and Dad exchanged a look before she said, "We've got enough for tonight. We'll run it through at the lab tomorrow morning and take it from there." She raised one eyebrow. "In other words, yes, you two have some free time."

This was less of a treat than they seemed to think. Making out in my room isn't as much fun when I have to wonder if my parents can hear, or worse, if they're cheering us on. I used to be considerate and listen to my music on headphones. These days, I turn the speakers up to eleven.

Paul stood there awkwardly; he still hasn't figured out how to navigate the path between "respect for his mentors" and "desire for their daughter." So I did the talking. "Okay, we'll just—"

That's when we heard a thump on the deck.

"Theo?" I let go of Paul to walk toward the sliding door, but Dad got there first. He pulled it open, startled, and swore as he rushed outside. I hurried after him, then stopped short, frozen in horror.

Theo lay sprawled out on the deck. His laptop rested

where it had fallen a few feet away, and the light from the screen illuminated Theo's face—the blankness in his eyes, the slackness of his mouth.

Oh God. Is he dead? He looks dead—

Theo's body shuddered, then convulsed. His limbs tensed as they started shaking so hard they hammered against the deck. I gasped. "Oh, my God. He's having a seizure."

"Call 911," Paul said, just behind me, and I heard Mom's footsteps pounding as she ran for her cell phone.

"What do we do?" Dad said as we both kneeled by Theo's side. "Do we put something in his mouth so he won't swallow his tongue?"

"No! Definitely don't do that." I'd heard that was a bad idea with seizure patients, but I didn't know what else to do. "Just—be here with him." Could Theo hear us? I had no idea. I only knew that my blood seemed to flush hot and run cold, back and forth, over and over again. My hands were shaking. As frightened as I was, I knew Theo had to have been so much more scared than me. So I whispered, "It's all right. We're going to get you to the hospital, okay? We've got you, Theo."

Dad muttered, "Has he ever mentioned—any illness, any other episodes—"

"No." Paul looked grim.

Could he be sick? Please just let him be sick. But we all knew Theo didn't have epilepsy. We knew what was to blame.

Nightthief. The drug Wyatt Conley's spy had pumped into Theo's body over and over again, for months—the stuff he had told me still gave him the shakes—it had done more damage than we knew. Theo hadn't been getting better; he'd been getting worse.

Conley had told us he didn't like relying on Nightthief for his dimensional travelers; we knew the drug could be harmful. But that night was the very first time I realized just how serious this might be.

The first time I realized Theo might die.

And the night Paul decided to do whatever it took to save him.

4

THE WIND BLOWS THROUGH THE GLASSLESS WINDOW OF the Castel Sant'Angelo, ruffling the veil I wear over my curly hair. "You knew Paul would have to come to the Triadverse," I say to Conley. "To look for a cure, for Theo."

"I can give you that, too. You can save them both." He chuckles softly. "You'll be rescuing Theo from the effects of his Triadverse self's journey to your dimension—and rescuing Paul from the consequences of his journey into mine."

"You deliberately . . . splintered Paul?"

Conley just grins wider. "Guilty as charged."

Now I know why the reminder didn't work. It could only have awakened Paul's soul if—if his entire soul were within this world's version.

But Wyatt Conley has torn Paul's soul apart.

Nothing I could scream at Conley would be foul enough.

There are no curses to carry the obscenity and fury in my heart.

Instead, I throw myself at him.

Our bodies collide as I slam him against the wall, knocking the breath out of Conley in a surprised huff. We both topple to the side, but I'm able to catch myself. He lands flat on the stone, red robes a puddle around him. I wish they were blood.

A terrible calm comes over me. Maybe this is what people feel like before they commit murder. "You *killed Paul.*"

"Not kill," Conley pants. He's still fighting to breathe normally. "I splintered him. Not the same thing at all."

"You tore his soul into pieces! You broke him apart!"

Conley's grin isn't as cocky when he's sprawled on the floor. "But you can put him back together again."

What does he mean? Then I look down again at the Firebird, at that reading I've never seen before.

"Reminders can serve another function, it turns out," Conley says. "They can reawaken someone's soul *or* capture an individual splinter. You thought you'd lost Paul, but you've already rescued him—part of him, that is."

A splinter of my Paul's soul hangs on this chain, in a locket I hold in my hand.

I lean over Conley to grip his robes in one fist. "Tell me where you hid the other splinters of Paul's soul."

"If you want that information," Conley says, "You'll have to earn it."

★ ★ ★

Five nights ago, at the hospital, my parents were able to stay with Theo, while Paul and I were stuck in the ER waiting area. If I ran a hospital, I would try to make a space like that feel comforting. Instead, the room seemed like it was designed to punish us: stark fluorescent light, uncomfortable chairs, a pile of dog-eared magazines at least a year old, and a television blaring in the corner with some obnoxious TV judge yelling at people stupid enough to go on the show.

Paul and I held hands, but we were too freaked out to comfort each other. We just hung on.

I whispered, "Theo never said anything about still feeling bad. He admitted he still craved Nightthief, but nothing like this."

"He hasn't confided in me much lately." Paul stared down at his beat-up gray tennis shoes; he even has to buy his footwear secondhand. "I believed his silence was about you. About us. It never occurred to me to think he might be more worried about something else."

All the awkwardness of the past three months—all the odd silences, the times Theo didn't come around when we expected him—why did I assume that was all about my relationship with Paul? Because I thought Theo was jealous, or at least hurt, I never looked deeper. I didn't ask the questions I should've asked. All the while, Theo suffered alone.

Paul murmured, "I should have known."

"He hasn't been around enough for us to see it." True. But it was amazing how little that helped.

"The signs were there. I failed to put them together." He

slumped forward in his chair, shoulders hunched, like he'd just picked up something heavy. "I noticed that he hasn't been driving as much. That he went out less. I thought—after what happened, I thought Theo simply wanted time to pull himself together. But I should've known he'd never skip spring break."

With that, Paul buried his head in his hands, and I leaned against his shoulder. I don't know whether I was trying to give him strength, or take some from him. Either way, it didn't work.

My parents didn't emerge until nearly one in the morning. The light washed them out, highlighting every wrinkle and gray hair, but that's not why they seemed to have aged ten years in three hours. Fear had hollowed them out.

My voice cracked as I said, "How is he?"

"Not good." Dad sank into a chair across from us. "Theo's in no immediate danger, but his vital signs, his blood work—the doctors have no idea what to make of it."

Mom started counting off points on her fingers as she paced between the rows of chairs. "He's anemic. His lungs show signs of damage, as if he'd been suffering from untreated tuberculosis for years, which of course he hasn't. And the muscles in his feet and lower legs—the degeneration made one physician suggest Theo might have early-stage distal muscular dystrophy."

I bit my lower lip, hoping the pain would keep back any tears. Paul's voice sounded thick as he said, "He doesn't, does he?"

My mother shook her head. "Possible, but doubtful. We all know the most probable cause."

Nightthief.

"Whatever negative effects the drug had on Theo's body didn't end when he stopped taking it," Mom said. "Apparently the damage had already reached a point of no return."

Her meaning was obvious, but I didn't understand. I wouldn't let myself understand. Something in my brain refused to take in the words. "He'll get better, though. Right? Now that he's finally seeing a doctor?"

Dad spoke gently. "At this point, we don't know. The medical team doesn't understand his condition, which means they can't form any meaningful prognosis. But the fact that his condition has continued to worsen this long after his final dose of Nightthief . . . well, that worries me."

Mom made a small sound in her throat—the sound she makes when she won't let herself cry out in pain. I'd heard that sound from her only once before, when she opened the door to see a policeman standing there, his hat in his hand. It was like she'd known she was about to be told that my father was dead, but she refused to believe it until the moment she had to.

That night, she believed the worst about Theo.

He might die because Wyatt Conley sent a spy to drug him over and over and over again, for months. Because of Conley's power play. Because of his grandiose dreams of dominating the multiverse.

I hadn't thought it was possible to hate Wyatt Conley more than I already did. I was wrong.

I beat myself up about it that whole night.

Why had I acted so stupidly around Theo? He accepted that I'd chosen Paul, and he never once tried to make either of us feel weird about it. If I'd taken Theo at his word, believed him that he was okay with Paul and me being together, maybe we would've spent more time with him. Then maybe I would have noticed things going wrong.

The next day, after Josie arrived, I told her as much, but she didn't buy it.

"Listen, Marguerite." Josie stood in our kitchen, drinking her third cup of coffee. The caffeine was supposed to make up for the fact that she'd changed her flight to 6:30 a.m. to get home ASAP. "You didn't know because Theo didn't want you to know. He hid his symptoms from everyone, and that's on him."

"It's not like Theo to keep that kind of secret," I protested. Paul? Sure. He locks his feelings and his fears inside, sometimes for too long. But Theo likes to gripe about everything from hockey teams to parking in Berkeley. "If he didn't feel strange about being around me and Paul, he would've said something."

Josie put down her mug and placed her hands on my shoulders. "I know it's been easy to lose sight of this lately, what with Triad treating you like the Holy Grail, but not everything is about you, okay?"

That stung. "Then why did Theo stop telling us everything all of a sudden?"

"Honestly? My guess is the symptoms scared him. Probably he was trying to deny anything serious was going on. He couldn't tell you guys what was happening until he admitted it to himself."

I weighed what she said, and sensed there was truth to it. No, it wasn't the whole story. But at least I felt like I could breathe again.

"When can we see Theo?" Josie asked. "Gotta be visiting hours already, right? When do his parents get here from DC?"

"Didn't Theo tell you? They're not in DC anymore." The Becks work for the US Foreign Service, which means they move all around the globe. Most of the time they're in Washington—learning new languages, doing diplomatic work there—but Theo was born in Chile, went to kindergarten in the Philippines, and attended middle school in Iceland. Sometimes I think that's why he's such a hipster; he's trying to prove he's mastered American culture, that he's even better at it than the rest of us. "Two months ago, his parents got transferred to Mongolia. It's not exactly a quick trip back. They won't be able to get here for a couple of days."

"His mom and dad have got to be freaking out." Josie sighed and rubbed her temples. "Well, we can take care of Theo until they get here. So where's loverboy?"

"Please stop calling Paul that."

"Why?" Josie smiled for the first time since we picked her up at the airport. "He's not your loverboy yet?"

The pacing of my sex life is none of Josie's business. Although I can tell her pretty much anything, Josie doesn't understand the need Paul and I have to take it slow. She's always gone for brief, intense romances herself.

So that morning I said, "You'll embarrass him. He's still figuring out how to navigate—this." I made a vague gesture meant to take in the house, the tangled interrelationships we have, all of it.

"Paul never went out with anyone before, did he?" Josie asked.

I shook my head. He'd confessed that he'd kissed only two girls before me, and one of those was a single-second, closed-lips kiss that hardly even counts. This is what happens when a guy goes to college before he even hits puberty. Paul spent most of the past decade surrounded by girls five to ten years older than him.

That said, Paul got extremely good at kissing very, very fast.

Josie nodded, her expression overly innocent. "And you and Paul—you're good?"

"Yeah, we are."

Paul drove me up to Muir Woods once, where we held hands while he explained the origins of the cosmos. I took him into San Francisco to see the Golden Girls Drag Show, which confused him nearly as much as it would've puzzled an extraterrestrial visiting Earth for the first time. We ride the bus into Oakland so we can watch movies at the elegant old cinema at Grand Lake, then have coffee and doughnuts at this cool old bakeshop nearby. So we have our special occasions. But in some ways the best part is that Paul and I can just *be*. Some evenings, I'll paint for hours while he reads or works with equations, and by now we drift in and out of conversation easily, naturally. We're good together—better than I would ever have dreamed possible six months ago.

"I still can't wrap my head around it," Josie admitted as she walked past me to flop down on the sofa. She wore the same fleece pullover and leggings she would for a 5K run. "You couldn't stand the guy, and now you're in love with him."

"That's not true."

She raised an eyebrow.

"*Can't stand* is way too strong. I just thought he was . . . kind of weird. That's all."

"Paul *is* kind of weird," Josie said. "But in a good way."

"Then why are you being so strange about my getting together with him?"

Instead of answering right away, Josie sipped her coffee, deep in thought. Finally she said, "Right after you came home with Dad, when you'd first fallen for Paul—you told me you realized you loved him while you were in the Russiaverse."

I remembered Lieutenant Markov waltzing with me alone in an enormous, ornate room of the Winter Palace, music playing from a phonograph in the corner, his hand warm against the small of my back. "Yeah. I did."

"Okay." She hesitated, and I realized she was worried about offending me. Josie usually doesn't worry about offending *anyone.* I knew it would be bad. "Are you sure it's not just that world's Paul you loved? Because when you told me about it—Marguerite, you fell really deeply for Lieutenant Markov. And even though he's another version of Paul, they're *not the same guy.*"

Obviously she expected me to blow up. But I wasn't angry. Josie hasn't traveled to other dimensions yet. That means she can't grasp what I've learned.

"Lieutenant Markov isn't identical to my Paul Markov," I said. "I know that. Still, something in them is the same. Something deep—the deepest, most meaningful part of who we are, that's the part that lives in every universe. In every person we could ever be. I fell in love with that Paul, and my Paul, because I fell in love with what's the same inside them—their souls, if you want to call them that. Or soul. Singular. One."

My sister didn't look convinced. "You really believe that? That you're in love with every Paul, everywhere?"

"I don't believe," I said. "I *know.*"

When we visited Theo at the hospital that afternoon, everything about his room there was depressing: the plain, cheerless walls; the TV hanging from a black metal adjustable arm, showing a generic action movie from cable; and above all the plastic-framed adjustable bed. Theo had propped himself up, and he grinned when he saw us, but he was still so pale. Yet he sounded cheerful, for our sakes. "About time you two showed up."

"I brought some things from your apartment," Paul said.

"Not that you'll be here very long!" I quickly added. "But you might want your stuff."

"All the comforts of home, huh?" Theo smiled. God, we were all trying so hard to be upbeat, and failing. "Okay, hit me."

"First of all," I said, "that blue hospital gown? Not your best look. So, here." From the cardboard box I took Theo's straw hat, the one he bought at the beach last summer.

He let me set it on his head, then reset it at a rakish angle. "I don't even need a mirror to tell me how much better I look."

"Smokin' hot," I promised.

Paul didn't bother reassuring him, just plowed on. "I also brought your e-reader, your cell, some headphones, and a pair of argyle socks."

With a frown, Theo said, "Socks?"

"In case your feet got cold," Paul replied, like that should be obvious.

Theo sighed. "You're worrying about my toes getting chilly, little brother? Trust me, we have bigger problems to deal with."

I think he meant it as a joke, but Paul and I looked at each other with growing dread.

We already knew what we had to do. In the car afterward,

we didn't even discuss other options—just argued over who would get to save Theo. I said, "You know I should be the one to go."

"No," Paul said, in that zero-arguments tone that sometimes drives me crazy.

"The version of you in the Triadverse ran off to South America, remember?" We appear in our alternate selves, wherever they happen to be, and we have to deal with whatever situation we leap into. I've fallen down staircases, woken up underwater, you name it.

Paul insisted, "I wouldn't have to be in Triad headquarters to get the information. All I need is a computer, a wireless link, and the ability to get through Triad's security."

"You know Conley has to have beefed up his systems since then."

"That would be the logical move, yes."

"So you see the problems?"

"I may not be the ideal candidate, but you're even worse."

Paul's bluntness felt like a smack in the face. I've learned not to get my feelings hurt too quickly, though. He never means to be hurtful; he just doesn't know how to phrase things. So I said only, "You want to explain that?"

"At least I have a chance of getting the information while remaining undetected," Paul pointed out. "You have none."

I didn't want him to be right, but he was. My knowledge of computers begins and ends with *hit power switch, magic box comes on*. Why do I have to be the only right-brained person in the family? Paul is hardly an expert hacker, but he knows a thing or two about getting past firewalls. "When did you get so good with computer security, anyway?"

Paul sighed. "Theo taught me."

His free hand rested against my leg; I tangled my fingers with his. "He took you under his wing from day one, huh?"

"Not day one. But early on—after I called out an error in one of his equations. At first he was pissed off, but the next afternoon he said he'd rather have me on his side."

That sounded about right. Theo has an ego the size of the Golden Gate Bridge. His saving grace is that he's as ready to admire others as he is to admire himself.

Paul spoke so tentatively, like he'd never tried to say any of this out loud before and didn't know how. "I'd never gone out to a club before Theo took me. Never even drank a beer. So he took me out with him. He called it 'remedial adolescence.'"

No wonder Paul idolized Theo. But he didn't know the *other* Theo. Not like I did. I was the one who'd been led into Triad headquarters for Wyatt Conley to take captive, the one who was physically attacked in a submarine. The one Theo kissed and claimed to care about while he was faking Dad's death and framing Paul for the murder.

Theo has so much goodness in him—but there's darkness there too. Even that afternoon, when I was more afraid for him than I'd ever been, I couldn't help questioning how much the Triadverse's Theo and our own have in common.

Paul had no such doubts. His loyalty to Theo was, and

is, absolute. If he had to break Wyatt Conley's truce to save Theo, so be it.

Conley had said only that we had to stay out of the Triadverse. But the Triadverse invented Nightthief—which meant if any cure or treatment existed, that was the only world where we'd be able to find it.

First the two of us headed back to Paul's dorm room. Since we had no idea how long his journey would be, we needed him to leave from a location that could be sealed off to be sure nobody was in the wrong place when he returned, and his physical body once again started interacting with our universe. Like, if he left from our couch, but somebody was sitting on that couch the moment he came back—my parents aren't one hundred percent certain what would happen, but it could lead to both bodies being fused together in a very permanent, possibly fatal, and definitely gross way.

By traveling from his dorm room and having me lock the door behind me, Paul was doing his part to make sure we never found out whether that fusion thing would be for real.

We got him settled on his bed, stretched out and comfortable; after a few rough landings in other dimensions, you learn the value of a soft reentry. I sat beside him and leaned over so that our faces nearly touched.

"If you think Conley's onto you—even for a second—come back," I pleaded. "We can figure out other ways of getting a cure."

"Not without bargaining for it, and that's not going to happen." Paul brushed a curl away from my cheek. In almost a whisper—because he was still shy about saying it—he told me, "I love you."

"And I love you. In any world, any universe."

His smile was crooked. "This world is enough." Then he became more serious. "Sometimes I look at you, and I think—if I didn't know we shared a destiny, if I hadn't seen the proof for myself, I'd never believe this was real. That you could love me as much as I love you."

I've felt exactly the same. "We do share a destiny. We're meant to be. Which means you're meant to come back to me. Got it?"

"Got it." When Paul settled his hands on his chest, he put his fingers on his Firebird. Our eyes met, and then—

Then nothing. Paul didn't vanish; there was no light, no pop, no sign that he had even been there. Of course, his body remained in our dimension, remains there still, right on his dorm-room bed, but unseen, untouchable. No scientific instrument on Earth could find it.

Slowly I rested my hand on the space where he'd lain, where only a moment before I would've been able to feel his heartbeat. His blanket was still warm. I told myself that Paul could do anything, that he'd save Theo and come back home.

But Conley was waiting for him. Even as I pressed my palm against the warmth Paul had left behind, his soul was being torn apart.

5

AFTER MY PARENTS FINISHED CHEWING ME OUT FOR NOT telling them about Paul's trip to the Triadverse to find a cure for Theo, they settled in with me for the wait.

"Paul said he'd come back after twenty-four hours," I told them as we sat up late on the back deck. "Or as close to it as he can manage. Even if he hasn't found a cure for Theo yet, he'll check back in just to let us know he's safe."

"Twenty-four hours!" My father shook his head, expression grim. "If Conley's figured out how to monitor dimensional traffic, his people could be on Paul within minutes."

"But that dimension's Paul already got away from Triad," I protested. "He escaped to Ecuador."

This placated my dad not at all. "You think a global tech mogul like Wyatt Conley can't hire operatives in Ecuador?"

Mom laid her hand on Dad's shoulder. "Henry, please. This isn't helping."

I imagined Paul being held prisoner. Being interrogated by men to whom the Geneva Convention wouldn't apply. My stomach cramped, as if in sympathetic pain. Had we been stupid to leave my parents out of it? I said, "Could you have done something to help him get into the Triadverse without being detected?"

"Nothing Paul isn't capable of doing himself," my mother replied. "He has a chance. Paul knew the odds. He did this to help his best friend. We should respect his decision."

She was speaking to my father then, who didn't reply. I figured it would be a long time before we were forgiven—or, at least, that it wouldn't happen until Paul had given Theo a miracle cure that restored him to health.

But it didn't take that long.

By the time thirty-six hours had passed and Paul still hadn't returned, Dad was beyond yelling at me about it. Like the rest of us, he was too frightened for that.

"They wouldn't kill him," I said, pacing through the great room. "Would they?"

"Unlikely. Conley would be a fool to simply eliminate Paul rather than taking him captive as leverage." My mother turned out to have an instinct for criminal behavior. "Yet Conley would also be foolish not to tell us he's taken Paul captive. My instinct is therefore to assume that Paul remains at liberty. But if he is free, why hasn't he returned?"

"Maybe he's in the heart of working on Theo's cure," Dad said.

"Maybe," I repeated. But none of us believed it.

Two full days after Paul's journey into the Triadverse, none of us had slept more than a couple of hours at a time. Dad now believed Conley had captured Paul but was making us sweat it out; Mom theorized that Paul could have experienced a Firebird malfunction.

In either case, we knew there was only one way to find out for sure.

"I should be the one to go," my father said. "I've left these travels to the young ones for long enough."

"Dad, no. I'm the perfect traveler. It should be me."

For the past three and a half months, Paul and I had periodically visited brand-new universes, to further test the Firebirds and to see more of the multiverse's wonders. Mostly I saw a lot of dimensions very similar to my own, but where my parents were working on different research, teaching at a different university, et cetera. But even those worlds could offer a wealth of data the Firebird project team could use. I went because I could travel more effectively than anyone else; Paul went with me because he had the experience, and because it was dangerous to travel alone.

Now, however, I would have to make a trip on my own—the riskiest one of all.

Mom sat at the rainbow table, her hands steepled in front of her. "You go in. You *immediately* use the locator function to find Paul. As soon as you know where he is, you return and give us the full report. We'll decide how to proceed from there."

"Okay." Did that mean actually reach Paul if I could, or

just get the information? I decided I'd make that decision when I arrived in the Triadverse.

"If Paul's Firebird malfunctioned," Mom continued, "he may have tried to return to our universe but instead traveled to a new dimension. Your Firebird is set to track his. You'll be able to follow in his dimensional footsteps, so to speak—to travel to whatever world he might have ended up in."

"Please." Dad's voice broke. "Let me be the one to do this. For all three of you to be in danger at once—"

My parents love Paul and Theo only slightly less than they love Josie and me. They're the sons Mom and Dad never had. I knew they were as afraid for Paul as I was, but seeing my father this upset ripped me open inside. "Dad, I can do this better than anyone else. I have the ability; I have the experience. Meanwhile, you have the actual scientific knowledge about the Firebirds. If you go, and Conley winds up capturing you, too? We're going to be totally screwed."

This made him laugh a little, as it was meant to. I knew I couldn't make this situation easier for any of us, but at least I could get my father to accept what had to be done.

Or maybe not. Maybe Dad still hated the idea of my going to rescue Paul as much as he ever had. But he didn't object again, not even in the moment when I embraced them both and leaped out of my own world—

—and thudded into my Triadverse self, who was at a coffee shop, staring at her phone. I gripped the side of the table and looked around, half expecting Triad goons to barge through the door with tasers. Instead, I only saw the usual crowd of people tapping on laptops or talking over their cappuccinos.

Immediately I used the Firebird locator function—and it came up zero. My Paul was nowhere in this dimension.

At that moment, it seemed like good news. Conley hadn't captured Paul! It was just a Firebird malfunction, like Mom said. With a smile on my face, I set the tracker into motion, so the Firebird would travel along Paul's path and take me to him.

Which is how I wound up in medieval Rome, questioning everyone I could find about "Paolo Markov of Russia" while trying to dodge accusations of witchcraft.

How I ended up here, and now, bargaining with Wyatt Conley for Theo's cure and Paul's soul.

Cardinal Conley gets to his feet and straightens himself. It hits me for the first time how ridiculous Wyatt Conley looks in clerical robes. It seems as if no universe could ever allow him to be a man of the cloth; whatever else Conley is, he's not a religious, moral person. Then again, in the Middle Ages, most cardinals weren't. The position let men gain tremendous influence and political power. No wonder this universe's Conley became a cardinal.

As solemnly as the church elder he pretends to be, Conley says, "If you're worrying about being splintered yourself, Marguerite, let me put your mind at ease. Perfect travelers *can't* splinter—it's yet another of our advantages. But generally, a soul can be broken into as many pieces as you'd like.

Dozens, even hundreds."

The horror dizzies me. Is Paul torn apart even now, scattered across the entire multiverse?

"Don't worry," Conley says, in a tone that could be mistaken for concern if you didn't know him well. His red robes look almost satanic in the firelight. "I went easy on you, didn't smash him up too much. Four pieces, in four different dimensions. You just rescued the first one! See how easy it is? I gave you this splinter as a sign of good faith."

Does he want me to thank him? "What do I have to do to get the coordinates for the other three dimensions?" Three more pieces of Paul's soul. Three more worlds I have to find, and three more rescue missions.

Disgustingly satisfied with himself, Conley says, "I have a few errands for you."

There it is—Triad Corporation's iron fist closing around me.

But if this is the price of Paul's soul, I have to pay.

"Let me explain precisely what I need." Conley stands up straighter; his cardinal's robes lend him an authority he doesn't deserve. "Out there in the multiverse are two other dimensions where your parents are very close to developing Firebird technology. I would prefer that they didn't."

I fold my arms. "You mean you want to have all the power."

"Who wouldn't?" He shrugs. "Here's how this is going to work. I have two dimensions working on Firebird research that need to be sabotaged as soon as possible. The next two splinters of Paul's soul are hidden in those dimensions."

Conley's thin fingers point at my own Firebird locket. "If you allow it, I can program your Firebird. You'll receive the coordinates for the first of those dimensions—as well as a program you can use as a computer virus to destroy your parents' research and your most valuable hardware."

"How do I collect each splinter?" I clutch the spare Firebird more tightly. "The same way I'd give him a reminder? Just hold it against him, hit the combination on the locket?"

"Exactly. See? Easy as pie."

Someday, when I have the luxury, I'm going to punch Wyatt Conley in the face. *Hard.*

Oblivious to my anger—or amused by it—Conley continues, "Collecting the second splinter of Paul's soul will unlock the coordinates for the next dimension I need you to sabotage. Lather, rinse, repeat. Once you've done what I need you to do in each dimension, and gathered those two splinters, then you'll come to the home office. Coordinates will be programmed into your Firebird with the rest."

"The home office?" He must mean the Triadverse. "I don't want to go there."

"I have to check your work. When I go through your Firebird data, I'll know whether you deployed the virus. If you've been a good girl—"

If there is any phrase I hate more than "good girl," I don't know what it is, and the words sound even more loathsome coming from Conley.

"—and you've stalled those dimensions' research for a while, I'll give you both the formula for Theo's treatment and the coordinates for the final splinter of Paul's soul. That final splinter is my insurance, you see. Your job is quite simple."

Like it would ever be "simple" for me to betray my parents, much less while I'm afraid for both Paul's and Theo's lives. "You could have sent anyone to be your saboteur, or gone yourself."

"There are dimensions where my reach is . . . limited." It seems to gall Conley that he has to admit that he's not omnipotent. "And yes, I could send certain other emissaries, but in order to do the kind of tricky work I'm looking for, they'd have to take Nightthief for a very, very long time. You know what that does to people now, don't you?"

I remember Theo thrashing on our deck, body in spasm, skin pale. "Yes, I do."

"We didn't expect this one side effect. See, after a while, exposure to Nightthief takes away your ability to dream—hence the name. Sleep researchers still aren't sure exactly why the ability to dream is so vitally important, but it is. Once you've lost it . . . let's say mental processes start to break down rapidly, and dramatically."

There's something uniquely cruel about Theo dying because Wyatt Conley will no longer let him dream.

"As for the physiological damage—well, I don't have to fill you in on that, do I? You've found out for yourself what Nightthief does to the lungs, the muscles, et cetera. But don't worry about that. The lack of REM sleep will kill Theo before any of the rest progresses much further." Conley smiles, though I don't know what he thinks is so funny. I imagine taking one of the swords from the castle guards outside and stabbing it straight into his gut. He continues, "So, to sum up, do these errands for me, and in return, you get not one but two grand prizes. Once you report in to the home office, I'll give you the formula for a solution that should ease Theo's symptoms, maybe even reverse them."

"That doesn't sound like a cure." If Conley intends to keep Theo sick—use him as a kind of hostage—I swear I'll go for one of the swords right now.

Instead, Conley becomes serious and—possibly—sincere. "Marguerite, this is the best we have. If I could cure Night-thief exposure quickly, I wouldn't need you, would I? But this treatment gives him a chance to heal. Keep treating him, and eventually, his body's immune system should take care of the rest."

Should. Not *will.* Still, I believe he's telling the truth, only because he really wouldn't need me if he had a cure.

Even more earnestly, Conley says, "And at the home office, I'll also give you the coordinates for the final splinter of Paul's soul—for the universe where you can put him together again. No errands to run there; that dimension isn't one of my problems. You can just go get Paul and bring him home. Sound good?"

I imagine reawakening Paul, holding him in my arms, and telling him I'll never let him go. I need that even more than Conley will guess—more than I can ever let him know. "It sounds . . . necessary."

There's that smirk again. "Is that a yes?"

Someday, I'm going to make Wyatt Conley sorry he ever screwed around with us. For now I have to play along. "Yes. Now give me what I need to get the job done."

He holds out his hands to gesture at the stone walls and flaming torches. "I'll give you the data, but I need a little more sophisticated setup than this. Shall we return to your home turf? I can transmit the first coordinates from there."

My dimension, he means. I'm relieved to hear him suggest it. Mom and Dad deserve to know what's going on. By now they must be frantic. "Okay."

Conley takes his own Firebird from the collar of his robe. With its intricate design and dull bronze color, his Firebird looks . . . mysterious. More antique than cutting edge. It seems to belong to this dimension more than our own. "Shall we?"

"I want to say goodbye to Paul. *This* Paul."

"You get so sentimental about the duplicates," Conley says, shaking his head. "But I won't tease you about it. My other self is just as bad."

That's definitely not the vibe I've gotten from our world's Conley, but whatever. "Besides, you need to give that order protecting my parents. From the 'witchcraft' mobs. Right?"

"Oh, right! You got it." He thumps the side of his head, like *Duh*. "I'll talk to Her Holiness right away. Pope Martha the Third. Rumor has it she puts our Borgias to shame." As he begins to walk away, Conley adds, "Listen, someday, when you're on board with this and we've been working together for a while, you and I will look back on this and laugh."

I don't dignify that with an answer. Instead, I wait for him to leave, and then search for Father Paul.

As I guessed, he's been waiting. Paul kneels in a small room off to the side that turns out to be a private chapel. A mural of Jesus raising Lazarus covers one wall, perspective wonky and faces stylized—the art, too, looks older than the Renaissance. They haven't rediscovered the techniques of the ancient world yet; this civilization is still crawling away from the Dark Ages. Light flickers from a handful of tallow candles in iron stands. Paul—Father Paul—is praying, but when I walk in he quickly murmurs something in Latin, crosses himself, and turns his face to me. "Is everything well? The cardinal will take care of your family?"

"I hope so." This chapel has no pews, only kneelers. So I go to my knees beside him; it's the only way to be close enough.

Paul glances at the doorway, no doubt worried we'll be seen. "You could claim sanctuary here. The sisters would keep you safe until your parents fall under the cardinal's protection."

Nuns? I'll be spending the night in a convent? This world's Marguerite doesn't get to have nearly enough fun.

She'll be near her Paul, though. That's enough. All I want now is to be back with mine.

I bring my hand to Paul's face and brush my fingers along his cheek. He draws in a sharp breath. Have they even kissed? Paul tentatively covers my hand with his, so that I'm cradling the side of his face. If I were to kiss him right now, he wouldn't resist. He'd kiss me back so passionately that—well, this chapel might be deconsecrated.

But I stole the Grand Duchess Marguerite's first and only night with Lieutenant Markov. I won't steal any more firsts with Paul. Each me should get to experience that moment.

"Everything's going to be all right," I say, to myself as much as to him. "You and I—we'll figure it out."

"Ours is not an easy path."

Paul's old-fashioned, elegant phrasing reminds me of Lieutenant Markov, which reminds me of falling in love with Paul in the first place, and now I can't take it anymore. I have to go home; the journey to save my Paul has to begin.

"The path isn't easy," I tell him. "But we're walking it together."

It's true in every world, everywhere. I have to believe that.

I take hold of my Firebird and Paul's—the two of them around my neck, one of them carrying a splinter of Paul's soul—and leap back home.

I fully expected my parents to freak out about what Wyatt Conley had done and the bargain we'd struck. What I didn't expect is that they would flat-out refuse to let me go.

"Dad—" I pull my hair back with both hands, trying to calm myself. "You know we don't have any other choice."

"We don't know that," Dad insists. "We have to at least

try to get Paul out of this ourselves. We tracked him to the—Medievalverse, didn't we? So we could figure out a way to trace the other splinters. We don't need Conley's bloody coordinates."

"We already *have* the coordinates." Theo sits on the sofa in a plaid shirt and jeans, a pale shadow of his usual self. His plastic hospital bracelet still hangs around one wrist. "Why wouldn't we use them?"

The data packet arrived from Triad Corporation a couple of hours ago, just after I returned. While we can already see the first coordinates, the ones that will lead us to the second two dimensions have to be "unlocked"—by storing data that proves I've done Conley's dirty work. Each betrayal wins me one more dimension, one more piece of Paul's soul.

My parents don't even want to download the information into the Firebirds. Dad insists, "We can manage on our own."

Theo groans. "Come on, Henry. We didn't even know splintering was possible until a couple of days ago. Tracing those splinters in alternate dimensions? We could be months away from cracking that."

"Or days," Mom says. "The only reason we haven't solved the puzzle is because we haven't yet tried. Obviously our counterparts in another universe managed to master this; if they hadn't, Conley wouldn't have the technology to splinter Paul in the first place. What they did, we can do. We only need to begin."

Dad nods, becoming encouraged. "And if Triad could

think of a treatment for Theo's condition, well, then, so can we."

"We're not physicians, Henry." My mother glanced at the bottle of Nightthief on the shelves, the one they'd hardly begun to study. "Still, we must make an attempt. Obeying Conley has to be our last resort."

"This *is* the last resort!" I don't argue with my parents that much anymore, but right now I feel like I could scream. "Don't you get it? Paul has been *torn apart*. If I don't do this, we might never get him back. If even one of Paul's other selves dies, then—then we've lost him forever."

Mom's expression is more sympathetic, but she still shakes her head. "That is a risk, yes. But a fairly remote one given his age and health."

I remember Lieutenant Markov, bloodied and weak, dying in the Russian snow. "That depends on where he is. He could be somewhere dangerous; Conley would do that. You know he would."

My parents exchange a look, and Dad sighs. "We'll give it one week. If we can't make substantive progress on finding Paul ourselves in that time, then—well, then we'll consider it."

"*Consider* it?" How can they do this? I step away from them, hurt and confused.

"Enough of this," Mom says sharply. "You know how much we love Paul. We loved him even before you did, if you'll recall. We aren't standing our ground because we don't want to get him back as soon as possible. We're doing this because the price of cooperating with Conley is too high."

My father adds, "Conley has his hooks into Paul already. That doesn't mean we should hand you over too."

I close my eyes tightly until the wave of anger passes. "Dad—"

"This discussion is over." Mom heads toward the rainbow table. "If we're going to save Paul, we need to get started."

Dad follows her, as does Theo. But when Theo walks past me, our eyes meet, and I realize he knows what I'm thinking. I expect him to rat me out to my parents—that's what the Triadverse's Theo would do. Instead, he sits down at the table, pretending he doesn't understand what's about to happen.

They work until almost midnight. By that point I'm lying in bed, twisted up in the sheets, unable to sleep. All I can think about is the last time Paul and I were alone together before Theo collapsed—the last moment our lives seemed normal.

We lay together on the narrow twin bed in his dorm room, my head pillowed on his chest. Soft classical music played from his phone deck, almost covering the noise from other grad students down the hall. His dorm room is as stark as any other cheap student housing, plus Paul isn't the kind of guy who would fix it up even if he had the money. He owns this utilitarian navy-blue bedspread, and there's only one piece of decoration on the walls.

Hanging above us that night was my portrait of Paul. Not the one I'm painting now, but the first one I ever attempted.

I cut it to ribbons when I thought Paul had betrayed us and killed my father. To my surprise, Paul insisted on keeping it just as it is. *It reminds me how close I came to losing you*, he said. That's the kind of thing I'd want to forget, but that he always wants to remember. At least he let me patch it up.

Paul stroked my hair, his fingers untangling my curls. It's the gentlest, most comforting touch in the world. "I heard from a few more universities today, about my postdoc."

One of the weird things about being a scientist is that you have to get multiple college degrees—and even after you get your PhD, you remain a student for another year or two, usually at a different college than the one you studied at before. The point of the whole postdoc thing? I have no idea. It's a hoop they all have to jump through.

It would drive me crazy that Paul has to leave, if I weren't headed to college myself in January. "Which ones?"

"Oxford made an offer; so did Stanford. I expect to hear from Cambridge and CERN soon."

This is information that would make most people jump for joy. Paul takes it in stride, but my stomach knots. "Nothing from Harvard or MIT? Or maybe Princeton?"

"Not yet. MIT is a possibility, but—professors at Harvard and Princeton are skeptics."

About Mom and Dad's work, he meant. Those are the professors trying to tear them down, the ones who don't believe us about what happened in December. "Okay, so, we think about MIT."

His gray eyes met mine. "It doesn't matter where I go. I'll still be yours."

I kissed him softly, enjoying the way we were tangled together, the soft sound of his jeans against mine as we shifted to get closer. "But I'd like it if you could be mine, like, every weekend. Not just at Christmas and spring break."

What with all the craziness of December, I'd deferred starting college until next January. The Rhode Island School of Design had agreed to that; they preserved my scholarship and everything. January is when Paul's likely to start his postdoc. If he goes to MIT, we won't be far apart at all.

Paul said, "Are you still unwilling to apply to any schools besides RISD?"

"RISD's the best in the country for art restoration."

"What about fine art?" His thumb brushed along the line of my cheekbone. "Forget taking care of other people's paintings. Create your own."

"See, this is how I know you're a genius in physics but not economics. Ever heard the phrase 'starving artist'?"

"I doubt you would starve, as both your parents and I are gainfully employed." Paul went from adorably literal to practical. "If you could study art anywhere in the world—to be an artist—where would you go? I've heard Josie tell you to think about the University of Chicago—"

"Not Chicago." The words came out too easily, for something so hard for me to admit. "I mean, that's a great school, but if I could go anywhere? I'd pick the Ruskin

School of Fine Art, at Oxford."

"Why Ruskin?"

"They teach everything there." I couldn't keep the envy from my voice. "You study anatomy as in-depth as medical students do, so you understand what's under the skin of the people you're trying to paint or sculpt. They have professors who teach just about every technique, ancient or modern or experimental. They're better than anyone."

"So go there," said Paul the genius who has the world's top physics departments fighting over him.

"I'd never get in. Remember, I haven't even been to high school, really." The downside of homeschooling: Colleges find it tougher to evaluate you. RISD got with the program, but a foreign university would probably find my record harder to assess.

Paul shook his head. "You'd get in when they saw your work. Oxford would admit you immediately."

Would they? We both glanced up at the shredded portrait of Paul; his eyes stare from the portrait as intensely as in real life. Yet I couldn't imagine the professors at the single best art school in the world would understand this painting in the same way. "The important thing is getting you into the right postdoc. I know that. You're doing groundbreaking research. I'm just painting."

"I'm just solving formulae. You're creating works of art that might be meaningful long after my scientific work seems mundane."

I laughed. "Not likely."

"But possible. Your dreams are as important as anyone else's. Your future is as important as mine. I'm willing to make compromises, if that's what it takes for us to remain together—but we shouldn't compromise before we even start."

"It's different for me," I said. "I'm not brilliant like the rest of you."

"You have no particular aptitude for science. But there are many kinds of intelligence. I'd never want to take your career as an artist away from you, any more than you would take my research from me." Propping himself on one elbow, Paul looked down at me, almost grave. "Stop measuring yourself against us. It's not the right scale. You have your own gifts, your own talents. Show the world everything you're capable of, Marguerite. You don't even see how amazing you are."

There are moments when Paul's awkwardness drops away and he suddenly says the exact right thing. Those moments make me feel like I'm melting—like we're fusing together, ceasing to be two separate people, turning into one.

That night was one of those moments.

"Hey," I said, more softly. "Mom and Dad are going to that conference in Tokyo in a couple of weeks. You're not traveling with them, right?"

"We decided against it."

"Well, then, maybe"—my cheeks flushed with heat—"maybe you could stay over."

We could be alone in the house. Nowhere near family members who know way the hell too much about my love life already. Instead, we'd be together with absolutely nothing between us, all night long.

He looked at me for a long moment, eyes darkening in a way I remember from that night in the dacha with Lieutenant Markov. Slowly, he nodded. "Okay."

I laughed softly, self-conscious. "It feels like we haven't done this before."

"We haven't. Well. Not here."

My Paul was only a sliver of consciousness within Lieutenant Markov that night in the Russiaverse, because he was separated from his Firebird and unable to receive any reminders. But he was there throughout that entire night—so he remembers having sex as vividly as I do. I said, "Does it still count as our first time? Since it's just our first time in this dimension?"

He brushed his lips against my temple. "I guess it does."

I slid atop him, my legs on either side of his hips. Paul's hands caught me at my waist. When I leaned over him, my hair fell past my shoulders, and he shifted slightly beneath me, enjoying the feel of me above him. I couldn't help imagining us just like this—without our clothes in the way.

Smiling, I teased, "You realize this means we're going to lose our virginity to each other . . . twice."

He thought about that for a moment before he started to grin too. "Our lives are strange."

"Deeply weird," I agreed, just before we kissed. Paul's hands slipped beneath the hem of my shirt, slow and sure and hot.

We may not have spent the past months having sex, but that didn't mean we hadn't had fun. He knows how I kiss. I know how he touches me. We've learned each other inside and out.

And now I have to lie here in bed in the middle of the night, alone and terrified for Paul's soul—until I'm 100 percent sure my parents are asleep.

By 2:00 a.m., I feel pretty sure Mom and Dad have drifted off, no matter how worried they are. So I get up, tiptoe into the living room in my T-shirt and leggings, and find Theo waiting for me.

He's sitting at the rainbow table, all three working Firebirds lying in front of him. "I've been double-checking each one to make sure they're operating normally," he says. Theo picks up the one I took along for my Medievalverse rescue attempt, studying the sheen of the light against its coppery surface. Softly he adds, "Part of Paul's soul is in this thing. Gotta make sure it keeps ticking, right?"

I nod. As worried as I am for Paul, as determined as I am to begin, I can't help noticing how exhausted Theo looks. No doubt he told my parents he was going to bed right after them; instead, he sat up, waiting for me.

Then again, maybe sleep is meaningless for him now. "Theo—what Conley said about the dreams—you really haven't had any?"

He remains bowed over his work. "I haven't remembered any dreams in a while. Doesn't necessarily mean anything. I don't remember them often." His dexterous hands hesitate, and I can sense him weighing his words. "Thanks for making me part of the deal, by the way."

"What do you mean?"

"Telling Conley you wanted a cure for me."

"Paul's the one who risked everything for you."

"And I intend to thank him too, once we've got him back. But right now, I'm thanking you." The brighter light he's aimed at the Firebird silhouettes Theo's face, and the starker lines reveal that he's lost weight. It's not like I never noticed before, but I thought it was the usual grad-student grind. Now I realize Theo's been fading away. "Sometimes I've wondered if you'd ever fully trust me again. Then you stood up for me. Put it all on the line. It was . . . Marguerite . . . you know, let's stick with thanks."

I don't know what to say, so I nod. His eyes meet mine, only for a moment, before he turns back to the Firebird, nods in satisfaction, and snaps it shut again. "They're ready?" I ask.

"Ready as they're ever going to be."

"No point in waiting around until Mom and Dad wake up." They'd stop me from doing this if they knew, even if it meant locking me in my room or smashing the Firebirds to gold dust. "I should go."

Theo says, "Correction. *We* should go."

"We?" I know I heard him right, but it takes a minute to wrap my head around it. "Conley didn't say anything about you coming along."

"He didn't say I had to stay home, either." Theo's grin is sharp enough to cut.

I'm still in shock. "You said—you said you weren't ever going to travel through the dimensions."

"That was before they kidnapped my little brother."

The old nickname—and a reminder that Theo's not doing this for me. He didn't even mention saving his own life. Only Paul's.

Yet I can't help recalling what Theo said to me. *Apparently, when I get a little bit of power, it goes to my head.* He sees traveling as a temptation, and Theo's not good at resisting temptation.

Still, if he's willing to take this chance for Paul, I have to be willing to take a chance on him.

"All right," I say. "Let's go."

We walk together to my room, where I've already posted a KEEP OUT note; my parents will understand the need to keep the room clear for Theo and me to return—if and when we can. I slide two of the Firebirds around my neck, mine and Paul's; though I know it's only my imagination, I can't help thinking Paul's feels heavier. I remember the Enlightenment scientists who tried to determine the weight of one soul. Now I could tell them.

Theo takes the last Firebird in hand. He stares at it for a moment. Takes a deep breath. Then puts it around his neck—ready for the journey at last.

"Okay?" I say to Theo.

His old bravado returns. “Let’s blow this Popsicle stand.”

My hand closes around my Firebird—the world falls away—

—and I slam into my other self.

This time I’m in bed—definitely one of the better places to arrive in a new dimension. The room is dark, so I can’t really get a look at much. Mostly I just notice that I’m stark naked. Okay, whoever I am in this dimension, I sleep in the nude.

Except . . . I’m breathing hard. My skin is slightly sweaty. I feel faint scrapes along my throat and breasts and thighs—those could be from fingers, or teeth. And there’s a pleasant kind of soreness that tells me this Marguerite just had sex. As in, not even two minutes ago.

I turn my head toward the naked man lying next to me—and see Theo.

6

I SCRAMBLE TO THE FAR SIDE OF THE BED, CLUTCHING THE sheet to my chest. This covers me—but pulls the edge away from Theo, who's totally exposed, and totally nude.

"Jesus!" Theo grabs a pillow to hold over his lap. "Aaaaand this is awkward."

My cheeks flush hot. I try to look anywhere but at Theo, but every glance shows me something else I'd rather not see. My bra on the floor next to a pair of boots that must be his. A condom wrapper at the edge of the bed. An old-fashioned alarm clock on the bedside table, knocked onto its side next to a lamp with its shade askew.

Apparently what just happened here was . . . extremely energetic.

For a few long seconds, maybe a full minute, neither of us can speak another word. We can't catch our breath, and besides, what could we possibly say? Would this moment be less cringe-worthy if Theo had never had feelings for me, and I'd never been curious about him?

Nope. Nothing makes this better. *Nothing.*

I stammer out, "This—this has to be—this is the most embarrassing way to jump into a dimension. Ever."

"We could have jumped in about five minutes earlier."

When we still would have been— "Okay, that's worse."

"Guess this version of me has better luck." Then Theo goes quiet for a moment. "Sorry. Dumb joke."

"I don't understand this."

With a raised eyebrow, he says, "You don't? Apparently I need to give Paul the sex talk again."

Wait. Theo gave Paul a sex talk? I'll deal with that later. "That's not what I meant."

What I can't understand is—how can Theo be in my bed? Paul and I have found each other in so many dimensions. The connection between us endures through all the worlds. Fate and mathematics bring us together, time after time. There's no room in that equation for Theo.

But then I think of some of the first universes I traveled to. In the Londonverse, Paul and I both lived in England, but we'd never met. And in the dimensions where I lived on a deep sea station, Paul and my parents were both in oceanography but didn't know one another. Even if there is a kind of destiny bringing me and Paul together, each world evolves at its own pace. We just haven't found each other here yet.

None of that explains why I'm in bed with Theo. At this moment, though—with the two of us undressed and close and unsure—I can't help remembering that one moment in London where I came *this close* to sleeping with him. (I mean, a version of him. I didn't know the difference at the time.) The way I felt then is a lot like the way I feel now: embarrassed, vulnerable, and a tiny bit turned on.

The turned-on part is probably left over from the other Marguerite. It is. Has to be.

Theo breaks the silence. "So. We ought to check the Firebirds, right? Make sure we went to the right place?"

They did, and he knows it; by now Paul and I have traveled enough to prove how they work. But testing the Firebirds is something to do besides freaking out about being stark naked in the same bed.

Well, not entirely naked if you count the Firebirds; one hangs around Theo's neck, two around mine. I tuck my sheet more firmly under my arms to keep it from falling, take one of the Firebirds in hand, then press the combination for a basic systems check.

It glows softly gold for a moment—the locator function at work—and my heart swells with stupid hope before I realize that it found Theo. Of course.

"Looks like we're in good shape, kid." The gold light from Theo's Firebird paints the side of his face for a moment longer before it goes out. He reaches up to run his hand through his hair, but it's shorter here, practically a crew cut. "Listen—what's a delicate way to put this—if you'll excuse me, I kind of have to remove, uh, something worn by someone else."

It takes me a minute to realize what he means. "Oh, *ew*."

"Tell me about it."

I cover my face with one hand. "I'm not looking."

The first door Theo opens leads into a closet, but he finds the bathroom on the second try. He scoops up something from the floor—his clothing, I'm sure—and goes inside without another word. As soon as I hear the doorknob click, I scramble out of bed to find my own clothes. The stuff on the floor will have to do. Plain dark skirt, scratchy blouse—it's all pretty utilitarian stuff. Doesn't seem like the kind of thing I'd choose to wear, but right now I'd put on a Big Bird costume if I had to.

Once I'm dressed, I finally calm down enough to start really studying my surroundings. Is this my bedroom or Theo's? I can't tell from the decor alone, which makes Paul's sub-basic dorm room look like it belongs on HGTV. There's a pale blue blanket at the foot of the bed, no headboard, white walls, plain venetian blinds for the windows, and no art. This room is smaller than the one I have at home, but it doesn't look anything like the graduate student dorms either. A small, unframed mirror hangs on one wall. I take a glance and realize that my hair's shorter here, cut in a bob. At first I think that looks awful with my curls, but then I realize my hairstyle might have been neater before Theo and I . . . well, before.

A soft rap on the bathroom door makes me smile despite everything; the poor guy has to knock to come back into the bedroom. Theo whispers, "Coast clear?"

"Yeah. Come on."

He steps out wearing what looks like a black coverall. He brushes his hands down the front, mock-modeling it. "Think I'm a mechanic in this universe? I mean, I like fixing up cars, but it never seemed like my ideal career choice."

"Doubt it, but who knows? We'll have to figure things out as quickly as we can."

He nods but doesn't move. Hesitating isn't like Theo. Then I remember that this is his first journey through the dimensions—the very first time he's found himself in another world. When our eyes meet, he breathes out sharply. "Still getting used to this."

"You feel just the same," I say. "Nothing changes, except you wake up someplace new."

"I *don't* feel just the same. I feel better. Like, a lot better."

Of course. Only Theo's consciousness traveled through the dimensions; that means he's in this Theo's body now. This body was never exposed to Nightthief, which means the damage Theo's been suffering from for months now—here, it doesn't exist.

He shakes his head, smiling at something that isn't funny. "I didn't realize how bad it had gotten until right this moment."

I put one hand on his shoulder. The touch is charged now in a way it wasn't before, but I don't care. Theo's scared enough to let me see how freaked out he is, which means he needs some kind of comfort. Once he's breathing more normally, I bring him back to the here and now. "You still remember yourself?"

"Yeah. But I programmed a reminder every ten minutes for the next day. Seemed like a good first step."

"You'll run down the charge." Firebirds can operate for a long time; Mom made sure of that. But reminders require a lot of energy. You have to limit them.

"I'll set them further apart once I get my bearings. Let me get a handle on this first, you know?" Theo brings his hands together. "So, you're the expert. Where do we start?"

"We start with this room, learn everything we can from it. That's always the best way to begin, with your immediate surroundings." It helps a little, Theo calling me the "expert." That's not exactly true, but at least now I'm thinking productively instead of standing here blushing. "Okay, the number one thing we ought to figure out is whether this is your room or mine."

Theo gestures toward the open closet door. Now that my eyes have adjusted to the darkness, I can see that plain dark dresses and skirts hang inside. He says, "Either this is your place, or in this universe I'm the world's most boring drag queen."

That makes me smile, and we're at ease with each other again. I point at a dark square of leather on the floor. "That must be your wallet, right?"

"Gotta be." Theo kneels down to check it out.

I steal a glance out the window to look around. Although there are few streetlights here, the moon overhead shines bright enough for me to see. This clearly isn't our same house, but I think it's still near the Bay Area—even in such a different neighborhood (smaller homes, fewer trees), the rolling ground is unmistakable. My bedroom is on the first floor of the house. Outside my window is a lone sweetshade tree; tethered to it, with a chain lock, is an old beater bicycle with fat tires.

"Check this out," Theo says as he gets to his feet. I turn around to look at the wallet he's showing me. At first I don't see what the big deal is—okay, so driver's licenses look different here—and then I realize that's not his license. It's a military ID.

"You joined the *army*?" That seems so . . . not Theo.

"I was wondering why the hell I practically shaved my head. Now I know. But there's more—"

Frowning, I realize that Theo's wallet is stuffed full of photos, all of them in black and white. I try to ignore the picture in front, a snapshot of me and Theo, the two of us standing with our arms around each other.

He continues, "We have black-and-white photography. We have a conspicuous lack of any smartphones or other modern tech here in your room. That means we're in one of the worlds that hasn't advanced as far, right?"

"Normally, it would mean that," I admit. "But Conley said he was sending me to dimensions where my parents were on the verge of inventing the Firebird."

"How can they do that if nobody's even come up with color film yet?"

"We'll have to see. Every world develops in its own way."

I lean closer, trying to get a look at more of the images in his wallet. "Do you have a photo of Paul?"

"Doesn't look like it."

Of course I don't know Paul in this universe, at least not yet. If I did, I wouldn't be with Theo. We'll have to figure out where he is in this world. It would be just like Conley to play a dirty trick and hide the next splinter of Paul's soul in a dimension where we live in different cities, or countries, or continents.

It doesn't matter. However far I have to go to rescue him, I will.

"I can't get over this," Theo murmurs. "It's so different but so not, all at the same time."

"Yeah, the changes can throw you off."

"Not as much as some of the stuff that hasn't changed."

He says it quietly, without looking at me, but for some reason I am suddenly, vividly aware of the mussed bed—still rumpled from when this Theo and this Marguerite made love. Theo wanted this for us. What must it feel like, for him, seeing that in one world we're actually together?

Maybe it's painful. Or maybe he sees it as vindication. Proof that we could have worked out, if I hadn't fallen for Paul instead.

I turn away, meaning just to give us both some space for a moment. Then a dark shape on my dresser catches my eye—a picture frame that had tipped over, face forward. I try not to think about what Theo and I might have done against the dresser. Instead, I right the frame and breathe out in relief; Mom, Dad, and Josie all smile out from the picture, in black and white but recognizably themselves. The photograph looks recent enough that they're probably all alive. I don't take that for granted anymore

"Come on," I say. "Let's check out the rest of the house."

We tiptoe from my bedroom, down a hallway, until we reach the kitchen. This house is smaller than our home in Berkeley—one story, low ceilings—and way more boring. No philodendrons in terra-cotta pots; no wall covered in chalkboard paint; no suncatcher in the window. The kitchen has a stove, oven, and refrigerator, but they all look sort of clunky. On the wall hang an actual paper calendar, annotated in at least four different colors of ink, and an old-fashioned black plastic phone, complete with a long spiral cord.

When I get closer to the calendar, I'm able to make out some of the entries, both the ones in Dad's scrawl and Mom's tiny block print. *Josie flt demo 4/17. Presentation AF HQ 4/19. Marg shift change 4/20.* None of this makes a lot of sense to me, but at least I know all of us live here together.

Next we head into the living room. The furnishings are pretty bare-bones here too, but I smile when I see a pile of sketches on a small table. Even before I pick them up, I know they're mine.

In the large majority of the dimensions we've visited so far, I'm still an artist—whether that means a professional, a student, or just an interested amateur. My love of creativity is one of my constants, a pole star amid the many constellations of possibilities and personalities that make up all the people I could be.

Besides, I learn a lot from my art. Each Marguerite sees the world in a whole new way.

The first thing I notice: These sketches are on really awful paper. Not only is it cheaper stock than you'd get at an art store, it's thin and coarse, not even printer-quality.

Next, as I squint to examine the drawings in the dim light, I realize that these are all works in pencil only. Usually color is one of the most important aspects of my work, but a few of the other Marguerites stick to black and white. Slowly I flip through the drawings. While I don't recognize some of the faces, others are more familiar. There's Mom, with her curly hair drawn back into a severe bun. Josie, with her hair cut nearly as short as Theo's. This is the only portrait I've seen of Josie in any world in which she wasn't smiling. Dad, wearing wire-rimmed glasses that look like something from bygone days.

And Theo. She's drawn him perfectly, capturing both his intelligence and his mischief just in the expression of his eyes. The warmth she's put into this sketch suggests that Theo's stayed over before, and that their relationship isn't some casual, careless thing.

"Nice," Theo says quietly. He's looking over my shoulder at this other version of himself—a version who has a relationship with me that he never will.

So do I break Theo's heart in this universe when I finally meet Paul?

Because Paul's face is nowhere to be seen in these sketches.

Carefully I put the drawings back in order and set them on the table. I walk to the window to look outside; the view is of the backyard, and I can make out a whole vegetable garden. That's new. Mom loves her houseplants, but aside from a few pots with fresh herbs in the kitchen, she's never bothered growing stuff for us to eat.

Okay, great, you've learned that in this world you guys get your carrots from your own yard. I'm sure that's exactly the information Wyatt Conley wants. You'll have rescued Paul in no time.

I take a deep breath and try to stay focused. Maybe Conley sent me to the wrong universe. Very dissimilar worlds are sometimes "mathematically similar"—so sometimes it takes a couple of tries to get where you want to go.

Then Theo whispers, "Check it out." I look over my shoulder and realize what's sitting in the far corner of the room: a computer.

A *real* computer, not some antiquated thing the size of a fridge with reels of tape and blinking lights. The slim black rectangle of the screen rests so deep in shadow that I didn't see it before. It seems bizarrely out of place, but the main thing is that I now have a chance to learn a whole lot more about this world. To figure out if this is where I'm supposed to be or not. To look for Paul.

I touch the screen, but nothing happens. Theo gives me a look before grabbing the mouse.

One click and the screen lights up. Instead of the usual folders over my dad's Sergeant Pepper wallpaper, there's a flat red-and-gray box with the header ARPANET. The cursor blinks at the front of a line asking for a password I don't know. "Can you get into the system?"

Theo nods. "Maybe, given time. I want a chance to check it out first; you only get so many tries before you're locked out."

ARPANET. I know that word, don't I? Then I recall the grad student who taught Josie and me about the history of computing. The ARPANET was essentially the first version of the internet—a version that existed only for military use.

Since when are my parents in the military? Them and Theo?

That's when I see what's hanging on one of the hooks by the door. I get to my feet, unable to believe what I'm seeing until I touch it and feel heavy rubber, thick plastic lenses. "What is that?" Theo says, not able to see past my shoulder.

"It's—a gas mask."

"Why do we need a gas mask?"

The puzzle pieces suddenly come together, the solution instantly taking shape in front of my eyes. The gas masks, the cheap paper, the vegetable garden—the fact that everybody I know seems to be in some version of the armed forces—

A siren begins to shriek, so loud the vibration ought to shatter the windows. Both Theo and I clamp our hands over our ears. It doesn't help much.

Tsunami alert, my mind supplies. *Or wildfires, or maybe a tornado.* That's what sirens would mean at home.

But we're not at home.

"What the hell—" Theo starts to say, but then Dad dashes into the living room in his pajamas.

Instead of asking why Theo's here after midnight, particularly with both of us this rumpled, my father yells, "Come on! We've no time to waste!"

Mom runs behind him, a plain beige robe knotted over her nightgown. She goes for the desk and slides open a panel on the computer to withdraw the hard drive. "What are you two waiting for?" she says. "Move!"

I start running after them, Theo only steps behind as we exit the house. Josie's the last one out of the house, racing past us with a helmet under one arm. "I'm headed to the base!" she yells, racing for a small black car that must be ours. "I love you!"

"We love you, too!" Dad says, looking back over his shoulder for only an instant.

By now dozens of people have joined us on the sidewalks, all of them running like hell. Parents hold their small children in their arms, to make better time; one little boy, maybe nine years old, clutches his kitten to his chest. Nobody has changed out of their nightclothes. Nobody has brought any physical object, except Mom and her hard drive. And everyone's headed in the same direction.

"What the hell is going on?" Theo yells, his voice almost lost in the shrieking of the sirens.

"I'm not sure," I say, "but I think—I think it's an air raid."

"*What?*"

That's when we hear the buzzing overheard. Thunder that

is not thunder. Fire in the sky illuminates the clouds so that we can see the outlines of airplanes overhead.

Bombers.

I realized as soon I saw the gas mask—this is a world at war.

7

I'M RUNNING AS FAST AS I CAN, BUT IT'S NOT FAST ENOUGH.

Shouts and even screams echo through the streets as we race toward whatever counts as safety. By now hundreds of people have joined the stampede. If I stumbled and fell right now, I'd get trampled to death.

Worst of all, over the din, I can hear the distant thunder of bombs.

"What do we do?" Theo yells.

"Follow Mom and Dad!"

"I mean—do we stay here? Do we leave? What?"

He's hoping I'll say we should leave this universe altogether, leap away and escape the consequences of the bombing. Go home.

When I'm the reason one of my other selves is in trouble, I feel obligated to stay so they don't have to face the consequences of my actions. Here, though, this Marguerite would be screwed no matter what. I didn't endanger her in any way; this is just the reality of her world.

But if we leave this dimension without completing Wyatt Conley's work—without retrieving this splinter of Paul's soul—then Paul is lost to us forever, and Theo might die.

"Keep going!" I shout back to him. "Hang on!"

If this gets bad enough, I'll send Theo back to safety, and face whatever comes.

The sirens scream louder now, sound reverberating from every building until my ears hurt. I'd had a vague impression of this street as derelict, run-down; only now do I realize that these buildings haven't fallen apart over time. They've been bombed.

"Come on!" shouts a man standing at the door of what looks like a warehouse. He wears a bright red armband and a helmet, which I hope means he knows what he's doing. "We've got to seal the doors in four minutes!"

People press in desperately. Mom tries to reach for me, but the crush pulls us apart. Suddenly I'm wedged in among dozens of strangers in nightclothes, in regular outfits, even a few in their underwear; I'm not even facing forward anymore, being carried along by the tide of bodies around me. It's hard to breathe. Gasping, I try to push myself toward the doors, only to get an elbow to the chin from someone who didn't even realize I was there.

"Hey!" Theo's voice cuts through the shouts. I crane my neck to see him shouldering his way toward me. One of his arms hooks around my waist, so tightly not even this crowd can tear us apart. "You okay?"

"Yeah." Which is not even close to being true, not with bombers flying overhead, but thanks to Theo, I can at least stay upright.

I shove myself forward and somehow manage to slip us through the doors. Then it's a mad scramble down concrete steps, into a basement. Though the space is enormous, it's crammed full of people—all of them breathing hard, sobbing, or both—and more are behind me. The only thing we can do is try to reach one of the walls so we won't be knocked over.

Once my shoulder makes contact with one of the cinderblock walls, I take a deep breath. *Stay calm. There's nothing you can do now but hang on.*

"There." Theo points farther down the wall, where my parents huddle together. Mom slumps against Dad when she sees us, as if she's weak with relief. But this air raid hasn't ended, so I don't know what she's so relieved about.

Just that I got in, I guess. That I have a chance.

I expect instructions on what to do, but in this situation there's only one thing we *can* do: wait.

We all huddle together, catching our breath; a few people are still crying, and others are attempting to hush upset children. One man nearby is whispering a prayer. The outdoor chill of early-spring air has vanished in the heat of hundreds of bodies pressed too closely together. Theo still has his arm around my waist. I wonder if he's trying to comfort me, or taking comfort himself.

I've been afraid for my own life before. It's terrible—a cold knot in your gut, your heart hammering at your ribs. Movies show people panicking and screaming like idiots. In reality, it's nothing like that. When you fear for your life, you're overcome by this ghastly clarity. You calculate your odds every instant. You invent options and see possibilities you wouldn't have considered at any other time. You realize as never before that your life is the only thing that is absolutely, truly yours. There is strength within us that we can't even comprehend until it's called upon. We are, at our core, built to survive.

Worse by far is being afraid for someone else. We can face our own risks with an unbelievable calmness. Risks to the people we love? They turn us stupid. Drive us mad. Fear and hope take turns telling us lies, each more improbable than the last. Our imagination kills the one we love in our mind, over and over again, and we have to witness. Yet somehow even that isn't as unbearable as the foolishness of hope. It's hope that makes us believe in miracles that haven't come to pass. Hope that crushes us with the unbearable truth.

No danger I've faced torments me as much as knowing the people I love are in danger. Mom, Dad, Josie, and Theo—any one of them could be blown to shreds in front of me and there's nothing I can do. And Paul, wherever he is in this world, is in the greatest danger of all.

Standing here, waiting to find out if we'll get blown to bits, is the most helpless, frustrating, frightening feeling in the world. Theo's presence is my lone comfort, but even that only helps so much. After a couple of minutes, I can't bear it anymore. *Okay, so, use the time. Look around, and see what you can learn about this world.*

Observing the people around me doesn't help much, because everyone's upset, and nobody's dressed normally. But I notice one old woman wearing a military jacket too big for her, something she must have grabbed on her way out the door. The flag stitched on the sleeve isn't the American stars and stripes, or any other nation's flag I've ever seen before. Apparently the geopolitical situation in this universe is dramatically different. I make a mental note to find a history book.

I light up as I see that a man near me has tucked a newspaper into the pocket of his bathrobe. "May I look at that?" I ask him, pointing at the rolled newspaper. A few people stare; no doubt they think a bombing raid is a weird time to catch up on current events. But the guy hands me the paper, hardly even glancing away from the ceiling.

"Good thinking," Theo murmurs as I open it. "Let's see what we're dealing with here."

The front page reads SAN DIEGO STANDS STRONG: SOUTHERN ALLIANCE REPELLED AT SAN YSIDRO MOUNTAINS. A grainy monochrome photograph shows the SoCal shoreline—but instead of the usual parasailers and beach umbrellas, dead soldiers lie on the sand. It's so graphic that I can't believe they would run it in a newspaper, period.

But I'm in a world where virtually every person is caught

up in this war. Images like this have lost their power to shock.

What the hell is the "Southern Alliance"? Theo gives me a look; I know he's wondering just as much as I am, but that's not the kind of question we can ask out loud without immediately tipping off everyone around us that something's up. Flipping through pages turns up no answers. Of course not. Everyone here knows about the Southern Alliance. It's too obvious a fact to print in newspapers; it would be like going onto the CNN home page to find a big article explaining what France is.

This newspaper is a lot more . . . news-focused than most of the ones I've seen. No sports section; no horoscopes. They do print movie listings, though, and I smile as I see an ad for some big melodramatic romance starring Leonardo DiCaprio and Keira Knightley. People tend to find their destiny, no matter what world they're in.

That means Paul has to be a physicist, at least a scientist of some kind. Mom and Dad must have heard of him—or they're going to. Maybe I could ask them to find out about him. What excuse can I come up with for that? I'll think of something.

Weirdly, there *are* articles about technology, about how the military is expanding its use of wireless internet, building drones for combat, and improving satellite navigation to better direct the troops. All of that sounds totally modern.

Theo, reading the article over my shoulder, whispers, "So how come their phones are still connected to the wall?"

The same reason they have to grow their own vegetables,

I suspect. The same reason eggs are rationed and paper is too thin. This war must require every person, every resource. They've made many of the same advances we have, but that technology is reserved for military use.

My parents have access to that; they're doing Firebird research. Which means that in this world, my parents are doing the exact same thing Wyatt Conley is doing in ours: trying to find technology that will allow them to dominate. To control. To win.

Conley's only doing it for profit, I think. *My parents are probably just trying to keep their country from being destroyed.* Big difference in motives.

A deep boom shudders through the room, and several people moan in dismay. It wasn't much of a shake, though—more like one of those earthquakes you hardly notice until it's over. The planes aren't too close to us. Yet.

I try to imagine what's happening out there. All the pictures in my mind come from bad movies or old World War II newsreels; none of them help me wrap my head around it. I only realize I'm shivering when Theo hugs me more tightly. Closing my eyes, I lean my forehead against his shoulder and take slow, deep breaths.

Another boom, louder and deeper. Cement dust falls from the ceiling and cinderblocks, and the impact jars us so much that some people fall down. Theo keeps us on our feet, but barely.

Where is Paul right now? What if he's *not* a scientist? The Paul in this world might have to be a soldier, too. He could be in this same battle—his life in danger, even now.

If he's killed with part of my Paul's soul inside him, that splinter will be forever lost. I could never re-create his soul, reawaken him. It would be like he died too—

It's less like I hear the explosion, more like the sound takes over the whole world. The floor convulses beneath our feet. I'm horizontal before I know it, one in a tangle of frantic, disoriented people. As I struggle to get up, towing Theo after me, water flows over my foot. A main must have broken. I imagine the entire room filling up, all of us struggling to swim and breathe the last inch of air.

But the water isn't flowing that fast. Even though much of the crowd is still crying or screeching, I can tell the shelter remains more or less intact. That was a close one, but we're okay for the moment.

Theo gives me a look. "Are you *sure* we should stick around?"

"We have to!" I whisper.

"Marguerite, we can't save Paul if we die here."

"Keep one hand on your Firebird. We don't leave unless we absolutely have to. The absolute last second. All right?"

"Yeah. Got it."

Then I hear the planes through the cement, from underground. The sound could only reach us if the bombers were directly overhead.

I turn toward Theo; his eyes meet mine. He grips my hand tighter and says, "Just in case—I love you."

And the world turns white, and disappears.

★ ★ ★

All those movies you see, where action heroes coolly stroll away while buildings explode right behind them? They're total crap.

When something explodes near you, a wall of hot air hits you so hard it feels like stone. Your eardrums seem to shatter, like the bomb's gone off in your head; you can't hear anything but a dull roar, and a ringing. The explosion knocks you down, sears your skin.

I manage to push myself up on my elbows, above most of the dazed people lying around me. Smoke lingers in the air, and I look up to see the exposed night sky, ringed by rubble that must have been the building we ran into before. Fire flickers up there, but nothing's burning down here. My palms sting, scraped and bloody, but I don't think I'm hurt worse than that. Next to me, Theo's lying on his back, coughing so hard from the smoke that he clutches his gut. Nearby I see Mom sitting upright, shaking her head like she's trying to clear the ringing from her ears. Dad brushes stone dust from his hair.

As the air clears slightly, I see the people on the other side of the room—torn skin, unnaturally bent limbs, and blood. So much blood.

"We need help!" someone shouts. It's not like I have any idea how to handle medical emergencies, but it's impossible to look at this and not feel the need to do something. By the time I reach some of the injured, a few nurses and one doctor are already working to help, so I fall in with them and follow their lead. The next several minutes are a blur: ripping apart spare pieces of clothing to use as bandages, bracing people in whatever posture will allow them to protect their broken limbs and experience the least pain. One elderly woman seems to be having a heart episode, but with no drugs to give her and no ambulance to call, all I can do is sit by her side and talk her through it. "Deep, slow breaths. Try to calm down."

She gives me a look like I am a total dumb-ass. Yeah, I get that "calm" isn't really an option with bombers circling overhead. But we have to try.

When she's as settled as she can be, I look around to find Theo standing behind me. "Anything I can do?" he calls over the clamor and the crackling of flame overhead.

Surely there is, but the way wounded and panicking people are crushed in here reminds me of a Hieronymus Bosch painting: nonsensical and grotesque. Who can tell what we should or shouldn't do? "Just hang on."

The air whistles as I hear another bomb fall. Theo and I look at each other in panic, and I clutch his hand. But the next impact is farther away. The one after that is even more distant. We begin to breathe a little easier, and the people around us visibly relax. Theo murmurs, "Does this mean we made it?"

"I hope so." Only then do I realize we're still holding hands, and I let go. We don't look each other in the eye.

Near us, a little girl asks her mother, "Is it over?"

"We'll get the all-clear soon enough," the woman says. "You wait and see."

From the weird glances she gets, I can tell not everyone is as optimistic as she is, but as long as I can't hear bombs, I'm taking it as a positive sign.

I keep offering what makeshift nursing I can, which isn't much. Within the hour, a doctor who's taken charge tells me to take it easy for a few moments. With a sigh, I lean back against the wall and slide my hands into my pockets.

Something's in my left pocket. I pull it out to see that it's a photograph, bottom up in my palm so that I see the back and the words written on it: *With all my love forever.*

I turn the picture over to see Theo in full uniform, smiling up at me.

"What's that?" Theo says from his resting spot nearby. He hasn't really glimpsed it; he's just trying to make conversation.

"Nothing." I put the photo back in my pocket.

We don't get the all-clear until hours later. By then my whole body is stiff, I'm starving, and the sunlight outside is so bright it feels like it could burn my eyes. I stumble around the street, squinting at the scene around us. Most of the neighborhood looks the same—except for the areas that have been instantly, totally obliterated. What were buildings are now smoldering holes in the earth. In the distance I can see smoke spiraling up from several new fires.

Through a megaphone, Red-Armband Guy shouts, "All commercial and manufacturing work is suspended for the day. Return to your homes and await further instructions."

"Thank goodness this happened at night, instead of during the day when you were at work," Mom says as we walk home along the ruined streets. All around us, smoke darkens the dawn sky. "I wouldn't like the thought of you at the munitions factory at a time like this."

My job in this universe is building bombs? How am I supposed to bluff my way through that? At this moment, I can't imagine anything I'd less want to do than make even one more bomb in this world.

Buildings I saw only an hour ago now lie in pieces on the street, having crumbled into smoldering piles of brick and rebar. Most of those houses were empty, surely, because of the air-raid siren, but I can't be sure. When I see a tricycle upside down in some rubble, I have to close my eyes tightly for a moment.

As the four of us reach our house—intact, untouched—Dad glances at Theo. "You know, Private Beck, during wartime, emotions run high. We live as if there's no tomorrow. So we overlook things we normally wouldn't, such as a young man sneaking out of our daughter's room in the dead of night."

For once, Theo is speechless.

Dad keeps going. "I myself am experiencing that sort of amnesia right now. I have *no idea* how you managed to find us in the bombing raid, since of course you were nowhere near Marguerite's bedroom when this all began. However, I suspect your commanding officer will suffer no such memory lapse if you fail to appear on base shortly."

“Right. Yes. Of course.” Theo’s hand steals toward his pocket, and his wallet, which we have to hope contains the address of this military base he’s supposed to report to. “I’ll just, uh, get going. I’m gonna do that. Now.”

Mom smiles crookedly at him. “Don’t you need your bicycle?”

Theo looks toward our house, and I glimpse the bike I saw last night. He sighs heavily, and I know he’s wishing for his Pontiac. “Yes, ma’am. Marguerite, I’ll be by later, okay?”

My only answer is a nod. I’m silenced by the memory of the last words he spoke before the bomb fell—what he wanted to say to me if those were our final moments alive. He smiles slightly, then turns to go.

Once we walk inside, Mom and Dad act like everything’s normal. For them, this *is* normal. My father volunteers to make breakfast, while my mother takes the first shower. I just sit at the kitchen table, unable to move or think. The smell of burning still stinks in my nose.

After only a couple of minutes, I hear the door slam, and heavy boots tromping toward our kitchen. Dad breathes out a sigh of relief.

Josie strides in, wearing her coverall, a grin on her face. “Hey, looks like we still have a house.”

“Fortunately,” my dad says. “That’s handy, isn’t it? Otherwise I have no idea where I’d keep my shoes.”

They’re both pretending all our lives weren’t in danger during the raid; they have to. If they didn’t pretend, the fear would be too much to live with. I haven’t been here long enough to match their bravado, but I muster a smile for my sister.

Dad gets out a frying pan and spatula. "Genuine scrambled eggs coming up. Last ones for a while, too, so enjoy."

"Can't we trade for some more ration cards?" Josie makes a face. "Reconstituted eggs are so awful."

"Don't be greedy, Josephine. We receive more than most people as it is." Mom comes into the kitchen, and there is nothing weirder than seeing her in a military blazer, skirt, and necktie.

As my parents hug each other, and the frying pan sizzles, Josie leans close to me and whispers, "Hey, Mom and Dad might be cutting you a break on the young-love-in-wartime thing, but could you and Theo watch the decibel level? I need my sleep."

Oh, my God, my sister heard me having sex, no, no, no. "Sorry."

Josie's already moved on. "You know what we need? Caffeine."

"Coming right up," Dad says, placing mugs of something warm, brown, and steaming in front of us. But the smell is all wrong. Whatever he just gave me, it isn't real coffee. When I take a sip, the stuff's so bitter I have to force myself to swallow.

"Maybe you should cut down on coffee, Marguerite," Josie deadpans. "You don't seem to be sleeping well lately."

Mom comes to the rescue—deliberately or not, I don't care. "Was it at least good flying this morning?"

"Better believe it," Josie says. As she keeps talking, I

realize my sister isn't just in the military. She's a freaking fighter pilot.

At first that seems impossibly strange, but then it doesn't. My big sister is the definition of a thrill seeker. Surfing, snowboarding, zip-lining—if you have to sign a liability waiver before you do it, Josie thinks it's fun. No matter how much this dimension has changed, my sister still found a way to get her adrenaline rush.

"I wish someone would call us about the lab," Dad mutters as he works with the eggs.

"Phone lines are probably down," Mom points out. "They'll send someone. Until then, it's no use worrying about it."

She always says that, back home. My dad answers like he always does: "I don't worry because it's *useful*. I worry because I can't help it."

Mom pats his shoulder. "Just eat breakfast."

"Come on, Dad." I want him to stop talking about the war. I want him to sit down and make bad jokes over our meal, like he always does. It seemed so strange when they all first started pretending we'd never been in any danger, but now I wish they'd go back to it.

They don't. "We've got to move forward," Dad says as he puts my mom's eggs on her plate. He's talking to her, not me. "We could do more theoretical work, but if the Firebird project is ever going to help the war effort—we *must* build a prototype soon."

Mom nods. "I know. We'll have to start tomorrow. We'd

be ordered to within the week in any case. I doubt the generals would be willing to wait any longer."

"You can do it, Sophie," Dad says. "We'll make this happen. It's our last chance."

That's when it hits me. Conley sent me here to sabotage my parents' work on the Firebirds. I can't get Paul back any other way. I can't cure Theo.

But if I steal that technology from my family in this dimension—I might be condemning them all to death.

Someone knocks on the door. "That will be someone from the lab," Mom says.

I get to my feet before she can. "I'll get it." Right now I just need to do something. Anything.

Or so I believe, until I open the front door, and Paul is standing there.

8

PAUL SITS IN MY FAMILY'S LIVING ROOM, ON THE MOST uncomfortable chair. He took off his uniform hat when he walked inside, but otherwise he could have stepped right off a recruiting poster. The navy-blue jacket frames his broad shoulders; his trousers are sharply creased. Even his shoes shine. His posture is so rigidly straight I wonder if his back hurts.

I want to run to him, use the reminder and capture this second splinter of Paul's soul—halfway there! Almost done!—but I can't. In this dimension, he and my parents know what Firebirds are; they'd understand what I was doing, and that I was from another universe. In other words, I'd be busted.

The warm rapport I'm used to between Mom, Dad, and Paul is absent now. Here, my parents appear to be his superior officers, no more.

"What about our electron microscope?" Mom asks.

"Minor damage," Paul says. "Or damage that would be minor, if we could get the replacement parts more swiftly."

Dad puts his head in his hands. "Bloody hell."

"It's all right, Henry. We can still run the resonance test. But not here." It's weird, seeing my mother act so *official,* especially with Paul. "Lieutenant, is the San Francisco facility ready?"

Paul nods. "Very nearly, ma'am. I could travel into the city tomorrow to personally supervise the modifications. Within five days or so, we'd be ready. A week at most."

"Then we should review the plans," Mom says. "Normally we'd do this on base, but I trust you won't object if we meet here today, Lieutenant Markov."

Even though this is an entirely different universe, an entirely different Paul, something in my heart still sings when I hear those two words: *Lieutenant Markov.*

Couldn't I reclaim this splinter of his soul? If Mom and Dad figured out what I was doing, would that be so terrible?

Yes, it would. My heart sinks, imagining my parents' reaction. This is a world at war; I am an invader, one wearing their daughter's skin. If they reported me to the authorities, I could wind up in a military prison. Regardless, once they knew I was a traveler from another dimension, I would have no chance to sabotage their work. If I can't prove I did that when I go to Triad's home office, Conley won't give me the final coordinates, or the cure for Theo.

"Of course not, ma'am. I'll set up at this table." Paul

reaches for the stuff lying in front of him—my sketchpad, open to the portrait of Theo. He hesitates. "That is—if you wouldn't mind, Miss Caine."

Miss Caine?

"No, it's fine." I step forward to take my art supplies myself. My hand brushes against his, an accidental touch, but Paul reacts to it. His eyes search mine, hoping for meaning.

The look in his eyes is one I know. One it took me a long time to interpret. But once I understood him, I could never miss that look again.

He loves me. At the very least, he cares about me deeply. And obviously Paul and I have known each other for a long time in this dimension.

So why is it still "Lieutenant Markov" and "Miss Caine"?

More than that—if Paul is here, in my life, why am I with Theo?

Our home turns into a makeshift physics lab, which for me is nothing new. But my parents aren't as warm and welcoming in this universe. Not that they're unfriendly to Paul or anything; everyone is almost excruciatingly polite as they work. But the warmth my parents showed to Paul from the very beginning, the affection that led them to bake his birthday cake and buy him a decent winter coat—in this dimension, I see no sign of that. Maybe this is the difference between a university setting and the military. The professors who would befriend you in a graduate program have to keep their distance when they're your superior officers.

While they're crunching numbers, I'm left with nothing to do. Word comes that the munitions factory where I work was destroyed in the air raid, which is an enormous relief. Me building bombs? That would've been a recipe for disaster. The way Dad tells me this, it's obvious he expects me to receive another duty assignment soon. But "soon" is not "today," so my day is my own.

Normally, I spend any free time in a new dimension searching for background information. That means web pages or other, more sophisticated sources in universes that have developed that far; in universes not quite so far along, I turn to books. Mom and Dad almost always have plenty lying around, because they're curious about everything from the ancient Incas to origami. In this world, however, it seems that paper is rationed as strictly as everything else. No encyclopedias or histories are to be had. My parents own only a handful of books, most of them novels. Even reading those might tell me something—but would I be able to figure out what's true and what's fiction in each one? So instead of obtaining vital facts for my mission, I wind up reading a Jane Austen novel called *The Brothers*. I don't think we have that one in my universe, though, so at least that's something.

Late in the afternoon, as they're taking a break for a fairly depressing snack of canned peaches, my mother draws me aside. "You're not ill at ease, are you?"

"Um, no?"

"I realize how awkward the situation is for everyone involved," Mom continues. "Lieutenant Markov is essential to our work, and we have to work at home today, so there's no way around it."

She seems to expect a response. "Okay."

"He's handling his disappointment well, really. That's all we can ask. I just hope it doesn't put you in a difficult position."

It sounds like Paul tried to get me to go out with him and I said no.

Why would I say no?

"It's all right," I say to her. "Paul's a good guy. I know he'll always do the right thing in the end."

Mom stares at me like I just told her ostriches orbit Pluto. Is it because I slipped up and called him Paul? After a moment, though, she nods. "Sometimes I forget how insightful you are."

I hug her, remembering the long weeks when I was trapped in dimensions where she was already dead. Traveling through the worlds gives you perspective. It makes you value what you have.

Just at nightfall, while the ad hoc scientific conference is still under way, the doorbell chimes again. Dad answers before I can. "Why, Private Beck. I don't think I've seen you in *ages*."

"Good evening, sir. Is Marguerite at home?" Theo catches sight of me and lights up like sunrise. He's playing his role in this universe a little too well.

Still, the roles have to be played. "Theo," I say as I go to him. He pulls me into his arms, an embrace so fervent, so intimate, that I can't deal with the fact that my parents are watching this. In Theo's ears, I whisper, "That's enough."

"For now," he says in a low voice.

This isn't my Theo.

The Theo from this universe—the one who's been to bed with Marguerite, the one who loves her—that's who's holding me now.

I manage to part us without actually shoving him against the wall. My parents studiously stare down at their equations. From his chair, Paul watches us, then ducks his head when he realizes I've seen him.

"How did the telemetry systems fare in the raid, Private Beck?" My mother asks him this without ever looking up from her work.

"Very well, Dr. Caine," Theo says. Huh, so my parents got around to getting married in this universe. Good to know. "In the first rush—for a moment, it felt as though I didn't even remember how I'd gotten back to base. Strange."

That's because my Theo was in charge during that trip; this Theo's consciousness didn't reclaim his body until afterward. He must have spaced out the reminders like I told him to.

"We didn't take too much damage," Theo continues. "I've reviewed the entire system. We'll be back to full capacity by tomorrow."

"Have you eaten dinner?" Mom says. She's being a bit cool—probably because she remembers us running out of the house half-dressed last night. "I can't offer you much beyond cheese on toast, because we're at the low end of our rations. But it's yours if you want it."

"I ate already. Just wanted to talk with Marguerite for a bit."

Dad waves us off. "Fine. Go on out back."

Out back? Theo seems to know what this means, though; he takes my hand and leads us toward the rear of the house. As we go, Paul watches us, his gray eyes yearning—no. *Hungry.* Then he sees my mother looking at him, and returns his attention to the papers on the table.

I love our back deck at home, with its silly tropical-fish lights and the yard that slopes so sharply you can't even set up a lawn chair. I love the way it's ringed by tall trees, making it seem as though our house in the Berkeley Hills isn't crammed into an overpopulated neighborhood; instead, I feel like we're cut off from the rest of the world, in a quiet, peaceful place of our own.

In this dimension? No such luck. We have no back deck, only the one tree. Instead, there's a few inches of concrete that has to count as a patio, and one rickety bench. But from the way Theo pulls me down next to him on that bench, this must be our favorite place.

"I missed you today," he whispers, and he draws me close.

My whole body flushes, but I manage to hold him back. "Wait."

When I pull the Firebird from his uniform jacket, Theo stares. "What the hell is that?"

"You'll see," I say, punching in the sequence that will activate a reminder.

The charge jolts him. Theo swears under his breath and pushes himself away from me. After a couple of deep breaths, his eyes go wide. He's my Theo again. "Whoa."

"Are you all right?"

"I was like—I was in my body, but I wasn't. Like sleep-walking while you're awake. That is the weirdest thing I have ever—ever—wow." Theo shakes his head, as if trying to clear it. "How do you deal with this?"

"It doesn't happen to me," I remind him. "I'm always in control, no matter what world I'm in."

"Nice work if you can get it." Theo takes a deep breath, then refocuses. "What exactly happened inside?"

Since Theo's not a perfect traveler, he doesn't remember what happens during his journeys quite as clearly as I do. So maybe he's forgotten the passionate embrace. Or he's pretending to. Either way, I'm grateful. "Nothing much. You came to see me, Mom and Dad pretended you weren't here this morning, and sent us out here."

Theo says, "That was Paul with your parents, right?"

"Yeah."

"Why didn't you go after him? Rescue that splinter of his soul?"

"Because I have to be in contact with him to do that," I say, blushing again. "Close contact. It's not like I can tackle him in the middle of the living room."

Theo frowns. "What if that's what it takes?"

"Of course, if I have to, I will. But if I start acting weird before we get into Mom and Dad's computer systems, they might figure out something is up." I hook one finger around the two Firebird chains at my neck. "Remember, it's hard for people from another dimension to see our Firebirds, but they can, particularly if they know to look for them. In this world, they know."

"Right, right. I've got it." Theo hesitates, then says, "I thought—I figured you couldn't know him yet, in this universe. Paul."

"Well, I do know him," I say as lightly as I can.

My casual attitude doesn't fool Theo for a minute. "Am I allowed to feel good about this?"

"About what, exactly?"

His eyes are dark, unfathomable. "About the fact that there's at least one world in the multiverse where you picked me."

I'm grateful for the darkness around us. Maybe that keeps him from seeing how flustered I am. "I—it's like you guys always said. In an infinite multiverse, everything that can happen, does happen."

"So this—you and me—we were in the realm of possibility? Not sure how that makes me feel." Theo stares up at the sky. Maybe lights are turned down, for fear of more bombers, because I can see every star above. "Probably you never even met Paul before today."

I ought to agree with him and move on. Instead, I tell the truth. "No, I know him. And he—he cares about me. I can tell."

"Poor bastard." When I look at him, Theo shrugs, but he's no better at faking casual than I am. "Being in love with a girl who doesn't love you back? It sucks. I'd know."

There's nothing I can possibly say in reply.

"I wouldn't wish that on my worst enemy. So I definitely wouldn't wish it on Paul." Theo hesitates, then moves us along to a new subject. "Listen, when I was on base, I tried using the military computers to get at the Firebird data. No luck. Maybe that's just because I'm not part of the project, but I figure your parents are as security-conscious as ever."

Mom and Dad aren't the type to use passwords like *ABC123.* For a while, my mom's log-in code at home was the molar heat capacity of magnesium, and that's just for her email. To get into a classified military project, they're going to employ every barrier that exists. Still, I thought Theo's familiarity with them would give us an edge. "You don't think you can get through at all?"

"If I had unobserved access to a terminal for long enough, probably, but in this universe, those are hard to come by. I can't exactly hack into a military computer from a military base. I'd be arrested before I even hit Enter."

What are we going to do? We have to complete Conley's errand if there's any chance of saving Paul and Theo. The computer virus can do the work for us, but only if we can access the system the virus is designed to destroy.

The answer comes to me, and I turn to Theo. "We don't try to get in through my parents. We get in through Paul."

"How exactly do we do that?"

"He's going to San Francisco tomorrow to set up the lab for a test of the Firebird components. If we go to San Francisco too, we could sabotage the new lab. Right?"

"Maybe." Theo still looks doubtful, though. "But why would Paul give us access?"

I take a deep breath. "Because I'll ask him to."

For a few moments, neither of us speaks. Then he says, "You'd betray one Paul to save another."

"If I have to." But when I hear Theo say it, my plan sounds so much harder. Crueler. "Besides, it gives me a chance to get . . . closer to him. So in the end I can rescue this splinter of Paul's soul."

"Makes sense," Theo says flatly.

"I hate this, okay? I hate every minute of it. Probably Wyatt Conley thinks I don't give a damn about my family in any other dimension, but this version of Dad is still Dad. This version of Mom is still Mom. Josie, Paul—if I do what Conley wants us to do, I might take away their last chance to win the war. But I have to. Getting close to Paul isn't the worst thing I'm going to do in this dimension. It's not even close."

Together we stare into the distance, at the place where light streams through our window and paints squares on the scrubby grass. Even electricity is rationed here, so the night has become quiet and still. Instead of traffic noise, I hear only the wind through the trees.

Theo speaks first. "I eavesdropped on as much war talk as I could today at the base. Apparently the situation doesn't look good. We lost Mexico. Which I guess means this country had Mexico at some point, but, whatever. Supply lines from the Midwest have broken down."

"Is this like, if we lose the war, we have to rebuild? Like the Civil War?" Reconstruction and Jim Crow sucked hard, but even that sounds better than the alternative. "Or is this like, if we lose the war, Adolf Hitler rules the world?

"The way the guys at the barracks talk, it sounds more Hitler-y. Still, it's wartime. They could be exaggerating. Everybody hates the enemy, right?"

We have to hope.

"Listen, we don't have the power to permanently end your parents' research, no matter what Conley says." Theo takes my hand—for emphasis, probably, or simply for comfort, but I am vividly aware of his touch. "Say we manage to infect their project with the virus, screw up the computer system they have here—which is so tightly knit together, by the way, that taking the whole thing down would be a cinch. How long do you think it would take your parents to rebuild? A year, maybe? A little less?"

"Do they have a year left?"

From inside we hear the sound of Josie cackling, like she does at Dad's awful jokes. If I do this, I'm betraying my sister, too. Guilt feels like a fist closing around me, squeezing tighter and tighter until I hardly remember how to breathe.

I whisper, "If my Paul were here, I . . . I think he'd tell me to leave him and save them."

"If he were here, you'd tell him to shut up while you saved his ass."

Despite everything, I laugh. "Probably."

"Listen. This 'cure' for Nightthief exposure Conley's talking about—even he admitted it might not work," Theo says. "If you're forcing yourself through this for me, don't bother. But it's not just about me. We have to get Paul back. That means we do whatever we have to do. Right?"

"Right," I say, trying not to hear my family talking inside.

Theo brightens, like everything's all right, when it so obviously isn't. He's doing this to help Paul, and I feel a wave of unexpected tenderness for him. "Okay," he says. "Now all we have to do is figure out how to get you to San Francisco."

We pitch it as a romantic getaway, claiming Theo has leave. (Hopefully he can get it.) Until I'm assigned new war work, the destruction of the munitions factory means I've got some free time. So—why not San Francisco?

Before we talked to my parents, Theo had said, "Are you sure they're going to say yes instead of taking a shotgun to my head?"

"Dad's not the shotgun type. Mom—maybe, but probably not." Besides, I remember how they reacted when I told them Paul and I had fallen in love. Maybe Mom and Dad aren't cozy with Theo in this universe, but they like him. They're not prudes. They're . . . realistic. "Anyway, if she were going to shoot you, she would've done it this morning."

"That isn't half as comforting as you think it is."

But asking your parents to let you go away for the weekend

with the guy who's been sneaking in and out of your room—no matter what universe you're in, that does *not* go over well.

"I can't believe you'd ask us this," Dad says as he paces the front room. "Not knowing what you know. Traveling down to San Francisco! It's outrageous."

Theo and I dare a glance at each other. His expression says what I'm thinking: *We screwed up.*

Mom speaks for the first time since I asked her about the trip. "Henry, we've had no problems with the train lines this far north."

Dad is not appeased. "Not yet. But at any moment—Didn't today's raid teach us anything? We don't know when the next attack will be. We don't get to know."

Wait. He's not freaked out by the thought of my staying in a hotel with Theo. Dad's upset because I want to travel away from home, period.

I venture, "Dad, the raid last night—we came *this close* to being blown away."

Mom's voice is sharp. "Don't remind us."

"Don't you see? We're in danger everywhere. All the time. It's not like I'm safer if I stay here."

After a moment, my mother nods, but Dad keeps pacing. "You remember what happened to your aunt Susannah. Everyone said the passenger ships were safe as long as they sailed under a neutral flag, but still—" His words choke off, and Mom takes his hand.

Aunt Susannah is dead.

I can't wrap my head around it at first. She's my giddy,

spoiled London aunt, who never seemed to care about much besides fashion and high society—but she loved all of us, and welcomed us whenever we visited Great Britain. One time when I was little, she took me to tea at some fancy hotel, and I felt so grown up. So special.

The last time I saw Aunt Susannah was in another dimension, the futuristic London where my parents had died during my childhood, and she had raised me. It was clear that she hadn't done the best job at mothering; maternal instincts and Aunt Susannah don't mix. But still, she took me in. She did her best.

Now I have to imagine her on a ship on the ocean hit with torpedoes, sinking fast. She would have been so scared, and there would have been no hope of rescue. No escape.

Mom strokes Dad's hand. "Marguerite is right. Safety is a luxury none of us have had in a long time, and may never have again."

He doesn't argue, exactly, just changes strategy. "She's eighteen, and we're sending her off with her boyfriend?"

"We should live life to the fullest," Mom says. We all hear the unspoken *while we can*.

Dad shrugs, and I know then that we're more than halfway to a yes. My mother always wins in the end.

Theo had been willing to lie about accompanying me to San Francisco, but it turns out he didn't have to. He *was* up for leave, and his superior officers gave him three whole days off. As glad as I am not to have to do this alone, Theo's presence complicates things in ways neither of us has to speak aloud.

It's one thing to pretend to be a couple when we're sitting on my parents' sofa. Another to carry that pretense all the way to a hotel for the weekend.

"I can't believe they're letting you do this," Josie fumes as she drives me to the train station Friday morning. "Mom and Dad practically handed you condoms for the trip."

"It wasn't *that* easy," I protest. My small suitcase sits in my lap; it feels like it's made of something not much sturdier than cardboard.

Josie shrugs. "Well, there's a war on."

Which is pretty much what she said last night, when she let me borrow her one good dress—dark red, and made out of fabric soft enough to almost feel silky. *For your romantic getaway*, she'd said, and of course I couldn't contradict her.

The train station buzzes with activity, but I glimpse Theo right away. When I wave to him, he jogs to us and—fulfilling his role—gives me a hug. "Hey. Was starting to think you'd ditched me."

"Never," I say. I hope that sounds flirty enough.

"Have a good time, you two," Josie says. Already she's turning to go. "Bang those hotel walls even louder than mine."

Oh, my God. My cheeks feel like they're on fire.

Theo waves goodbye to her, then crooks his elbow. I slip my arm through it. Like a man and woman would if they wanted to touch each other every moment. Like we were in love.

9

FROM THE TRAIN WINDOWS, I FINALLY GET MY FIRST REAL look at the damage done to this battered world. The bombed-out neighborhoods I drove through the other day—the one I walked out of on shaking legs—that seemed like one terrible thing that happened in one devastated place. Even though I'd learned about the war, I still couldn't envision what that truly meant.

Now I don't have to. The evidence spreads out on either side of the train.

We must live farther than I'd thought from the Berkeley I know, because our train ride lasts awhile. Then again, we're moving very slowly, which gives me a chance to look around. Instead of the urban sprawl of my world's Bay Area, we pass through only a few small towns, each one of which looks sadder and more broken-down than the last. Paint peels from buildings; litter lines the potholed streets; and nobody seems to be driving, or walking around, or doing much of anything. Mostly, though, the train travels through fields that look almost too abundant. Clover and weeds have grown as high as the train itself, sometimes higher. Vines have reclaimed what remains of old fences. Nobody has farmed or built or even mowed grass around here for a very long time.

Often, in a new universe, I try to decide which artist would have been most likely to create a world like the one before me. This time, I can't think of a single painter who would have created a world so gray and hopeless. Though maybe Andrew Wyeth could have captured this if he'd wanted to—nature and the countryside, but strangely haunted.

"How long do you think this war has been going on?" Theo says, quietly enough not to attract attention from the other passengers in the train car.

"Years. A decade? Maybe more." Looking at the utter deadness around us—in what used to be some of the most expensive property in the entire country—I could believe the war has lasted an entire generation.

Theo and I sit together like the lovers we're supposed to be. The lovers we *are*, in this dimension. Most of the people around us wear dark, practical clothing like the cheap dress I've got on, though several men are in uniform like Theo. I take another look at him in his crisp, dark green uniform, complete with the folded cap on his head, and can't resist a smile.

He smiles back. "What's so funny?"

"Your uniform. It's not exactly a Lumineers T-shirt and a fedora, is it?"

"You mock my fashion sense." Theo puts one hand over his chest, pretending to have been shot through the heart. "But I for one happen to know I am stylin'. Well, usually. Not today."

As innocently as I can, I say, "Aren't most of the hipster guys growing beards now?"

Theo makes a face. "Not me. I mean, I could maybe have a goatee or something sometime. But the beards you see right now? Halfway to Amish."

I laugh out loud. Several other passengers turn to look at us, but instead of looking annoyed, most of them smile. Maybe people have a soft spot for wartime romance.

If Theo notices, he shows no sign. "Listen, I meant to wait until we got to San Francisco, but it looks like that's going to take longer than I thought."

No timetables were given at the train station. Apparently you're supposed to count yourself lucky if you even reach your destination. "Wait for what?"

"To go over the files I pulled." From his rucksack Theo tugs a manila folder, which is thick with more dot-matrix printer paper.

"I thought you said you couldn't get through the security," I say, leaning closer.

Theo replies, "I couldn't get through to the classified stuff, no. But more general information? Not a problem."

As soon as he opens the folder, my eyes find the name on

the top sheet: LIEUTENANT PAUL MARKOV.

"So here we have Paul's assignment, his service record—which is golden, by the way—and even his address in San Francisco." Theo frowned down at the paper. "Military Housing, it says. I get the impression that's somewhere between a barracks and an apartment."

"Do we have his phone number there?"

"Yeah. At his office on base too. So you'll be able to reach him one way or another." Then Theo sucks in a breath, and his hand tightens around the folder until the cover crumples. "Dammit."

"What?"

He points at a name on another page, one he just pulled out. It's in small print, in one entry like all the others, but as soon as I see it the world turns cold.

Lieutenant Colonel Wyatt Conley.

"What is he doing here?" I say, but the answer comes to me immediately. He's doing the same thing he always does: inventing the latest technology and marketing it to whoever will pay the most to get it. In this world, that's the military.

Once, in the Londonverse, I heard Conley give a speech about how war evolved over the centuries. He said then that the next weapons and strategies would go beyond anything history had ever seen.

As strange as this war is to me, I don't get the sense that it's so incredibly different from the ways wars have been fought before. Conley doesn't have the technology he needs here to do what he wants to do.

Then it hits me. "He's connected to the Firebird project, isn't he? But—he can't be. If so, he wouldn't need me. He could sabotage the Firebirds himself."

"He's requested transfer to the project multiple times. Always been turned down." Theo keeps scanning the files. "Conley and Paul have worked together on some other projects, though. Now he's trying to get Paul transferred over to his department, but no success so far."

"Do you think that's this dimension's Conley trying to get control over Paul? Or our Conley trying to screw things up and failing?"

"My guess? Both. But our Conley gave up, which is why we got this all-expenses-paid vacation in paradise." Theo makes a gesture like *Look at these amazing prizes*, and finally I can smile again.

At this point I notice an older man looking toward us with a puzzled frown. I whisper, "Remember, watch our volume control as long as we're talking about dimensions."

Theo swears under his breath. "I keep forgetting how *quiet* it is here."

Nobody's music is wafting over from earbuds. Relatively few people seem to chat with each other. There's no ambient noise of cars or city life from the world outside. Just the thrumming of the tracks beneath the train, the occasional crinkle of folded newspaper, and Theo and me.

More quietly, he continues, "So what's our plan here?"

"We get to Paul, and I find out what I can." Already I'm counting the minutes until I can be alone with him again.

"I could suggest dropping by the lab for a tour, and—I guess that's a place to start."

Theo frowns. "Not much of a plan there."

"It could work," I retort. Theo's already loaded the virus onto this dimension's version of a hard drive. All I'd have to do would be plug it into the right port—and once I was in their lab, I think I could figure out what that is.

"It could," he concedes, "but we can't afford to count on that. The project is classified. You might not be allowed in regardless of who your parents are."

As much as I hate to admit it, Theo's right. "What else should I do?"

"For starters, try to swipe his keys. His wallet too, if you can get it, or even just take a look inside. Since you're Sophia and Henry's kid, you can probably get him talking about the Firebirds without too much trouble. Find out how to get access to the computer system, and with this handy virus, we can take it from there. We'll have screwed this whole world over before you know it."

Our conversation has become so tactical. So—cold. "You sound happy about it," I snap. "Could you cut it out?"

"Hey," he says, more softly. "I know it's hard doing this to your parents. I love them too, you know. Just like you and I both love Paul. That's why we're here. If we have to choose between a version in another dimension and our version—there's only one choice we can make. Right?"

"You think they're totally different," I say, "but they're not. Mom is my mom, everywhere. Paul is Paul, everywhere."

"And I'm the homicidal psycho from Triad everywhere?"

That stings. "No. I didn't mean—they're not identical. But they're not as separate as you're pretending they are."

"If the pretense helps us get the job done, then I'm going to keep on pretending my heart out. Because that cure for Nightthief exposure—I need it, and soon. Are you with me?"

"I'm with you." I mean it, but saying the words still hurts.

"Don't listen to me, okay? Sometimes I snark about stuff because—you know. It's easier." Theo clearly sees that I'm still affected, but he doesn't press further. "Okay. You go meet Paul. You learn everything you can. You bring me keys or a pass to his lab. I can take it from there."

"You?"

"Don't act so surprised. This might be my first long-distance trip, but I think I'm getting the swing of it. Of course, I had to cut way down on the reminders—you were right about the charge, and also, *damn* do reminders hurt." His smile is crooked. "What did you think I was here for? Just to provide an excuse for you to get on that train?"

"Moral support, I guess."

It's his turn to laugh. "Immoral support, more like."

How can Theo make me smile even when the situation is so grim? Somehow he always does.

Then he adds, "Besides, like you said, while you're nabbing Paul's stuff—you'll be close to him. You'll have your chance to rescue that splinter of his soul."

The thought of being close to Paul—both this world's Paul and my own—sends a shiver through me. But I don't lose focus. If I act too early, Paul will catch on. We have to complete our terrible mission here before I have my chance at Paul. "Not until the very end."

"Two rooms? What's a guy with a pretty girl want with two hotel rooms?" says the desk clerk.

With a straight face, Theo replies, "I'll have you know I'm a gentleman, sir."

The guy gives him a look. "You know how many refugees from SoCal we've had coming through here the past couple of weeks? You're lucky I've even got one room available. Nobody else is going to have many vacancies either. Take this one, and you can be a gentleman on the floor."

As we silently ride up in the elevator, Theo holds our suitcases. I hold the hotel key—old-fashioned, metal with an aquamarine plastic tag dangling by a chain. Finally Theo says, "The floor's fine. Really."

"We can take shifts. Four hours bed, four hours floor."

"That works too."

The problem is, there's not even a lot of floor in this hotel room, which is the smallest I've ever seen. Although I guess this is technically a double bed, it's narrower than most, and yet it covers almost the entire length of the room. We barely have room to slip inside, stash our suitcases in a closet almost too shallow to hold them, and to open the door to a bathroom not much bigger than the closet. The carpet is beige industrial stuff, and the paint on the yellowing walls is chipped.

"Well, it ain't the Ritz." Theo sits down heavily on the bed, then frowns. "Wait. Where's the phone?"

Turns out this hotel has only one phone per floor. If you want to make a call, you have to wait in line to step inside the "phone booth"—actually just a cubby with a little bench. The guy in front of me has a ten-minute argument with a woman (wife or girlfriend, I can't tell) who apparently feels like he doesn't make enough time for the two of them. I hear enough of the conversation to agree with her, but nobody's asking me.

Finally he slams down the receiver and stalks off. The phone is mine. For a moment I sit there, staring at the print-out with Paul's number on it, wondering how I go through with this.

Then I read the title again: *Lieutenant Markov.* And I dial.

Three rings, and—"Markov."

Paul's voice feels like rain after a drought. Just hearing him makes my throat tighten. I manage to say, "Lieutenant Markov? This is Marguerite Caine."

"Miss Caine?" He sounds like he thinks this might be some kind of prank.

"Yeah. Hi. I—I hope it's okay that I called."

"Of course. Has something happened to the Doctors Caine?"

"No, no, they're fine! I was calling because, well, I'm in San Francisco, and I'm on my own. So I thought maybe we could meet up."

After a brief pause, Paul says, "You came to San Francisco by yourself?"

"No. I came here with Theo." Do I sound angry? I'm trying. "But he got upset because I—well, he stormed off. So now I'm all alone in the city for a couple of days."

"Private Beck left you on your own?" At least one of us is genuinely angry.

"I'm all right!" I feel the need to make excuses for Theo, even after an argument that's totally imaginary. "I've got a hotel room, and my suitcase, and a ticket back home in three days. But until then—well—I could use some company."

The silence that follows stretches so long I start to wonder if we lost our connection. Finally Paul says, "Would you allow me to take you to dinner?"

He speaks so formally, sounds so unsure. I'm reminded of Lieutenant Markov, and the way he loved the Grand Duchess Margarita for so long without ever saying a word. I can feel my smile like sunlight on my face. "I'd love that."

Next up in this dimension's never-ending parade of awkward: getting ready for my hot date with Paul while Theo is in the same room.

Technically I get dressed in the bathroom, but he's right outside the door, critiquing the other elements of my outfit. "Your shoes are awful," he calls as I struggle with my zipper. "These are hug-me pumps at best."

"I'm not going out to *seduce* him." Paul and I never discussed whether getting together with other-dimensional versions of ourselves would count as cheating. Our relationship issues are not like most people's. "I just need him to be, you know, flattered that I'm paying him attention."

"Trust me," Theo says, more quietly. "He's gonna melt the minute he sees you."

I pretend I can't hear him. Instead, I finally conquer the zipper, then step as far back as I can to look at myself in the small mirror.

Josie's slightly shorter than I am, and her boobs are way better. But the way this dress is cut, the differences in our sizes don't matter. The neckline cascades in soft folds, Grecian-style, then flows freely down to slightly past my knees. Although the dress has no sleeves, some of the red fabric drapes over my shoulders almost to the elbow. It doesn't show much skin at the neck or arms or legs, and the fabric remains cheap, but the overall effect is undeniably sexy.

My short hair makes me wince. If I could tie it up in a messy bun, that would look perfect. Instead, I work with the bob as best I can, pulling one side back with a shiny metal clip.

Lipstick here is almost always worn dark red. The shade matches the dress, so I'm happy with it. I have no jewelry besides the Firebirds, tucked beneath my neckline so that only a hint of the gold chains shows at my throat. I fluff my hair again, step out of the bathroom, and smile. "How do I look?"

Theo just stops. He stares at me like he can't move, or maybe even breathe. His expression reminds me of the picture I found in this Marguerite's pocket.

I think maybe the tiny bathroom mirror didn't do justice to this dress.

Then Theo snaps out of it. "You look smashing, my dear."

"Very British of you." Stupid joke. I have to joke, distract him, do something to break the tension between us.

"Should I say ravishing? Gorgeous? How about lovely? Lovely works."

I manage to smile. "Thank you."

When I step into the shoes, I wobble—heels aren't my thing. Theo leans close, so that I can brace my hand against his shoulder. Once I've got them on, though, he doesn't move back. I don't take my hand away, either.

"You know . . ." His voice trails off.

"What?"

Theo shakes his head. "Better left unsaid."

Normally I would let him get away with that. Tonight I don't. "Tell me."

His eyes meet mine. "I'm in this extremely weird position where I'm jealous of myself."

It's hard not to look away, but I don't. Remembering London, I admit, "We came close enough before."

"But that wasn't me either!" Theo starts laughing, and I can't help but smile. "Do you think we're serious? This Theo and this Marguerite? Or is this just, you know, seize the day, seize the girl, because tomorrow never knows?"

At first I think I won't even be able to say the words, but Theo deserves this much of the truth. "We're in love."

"You think so?"

"I know." I fold my arms in front of my chest, one tiny barrier between me and Theo as he stands so very close. "During the air raid, I found a picture of you in my pocket. You wrote on the back, 'with all my love.'"

Actually he said something about *eternal love*, but maybe I can leave that part out.

"I can believe that," he says evenly. "Doesn't mean the feeling's mutual, though."

"It is. I found my drawings of you. The way I sketched your face . . ." I switch out of first person. "She loves the Theo from this dimension. Deeply. Completely."

"Lucky guy."

When our eyes meet again, we're both listening to the words we haven't said. Even though I don't feel the same way Theo does, he's important to me—and apparently there was more potential between us than I ever realized. He wasn't wrong to fall for me. Just in the wrong universe.

I summon the courage to say, "In the bomb shelter—right before the blast—"

"I said the kind of thing people say when they think they'll never have another chance," Theo says. "Let it go, okay?"

I should. I will. Just as soon as I figure out how.

10

NO TRANSAMERICA PYRAMID. NO COLUMBUS TOWER. Either Ghirardelli Square was bombed to oblivion a while ago or they never built it in the first place. People walking by me on the street seem quieter, more furtive, less themselves—it's like I'm surrounded by the same hundred black coats with changing faces. This isn't the San Francisco I remember.

Something of the city's spirit survives, though. I'm able to take a cable car part of the way, and the place where Paul asked me to meet him is in the neighborhood still known as Chinatown.

I stand on the corner, my long dark coat pulled tightly around me. The temperature turned colder today—winter's last futile howl against spring. I wonder if weather conditions are the same in alternate dimensions, if at home Mom and Dad have pulled their sweaters back out of the closet. Or maybe the "butterfly effect" holds up, and the tiniest possible changes in each world create new climates, new storms.

Meanwhile, Theo's stuck in our hotel room, waiting for me to come back and tell him all about flirting with Paul.

I keep remembering that picture I found in my pocket, and what was written on the back. Theo and the other Marguerite love each other so much here. I guess—I guess I fell in love with him before I even met Paul.

The strange part isn't that I'm with Theo. To myself I can admit that I understand how I could fall for him, with his sense of humor, devilish eyes, and the kind of full lips most girls would kill for. Despite the darker side of his character I'm still coming to terms with, Theo has a lot to give.

The strange part is that I didn't fall for Paul.

This Paul's love for me might as well be tattooed on his skin. Anyone near him can see it, no matter how hard he works to remain at a polite distance, to show me no more attention than he should. But he's *always* paying attention to the details and emotions other people miss. Paul sees the real me in ways no one else ever has.

Did this Marguerite just not understand how much he cares?

I tamp down my frustration. *You didn't understand him either at first, remember? It took you nearly a year to realize who Paul really is. This Marguerite got involved with someone else first. So it's going to take her longer. But she'll get it eventually—won't she?*

The question, I guess, is how much this Marguerite loves Theo.

If our souls are the same in world after world, then Theo must in some fundamental way be the same person as the one from the Triadverse who betrayed us all. I've fought hard not to measure my Theo by the actions of another, but that silent judgment has lurked in the back of my mind.

Yet he stayed silent about his own pain. Came on this dangerous journey, breaking his own resolution never to travel between the worlds. Helped me come to San Francisco and set up a date with another man. The Theo from the Triadverse—I can't imagine him being so brave. But, of course, we're not only here to save Paul; we're also after the cure for Nightthief. So far I have no idea whether this world's Theo is more like the one from the Triadverse or more like mine.

At that very moment, amid the dull, faceless crowd, I glimpse Paul.

His uniform is different from Theo's or even the one he wore to our house the other day: crisper, all in spotless white, except for navy and gold stripes at the sleeves—an officer's insignia. The hat he wears has a brim and a small flag on the front. He could almost have stepped out of the 1940s.

It's like Paul was built to wear uniforms. I remember how he looked in Russia, when he was a soldier and my guard.

Which makes it even sweeter to lift my hand and wave.

He stops short. "Oh, Miss Caine. I didn't expect you to be—" *Dressed up*, maybe. Or *smiling.* But Paul says only, "—here so soon."

This is the time we chose, almost to the minute; he's punctual in a scary, inner-atomic-clock way. I let it slide.

"Hey, let's make a deal. If you'll call me Marguerite, I'll call you Paul."

It takes him a moment to say, "All right. Marguerite."

"All right, Paul."

"Well," he says, then doesn't seem to be able to come up with anything else right away. I stifle a smile; Paul's as awkward in this dimension as he is in mine. "So. Dinner. I made reservations."

"Wonderful." He must be taking me someplace special.

Then he adds, "Very few places are able to cook well with the new ration standards. This is an exception."

Restaurants that have to feed you off a ration card? I remember the dismal meals at home—cheese on toast, canned peaches, eggs that are not real eggs—and lower my expectations.

Apparently cheesy Chinese-restaurant decor has the power to travel through dimensions unchanged. Red-and-gold fans unfold across the walls, and small paper lanterns dangle in the corners. They're all a little faded, like nobody's replaced them with new ones in a long time, but they still add color to the room. Paul and I are seated in a curved booth just beneath one of the lanterns. The setting is perfect—intimate, so I can ignore the noise and activity around us and just be with him.

And betray him, whispers Theo's voice in my memory.

"At first I didn't understand why you weren't working at the munitions plant," Paul says, instead of normal human conversation like *what happened with Theo* or *how was your trip*.

"But it was destroyed in the air raid. I'd forgotten."

"I'll get another duty assignment soon, but not yet," I say, which is probably the truth. Mom and Dad would have told me if I were going AWOL.

Paul nods. "I heard the younger workers were on shift. The thirteen- and fourteen-year-olds. It's terrible." A lot of people say stuff like that about tragedies only because they think they're supposed to, but Paul closes his eyes briefly after he speaks. Like it hurts to remember it.

When I think about a bunch of middle-school kids blown to bits in a factory already filled with explosives, my heart hurts too.

Also—kids as young as thirteen are working in factories? The war has already closed the schools, then. This dimension—at least, this nation, the one containing my family and friends and everyone I love—it's even closer to the brink than I realized.

You're the one who's going to push them over the edge, I remind myself. My parents believe the Firebird project is their last hope; my job here is to take that hope away.

I hate Conley for making me do this. I hate myself for doing it.

But as I sit here, looking across the table at Paul, I remember that a splinter of my Paul's soul is trapped within. Lost and utterly alone, in a world he can't escape. For him, I think I could do anything. Even this.

"I'm glad you phoned today. It gives us a chance to talk." He takes a deep breath, obviously gearing himself up to say something he's planned. "When I spoke to you a few months ago—if I made things difficult between us, I'm sorry."

Can I forgive Paul before I know what I'm forgiving him for? I try, "What were you thinking?"

Paul's hands twist the napkin across his lap. "My father always told me not to let anything get between me and something I truly wanted."

I blink. That sounds . . . encouraging. Always before, I've had the impression that Paul's father was anything but supportive.

He continues, "So I thought I would ask you out, regardless of what your parents might think or—or whether you were already dating someone. I misunderstood the depth of the commitment between you and Private Beck. If I had realized, I would never have said anything. Please forgive me."

I can picture the entire scene: Paul standing in front of me, probably scrunching his cap in his hands the way he's twisting that napkin now. Me, so addled with love or lust for Theo that I couldn't see the good man standing right in front of me. The depth of what he felt went unnoticed, unreturned. My heart breaks for him a little. At least I can give him tonight.

"It's okay," I say. "Really."

"Oh. Good. I'd thought—well, I'd been afraid you weren't at ease with me anymore. Even intimidated."

Paul's an intimidating man: his size and his rugged features make him look more like a firefighter or a SWAT team member than a scientist. I've seen people glance at him when we're walking around Oakland after dark. In shadow, he looks like someone who could take you down in about five seconds. Yet I've seen how gentle he can be, and the memory makes me smile. "You've proved you're not the big scary guy I thought you were."

He looks skyward, like he wants to laugh but can't. "Big scary guy," he repeats.

"Nope. That's not you."

"Glad to hear it." That's as close as Paul can come to banter. He's so endearingly unsure of himself that it reminds me of my own Paul. The pain of missing him mingles with the strange delight of being with this world's Paul Markov, and suddenly it's hard to remember where one ends and the other begins. Is that glimmer of my Paul's soul at work here, drawing us closer together? "I hope your parents aren't upset with me. They might have seen my behavior as disrespect."

"Of course not. My parents know you're okay. They wouldn't work with you otherwise."

"We all have our duty."

"It's not just duty. Mom and Dad think you're brilliant," I say. It's the truth in my world, and probably in this one as well. "She even calls you a genius. Which for most people just means, 'someone really smart,' but you know Mom. When she says genius, she means it."

Genius isn't just intelligence, she explained to me once. It's the ability to see further than anyone around you, to put together different concepts in a way no one else has imagined. Genius implies originality and independence. It's her highest compliment, and Paul's the only one of her students I've ever heard her describe that way.

Paul ducks his head. But I can see his small, almost disbelieving smile. "That's good to hear."

"Tell me about San Francisco," I say. The file Theo found listed Paul as having military housing here in the city; he must only visit the base in my hometown from time to time. "What it's like to live here. Tell me everything."

Paul is normally so taciturn that "tell me everything" is likely to get you about two short sentences, max. Either this Paul is more willing to talk, or Josie's red dress has magic powers. Because he starts telling me how he came to the city in the first place—and since I'm able to read between the lines, he actually tells me a whole lot more than that.

He came here "after New York fell." Apparently he was born in NYC, just like my Paul, only a few months after his parents immigrated. His military service began three years ago, "two years before the compulsory age." The advanced weaponry program had recruited him based on his scores on the "usual mandatory tests," which I'm guessing don't have much in common with the SATs. When I ask him about music, he loves Rachmaninoff as much here as he does back home—but has never heard of anyone from the past fifty years or so.

Then again, Paul is so adorably clueless about pop culture in every dimension that he wouldn't know any performer from the past fifty years anyway.

Even this more talkative version of Paul isn't comfortable

monopolizing the conversation. So I try to do the thing I suck at the most. I flirt.

"You ought to sit for me sometime," I say.

"Sit for you?"

"As a model, for my sketches. You have the face for it." My mind flashes back to one time my Paul sat for me—and showed off much more than his face—but if I start thinking about that in depth, my face will turn as red as my dress.

"A face like a model. Hardly," Paul says, but I can tell he's flattered, and so embarrassed about it that he doesn't know what to say. Paul has no more game in this universe than in my own.

Might as well lay it on thick, have a little fun. "The lines of your face would work well, for an artist's subject. Your jaw, your brow, your nose—straight and strong. Plus you have amazing eyes."

Paul's expression is caught halfway between disbelief and pleasure. Probably he'd be more comfortable if I changed the subject, but I've hardly even gushed to my Paul about how much I love every single inch of his face. Might as well enjoy this. If I'd known it was so easy to bowl him over, I might have tried it long ago.

"Your eyes are actually gray," I say, more softly, so he has to lean closer to hear. "At first I thought they had to be blue, a very pale blue, but they're not."

"It says blue on my ID form." He's even worse at flirting than I am.

"But you know they're gray, right?" Maybe he doesn't.

Paul has never been a guy to spend much time looking in a mirror. "What color does your ID form say your hair is?"

"Brown," he replies, which isn't exactly a wrong answer. But it isn't exactly right, either.

"Light brown, but also a little red, and a little gold." The hours I've spent mixing paints, trying to get the right shade. Paul is a difficult man to capture. "You have good shoulders, good skin—good everything, really."

"You make it sound as if I were very handsome."

"You are."

This gets me not a smile but a skeptical glance. "Most women seem to disagree with you."

There was a time when I wouldn't have agreed either. His beauty isn't boy-band cute; he's rougher than that, his appeal not as easy to see. Once I'd seen it, though, I became drawn to him on a primal, instinctive level I couldn't deny.

I suspect Paul is feeling much the same way now.

We eat our chicken chow mein; it's a messy meal for a date, but I'm pretty good with a pair of chopsticks, and so is he. I keep the conversation going, and Paul—well, he tries to flirt back, clumsy as ever, but for me it's enough just to see how much he's enjoying himself.

Halfway through the meal, though, it hits me. What happens after?

As soon as Theo and I have done our job here, we'll leap out of this dimension forever. I'm not too worried about our other selves; they'll be freaked out to find themselves in San Francisco, on the train, wherever—but they can find their way home easily enough. I doubt they'll be in any more danger because of the war than they are already.

But Paul will probably guess what really happened. He'll know that I wasn't his Marguerite. All the hope I see in him now—this light in his eyes as he looks at me—that will be destroyed.

Maybe not. Maybe he'll react more like Theo and take some satisfaction in knowing that in another world, I loved him. In so many other worlds . . .

No. Because he won't only be dealing with a broken heart. He'll be dealing with the catastrophic destruction of the Firebird project, and this nation's last hope for winning this war.

You deserve so much more than this, I think as he tells a story about traveling through the battle lines that cover the continent, on his journey from New York as a boy. *We all do.*

The tragedy of this world is just one more sin to lay at Conley's feet.

But I'm the one doing it. I'm the one prioritizing Paul's life over that of an entire world.

No. I won't think about that. I can't. The war began a long time before I got here, and I don't understand how they'd use the Firebird to help anyway. They're clutching at straws, that's all. I'm simply . . . taking the straws away.

So I tell myself. But the words ring hollow.

At least I've given this Paul tonight—one night when it seems like his dreams are coming true.

When we leave the restaurant, I slide my arm through

Paul's, for the two of us to walk together that close. The silence on the streets of San Francisco is almost eerie—to me, at least; Paul seems to expect the quiet.

Although I gleaned a lot from Paul's dinner conversation, I didn't get any information about getting onto the base. Theo acted like it would be no big deal for me to steal Paul's wallet in the middle of dinner. It's not like I took Pickpocketing 101 with Fagin and the Artful Dodger.

Only one solution presents itself: Stay with Paul. Take this further than either Theo or I was willing to openly discuss.

"Are you all right?" Paul says. "You seemed far away for a moment."

"I guess I was." *Focus*, I remind myself. I won't get many other chances at this.

"Tonight—I'm glad this happened." Then he pauses, trying to find the right words. "I mean, I'm sorry things went wrong between you and Private Beck, but I'm glad you called me. That we spent the evening together."

He may not have game, but most of the time, simple works better than smooth. Paul's clumsy, honest pleasure in my company charms me more than any player's lines ever could. Even if this were the first time we'd ever met—if I weren't already in love with him—I'd still feel an irrepressible smile spreading across my face. "Me too."

Paul keeps struggling to find the right words. "This isn't—I haven't gotten to do this very much. Go out, have fun."

"With women, you mean?" I toss this off lightly, knowing how utterly inexperienced my Paul is. Then I realize that might not be true here. What if he tells me about some other girl, some other relationship?

But he says, "With women, or with anyone. All of us have to work so hard; we seldom have time for anything else. You know as well as I do."

Maybe I do. This Marguerite seems to have made time for Theo between shifts at the munitions plant, though.

Thinking about the other Theo and the other me distracts me for a moment, but I'm snapped back to the present when I hear Paul say, "Where are you staying?"

Paul's just asking, probably wondering whether he should walk me there, or wait for the bus with me. From any other guy, though, that would be a hint—suggesting he wouldn't mind an invitation to my room.

Theo's in my hotel room, so that's out. However, if Paul and I could be alone—if I could distract him completely—I'd have all the time I wanted to go through his things, rummage through his wallet, and otherwise be the Mata Hari Theo told me to be.

But I'm not going to bed with him. No way.

With Lieutenant Markov, I thought I might be trapped in the grand duchess's body forever; because of that, I acted for myself, not for her. And I've always known the grand duchess loved him, and she would have chosen to spend that one night with him, if she'd had the chance. But this Marguerite isn't in love with Paul yet, and I won't have sex with someone she wouldn't consent to normally.

Even kissing is a step over the line. This Marguerite

wouldn't like that, and I'd sworn I would never steal another first kiss between any of the Marguerites and her Paul. But this is different, a necessity rather than pure desire. With this plan, I can slip the Firebirds in my purse so he won't notice them, kiss Paul until dawn, and search for info about the labs once he falls asleep. *This is the smart move*, I tell myself. *The tactical move.*

Which it is. But I can't deny that I also want to be with Paul so badly it almost hurts. If I could just hold Paul close, feel him against me, then for a little while I wouldn't be afraid for him. I'm so sick of feeling afraid. Paul makes me feel strong. Whole.

And my Paul is within him—that one splinter of his soul.

"My hotel's not far," I say quietly. "But I bet your place is closer."

Paul stops in his tracks. He stares at me, clearly astonished. "I—" It's almost fun, watching him struggle for words. "Are you sure?"

"I don't mean— I couldn't spend the night. Not yet. But I'd like to stay with you for a while longer, if that's okay."

There are really gross guys who assume a woman would never go to a man's room for anything but sex, and wouldn't hesitate to take advantage of someone alone with them behind a locked door. But Paul isn't one of those guys, in this world or any other. "Whatever you want."

I look into his eyes, and the hope I see there slashes across me like claws. If only I could keep him from ever learning the truth about tonight.

Paul hesitates before he says, "Is this about, well—revenge?"

"Revenge?" I want my vengeance against Wyatt Conley, but how would Paul know that?

I understand once Paul continues, "Against Private Beck. For leaving you alone in the city."

"Oh! No, it isn't." Will he believe that? Would I? "Maybe that's why I called you. But it's not why I had such a good time tonight, or why I want to stay with you longer."

"I wouldn't want you to do anything you'd regret."

Paul, do you *have* to be such a perfect gentleman right now? "I won't."

"It's just—" He takes a deep breath, weighing the words he's going to say. "Do you know when I first fell for you?"

I shouldn't hear this. Only the other Marguerite should hear this, ever. Paul shouldn't be saying it out loud to someone who's tricking him. But there's no way for me to tell him to stop.

He takes my silence as permission to go on. "You remember the warehouse in Miramar we used as the first makeshift lab? Concrete walls and bare rebar. I don't pay much attention to how places look, but that place depressed me."

"It would've depressed anyone," I say, because that's what it sounds like.

Paul smiles. "But there was that one skylight that hadn't been painted over, remember? With the panes that had been broken and taped so many times?"

I nod, wondering why Paul would fixate on an old window.

"You probably don't remember, but there was one

day—back early on when we were cleaning out the warehouse and getting it ready, you and Josie too—this one day, I saw you staring upward. I asked you what you were looking at, and you said, the light. You told me to watch the pattern of the light."

Paul's entire expression has changed as he tells this story. The awkwardness is gone. It's as if something is dawning inside him.

He continues, "The shafts of light cut across the top of the warehouse just so. You said it was beautiful—that you'd like to try and sketch that someday. And as long as we worked in that warehouse, I never forgot to look up at the light. Sometimes it felt like the one scrap of joy I could still have. And I thought, if Marguerite could find something, even here, that's beautiful, she could make every day beautiful."

"That is—completely amazing."

"I always wondered if you would laugh at me, if I told you that." Paul's crooked smile pierces me through.

Leaning closer, I shake my head. "I would never laugh at anything so perfect."

"Marguerite," Paul murmurs, his voice reverent, as his fingers brush under my chin, lifting my face to his for a kiss.

His mouth covers mine, strong and warm. All the voices inside me—guilty, afraid, unsure—they all go silent. There's no room left in my head anymore for anything or anyone but him.

I've missed you so much. My hands fist in the lapels of Paul's uniform jacket. He pulls me into his embrace as our kiss deepens, and I feel the safety and comfort that only comes when I'm in his arms. The silence of the night around us lets me hear the slight catch in his throat, the little sound of pleasure as we wind ourselves around each other. He slides one hand over my shoulder, fingers brushing against my neck. Any moment now, he'll back me against the nearest building, and I want him to.

But instead he keeps caressing my neck, only that, which is so—chivalrous, and sweet, that it ironically only makes me want him more—

—until his fingers wrap around the chain of a Firebird.

I jerk back as he pulls; the chain snaps, stinging my skin. While I still have one of the Firebirds (which one? His or mine?), the other is in his grasp. Paul steps away from me, half turning to look at the Firebird in his hand. As he does, the expression on his face changes from disbelief to anger.

The Firebirds have that quality of things from another dimension—visible, tangible, but unlikely to be noticed by anyone in their home dimension unless their attention is called to it.

Or if you knew about them already. Like this dimension's Paul, who works on the Firebird project.

"Give that back," I say. If I'm going to get home and save my Paul, I need both my Firebirds. "Give it to me!"

"Earlier, I caught a glimpse—" Paul shakes his head. "I thought, it can't be. If the Doctors Caine had completed a Firebird, they would have told me. Nor would they have given it to you. But now I understand. This Firebird came from another dimension." When he looks at me again, his eyes are the color of steel. "Like you."

Busted.

11

"PLEASE." I HOLD OUT MY HAND FOR THE FIREBIRD. "I NEED that."

"To get back to the dimension you came from." I've never seen Paul's face like this. Most people grimace when they're angry, as if the rage is twisting them up outside as well as inside. Not Paul. He goes still, turns cold. Right now he might as well have been carved of stone.

Paul always values honesty. So I just say it. "Yes. To go home again, and for lots of other reasons too. Don't leave me stranded here."

His jaw drops slightly, and I realize that he didn't expect me to admit where I'm really from. And maybe, within his anger, there's a hint of the wonder I felt the very first time I traveled with the Firebird. Realizing that it works—that travel between dimensions is actually possible—was one of the most mind-blowing moments of my life. It must be for him too.

Maybe I can use that. I venture, "Everything Mom and Dad thought they could do—everything you believed they were capable of—the Firebirds are all that and more." He gives me a look; I can't tell if he's feeling less hostile or not, but he hasn't moved. I hope I can take that as a good sign. "People are depending on me. I have to keep going; lives are at stake. Please don't trap me here."

"How long have you been in our dimension? Weeks? Months?"

"Only a few days, I swear." The lone streetlight nearby paints the scene in chiaroscuro—deep shadows, and the stark lines of light that reveal his anger. I wonder what he sees in me. "I was forced to come here."

Paul's stare bores through me. I've never sounded less convincing.

So I change tactics. "Can we just sit down and talk about this? I'd never want to hurt you, Paul. Never. Back home—in my dimension—you and I got off to a better start, and—"

"How convenient." The tone of Paul's voice could lower the temperature by twenty degrees. "That we're all such good friends."

"Of course we are. The patterns between the dimensions, the way they bring people together, over and over again—it's like destiny." My Paul believed in fate even before we began traveling with the Firebirds. This one doesn't.

He turns the Firebird over in his hand, even more curious than he is angry. Then it hits me: The very thing Paul's been trying to create for the past few years—the thing he and my parents believe can turn the tide of this horrific war—it's his now, not mine, and there is *no way* he'll ever give it back.

"Please!" I take a step closer, but when he turns to look at me, I know I'd better not come any nearer.

"What was tonight about?" Paul says. "Coming on to me? Seducing me? What kind of game are you playing? Why are you here?"

"I'm here to save you. Not—*you* you. My Paul, from my universe. He's been splintered. Have you guys discovered the risk of splintering yet?"

"Consciousness becoming divided during interdimensional travel?"

"Yes! Exactly!" Oh, thank God for that, because I'd never have been able to explain the science behind it. "My Paul splintered. I mean, he was splintered, on purpose, and he'll never be able to come back home again unless I rescue him." Talking about him in the third person, to his face, feels strange. Worse, it feels futile. My legs have begun to shake. This has to sound crazy, spilled out all at once like this, and I can tell Paul doesn't believe me. In desperation, I say, "Couldn't you tell? The way I was with you—I wasn't pretending, not really. I love him so much."

"So much you seduced someone else?" Paul tilts his head as he studies me, with distaste. "How touching."

"I wasn't going to *sleep with you*. Besides, you're not someone else! A splinter of his soul is inside you, and—and it wouldn't matter, even if it weren't. You're him, and he's you."

Paul flinches when I tell him about the splinter within him, but he doesn't respond. "You were with me just because you missed him so much? You wanted the next best thing? Somehow I doubt it. You've confessed to being from another dimension. You have a fully operational Firebird—the technology we've been trying to create here for a long time. Technology we need very badly. If you've been in this dimension for as much as a day, you know how the war is going."

I nod. "The air raid was my first night here."

"Then you have no excuse. If you're your parents' daughter—and in love with another me, one so similar you find us interchangeable—you should have turned this technology over to us immediately."

I remember the lesson I learned the hard way as a little kid, when I tried to sneak around my parents' rules: Trying to outsmart a genius rarely ends well.

Paul takes one step toward me, reminding me powerfully of his greater size and strength. "Do you want to change your story? Or stick to the original lie? The latter technique works better during interrogations. That's what they tell us."

In this dimension, they prepare people for being captured and tortured. If I'm turned in as an invader or a spy, this is what will happen to me. Paul wouldn't hurt me—I know that much—but he might report me to people crueler than he is. I'm so far out of my depth here that I have only one possible defense left: the truth.

"No. I wasn't with you only because I missed you. I do

miss you—him, okay, him. I love him. That's why I'm doing this. The only reason I'd *ever* do this." The cold wind whips around us, making me shiver. We seem to be the only people on this entire street—otherwise deserted and desolate. "My Paul really was splintered against his will. The people who did it won't give him back unless I do what they say. They told me to . . . to sabotage your work here. To ruin the Firebird project if I could. That's the only way they'll let me know the other dimensions Paul is hidden in."

Paul believes me. I almost wish he didn't. "You're here to sabotage us?" His fist tightens around the Firebird; the metal corners must be cutting into the skin of his palm. But he doesn't even notice it. "That's why you cozied up to me tonight? To get information?"

I feel so cheap, so small. But I shout back, "To save my Paul? I'd do worse than that. I would do anything to get him back home and safe. Anything in the world—in all the worlds. And that means I need the Firebird."

He stands completely still for a moment—long enough to give me hope—before he says, "Not as much as I do."

"Paul, *please*."

But already Paul has turned his face from me and begun walking away. No goodbyes.

I want to chase Paul down, plead with him, but I already know it wouldn't do any good. If I could only prove to him how deeply I love him, how well I know him.

So I call, "You—you don't get along with your parents! You think your dad's a bad person, and your mom won't stand up to him, so you try to stay away from them. You won't even tell me anything else about them. You always sleep with one foot outside the covers. And you—you don't enjoy porn that much because you think the men and women never seem to actually like each other, and that ruins it for you, which is basically the sweetest thing ever. But naked pictures are okay! You're into those." No—stupid subject to pick—it just makes me sound crazier. "Your favorite cake is chocolate with caramel icing! You like rock climbing—"

But he wouldn't have any time to go rock climbing in this universe. Ration cards wouldn't allow for much chocolate cake or caramel icing. I'm calling out things about my Paul that this one doesn't remember or understand.

I'm calling to my Paul, really. The one who's lost to me. The one hidden deep within the man stalking away into the dark, leaving me alone.

The entire walk back to my hotel, I feel like I ought to be crying. Or panicking. Instead, I trudge forward, almost numb with shock and despair.

I screwed up *everything.* My Paul is still in danger, and I may have just made it impossible to ever get him back. I would've thought that was the worst feeling imaginable—but the reaction of the Paul from this dimension burns it in deeper. Salt in the wound. He caught me trying to betray him, my parents, everyone in this entire world—and called me out about flirting with him, which now seems so cheap and stupid and small.

It's one thing to fail, another to fail in a way that makes you ashamed you even tried.

The single Firebird hanging around my neck now is Paul's—so I still have that sliver of his soul. It helps a little to think that he's still safe. If this were the Firebird about to be disassembled and broken down into component parts for study, then I would have lost him forever. One Paul would have unknowingly murdered another.

But losing my own Firebird is catastrophe enough.

The old-fashioned clock in the hotel lobby says it's after midnight by the time I come in the door. As I ride up in the elevator, I think, *Theo's our last chance.* How would Theo be able to get close to Paul, especially now that Paul is going to distrust every single person he meets? How could Theo use the computer virus to tear the project apart? I don't know, but he's going to have to figure it out.

When I enter the hotel room, the lights are off. Of course—Theo went to sleep already. He's lying on the bed, on his side, and somehow his face looks innocent. That's a first.

I have to wake him up. He has to know how badly this went wrong, so he can help me figure out a Plan B.

Even though I still can't fully trust Theo, I know I need him now.

Remembering his reaction to the red dress, though, I go ahead and change in the bathroom, wrapping myself in the white robe I brought. The robe's fabric is as thin and cheap as I've come to expect in this universe, and the hotel doesn't seem to consider "heat" one of the guest amenities. So I'm shivering as I sit on the edge of the bed and whisper, "Theo?"

"Mm." He stirs slightly, but then snuggles back into the pillow.

I put one hand on his shoulder. The remaining Firebird dangles from my robe as I lean closer. Theo's skin is warm through the white fabric of his undershirt. "Hey. Wake up."

He half turns, opens his eyes, and gives me a groggy smile. Then he slings one arm around my waist and tows me down onto the bed.

I try to protest, but I can't speak, because his mouth is covering mine.

Theo and I kissed only once before, and it was a pretty good kiss—but nothing like this. This is passionate, warm, searching. At first I'm too startled to react, and before I can even speak, he rolls over so that he's on top of me. This isn't my Theo.

"I was having the weirdest dream," he murmurs as his hands press mine against the mattress. "Sorry I fell asleep. Let me make it up to you."

He kisses me again, and I feel the weight of his Firebird against my chest. I pull back and turn my face from his. "Theo, wait."

"Hey, what's wrong?" He pulls back and props up on one elbow—even as his other hand trails down my body, casually curving over my breast before coming to rest on my belly. "Are you all right?"

"Hang on." I grab his Firebird, quickly set a reminder, and—

"*Gahh!*" Theo shoves himself backward, slamming into the headboard. The pain of the reminder makes him clutch his chest, but it's the sudden rush of memories that make his eyes go wide. "Oh, I—I just— I didn't mean to—oh, crap."

"It's okay." I'm so grateful to have him back with me that I don't care about what just happened here.

Theo, however, does. "Listen, Marguerite, I'm so, *so* sorry about—the kissing, and the hands, and—I'm just really sorry I did that."

"It's all right. You weren't yourself. Literally." I straighten my robe as I sit up, trying to make myself forget it all.

"Right. Got it. Moving on." Then Theo stares at my throat. "Wait. You're missing a Firebird. Where's the other one?"

"Paul has it. Theo, he figured it out. He knows everything, and he took my Firebird."

I vent the story to him, holding nothing back; I tell Theo what I felt, what I did, from the first smile on the sidewalk to my brazen offer to go to Paul's place, all the way to shouting out the things I knew about my Paul as the other one walked off. By the end, my voice is shaking—from fear, rather than any urge to cry. I'm so scared for my Paul now that it eclipses everything else.

Our eyes meet, and I know we're both worried about the same thing. If I tried to travel home with Paul's Firebird—the one storing a splinter of his soul—would I destroy it? If so, then my choices may be living in this universe forever or killing Paul.

"We have to think of something," I say. "Some way to get to Paul, to get that Firebird back. I don't know how we even start to—"

"Hey." Theo takes my hand in both of his. "We're going to figure something out. All right? Don't panic."

"I'm not panicking." Even as I say it, though, I'm trembling so hard my entire body shakes. "But I don't know what to do."

"It's late. You're tired, and you've had one hell of a night. Right now you need to calm down. Take deep breaths, try to sleep. We'll tackle this in the morning."

"How am I supposed to sleep? Even if we could get Conley to tell us the other two dimensions we need to search, we can't save Paul and get home. Not without that other Firebird."

The springs of the mattress creak as he leans closer to me, and his fingers tighten around mine. "If we figure out where Paul is, and we only have two Firebirds, then I'll give you mine. You'll be able to take him home."

"But—you'd be left behind."

"You'd come back for me," Theo says simply. "Or Paul would. One way or another, I'd get home in the end."

He says that knowing how strange it is to be lost in another version of yourself. Knowing how dangerous other dimensions can be. "I can't let you do that."

"The hell you can't. You're not the only one who loves

Paul Markov, okay? Anything you'd do to get your boyfriend back, I'd do for my best friend." He shakes his head; in the moonlight filtering through the window shade, I can see his rueful smile. "Or do you still think I'm the same as that other Theo? Always looking out for number one?"

"You're not him," I say, just as I've said many times before. Maybe I'm finally starting to believe it. "But . . . do we even have the right to do this? To sabotage this technology when they feel like it's their only hope?"

"They don't know that. We don't know that."

"If there's any chance they're right, then I'm basically prioritizing my Paul's life over the lives of every other person in this dimension."

Theo scowls in irritation. "I have two words for you. *Global* and *warfare*. We didn't start the fire, Marguerite. The war going on in this dimension is bigger than the people we've met here. Bigger than this country. Could the Firebird help them? Maybe. But from what I can see, no one weapon could win it for them. So we can't tie ourselves in knots worrying about these guys. We have to look out for ourselves. I need a cure, and Paul needs to come together and get back home. Right?"

I believe what he's saying, mostly. Yet guilt still weighs me down. "I guess."

More gently, he adds, "Now, come on. Try to sleep."

Even though I want to argue with him, I can feel exhaustion creeping over me, dark and heavy. I ease down onto the bed, lying on my left side so that I can look toward the moonlight. The second my head touches the pillow, I know I won't be awake long.

The mattress shifts as Theo moves toward the floor, but I reach back and catch his arm. "Don't go."

After a moment, he lies down behind me, spooning around my back as he wraps one arm around my waist. It could be a lover's embrace, but it's not. He's simply here with me, close enough for me to hear him breathe, so even in sleep I'll know I'm not in this alone.

Yet I can't stop my imagination from wandering across San Francisco. I envision shabby military housing, and Paul sitting on the edge of his bed, alone. The Firebird is in his hand, and he's mad as hell. But his heart is broken just the same.

12

BY NEXT MORNING, THEO AND I ARE IN STRATEGY MODE.

"First thing we have to figure out is whether Paul has talked to your parents," Theo says as he combs his wet hair wearing just his undershirt and uniform pants.

"My guess is yes." Then I think about that for a moment, pulling my rumpled robe more closely around me. "Actually, no. Not yet. They aren't as close here. Besides, Paul would want to think through everything, examine the Firebird, all on his own, before he said anything. But he *will* tell them."

"And soon. It won't take Paul long to figure that thing out, especially not if they were on the verge of the breakthrough here already." Theo sighs. "Never thought I'd be pissed off that my research partner is so freakin' brilliant, but here we are. Anyway. Second question is, will your parents believe him?"

"Maybe? At first, they'd have to wonder. But as soon as he's able to show them the Firebird itself—or the schematics—Mom and Dad will realize what it is. Then they'll know he's telling the truth."

"Then we need to work fast."

We have two goals we must accomplish, and they work against each other. I need Paul to trust me enough to hand the Firebird over again, and yet I also need to betray him and destroy his work. There's no way to make both of those happen—

—or is there?

"Hang on," I say to Theo as I jump from the bed and slide my feet into a pair of shoes.

While I straighten my robe, Theo says, "Where are you going?"

"To the phone!"

Happily, nobody's waiting to use the one telephone on the floor, so it's all mine. After the seemingly endless process of using a rotary dial, I get the military base. "Extension, please," says the bored-sounding operator.

"No extension. I want to leave an urgent message for Lieutenant Paul Markov. It should say, Meet me at nine a.m., at Fisherman's Wharf." Oh God, I hope they still have that in this dimension's San Francisco.

Apparently so, because the operator says, "Yes, ma'am. Who is the message from?"

"Marguerite Caine. The daughter of the Doctors Caine."

This mention gets the operator's attention, just like it was supposed to. "Yes, ma'am. We'll get this to him right away."

"Thanks," I say. As soon as I hang up, I run toward the hotel room to shower and dress in a hurry. We'll have to rush to get to Fisherman's Wharf on time.

On our way there, Theo and I could pass for any other couple in this world. He wears his military uniform, complete with green cloth hat on his head. My navy-blue dress isn't nearly as slinky as last night's outfit, but honestly that's a relief. The red one should really be kept in a glass box with a little hammer and a sign that says DO NOT WEAR EXCEPT IN EMERGENCY.

When we get to Fisherman's Wharf, I'm astonished to see that it looks like—well, a wharf. Used by fishermen. Instead of the familiar touristy extravaganza of restaurant signs and funky sculptures and hop-on/hop-off buses, I see boats and a fish market. Not all the boats are fishing trawlers, though; several look more like coast guard vessels, complete with mounted guns. A few places along the wharf offer food, but rather than overpriced burgers, they sell the kind of stuff that comes in brown paper bags so people can grab them and eat as they go.

"I always thought I hated our version of Fisherman's Wharf," Theo says. "Now I kind of miss it."

"Yeah, me too." In the distance I can hear the bark of a sea lion; at least they're still here, sunning themselves. Not everything changes.

Glancing at the nearest food stall, Theo asks, "Think we've got time to look for doughnuts?"

"How can you think of doughnuts at a time like this?" Honestly, though, I'm hungry too. Our hotel didn't have room service, and probably hasn't for decades.

"How can you not? You want us to do some serious strategizing today? We're gonna need fuel. Preferably chocolate-glazed fuel."

I give him a warm smile—which fades in an instant as I look to the left.

Paul stands there, hands in his pockets, waiting.

Theo sees him only a moment later. He curses under his breath, and Paul raises an eyebrow.

"So," Paul says. "You two made up." Obviously he's unsure how much he can say in front of Theo.

Understanding this, Theo slips his finger under the collar of his shirt to pull up a short length of gold chain. "Actually, I rode with her."

"The two of you came here together." Paul's tone turns bitter. "How does this fit in with your so-called love for me, Marguerite?"

"Hey. Shut it, pal." Theo steps forward. "I'm not with her—not in our dimension, anyway. I'm a friend of hers, and by the way, a friend of yours. I came here to help her out. To rescue *you*. Well, also myself, but definitely you too."

Paul, clearly taken aback by Theo's total understanding of the situation, snaps, "Stop talking about him as if he's me. He isn't. We're two different people."

"Okay, fine, sure," I say. It's not worth arguing about at this point. We need to get on the same page. "I'm glad you came."

He doesn't answer at first. Then Paul says, "I haven't slept."

Theo makes a scoffing sound, like *Why should we care?* He's too defensive. But I can tell Paul's telling the absolute truth. Now that I've recovered from the first shock of seeing him, I can see the stubble on his face, the dark shadows under his eyes. Quietly I ask, "Why not?"

"I stayed up all night with this." Paul pulls the stolen Firebird from his pocket. My first instinct is to lunge for it, but I remain still, except for holding out one hand to keep Theo back. Paul continues, "I ran the data over and over. I've learned a lot, but I have a lot further to go. In other words—if you want it back, the answer is still no."

"Listen to me." I step closer to Paul. "Remember what I said last night? This man, Wyatt Conley, intends to sabotage your work in this dimension. If we fail, he's just going to send someone else. Lots of someone elses. Conley's not a man who gives up until he gets what he wants."

Paul retorts, "So I should surrender to you now and save myself the trouble?"

Theo's eyes narrow. Obviously he'd like to rip into Paul. But I told him to let me take the lead on this, and he lives up to his promise, saying nothing.

"Here's the bargain I'm offering you," I tell Paul. "In our dimension, Theo works on the Firebird project too. He helped build this. If you agree, Theo will sit down with you and explain everything about how this works. He'll go over your own designs, critique them, whatever it takes to get you guys ready to make a Firebird of your own."

"You're a physicist?" Paul says to Theo. The amount of surprise in his voice isn't insulting—but it comes close.

"Hey, I might have been tracked into telemetry systems this time around, but in my dimension? I taught you everything you know." Theo grins. "Well. Almost everything. I have to keep a few things to myself. Maintain my advantage."

I cut in. "He can get you there, Paul. If you let Theo show you, you can crack the secrets of the Firebird within the day."

He doesn't even know what to say to an offer that good. "Then I'm supposed to give this back to you. And—and you'd take back the splinter of your Paul's consciousness. Is that all?"

I shake my head. "No. For this world's safety, and so I can get my own Paul back home, we have to make Wyatt Conley believe we've sabotaged your work. But maybe that doesn't mean we have to actually do it. Could you and Theo create a simulation?"

"A simulation of what?" Paul says.

I don't really know. "Whatever it would look like if your computer networks were destroyed. If your data were erased by a virus. If we had something like that—then, when Conley checks, he'll think you guys are defenseless, when really you'll be building your first Firebirds even before I get home."

Paul looks even less convinced than before. "You can do that?"

Theo, realizing it's time for him to step in, nods. "With

your cooperation. And also, that Lieutenant Colonel Wyatt Conley who keeps trying to work with you? You have to find a way to keep that guy one hundred percent out of the loop. Our Conley could get inside him, learn what he knows, and find out we faked the whole thing."

Even though I can tell Paul has begun to believe us, he still doesn't agree. "This could be a trick. Maybe you're going to lead me in the wrong direction, tell me things about the Firebird's construction that aren't true."

"Do you really not get it?" I could smack him upside the head. "I love my parents. I love my sister. And I love you. Do you think I'd ever leave you guys defenseless in the middle of a war, if I had any other choice? Well, as of this morning, I thought of another choice. So let's take it together, okay?"

"We're not the same," Paul says again. "Your Paul and me."

Shaking my head, I smile. "You are, in ways you can't even begin to imagine."

"Enough relationship talk," Theo says. "You taking the deal or what, buddy?"

Paul hesitates one moment longer before saying, "Come with me."

We spend the rest of the day on base; Theo's military ID and my status with my parents make it easy for Paul to get us access. For the next few hours, Theo and Paul get caught up in mega-dense scientific talk, while I drink awful fake coffee and watch them at work. Even here at the base, things are done low-tech when possible; Theo scribbles math equations on a chalkboard, occasionally brushing his hands free of yellowish dust, and Paul uses an honest-to-God slide rule. Theo's natural affection for Paul slips out from time to time; I can tell Paul both notices it and has no idea what to do with it.

So far as he can, Paul pretends I'm not even there. At first I think this is because he hates me for what I did last night. As time goes on, though, I start to wonder. The way he finds himself watching me, then suddenly turns away, awkward and unsure—it's not unlike the way Paul looked at me back at home, when we'd started to care about each other but didn't yet know what to do about it.

This Paul's feelings for his Marguerite are too strong to be pushed aside. Even when he's angry. Even when he's hurt and scared. He still loves her.

Will she ever fall in love with him, too?

They keep talking science. They set the Triadverse virus loose on a data backup that should pass for the real thing. They get to where they work together almost as smoothly as Theo does with my Paul back at home.

Finally, around two in the afternoon, Theo sits up straight and says, "You've got the data, now. Another few days of review, and you'll be ready to build."

After a long moment, Paul says, "Thank you."

That cost him; I can tell. So I say, "Thank you for giving me another chance. I know I didn't deserve it."

He looks up at me, and for one instant I glimpse the

disappointment there—the hope he felt so briefly last night before it was snatched away. Despite what he must be feeling, Paul holds the Firebird out to me. As I take it, he says, "I knew from the data that you were telling me the truth about—about most things. It made me think you might be telling the truth about it all. If there's a version of me in trouble out there, I'd like to think someone was coming for him."

"That sounds more like the Paul Markov I remember." Theo grins in relief.

To Paul I say, "We're going to bring him home. But he's not only out there. He's here, too."

He looks down at his chest, as if the splinter of my Paul's soul might be hidden inside his own heart.

I step closer to him. "No need to tense up like that. It's not going to screw with your head or anything."

"Theo says the retrieval method is the same as a reminder," Paul says. "Reminders hurt, and now I have to take one. How would that not make me tense?"

Theo leans against the nearest wall and shrugs. "You have to admit, he's got a point."

"Hold on." I slip my own Firebird around my neck, then press Paul's against Paul's chest. Even through his uniform jacket, I can feel the warmth of his body under my palm. When I raise my eyes to his face, he's looking down at me, and I know we're both remembering how we stood like this last night, just before we kissed.

Or maybe what I see in Paul's gray eyes is that splinter of

my Paul. The one I really love.

I hit the combination Conley taught me in Italy. Paul shudders from the flash of pain, but he makes no sound. The Firebird seems to vibrate in my palm. There it is—the faintest little flicker of heat, the proof that I've recovered the second splinter.

"We've got him." I breathe out heavily, then grin at Theo.

He grins back. "Two down, two to go."

Paul is by far the least enthusiastic of the three of us. "I don't feel any different."

"You don't?" I would've thought my Paul's soul would affect his more. Yet this Paul is already a scientist, already in love with me. Maybe he and my Paul are too much alike for him to feel the impact. "Well, it worked. I promise."

"You promise a lot of things," Paul says flatly.

I don't want to leave this universe when he's angry with me. Is that childish? Even selfish? Probably. Yet I want to heal the wound I caused—just like I want to heal all the others. "We're okay?"

"You unlocked the final secrets of the Firebird. So we're even." Paul doesn't smile as he says it. "Next time, consider asking for what you need, instead of treating me like a fool."

That stings, but maybe I deserved it. I keep my voice gentle. "Hang in there, all right? With your Marguerite, I mean. You never know when things might change."

"Hey. I'm standing *right here*," Theo protests.

"Sorry, Theo. I just meant— Paul, I told you there was such a thing as destiny. It brings us together, over and over again, dimension after dimension. Destiny won't let you down."

"I wish I could believe that." Paul stands up and walks to the door. Apparently emotional sharing time is over. "One of the men on security detail can show you two out."

"Why out?" Theo takes his Firebird in hand. "Marguerite and I can pop out right here. Then you can explain to our other, slightly lesser versions exactly what the hell is going on, because, trust me, they're gonna want to know."

Paul opens the door. "I don't want to watch," he says quietly. "I'll come for you both immediately. But when you—go back to the way things were—I don't want to see that happen."

He means he doesn't want to watch the moment when this world's Theo and I once again look at each other with love.

I walk out, knowing Theo will follow, and I don't allow myself to look at Paul's face again.

Once Theo and I are alone in the corridor, accompanied by the sound of typewriters clattering within office doors, he says, "Look on the bright side, chica. We've got the Firebird. We've got a good cover story in place. This is progress."

I swallow the lump in my throat to reply. "Conley might find out we didn't really sabotage them." Even before I suggested the plan, I knew that was a risk. That risk looms larger now, casting its shadow over my hopes.

"Yeah, he might. But we could make it seem like this Paul tricked us, something like that. And if this world's

Conley never learns the truth, we might get away with it completely."

"He has to learn eventually, doesn't he?"

"Eventually could be a long time from now." As Theo opens the door and we walk outside, he glances over his shoulder, in the direction we came from. "This Paul's kind of a hard-ass, isn't he?

"No. Just hurt." I think of the way he looked at me last night—hopeful, dazzled, halfway to being in love—and I feel even more like scum than before.

But Theo's right about one thing. We have the Firebirds. So far as Conley knows, we completed half the job. One more dimension, one more mission, one more betrayal. Then and only then will we go to the home office and learn the final universe hiding the last splinter of Paul's soul.

"At least we have something to use against Conley now." That was the idea I clung to when this trip began—that I'd find a way to undermine Conley, that instead of simply doing his bidding, I'd turn his own plan against him. "Conley wants to monopolize the ability to travel through dimensions. Now we've guaranteed that's not going to happen."

Slowly, Theo smiles. "There's that fighting spirit. Now, do we know where we're headed?"

Quickly I double-check my Firebird around my neck; the second set of coordinates have been unlocked. "Yeah, sending you the data now. Mission one-half accomplished. Let's go."

Theo pauses. "A whole other world." When I give him a look, he shakes his head. "I know that's the idea. But it's like I only just started believing this place was real."

"Soon it's going to seem like a bad dream," I reassure him.

"I don't know," Theo says as he takes his Firebird in hand. "This place had its benefits."

Our eyes meet, and I know he's remembering the way he kissed me last night.

But it's over in an instant, as the Firebird rips us out of these bodies, this world, forever.

13

WHEN I SLAM INTO MYSELF, I'M WALKING ALONG A CROWDED sidewalk, and I nearly trip over my own feet.

A beefy guy in a Yankees jersey bumps into me from behind. "Hey, it's a side*walk*. For walking. Got it?"

Another voice nearby mutters, "Tourists."

I flatten myself against the nearest building, where I won't be in anyone's way. Where have I wound up this time? It's daylight, and there are—wow, hundreds of people and at least three food carts just on this stretch of sidewalk.

I look up and start to smile, because even though I've never been here before, I know exactly where I am.

Times Square.

Visitors to the city clutch shopping bags or record the scene on their smartphones, while locals in business clothes walk twice as fast as anyone else as they weave in and out. Although I can hear car horns nearby, the street right next to me seems to have been closed off a long time ago; the space is instead filled with shaded picnic tables, where people eat and hang out. Above me are tall buildings bearing billboards about the size of my house, and so many glittering lights that they shine even in the middle of the day. Nearby a news ticker scrolls headlines like:

PRESIDENT AND FIRST LADY TO MAKE STATE VISIT TO BRAZIL

NISSAN AND TOYOTA ANNOUNCE MERGER

UK PARLIAMENT VOTES FOR GENERAL ELECTION

OSCAR WINNER HUGH JACKMAN RELEASED FROM HOSPITAL.

Those all look familiar enough—except that I don't think Hugh Jackman has won an Academy Award in my world. Beside the fact that I'm in New York City, this dimension doesn't appear to be very different from my own. At any rate, it's better than the desolate world at war we left behind.

For a moment I remember Paul saying goodbye to me there—the distrust, the betrayal in his eyes. Just thinking about it burns. No, I don't ever want to see that Warverse again.

My clothes seem like exactly the kind of thing I'd have at home—though the dark green dress and the low-heeled lace-up oxfords are a little fancier than I'd generally wear for everyday. A cross-body bag hangs at my hip, and I start fishing around inside for clues. Keys, lip gloss, chewing gum: All that tells me is that Clinique and Trident exist here too.

Inside a silver leather wallet I find a New York State ID card—no driver's license—but my address is printed on the ID, so now I know I live on Eighty-Third Street. Also a yellow and blue Metrocard, which I'm guessing is what you use on the subway. Some cash, a case for the sunglasses I realize I'm wearing atop my head, and—*yes*. My smartphone.

It wants a code to unlock. At home I use Josie's birthday, so I plug that in and, boom, I'm in. *Maybe I should be less predictable,* I think, but I can't stop smiling.

Before anything else, I go into contacts and scroll down to the *M*s. Then the *P*s. Paul isn't listed.

Do I not even know him in this universe? This is New York City; in our world, that's where Paul was born. So he should be here, shouldn't he? If I can't get to this dimension's Paul Markov, how am I supposed to rescue the next part of Paul's soul?

Maybe you just haven't met this world's Paul yet, I remind myself. *Or you might already know him, but the two of you aren't close enough to exchange numbers at this point.* Paul had worked with my parents almost a year before I put his number in my phone; I didn't need to contact him on my own, and even if I had, he was at my house nearly every day. Texting him wasn't a big priority.

The tight coil of fear within me slowly relaxes. I shouldn't panic yet.

Resigned, I scan through the rest of my contacts. There's Mom, Dad, Josie—and yes, Theo, here in NYC so no need to use the locator on the Firebird—but that's when my phone buzzes and a calendar alert comes up: *Movie w/R at AMC 42nd*. Looks like that's in fifteen minutes.

I'm only a couple of blocks from Forty-Second, as it turns out. So I hurry through the packs of people gawking at the signs, the other tourists, and the Hello Kitty store. Obviously I'd rather spend the next couple of hours studying this dimension than sitting in a movie theater, but if I'm going to pass as this world's Marguerite, I shouldn't blow off her plans without a good reason.

When I get to the front of the theater, I'm not sure whether to go in or to wait outside for someone to recognize me—which is when I hear a woman's voice call out, in an English accent, "Marguerite! There you are!"

I turn around to see Romola.

Somehow I manage to conceal my astonishment. It's definitely her: same dark gold hair, same square jaw and stubborn chin. We've run into each other in a couple of worlds now, but never before have we been friends. Here, though, Romola comes up to me with a smile on her face. Instead of the expensive, glamorous clothes she wore in the Londonverse, she's got on normal jeans and a sweater. As she walks up to me, she smiles and holds up her phone, revealing a bar code. "Since you were running late, I went ahead and bought our tickets."

"Thanks," I say, but then I can't think what to add.

Fortunately Romola's ahead of me. "You can make it up to me by getting the popcorn. And M&M's! They're so good mixed together."

Her presence here weirds me out in a way I can't explain, even to myself. She's someone I've met before, but never known well. I thought of Romola as—an accident, a coincidence. Not a person who was supposed to mean a lot to me.

Just like Paul should be everyplace, everywhere with me, and he's not.

The movie turns out to be one I'd meant to see at home, and Romola's right about the popcorn-plus-M&M's mix. So by the time we're walking out of the theater in the late afternoon, my mood has improved. This world is no more dangerous than my own; Mom, Dad, and Josie are all alive and well; and there's a text message waiting for me from Theo, which says only, Turns out I live in Alphabet City. Headed your way.

"Tonight's the big dinner, isn't it?" Romola's smile turns almost wicked as she says it. "You have to tell me *everything*."

As casually as possible, I ask, "What do you want for the highlight reel?"

"Let's see. The absolute most awkward question your parents ask him. And oh, if he looks intimidated or even unsure at any moment, get a photo if you can, would you? I can't wait to see my big, bad boss being interrogated by your parents." She's joking, but not; her glee at the thought of this dinner is real.

So in this world, we met through her boss? Maybe she works for some other world-class scientist; that might explain how Romola and I keep coming together. Right now she's looking at me for a reply, one I'm not sure how to make, so I bunt. "Oh, sure, I'll film the whole thing, zoom in on his face. He won't notice that."

The sarcasm covers my ignorance well enough. Romola just laughs. "All right, all right, we'll talk next week, and you can tell me all about it."

"Okay."

Romola hugs me before she leaves. Somehow I manage to return the hug without stiffening up. Then I walk to the closest subway station and spend a while searching on my smartphone until I find an app that will tell me how to get to any address via public transit.

For the record: the New York subway is even more disgusting than Bay Area Rapid Transit. I didn't think that was possible. It's faster, though, because within ten minutes I'm staring up at the high-rise apartment building where I apparently live. A uniformed man at the door smiles at me. "Miss Caine. Welcome back. How was your day?"

That must be the doorman. "Great, thanks," I manage to say before ducking inside; it doesn't look like any more conversation is required.

Apartment 28G ought to be on the twenty-eighth floor, so I head up in the elevator. As I walk toward the apartment door, I hear the faint strains of "Here Comes the Sun" in the hallway, and I grin. Dad's home.

I walk into an apartment that's even smaller than the house we had in the poverty-stricken war dimension—but unlike that place, this is immediately recognizable as our home. A houseplant hangs from a hook in one corner, with its long vines trailing along the tops of the windowsills. Piles of books and papers sit on the table and in the corners. The walls are painted a sunshiny yellow, and on the leather sofa sits my father, laptop on his knees, typing away.

"There you are," Mom says, as Dad glances my way just long enough to smile. She walks out of what must be her bedroom wearing a dark blue sheath dress—simple enough, but pretty fancy for someone who normally sticks to jeans and threadbare sweaters. Head tilted, she puts on an earring as she says, "I didn't think you'd make it back before dinner."

"Here I am. Hey, you look nice."

Mom sighs. "I don't want Josie to think we're not taking this seriously."

"I only wish I could believe *she* wasn't taking this seriously," Dad says without looking up from his computer. "Honestly. After only two months?"

"Now, Henry. We made up our minds after less than a day." My mother rests one hand on my father's shoulder, and he closes his laptop to smile at her. She continues, "The speed of their courtship isn't the issue. Or it wouldn't be, if I had a stronger sense of who he is. But—there's something elusive about him. Something hidden. I don't like it."

"Tonight's our chance to question him," Dad says. "Don't think I don't intend to make use of it, no matter how la-di-da this restaurant is."

"You sound like a police investigator going after a suspect." Mom leans down and kisses his forehead. "Good."

The dots aren't difficult to connect. Josie's dating someone seriously—Romola's boss, from the sound of it. This isn't as remarkable to me as the fact that Josie's either engaged to him or about to be. Normally my sister seems to go for quantity over quality with her boyfriends; she's not a party animal or anything, but lots of guys love the same adrenaline sports she does, so she meets someone new all the time. Josie always swore she'd only get serious about a guy after she had some idea where she'd end up, professionally speaking. *I don't want to sacrifice my dreams for anybody*, she said once. *And I don't want him to have to sacrifice his dreams for me.* That's kind of hard core—but that's Josie.

Here, however, some guy won her over in just two months? This man I have to see.

"How long until we leave?" I ask.

Dad says, "Thirty minutes or so. I ought to grade a few more midterms, shouldn't I? Say no."

"Yes," Mom calls from her room. Dad sighs.

I find my room on the first try—and exhale in relief as I see my paintings on the walls. My style here is much the same as at home: very realistic, except for my use of color. Here, I stick to a muted, limited palette for each portrait, giving the finished work a definite mood. Josie's picture glows with reds and pinks; Mom's reflects cerebral silvers and blues; Dad's has soft sunny golds; and . . . then there's Theo.

For his portrait I used bronze, orange, burnt sienna—colors both grounded and yet somehow electric. His dark eyes seem to shine as he looks out from his picture.

I don't see a portrait of Paul.

Frustrated, I run a search on my tablet. "Paul Markov, physicist" comes up with zero results. So does "Paul Markov, scientist."

My fear comes rushing back. Wouldn't Paul be a scientist in any world he possibly could? In a dimension so much like our own, wouldn't he go into physics, just like before? It seems as if nothing could keep him from that destiny, unless he's seriously ill, or his parents never emigrated from Russia.

How am I supposed to find him if he's in Russia? Over there, his name is so common he might as well be called John Smith. Besides, how would I even get there?

I try again, with his name and his birthday. Then an image shows up—something from a school webpage, some years old now—but I smile as I see it. That kid in a plaid shirt, surely no more than ten years old: I'd know him anywhere. Paul doesn't keep any photos from his childhood, so I've never seen him as a little boy before. Of course he was completely *adorable.* My fingers trace over the screen, outlining his baby face.

Then I realize that the school is one here in New York City, and I laugh out loud in relief.

Encouraged, I search a little more online. He doesn't have a Twitter account or anything like that, but he doesn't in my world either. None of the universities list him as a student. He doesn't seem to participate in any of the rock-climbing or hiking clubs I can find in the area either.

Finally I locate a Facebook page, which is set to private. The one photo I can see shows him from the side, looking away from the camera; it's like Paul clipped the image from the background of a photo of someone or something else. Bad as the picture is, I'd recognize him anywhere—even here, when he's wearing a tailored leather jacket that seems entirely unlike anything he'd own. Same gray eyes; same broad shoulders. I look closer, seeking that lost, lonely expression that always touches me—but the shadows in the picture render his face unreadable.

It's easy for me to imagine this picture as an image of the Paul from the Warverse; something about the lines of the leather jacket reminds me of his military uniform. His stricken face as Theo and I walked away . . . I hurt him so much, giving him hope and then crushing it. Maybe I had no other choice; maybe the situation worked out for the best. Doesn't make it any easier to think about wounding Paul after Paul, in world after world.

Try not to screw it up this time, I tell myself.

Easier said than done. Without any school or job listed for Paul, I have no way of arranging an accidental meeting. Somehow, I have to get him to reach out to me.

Inspiration strikes, and I open a quick Facebook message to Paul. After chewing on my bottom lip for a moment, I type: *Hey, we've never met, but we have mutual friends.*

Alternate versions of him in other dimensions count as "mutual friends," right?

Basically, everyone says you and I should meet sometime. So how about this week? We could get together—

Where? I don't know New York City very well yet. But I know where my parents teach without even having to ask. Growing up surrounded by physics grad students means you're constantly looking over postdoc applications to the best schools in the world.

—on the Columbia campus and grab a coffee, if you wanted. Hope this is the right Paul Markov. If it's not, sorry for the mistake!

That works. Even if Paul's not intrigued by the idea of the blindest blind date of all time, he'll probably write back, if only to ask which one of his friends is trying to set him up. Then I'll keep the messages coming, ask a few casual questions that will tell me *something* about this world's Paul, and I can use that information to find him.

And who knows? Maybe he'd like the idea of a blind date.

I hug my knees to my chest, but my smile fades as I remind myself of my other reason for being here. Wyatt Conley didn't send me to this dimension to look Paul up for a latte. Not even to retrieve the next splinter of Paul's soul.

He sent me here to betray my parents, and this time, I can't take the risk of faking it. This time, I hurt them for real.

My dark errand weighs heavily on me as the three of us ride down in the elevator, on our way to eat dinner with Josie and the guy in her life. Apparently we're being treated to someplace fancy, because normally my father would never wear a tie for anything less than a wedding, a funeral, or a pitch meeting for a big research grant.

"We should've insisted on picking the restaurant," Dad says during the taxi ride across Central Park. "The Vietnamese place around the corner, maybe. We'd all be more relaxed, and ten-to-one I'd like the food better."

"If he's treating, then logically he should be the one to determine the restaurant." Mom looks out the car window at the darkening sky above. Day has begun fading into night. "We learn about people by observing their choices, Henry. The more control we surrender in this situation, the more we'll learn about him."

I'm wedged between the two of them in the middle of the backseat of the cab, with some obnoxious taxi-only TV channel playing on the same screen my knees are jammed against. "How much farther is it?"

"No idea," Dad grumbles. "Never bothered going anyplace so ritzy in my life, and my great-uncle was a viscount, you know."

Mom smiles. "Look at it this way, Henry. Now we know where to take Susannah the next time she visits Manhattan."

I feel a completely illogical leap of surprise at the news that Aunt Susannah—dead in the Warverse—is alive and well here. And *of course* they need to take her to the fanciest restaurant in New York. The more pretentious and overpriced something is, the greater chance Aunt Susannah will love it. I manage to hold back a giggle, but barely.

But being with my parents while they're acting like themselves—dorky and silly and so crazy about each other it's almost embarrassing—that only makes it more difficult to think of the task ahead.

I hug myself and shrink down farther in the seat.

The restaurant turns out to border Central Park. It's located in a stately, cream-colored building from the 1910s, one that doesn't proclaim its status so much as it quietly suggests it. As we walk to the front door, I see someone standing nearby, waiting; when he turns, I recognize Theo.

"Hey," I call. I'm about to lift my hand to wave when it hits me: What if Theo's here because *he's* Josie's fiancé?

That's crazy. They've never seemed like more than friends, not ever, even if he is closer to her age than mine. But this is a new dimension, with new rules. Is that why he's in my phone contacts? Because I've made friends with my future brother-in-law?

Then Mom smiles at him. "Theo. So glad you could make it."

"Glad to be here," Theo says. I can tell he's winging it, trying to figure out how well he knows my parents in this dimension.

The answer comes as Dad slaps him on the shoulder. "You needed to take a break from your dissertation—and besides, we'll need an objective point of view. Nobody we'd trust more than you."

Theo gets that *oh crap I have no idea what they're talking about* look. So I provide an assist, saying, "We can't let Josie marry just anybody, you know."

He visibly stifles a laugh, as astonished as I am at the

thought of commitment-phobic Josie getting engaged. My parents don't see; they're already walking inside. Once again, Theo crooks his arm for me, and I take it. He whispers, "Seen Paul?"

Only on a computer screen. I shake my head. Explaining my plan will have to wait for later.

We enter a hushed space, so carefully lit and perfectly decorated in cream and gold that I'd know it was crazy expensive even if Dad hadn't told me already. The carpet beneath my shoes feels as plush as if I were walking on clouds. Theo uses his free hand to straighten his mega-ironic '80s tie with the piano keys on it; this place is fancy enough to make even him self-conscious.

In the corner Josie rises from her seat to greet us. She's wearing flowing silk pants and a cowl-necked sweater—which, despite their elegance, still look like something my sister would choose to wear. *So Josie's herself here*, I think—and then I stop short. Theo sucks in a sharp breath as we see who's by her side—

—my sister's fiancé, Wyatt Conley.

14

JOSIE TAKES CONLEY'S ARM, HER FACE GLOWING. "EVERY-one, this is Wyatt. And Wyatt, may I present my parents, Dr. Sophia Kovalenka and Dr. Henry Caine; plus my sister, Marguerite; and my parents' graduate assistant, Theo Beck."

"A pleasure to meet you, Dr. Kovalenka, Dr. Caine. And Marguerite and Theo. I'm so glad you could make it tonight." Conley's manners are better than usual. If I didn't know what a manipulative, power-hungry snake he actually is, I could believe my sister had gotten engaged to a nice guy.

As my parents get through some small talk with the "happy couple," Theo and I take our seats. I lean toward him and whisper, "What's Conley doing?"

"From this angle, I can see what your parents can't see, namely that he's letting your sister grope his ass."

Somehow I manage not to gag. "I mean, why is he going after Josie? What's his game? And if Conley's got such a good in with my family in this dimension, why did he send us here?"

Theo raises an eyebrow. "Now *that's* a good question."

I look carefully at Conley, studying his neck and chest in particular. He's wearing a suit, one that's not closely tailored, so it still fits his "Bad Boy Wonder of Silicon Valley" image—but the subtle sheen of the fabric makes it clear his jacket alone probably cost as much as some cars. What interests me most is the lack of any rumples or wrinkles along his shirt, no telltale bulge beneath his silk necktie.

He's not wearing a Firebird.

Conley wouldn't necessarily have to wear it at all times; once you've stabilized in a dimension, you can take the Firebird off and put it aside almost indefinitely. But I've never removed my Firebird for more than a couple of seconds when I didn't absolutely have to, and neither would anyone else traveling through the multiverse.

Besides, he showed no flicker of recognition when he saw us. Conley loves to lord his power over people, to show off when he's got the advantage. So my guess is that we're sitting down to dinner with this world's Wyatt Conley—no passengers from other dimensions involved.

That would mean his romance with Josie is for real.

Everyone settles in. I hesitate before unfolding my napkin, which has been done up into some kind of origami swan. This tablecloth is made out of better fabric than most of my clothes. And when the waiter gives us the menus—gliding in and out almost unnoticeably, like a spirit—no prices are listed.

Theo murmurs, "If you have to ask, you can't afford it."

I'd laugh, but I'm too busy watching Conley and Josie.

"Well, I told you, Wyatt and I met when I agreed to help with his latest gaming system." Josie beams. Since when did she get into programming? Her next sentence answers that question. "The company needed someone to surf in a wave pool, so they could study the body kinesthetic, the kinds of motion, all of that. They'd already had a guy come in, but when they advertised for a female surfer too, I figured, what the hell. I'd been wanting to visit the Bay Area again, and I thought I might as well get paid for doing what I'd do for fun on the weekend anyway."

Conley cuts in. "And I was there just to see how the project was getting on."

"You had time for that?" Dad says, amiably enough. He's the only one of us totally at ease in these sophisticated surroundings—well, aside from Conley himself. My father's English-nobility background is showing. "I'd think running ConTech would keep you far too busy for that sort of thing."

I make a mental note. His company isn't Triad here; it's ConTech.

"I'm a busy man," Conley admits. "But I try to look in on various projects and teams throughout my company from time to time."

"Keeping them on their toes, huh?" Theo says.

That earns him a look from Conley, who clearly isn't sure why the grad assistant feels free to snark at him. But Conley keeps going. "Whatever made me show up that afternoon, I'm grateful. Because the minute I saw Josie surfing—she looked so happy, so confident, like she was having the time of her life—well, I guess that's why they call it love at first sight."

Oh, vomit.

"You know how I am," Josie says. She's speaking to all of us, supposedly, but she's looking at Mom. "I never wanted to be held back, and I never wanted to hold anyone back. Wyatt—he's already accomplished so much. I *couldn't* keep him from his goals. I'm not sure that's even possible."

Conley smiles as he puts one hand around her shoulders, not quite an embrace. His eyes flicker away only briefly, as he gestures to the waiter.

Josie continues, "I'm not leaving Scripps. I'm still going to get my doctorate in oceanography. And after that, Wyatt's talked about funding an expedition to Antarctica, where I could work on the iron content research we talked about, Dad."

"Really? What sort of methodology have you chosen?" Dad perks up. He's never regretted leaving oceanography for pure mathematics, putting aside his own promising career to support Mom in hers—but he's still a huge nerd about it.

The waiter arrives with champagne. With a nod of her head, Mom lets the waiter know he can pour me a glass as well. Special occasion, et cetera. She and Dad won't touch a drop, though. They don't drink much, and besides—despite the smile on Mom's face, and all my father's excited questions, I can tell they're analyzing Wyatt Conley every single second.

I take a sip, mostly to cover my own discomfort with the situation. Under his breath, Theo says, "I think Conley means it."

About loving Josie, he's saying. "This one does," I mutter. "That doesn't mean another one wouldn't use this to his advantage." Theo nods.

The rest of the night has a hallucinatory quality—half dream, half nightmare. For the dream, we have the hush of the room, the cloudlike elegance of the space, and food that tastes like the stuff you get served in heaven, in most world religions. For the nightmare: Conley's hand in Josie's, or around her shoulder, all evening long, holding tight. Like he *owns* her.

Yet I can't deny the energy they have together. Josie laughs when she tells her story about teaching him to water-ski; he lights up when he talks about how she gets him to stop thinking about business all the time and actually enjoy his life. And I notice the compliments he pays her. Conley never calls her *beautiful*, or *sweet*, or any of those generic terms that actually don't have jack to do with my rough-and-tumble sister. He says Josie's *dynamic.* That she's *filled with purpose.* Above all, she is *strong.*

I have to admit: He knows the real Josie. Maybe he even really loves her.

Silently I decide to stop thinking of this one as "Conley" and instead think of him as "Wyatt." That doesn't mean I trust Wyatt—not even close—but it reminds me that he's not the same guy as the one who's kidnapped and traumatized my family. I have to evaluate this one on his own.

Dessert arrives in the form of sorbets in flavors I've never heard of before: green tea, crème brûlée, even beet-and-lime. Tentatively I sample the beet-and-lime one—which is actually pretty good—then nearly choke on it when Wyatt says, "So where are you with the Firebird project?"

Next to me, Theo coughs into his napkin, trying to pretend he didn't just aspirate his dessert. Mom seems to think it's a natural question. "Not yet at the point of building a prototype, but I think we're ready to start construction soon."

"Depending on funding," Wyatt says, and Josie squeezes his fingers. I can tell what's coming next—the offer, the blank check he's ready to sign. The power he's about to seize over my parents' research.

Then Dad surprises me. "Josie's been hinting about this for a couple of weeks now, but I'm pleased to say that help is unnecessary. We just found out yesterday that we've been approved for a grant that ought to cover our next three years of research."

This is Wyatt's cue to start trying to talk my parents into letting *him* provide the funding. Instead, he grins and shakes his head. "I can see I'm going to have to invest at the IPO, like everyone else."

"IPO," Mom scoffs gently. "We're not doing this to make a profit, Wyatt. We only want to prove what's possible. To see some fraction of the infinite dimensions layered within the multiverse."

Josie murmurs, "Like climbing a mountain just because it's there."

"Do people climb mountains for any other reason?" Dad says. He gives Theo a look. "However, our assistant here thinks more like you do. His rationale is that if we can bring back advanced technology from alternate dimensions, we should—and in that case, money's going to be made and we might as well be the ones to make it. Right, Theo?"

"Yeah. I mean, yes, that's what I've always said. But lately I've wondered whether you and Sophia aren't right after all." Theo looks past us, at memories instead of the here and now. "Maybe the answer matters more than the reward."

My mother takes Theo's hand. "You're getting philosophical on us."

"Hardly." He manages to grin. "You know the old joke—a philosophy major winds up on the street with a sign that says WILL THINK FOR FOOD."

Everybody laughs, and the dinner tapers off into ordinary chitchat, like what everyone thinks of the sorbet, and Dad's token attempt to wrest the check from Wyatt. When we walk out into the night, I'm struck by the halved sky above me—to my right, Central Park's tall leafy trees are blacker than the sky above, and to the left, tall buildings reach upward, every window a sort of lantern. I think I'd like New York, if I ever got to visit for normal reasons.

My parents take it for granted that Josie's going to the

hotel suite she shares with Wyatt, which I didn't. It's not like I didn't guess that if they were engaged, they'd probably had sex, but that doesn't make me any happier to think about it. They stroll off alongside the park, enjoying a romantic evening in the big city.

Conley could get to my family here any time he wanted to, I think. *All he'd have to do is travel here, take over "Wyatt" for a few hours and he'd be done. So why hasn't he?*

I begin putting together a plan.

As the four of us stand there near the front of the restaurant, my mother's hand outstretched for a cab, Dad says, "I have to admit—she's happy."

"She is, and yet"—Mom shakes her head—"am I questioning it only because it seems too good to be true?"

"That's not like you," I say. "You should trust your instincts."

She gives me a look—questioning, but not disapproving. "What do your instincts tell you, Marguerite?"

How do I answer this? I can't let on how much I know; certainly I can't tell them the truth, not when I have to sabotage their work tomorrow. "I think he really loves her, but—something about it—I guess it all seems too easy."

"Yes, that's it." Mom combs her fingers through my curls, like she used to do when I was little and she helped me to go back to sleep after a bad dream. "We'll have to see. Of course, in the end, it's Josie's choice to make."

"Still, worth checking out," Theo says. "So. I ought to get going."

"You mean, *we* should get going." I improvise as smoothly as I can. "There's this really cool performance-art piece happening downtown tonight, in about an hour. Theo said he'd take me if I wanted to go. It's okay with you guys, right?"

My parents exchange a look. They've always been pretty chill, but my heading out into the wee hours is a little over their boundary lines. Of course, I'll have Theo with me—and apparently they're not sure what to make of that. Does that mean we've never flirted in this universe?

Or does it mean that we have?

Regardless, after a moment, Mom nods. "I realize not all art hangs in galleries. But text us when you get there and when you're leaving, and wake us up when you get in."

"And you'll see her all the way back to our building, Theo," Dad chimes in.

"Absolutely." Theo grins, hands in his pockets, like these had been his plans for the evening all along.

A bright yellow taxi finally sidles up to the curb for my mom and dad. As soon as it pulls off, Theo says, "This had better not be about *real* performance art. Because no."

I give him a look. "No. We're going to Josie and Wyatt's hotel."

"Thrilled as I am to hear you inviting me to a hotel, I bet you're going in a different direction with this."

My cheeks flush with heat as I remember Theo and me in the hotel in San Francisco, and the way he rolled me over, kissed me passionately. Thank goodness it's too dark for Theo to see my blush. "Conley hasn't come to this dimension. He can't have, or else he would have taken care of the sabotage himself."

"Sure. But this world's Wyatt Conley isn't going to know anything about that."

"No, but—he's a genius, right? In every dimension. And he might not be involved in the research about dimensional travel, but he's smart enough to understand it. If this version really loves Josie . . ." Still so weird to think about that, but I've begun to believe in his feelings for her. ". . . then maybe he could help us figure out why Conley didn't come to this world."

Theo frowns as we begin to stroll in the same direction Josie and Wyatt went. "Wait," he says. "You want to tell this version of Wyatt Conley the truth? Because that is risky as hell."

"The worst that could happen is Wyatt deciding we're nuts."

"No, the worst thing that could happen is Conley actually showing up in this universe, finding out we're trying to work against him, and retaliating by splintering Paul's soul into a thousand pieces instead of only four."

Instinctively I raise my hand to cover the two Firebirds hanging beneath my dress, next to my skin. A thousand dimensions—including some where we live on different continents, where reaching Paul would be nearly impossible—I could spend the rest of my life chasing him. Hunting for him. Reassembling the essential soul of the guy I love, bit by bit.

If I had to, then I would.

But I won't. "No," I insist. "If Conley were ever coming here, he would have done it already. He wouldn't have sent us. That's all there is to it. And if there's something unique about this dimension that keeps him out—"

"Then it would keep us out too," Theo says.

"Well, okay. But still, there's something here we're missing. Wyatt is the only person with any chance of helping us figure out what that is." I take a deep breath as I resume walking. "Except Mom and Dad. But we can't tell them."

"Because we still might have to saw them off at the knees." Theo says it dully. "Moving on. Found this dimension's Paul yet? I went through the whole Columbia student directory, and nada. He could be at Cambridge—"

"He's in New York. I don't know what he's doing besides grad school, but he's here. I sent him a Facebook message saying mutual friends wanted to fix us up." I take my phone out of my leather backpack to check it. But the Facebook app has nothing more to offer me than a lot of FarmVille updates. Apparently I'm really into FarmVille here. Kind of sad. "He'll write back. Probably." Maybe I should have put up a hotter profile pic.

But Theo says, "Of course he'll write. He'll be freaked out as hell, but you know Paul. He can't stand having incomplete data."

"You're right. He'll *have* to know." The thought soothes my raw nerves. I'll find Paul here; it won't be much longer. Another day, or maybe two. I can handle that.

"So," Theo says. "Josie and Wyatt Conley. There's not enough WTF in the world."

"Nope. But at least we know where Conley's vulnerable."

"You think that's true at home too? I mean, come on. They hardly know each other there."

True. Yet I can't forget how Josie's always joked that she thought Wyatt Conley was hot; maybe she wasn't joking. And now that I think about it, Conley's always managed to avoid meeting Josie face-to-face. Before it simply seemed unlucky. Now I can't help wondering if he avoided her on purpose because he knew she was a weakness he couldn't afford.

Slowly, I nod. "Yeah, I do."

Theo shrugs. His hipster-tight jacket crumples a bit at his shoulders, but that's all part of the look. "That's going to make for some interesting investigations back home. But for tonight, we try to talk with Conley about this without coming across as total lunatics. Tomorrow—I guess we go ahead and load the virus into your parents' data."

Although my heart aches, I can't think of another way to successfully fake that sabotage. "Yeah, we'd better."

If I told my parents the truth, they might help us; probably they'd play along just to stop anyone from attempting to dominate the dimensions. But I'm still heartsick to think that we didn't really carry out Conley's plan in the Warverse. I offered Paul that deal because we had no other choice, which means there's always a chance Conley will figure out the truth. If he does, God only knows what will happen to Paul.

I can't take that chance again. No, this time we have to play by Conley's rules.

Finally we approach the hotel Josie mentioned. Its brilliant sign glows gold in the night, at least two stories high. "Looks pretty swanky," Theo says, gesturing at the twin waterfalls on either side of the front door.

"Like Conley would stay anywhere else," I sigh. "Come on, let's—"

I hear the shriek of brakes just behind me, and whirl around, expecting to see a cabdriver getting into an accident. Instead, a black van runs up onto the curb before it skids to a halt.

Two men garbed in black, including ski masks that cover their faces, jump out and run in my direction—and I realize the person in trouble here is me.

Theo doesn't even hesitate. He charges, only to have one of the guys slam a fist into the side of Theo's head. Instantly he crumples to the sidewalk.

I turn to run, but a hand closes around my arm as tight as a vise. Even as I twist away, trying to scramble out of his grasp, someone else hoists me over his shoulder. I scream as loud as I can, which is when a black bag covers my head.

"*Help!*" I shriek. Someone's got to hear me through the bag, right? I try kicking at my captor, but he's running—and then there's a dizzying kind of spin as he throws me into the van. I kick out with both feet, going for the bag with my hands, but my arms are yanked down, and someone very heavy sits on my legs. *Oh God, oh God, what's happening?*

I hear Theo shout, "Marguerite! What— *Police! POLICE!*"

The van door slams shut, and my blood turns to ice.

I'm being kidnapped. Abducted. Taken against my will.

Again I scream, wordlessly, but it does no good. We accelerate so fast that I roll over and hit the side of the van, and once again, tires squeal against asphalt. I feel a plastic zip tie tighten around my wrists, and then someone does my legs. Thrashing, I try to shake off the bag, but two large hands push my shoulders down onto the floor of the van.

"Listen to me," says a heavily accented voice. "You get that bag off, you see our faces. You see our faces, you don't get to go home again. Maybe you like that bag now, huh?"

I hate the bag. But I'm keeping it on.

My heart pounds so hard it feels like my chest will crack. Tears well in my eyes, and I'm so scared I think I'm going to wet my pants.

Never let them take you to a second location. That's what all the self-defense classes say. It doesn't matter if someone holds a gun on you, you do not let them take you to a second location, because if they'd kill you where you stand, they'll kill you wherever you're going, except they'll have control of you for hours or days before you die, and you Do. Not. Want. That.

Will they rape me? Will they kill me? My mind seems to have shattered into something that can only show me the thousand horrible things that might be about to happen. That are probably going to happen. All the dangers of traveling through dimensions, and yet I never thought about how the same dangers from my own world might be the ones that killed me.

The Firebird, I remind myself. *You've got the Firebirds.* If I can manage to touch it at some point, even with my wrists bound, I might be able to leap out of here. But then that leaves this Marguerite to suffer a terrible fate—and means Wyatt Conley might decide I'd broken our deal. What would happen to Paul then?

Paul wouldn't want me to get hurt for his sake. I know that. But I'm not leaving him behind in this universe unless I have no other choice.

It seems like we drive forever. The van bumps and jostles me constantly, even though the guys continue holding me down; they talk the whole time, in what I'm increasingly sure is Russian, but in a dialect I'm not familiar with. Maybe my weeks in St. Petersburg will kick back in, and help me to understand them a little. All I know for sure is that we go over a bridge—the rhythmic thump-and-click unmistakable—and then keep driving for a long time more.

When the van comes to a halt, my pulse intensifies to the point where my chest hurts. I might be about to throw up. I don't want to throw up in the bag. My brain seizes on that—*don't puke, don't puke*—because it seems like the only part of this I might be able to control. Once again, I'm hauled over someone's shoulder and carried down a short set of stairs. Metal doors swing shut behind us; I hear locks being turned.

This isn't some random vacant lot or warehouse. This is a space designed to be secure, and secret. Oh, my God, is this human trafficking or something?

I'm dumped into a chair. The unpleasant screech of duct tape accompanies the pressure of it being wrapped around me, keeping me in place. If I knew what they wanted, I'd beg, I'd bargain—

Then it hits me. Maybe this isn't random.

A criminal operation—a professional one—that could be run by someone with a lot of money. A lot of influence. Someone who could get others to do his dirty work.

But no, I tell myself. *He's in love with my sister—for real, I'm sure of it. Conley wouldn't do this, unless—unless he realized I suspected him—*

"We've got her," says the man just by my shoulder.

Someone responds: "I see that." Only three words, but I recognize his voice.

Because it's Paul.

15

I CAN'T SPEAK. CAN'T SWALLOW. CAN'T BLINK.

The unbearable terror of the past hour expands, explodes. Every thought I have vaporizes. Nothing remains but the hard truth: Paul kidnapped me.

Who is he in this world? How can he be a part of this?

I hear him take one step closer, as if he's approaching. Yet he speaks to the others in the room instead. "She's just a girl. I checked. She's not even as old as I am."

"Leonid said to pick her up if we had the chance," says one of them—the one who grabbed me, I think. From the sharper diction of his words, I can tell he's pulled off the ski mask; I hope he stays behind me, because I don't want to see his face. I can't see his face. "We got the chance."

Paul swears under his breath; I remember enough Russian to know he's angry. Furious.

And I'm not the one he's angry with.

He didn't mean for this to happen. That has to be it. Someone else, this Leonid person—that's who kidnapped me. Paul's mixed up with some seriously terrible people, all right, but apparently he never meant for me to be hurt.

Besides, a splinter of my Paul's soul is within him. The guy I love is in there, just beneath the surface. I tell myself that he's influencing this Paul's actions. Playing a part in his decisions. My Paul will protect me.

So this will turn out okay. He'll get me out of this. And now I have the chance I need to retrieve the next piece of Paul's soul. But the terror of the past hour will take a long time to subside. My breaths come shallow and fast, my ribs straining against the duct tape every time I inhale.

He comes closer, and I feel his hand tug at the bottom of the black sack over my head. One of the men says, sharply, "What are you doing?"

Paul says, "The rest of you stay behind her. She already knows what I look like."

Then he lifts the edge of the bag. In the first instant, the light seems overwhelmingly bright—but my eyes adjust, revealing a dimly lit basement, and Paul standing in front of me. He's no monstrous version of himself, amused at my terror or eager to be cruel. Instead, he looks at me with much the same expression my own Paul would have in this kind of situation: worried for me, angry with my kidnappers, and determined to find the best way out.

Really, the only different thing about him is the clothing. Even if Paul could afford a slim-cut leather jacket like that, he'd never wear such a thing. Designer jeans, either. The outfit suits him, though, in a strange way.

"You've put us in a difficult position," Paul says to my abductors, then goes silent again, obviously thinking hard.

Analyze your surroundings, I tell myself. My terror-fogged brain clears as I focus on each element in turn. The chill of this room. Cement floor, with a drain at the center. Cinder-block walls. Pipes and some rebar stretch along the ceiling, confirming my earlier instinct that this was a basement. While the rest of the guys remain out of sight, I can see their shadows reflected on the floor. The swinging light overhead distorts their shapes, but I can tell all of them are as big and bulky as the men who abducted me.

As for Paul—I now notice he's been inked, a few blue-black lines apparent at the open collar of his shirt. It seems so incredibly unlike him to get a tattoo. His light brown hair is combed back and slicked with something that makes it seem darker. But he is still, fundamentally, the same.

"None of you have ever seen her before?" Paul glances around the room; nobody speaks. Finally he addresses me. "Who are these mutual friends?"

My mouth is so dry from fear that I have to swallow before I can say, "What are you talking about?"

"Your message." The dry humor in his voice is familiar. "You said mutual friends thought we should go out."

"Obviously I had the wrong Paul Markov."

Paul remains suspicious. "Did Tarasov tell you to make contact?"

"Who?" I can't remember a Tarasov from any dimension.

His frown deepens. "Derevko, then. Or Quinteros?"

"I don't know who any of those people are. Is this—is this because of that Facebook message?" Who the hell attacks someone because they messaged them on Facebook? "Like I told you, I made a mistake."

Paul inclines his head, like *It's possible.* Obviously he's still unhappy with the situation, but not . . . shocked. How can he not be shocked? These guys showed up with a kidnap victim. Namely, me.

This is obviously a criminal organization. I mean, they had a van, people watching me, waiting to see if they could kidnap me, all because I tried to get in touch with Paul in the most innocuous way, plus none of the others seem to have been born in the United States and *holy crap I'm mixed up with the Russian mob.*

How did *Paul* get mixed up with them?

He steps farther back, as if to study me from a distance, then leans against the cinder-block wall, like he's completely at ease.

But he's not. The tension in the way he holds his shoulders might be invisible to anyone who didn't know Paul as I well as I do. Deep inside, he's unsure of himself. Questioning what to do next.

I cling to this scrap of knowledge the way I'd grab a life preserver in the ocean. Is that uncertainty part of this world's Paul, or the soul of my Paul coming through? It doesn't matter. The only thing that matters is *I know this man.*

"Listen," I say, as calmly as I can. Paul responds to logic. "You said you researched me. So you know I'm eighteen years old, I live with my parents, and I'm not mixed up in . . . in whatever you guys are mixed up in." Time for a little creative invention. "Some friends of mine told me about a Paul Markov. Actually, now that I think about it, maybe I got the last name wrong. Obviously you're not the person I was looking for."

Paul inclines his head slightly. "Persuasive," he says. That's not the same as *I believe you*, but it's a positive sign.

"She knows your name, and she's seen your face," says one of the guys standing behind me, and the fear inside me once again boils over into panic. Every trashy true-crime TV show I ever watched has made it clear that they never let you see their face unless they plan to kill you, and while Paul would never do that, I don't feel good about the others—i.e., the guys in the room who are bigger, and stronger, and who probably own guns.

Yet they seem to defer to Paul.

Quietly he says, "The police would investigate the murder of a young woman from the Upper West Side. They wouldn't care very much about a kidnapping that resulted in no injury. Probably they wouldn't even believe any abduction took place; they'd think it was a story she made up. Cover for sneaking out to a party, maybe."

"There was a guy with her," grunts one of the men behind me. "We knocked him down. Out, maybe. Didn't have time to handle him permanently."

Theo. By now he will have phoned the police, my parents, everyone. They must all be so scared.

Paul says, "Then we don't have any time to waste. Either we have to get rid of the evidence, or we have to work out a deal." He steps closer to me. "I don't want police attention. How can I best avoid it, Miss Caine? By eliminating you as a witness, or by setting you free to tell the police you have no idea what happened to you?"

"Option two," I say. "Definitely."

"You can't trust her to do that!" objects one of the goons.

"I don't think she's stupid," Paul says. "She knows that if we found her once, we could find her again. The police might take me in for questioning, but by now she knows I have many friends. Don't you, Miss Caine?"

"All I want to do is get out of here." But not too quickly. "You'll drop me off? Don't send me with the others. I don't trust them."

If he's the one who drives me to God knows where, I'll have a chance to bring the Firebird into contact with his body and rescue that splinter of my Paul's soul. Then I can leave this dimension. Just leap out of here. Theo's Firebird will tell him that I've left; he'll follow me to the home office, where we can finally have it out with Conley. And this world's Marguerite can wonder why the hell she came to on a strange street corner, call her parents or the cops, and go home without suffering anything worse than a few bruises, some confusion, and a nasty rip in her tights.

"She'll stay quiet," Paul says to the others. "If she

doesn't—we can remind her of the bargain we've struck."

"Leonid has his ways," someone behind me says. Which is his way of agreeing with Paul. Even with the duct tape around my chest and arms, I feel like I can breathe better. Within a couple of hours, this will only seem like a bad dream.

Later, I know, I'll have to question how Paul got mixed up in this—I mean, seriously, the Russian mob? But I can't think about anything that complicated right now. My mind boils it down to the absolute basics: *Stay quiet. Trust Paul. Get home.*

But Paul hasn't said he'll be the one to drop me off—

A metal door slams. My entire body tenses so hard the tape pulls tight across my belly and my arms. Heavy footsteps walk through some kind of hallway—slightly behind me—and then I hear a deep, strongly accented voice. "You went fishing, I see."

While all the other men chuckle in a sheepish, brown-nosing kind of way, Paul's face falls.

I don't even need anyone to say the name. This is the man in charge. Leonid.

The footsteps circle around until I can see Leonid himself—still a shadow, mostly, lit from behind. He doesn't look directly at me; the guy knows better than to show anyone his face. "This is a child. My grandmother could catch this one."

Screw you too, I think.

But I know better than to say anything out loud. I'm

not even going to look directly at Leonid—*see, I can't identify you, it's okay to let me go*—and I don't want to draw any more attention. He's not getting any reaction from me whatsoever—

—until he steps into the light, and I have to bite down on my own tongue to keep from crying out.

Not because he's shown me his face, and proved he doesn't care whether I live or die.

Because the face looking at me now *is* Paul, through a mirror darkly.

He's older—rougher—hair as gray as his eyes—and coarser in every way, as if someone had taken Paul and stripped away everything that makes him beautiful, leaving only the brute behind. The nose has been broken a couple of times; his teeth are yellow from decades of coffee. Yet the resemblance is powerful, and unmistakable.

Behind him, Paul says quietly, "I'm handling this, Papa."

Leonid is Paul's father.

The puzzle pieces snap together at last. This is why Paul never goes home at Thanksgiving or Christmas. Why he doesn't like his parents, won't even talk about them. Why he has to get by on a modest grad student stipend, with no help from home ever. Paul's dad is mixed up in organized crime. The reason they cut him off must be because he refused to join the family business.

Except in this dimension, Paul stayed. Now he's trapped in the last possible life he could ever want to lead.

"You're handling it, are you?" Leonid says to Paul. "You

found out who she's with?"

"No one." Paul stands almost at attention. I always thought he was awkward with us—because, well, he is. But with his father, he's even worse. Tense and uncertain. Scared. "The entire situation arose out of a misunderstanding."

"You believe that?" Leonid's finger brushes against my cheek, a cold, impersonal appraisal.

Paul nods. "Yes, I do."

The guys standing behind me don't even seem to breathe. I realize they're nearly as terrified of Leonid as I am. Leonid's not just in the Russian mob; he's high up. Very high.

Enough so that he doesn't care if I see his face or not. He's too big a fish for the cops to net easily.

Leonid Markov cocks his head, and finally he speaks to me. "You're a sweet little girl who knows nothing about business? I think maybe you are. You don't remember any of this, even our names?"

My entire knowledge of criminal activity comes from *Law & Order* reruns. Probably not reliable. I stick to what Paul said before. "If I tell the police I don't remember anything, you won't come after me again. That's all I want."

He laughs out loud, pats my cheek. "Good girl."

Was that stupid, persuasive, or both? At any rate, Leonid is out of my face now, standing up and looking at Paul instead. Paul says, "I'll drop her off myself. Drive her to another borough. It doesn't have to be any more complicated than that."

He speaks so evenly that someone could almost miss the

fact that he's pleading for my life. Joy spreads its wings inside me. Paul's going to be the one to drive me away from this place. I have a chance at rescuing my Paul's soul. This will all be over soon.

"You're right," Leonid says. "It wouldn't have to be, if I didn't have such idiots working for me."

Silence falls. Danger has become palpable in the room, but suddenly the threat is no longer directed at me.

Leonid steps back. In the harsh light of the single bulb dangling down, the wrinkles on his face cast strange shadows. "Idiots kidnap a girl where people can see them, where they knock down a witness and leave him there to call the police. Idiots kidnap a girl in front of a building with a security camera in the front. Idiots get us on the news!"

At first my heart leaps at the thought the authorities know I'm in danger—but that's only instinct. In this situation, instinct is completely wrong. I was out of trouble; Paul had found the way to save me. Now those plans don't count anymore.

Leonid reaches inside his heavy coat, and something about the way he moves reminds me sharply of Paul. For a moment father and son are superimposed on each other—old over young, corrupt versus good—confusing me enough that at first I don't recognize the gun.

Then it's as if there's nothing else in the room. The gun makes everything else invisible, silent, irrelevant. The dull sheen of black metal stands out even in the darkened room. Then my vision focuses even tighter, on Leonid's hand as he squeezes the trigger.

When the sound of the gunshot explodes in the room, I scream—in fear, and in pain, because it's so loud my eardrums sting and I think they might have ruptured. Then I'm too scared to scream anymore. Through the ringing of my ears I hear a heavy, wet thud on the floor just behind me.

Leonid has one less henchman.

Every other guy in the room remains completely quiet, like if he shows Leonid enough respect, he won't be next. Paul is the only one who challenges his father. "What did you do that for?"

"I don't need idiots." Leonid slips his gun back under his jacket as casually as I'd put my phone back in my purse. "This wasn't his first mistake." His gray eyes—so like Paul's, yet so much colder—focus on someone else in the corner of the room, probably the other man who kidnapped me. "You—it was your first mistake. So you get another chance. One more. Understand me?"

Even as Paul clenches his jaw, flushed with unspoken anger, he looks toward me. His gaze is a message I think I would understand even if I didn't know him so well: *Don't react, don't move, and this won't happen to you. I won't let it.*

"Clean it up," Leonid says to his goons as he puts one hand on Paul's shoulder, the gesture of the warm, loving dad he so obviously isn't. "Come, Paul. We should talk about what happens next."

Don't leave, I think.

But he has to bargain with his father, probably for my life.

I force myself to remain calm as father and son walk away, and the heavy metal door behind me swings shut again.

Men grumble in colloquial Russian I can't quite catch as they remove their dead or dying comrade. I only glean a few words—*trash, hurry, silent.* Why didn't I study harder after I got back from my first trip? I'd gotten so good at Russian then, and I wish I spoke it fluently now. At my feet, I see a trickle of blood oozing toward the metal grid in the center of the room. With a rush of horror, I realize this is what the drain is for.

Finally I have to let the fear take me. A strange immobility sinks over me, and I know my expression has gone totally blank. This must be the way rabbits or deer feel when they see headlights coming on the highway. This is why they stand perfectly still as death rushes toward them.

All I can do is sit in this chair, feeling duct tape tight against my ribs, stealing my breath. My body shakes—trying to burn off the adrenaline shot into my blood so I could fight or flee. I can do neither.

I zone out. Time blurs. I am bound to this chair forever and for only a second before the metal door clangs again. My stomach clenches as I brace myself for Leonid—but when I see Paul, I can breathe again. Our eyes meet, but again, he doesn't speak to me. "We need to set up a more convenient place for her to stay. She'll be with us for a few days."

Days? I bite the inside of my cheek. But captive for days is still better than dead.

"Why the hell are we keeping her?" one guy asks. They're

still working; I can hear the crinkle of trash bags being wrapped around a body. "The sooner we get done with her, the better."

"Miss Caine turns out to be valuable," Paul says.

Surely he doesn't know anything about the Firebirds. They haven't tried to take them, anyway; both of the Firebird devices are still nestled against my chest, metal edges almost cutting into my skin from the pressure of the tape. Nobody from this dimension should notice them easily.

Paul answers the question I didn't ask aloud. "Her sister's engaged to a billionaire. Wyatt Conley, the founder of ConTech. Ten minutes ago, at a press conference, he offered a million dollars for information leading to her safe return."

I could scream in frustration. If Wyatt hadn't done that, they probably would have let me go within the hour! Even now, in a world where he's actually trying to help me, he's still screwing me over. Figures.

Yet I take comfort in one fact: The price of my life is one million dollars. Wyatt's reward might keep me imprisoned, but it might also keep me alive.

16

APPARENTLY THIS ISN'T THE FIRST TIME THESE GUYS HAVE kept a prisoner. Leonid's men prepare for my captivity swiftly and efficiently.

The bag goes back over my head before the duct tape is cut. They get rid of the zip tie around my ankles—blood rushes into my cold, tingling feet—but the one around my wrists remains. The large hand that closes around my arm doesn't belong to Paul; I know from the way the fingers dig cruelly into my flesh, even through my thick wool sweater. Many footsteps follow and surround me, a dull ominous cloud of sound. The loudest thing I hear is my own ragged breathing within the bag. My half-numb legs make me clumsy as I walk along some corridors, turning that way and this, until someone jerks me to a halt and growls, "Down the stairs."

I reach forward with one leg and feel the first step—then almost lose my balance and fall. One of the men near me laughs at my uncertainty, and rage swells inside so hot my temples throb. It's almost enough to turn me stupid, to make me start screaming at him. *You think it's so funny? I'm scared to death and I can't see where I'm going and you're trying to push me down a flight of stairs and if I ever get my hands free—*

But I remember the guns, and say nothing.

A gentler hand cups my shoulder. "Here," Paul murmurs. "I'll walk you down."

I lean on him the entire way, as I feel each step with my toes. The space where they're putting me is so damp I already feel clammy. Cold, too. I remain aware of the warmth of Paul's body near mine.

When I finally stand on a level floor, the door above us swings shut; several locks turn and click, sealing Paul and me within. One tug, and Paul lifts the bag away from my head. This room is smaller than the one I was originally held in, and quieter, too, farther from any sounds of the city above. More light shines from the few bulbs on the low ceiling, though, and the floor lacks a drain. Of the two rooms, I definitely prefer this one.

In one corner I see a cot with a blanket; in another, a bucket with a lid. Normally the thought of peeing in a bucket would gross me out, but I've been on the verge of wetting myself since the first moment I was grabbed on the street. By now the bucket looks pretty good.

Paul says, "We'll bring you some food soon. A few bottles of water. The blanket should keep you warm, but if you need another, tell whoever comes in here."

"You. I want it to be you."

Different emotions flicker across his face—surprise, confusion, even some pleasure at being chosen. He says only, "Why me?"

Because I have to get close to you if I'm going to have any chance of rescuing my Paul's soul. Fortunately I have other reasons, ones I can say out loud. "You want me alive. And you wouldn't hurt me."

"No one here is going to hurt you," Paul says. "They have their orders, and they'll follow them."

I lift my chin. "It wouldn't matter what the orders were. You wouldn't hurt me, no matter what."

He raises one eyebrow, just like Mr. Spock—one of his favorite characters. If the situation were any less dire, I'd have to laugh. "You don't have the necessary information to make a judgment."

A thousand memories of Paul flip through my mind: making lasagna together the night before Thanksgiving, riding in a submarine in an entirely new world, kissing in the train station, listening to music in the car as we drove to Muir Woods, simply holding each other in his dorm room and feeling the rise and fall of his breath beneath my hands.

That Paul is within this one.

"I know enough," I say.

Paul studies me a moment longer, then breaks the connection between us as he turns away. "You have the necessities. And—like I said—let us know if you need another blanket."

Even now he's trying to shelter me. "Okay."

"The door overhead will be padlocked. No one outside this building will be able to hear you, regardless of what you do. I argued that you should be given a cot, even when the others pointed out that you could break it down and use the pieces as weapons against anyone who comes into this room. If you're considering that plan of action, don't. It will be futile, because others will be outside, ready to stop you through any means necessary. Then you won't be able to keep the cot any longer. Have I made the conditions of your stay clear?"

My stay. Like I'm at the Hilton. "Crystal."

Paul hesitates a moment longer—like he thinks I haven't really understood, or that I'm not taking it seriously. I don't know how he can think that; somebody got shot to death while standing about three feet from me, less than an hour ago.

What he senses—what he knows, I think—is that I'm not afraid of him.

Paul says nothing else, simply nods as he heads up the concrete steps.

The door thudding shut ought to sound ominous; instead, when I hear it, I smile. I can smile because I know something the others don't, something Paul himself doesn't know yet.

Paul can't stand not understanding why something happens. It doesn't matter whether that's some freak behavior of subatomic particles in an experiment or people laughing at a joke he doesn't get; it drives him nuts. He responds to uncertainty by charging at it, determined to force the mysterious to make sense. This tendency of his can be frustrating—Paul wants people to behave logically, at least most of the time, and there's no way to get him to accept that they just don't. But it's also one of the reasons he's such an amazing scientist at an age most people are still picking a major. The easy explanation is never enough for Paul.

Right now, he's asking himself why I'm so sure he won't hurt me. Why I trust someone I met while I was duct-taped to a chair. Obviously he can't begin to guess the real answer.

Paul will want to talk. I can prove that I know him like nobody else ever has, or ever will. If I can win him over enough to untie my hands, while we're in here alone together—then I've saved the next part of my Paul's soul.

As I lie on this cot, I have no way of knowing how much time has passed. Forget a phone or a clock—I don't even have sunlight to go by, if the sun has come up yet, which I doubt. So maybe an hour passes, or maybe three do; it doesn't make any difference. I just have to stay here, studying my makeshift cell and waiting for a chance to talk with Paul again.

My surroundings don't give me much to work with. The room probably measures about ten by ten. Walls: unpainted cinder blocks. Ceiling: not sure, but whatever it is, it's solid—forget any removable panels or inviting air ducts. Floor: concrete, no drain, which is a good sign I wouldn't have known to look for yesterday. I'm lying on a sky-blue comforter, which was nice once but has seen wear; something about the cozy fabric plus the hard use makes me think this blanket belonged to a child, long ago. Who takes a blanket from their kid's bed and uses it when they're kid-napping someone? How can anybody be that schizo? I can't understand it. Add another entry to the extremely long list of reasons why I would make a bad mobster.

The eerie quiet is the worst part. This blank, cold room could stand in for a sensory-deprivation chamber. Once I didn't understand how solitary confinement could drive prisoners insane, but when I try to imagine being in a place like this for months or years, I see how it could happen.

But nobody comes down to harm me. Except for my wrists, I'm in no pain. I tell myself it's not so bad.

(So far, the worst part was I had to use the bucket once, which was about as gross as you'd imagine. At least the Russian mafia politely provided a lid.)

Honestly, I'm probably doing better than my parents right now. I close my eyes tightly, thinking about how scared they must be. Their only comfort must be Wyatt's reward offer.

But I can't rely on Wyatt Conley's "good heart." Yeah, it looks like he loves Josie in this universe, but that doesn't change the fact that he's corrupt to the core. If anyone could be callous enough to screw around with a ransom for my life, it's him. Maybe he's trying to get the Russian mob to give him a discount.

Some sense of time returns when the padlock clatters against my door. I sit upright as the door swings open. The hair on my scalp prickles in fear when I hear the heavy tread on the stairs. Within moments I realize something very good—they're bringing me food—and something very bad—Paul's not the one bringing it.

One of the ski-mask guys carries a paper sack and a plastic bottle of Sprite. From the paper sack he pulls out a damp-looking sandwich that has probably been Saran Wrapped for at least a couple of days, and a small bag of ranch-flavor potato chips. I hate ranch flavor, but right now? I can't wait to stuff the chips in my face as fast as possible.

"Can you take this off?" I say to Masked Guy, holding up my zip-tied wrists.

He laughs. "You want food badly enough, you can eat it with those on." Then, perhaps reconsidering, he leans down and opens the Sprite bottle for me. Thanks, Mr. Hospitality.

I start working on the bag of chips. Masked Guy just stands there, staring at me. Probably he's watching to make sure I don't do something brave/stupid, but I'm reminded how much I'm at their mercy. Paul is only one man in what appears to be a very large, very ruthless organization. He would protect me, but with all the others, I have no guarantees.

Then I hear Paul's voice from above, loud, and in proper Russian I understand, "*Stop wasting time down there. Come back.*"

Masked Guy huffs. I don't need any background knowledge to know exactly what he's thinking: *The boss's kid thinks he can order me around? Snot-nosed brat!* But he doesn't dare defy Leonid's son.

For the first time, though, I realize that Paul can't be with me every second. What do I do if someone escalates this? What if someone is on the verge of raping me, or torturing me? As long as Leonid's in charge, if Paul were gone for some period of time—that could happen. Could I really bear that for this world's Marguerite?

I'd like to think I wouldn't abandon her here no matter what. But even if I wanted to leave her behind and get out of this universe, at least for a while, I couldn't. While I can touch the Firebirds with my hands bound, even kind of get my fingers around one, I just don't have enough flexibility to work the controls. So there's no getting out of this one, no matter what.

As long as my hands are bound, I'm trapped here.

Masked Guy stomps up the stairs—wow, Russian mobsters are brattier than I would have thought. But he doesn't shut the door behind him. Instead, Paul descends the steps, returning to my side.

"He didn't bother you?" he says.

Still protecting me. "No. I'm all right."

The door overhead swings shut with a clang. Paul glances upward, eyes narrowing in irritation, or anger. Maybe he and Masked Guy have clashed before. At any rate, he didn't fully trust the guy with me. "If he ever says or does anything that scares you, shout for me. Or scream. I'll come."

Like this whole scenario doesn't scare me. But I nod, and Paul turns away, ready to go upstairs and tell Masked Guy to watch his step. I ought to be glad about that, but instead, I'm desperate not to lose contact with Paul again. The word comes out of my mouth almost before I can think about it: "Stay."

He stops. "Why?"

"It's so quiet down here I can't stand it much longer."

After a moment, Paul says, "I meant to talk with you anyway."

Don't overreact. Be casual. You have an opportunity here. "Okay. Good."

He folds his arms across his chest as he leans back against the far wall. "You trust me. And you shouldn't. Why?"

"You're not like the others." Should I risk it? Might as well try. "Not like your father."

His eyes narrow, but he doesn't disagree.

In my own dimension, Paul will never talk much about his family. Finally I understand why—but even when he learns I know the awful truth, he'll resist telling me more. I'd already realized how ashamed he was of his family. Not embarrassed. *Ashamed.* Like it kills him a little every time he thinks of it. When he told me his parents were "bad people," I thought they were alcoholics or maybe even abusive. Now I see how they actually failed him: Paul's parents never even gave a damn. If you love your kids, you don't live a life of total corruption. You don't expose them to violence. You don't try to shove them into following your own wretched example instead of going after their dreams. Mr. and Mrs. Markov did all that to Paul and more. His good heart had to be so strong to survive that intact, but it did. In my world, and in so many others.

Has he always thought I'd hate him if I knew?

Maybe this is my chance to find out the rest of the story. Then I can tell Paul I've discovered it all, and I love him even more.

"What's your mother like?" I ask him.

"Why should you care?"

"I've been down here too long. I'm bored. Is she in the family business too?"

"Family business?"

"What else should I call it?"

Paul doesn't provide another term, probably because most of the alternatives are worse. "She's not directly involved."

"Does she, um, approve?"

He laughs softly, in contempt. But only when he speaks do I realize the contempt isn't for me. "My father's word is law, for all of us. My mother insists on that even more than he does. She worships him."

"Did she want you to work for your dad?"

"Insisted on it." Paul shakes his head at some scene in his past that must be playing out in his mind. "She even gave me my first tattoo."

Okay, that took a left turn. "What does a tattoo have to do with, um, this life?"

For a long moment Paul stares at me, like he can't understand why I'm asking or why he wants to answer. But he does want to tell me; I can see it in his eyes. Finally he says, "In Russia, members of 'this life' are always tattooed. The images reveal the crimes they've committed, the time they've served in prison. Or the things they believe."

"What tattoos do you have?" He can't have done terrible things like his father, or those awful men upstairs. Paul's not like them, and never could be. Yet I see the lines of ink at his open collar, testament to a divergence between this Paul and my own.

Paul notices my gaze on his skin. He says, "This is just to show you. No other reason." And then he starts unbuttoning his shirt.

Once again I remember the day Paul posed for me as my model. Not what I need to think about right now. Instead, I concentrate on the fact that he told me not to be afraid, that he's trying to comfort me as much as he can.

He doesn't strip off his shirt, doesn't even open it all the way. But the top half of his chest is mostly exposed now and I can see the tattoos for myself. They're simple, drawn only in blue-black ink, but artfully done. The largest tattoo is in the middle of his chest, a surprisingly devout image of the Virgin Mary with baby Jesus. On one shoulder is a rose that looks withered, or dried; on the other, a dove perches on a twig.

In my mind I hear Lieutenant Markov whisper, *Golubka.* He called me his little dove as he held me in his arms.

"You like this one?" Paul gestures toward that shoulder. "It means 'deliverance from suffering.' The rose, that says I would prefer death to dishonor. And the Madonna tells anyone who understands that I was born into—what you call 'this life.'"

The Madonna requires no explanation. The meaning of the rose doesn't surprise me either; Paul's sense of decency and kindness holds true even in a reality where he didn't escape his parents' corruption. But the dove . . .

I look into his eyes. "What suffering were you delivered from?" I ask as gently as I can. "Or are you still waiting for deliverance?"

Paul stiffens. Immediately he begins buttoning his shirt. "You ask too many questions."

"But you want to answer me. Don't you?"

He pauses for a long moment, and I know he feels it too—the electric connection between us that spans the worlds. Yet Paul can't understand why he has this bond with a stranger, why he felt the need to show me the secrets inked on his skin, or why I reach out for him even now. Baffled, almost hurt, he simply goes up the stairs without another word.

As the door shuts and locks again, I take a deep breath and realize I'm shaking. I trust him so deeply, but this scenario is unlike any I've ever faced while traveling between the universes; I could make the wrong move at any moment and upset a very delicate balance.

Getting closer to Paul in this dimension means playing with fire.

17

WHEN THE HIGHLIGHT OF YOUR DAY IS SOMEONE GIVING you a fresh bathroom bucket—it's not a good sign.

Masked Guy hauled the old bucket upstairs. He seemed about as thrilled with his errand as you'd expect, but I was still sort of sorry to see him go. After so long in this featureless underground cell, seeing anyone—even him—was fuel for my understimulated mind. But by now he's been gone for a while, however long a while is, and I feel the room shrinking around me, sealing me farther away from the real world.

My sense of time has all but collapsed. I have no idea how long I've been down here. More than three hours since they brought me food, though, because I'm hungry. Beyond that, I can't tell.

I'm exhausted. At this point, this world's Marguerite must have been awake for more than twenty-four hours straight.

Surely the negotiations for my release have begun. Wyatt Conley might already have bankers bringing him a million dollars in unmarked bills. Or instead of collecting a cash-stuffed briefcase from under a park bench, Leonid's probably giving Conley the number of some Cayman Islands account that will mysteriously disappear the moment after the ransom deposits.

The door at the top of the stairs swings open. The same strange cocktail of emotions swirls within me—fear, hope, the peculiar happiness of knowing that at least *something* is happening—

—when I see Paul returning to me, and hope eclipses all the rest.

"Here," he says. He's holding a white Styrofoam container and a can of ginger ale. "You must be hungry again."

"I am. What time is it?"

"Does it matter?"

"I'd just like to know." My voice shakes, but I swallow hard and continue. "Being in this room for so long—it's weird, not knowing anything that's happening outside."

Paul hesitates. His gray eyes are almost unreadable, but I can see that he doesn't like realizing how scared I am. When he answers me, his words are simple and precise. "It's early afternoon. Cloudy. We had rain earlier, but it stopped."

Who knew it could feel like such a relief just to hear what the sky looks like? "Thanks."

"Your lunch is late. I'll make sure dinner gets here faster, if you're still . . . with us."

Does that mean "still with us" as in "not yet free," or as in "alive"? I'm about 99 percent sure he means the former. In this situation, though, 99 percent is not enough.

Paul pulls back the Styrofoam lid to reveal lasagna and garlic bread. The smell of tomato sauce, cheese, and garlic almost makes me reel; I'm that hungry.

But I also remember the night Paul and I made lasagna together in my family's kitchen. We listened to Rachmaninoff, and our shoulders brushed against each other, and we laughed every time we screwed something up, which happened constantly. That was the first night I recognized that my feelings for Paul had begun to change. Sometimes I think of it as the first night of "us."

"Any chance of taking these off?" I offer my bound wrists to Paul. "If I try to eat Italian food with my hands tied, I'm going to get it all over myself. Or do you need a chance to laugh at me?"

Paul would never laugh at someone for a thing like that. He'd be offended by the very suggestion, which is what I'm counting on.

But he doesn't cut through the zip ties. Instead, he says, "I'll help you."

As he takes the white plastic fork from its plastic sleeve, I say, "You mean you're going to feed me?"

"It's like you said. Otherwise, you'd make a mess." He hands me the thin paper napkin. "The ties have to stay on."

He starts to sit on the edge of my cot, then pulls back. No doubt he thinks I'll feel threatened if he comes close to me too quickly—which I would, under normal circumstances. Actually, as he finally settles next to me, I feel comforted.

This hesitation means he's thinking of me. Trying to make this easier.

And even though I can't make my move yet, it helps me to know he's this close to the Firebirds.

Paul carefully gets a forkful of lasagna, lets the first droplets of sauce fall, then brings it to my mouth. I feel weirdly self-conscious about taking the initial bite. After that, though, I don't care. The first taste of tomato sauce against my tongue makes me salivate so quickly my mouth almost hurts. I can handle the garlic bread myself, so I sop that in the sauce and eat some before he offers me the next bite. I could swear I've never eaten anything this good before in my life.

"You were hungrier than I thought," Paul says.

I must be wolfing this stuff down like a stray dog. Forcing myself to chew slower, I dab at my mouth with the flimsy paper napkin. "Sorry."

"Don't apologize. The fault was mine."

Paul feels guilty. Maybe I can use that. "Does this establishment offer showers? A bath?" He'd take off the zip ties to let me bathe, surely. "Between the crazy eating and the crazy hair, I bet I look like the Tasmanian Devil."

"You've looked better."

Ouch. I glare at him. "How would you know?"

"I would assume."

Once again I remind myself that Paul's rudeness is always a kind of honesty. Since last night, I've been thrown in the back of a van, terrified, imprisoned, and duct-taped. Plus I'm sleep-deprived. I *hope* I've looked better than I must right now.

"Why did it take so long for the food?" I ask. "You only get your ransom money if I'm returned safe and sound, right? Starved to death definitely wouldn't count as 'safe.'"

"It takes weeks for a human being to die of starvation. Thirst kills faster, within days." Another thing that's the same in this dimension? The way Paul's face looks when he realizes he's just said something amazingly tactless one second too late to take it back. "Nobody's going to deny you food or water. Let's leave it at that."

"Did you get some dinner too? I'd bet anything you love lasagna."

He hesitates. "Everyone loves lasagna."

"But you really love it." I say this as innocently as I can, between bites. "I bet you've even learned to make lasagna yourself."

He isn't fazed—at least, visibly. "You like to pretend that you know me very well."

"I have instincts about people."

"Unlikely. What most people call *instinct* in people is really the interpretation of small subconscious cues."

"Maybe I picked up on some of those."

"There are no subconscious cues that could tell you I enjoy lasagna."

I laugh out loud. Paul does that thing where he realizes something he's said in seriousness is funny—his expression clouds, and he tries to smile, but it never quite works. Moments like that make him feel vulnerable. So I quickly say, "It's like you said. Everybody loves lasagna. That's all."

"That's not all."

"What else could it be?" He offers me one more bite, and I take it, the conversation flowing smoothly around my meal.

"I don't know," he says. "But I don't believe in instincts."

"What about psychic powers?"

This earns me a stare as withering as the one I'd get from my scientist Paul back home. I decide to mess with his rational head, for once; besides, after hours tied up and freaking out, I need to remind myself how much I know. What power I still possess.

So I say, "For instance, my instincts—or powers, you decide—they're telling me you wanted to follow a very different path in life. Something that wasn't illegal. Something more than this, bigger and more meaningful. Personally, I think you would've been a good . . . scientist."

If the situation were less terrible, the look on his face would be hilarious. He puts down the Styrofoam container and stands up. "How could you guess that I wanted—?" His words stop as he catches himself.

How *would* I have guessed that? "The way you always seem to be analyzing things. You're smart. I can tell."

Paul paces in front of me, his footsteps loud in this small, dark cell. "Someone else has told you about me. There's no other way you could know that."

"Who knew that, besides you? Nobody, I bet. You don't open up to many people." Which means any people.

He takes a step backward to consider me from a different angle. "What else do your 'instincts' tell you about me?"

I remember the things I shouted after the last dimension's Paul. They were too intimate, too exact. This time, my answer will be simple. It will be honest. But it will still be some of what I love about him.

After all, a splinter of my Paul is within this man, even now.

"You like facts. You want to be objective. So sometimes people assume you're cold, but you're not. Not at all. I think you feel more deeply than most people ever do; you just don't know how to show it. You always feel—out of step. You're not like the people around you, and they know it as well as you do. And you think it's because something's wrong with you, so you retreat deeper into the background. That just means people don't get to know the real you."

Paul takes one step backward. I think he doesn't know whether to be moved or frightened.

"You're lonely," I say, more softly. "You've been lonely so long I think you've forgotten there's any other way to be."

He breathes in deeply. By now the way he looks at me reminds me more of my own Paul—that mixture of uncertainty and awe I remember from our first days together.

Is that part of his soul shining through? Will he save me after all?

I lean forward, willing him to understand it's okay for

us to be close. "You want a family. Not your own—a real family, made up of people who take care of each other. And when people are scared of you, because you're so big, it kills you a little inside. Because you can be so gentle. So kind."

"You don't know me," Paul says, as if by pronouncing the words he can make them true.

"I wish you could learn how to show more people the real you. If you could, nobody would ever be scared of you again." *Nobody could help but love you,* I want to add. But that's a step too far.

After a moment, he laughs, a hard, strange sound. "You learned all this already?"

"First impressions can tell you a lot." I smile. "So, what do you see when you look at me?"

I'm not expecting much of an answer—but I get one.

"You're insecure," Paul says flatly. "So you exaggerate your knowledge or emotions to draw attention you think you won't get otherwise. You have genuine talents, however. If you didn't, you wouldn't be willing to put yourself forward. Why they're not enough for you, I don't know. You're sophisticated for your age in some ways, naive in others, which makes me think you went to one of the experimental schools—a Waldorf school, maybe—or you could have been educated at home by intelligent people. You come across as a normal young girl, but when angered, I suspect you're dangerous. I say that even though I'm the one with the gun."

His little joke gets lost in all the rest. I'm too astonished, too hurt, by this bald accuracy. Naive? Insecure? Is that what my Paul thinks too?

The last part is the only one I can bring myself to talk about. "Dangerous?"

"You're calm under pressure. Calmer than you should be." Paul's gaze rakes over me, as though his perception alone could scour me raw. "Maybe you did reach out to me by accident. But now you taunt me with this life I can never have—that's either courage or madness. I don't know which. All I know is that you're not an ordinary girl. You've seen things others haven't. Done things others couldn't."

I feel like I'm going to cry, but I won't. Not in front of him, not now.

He sees my weakness, but doesn't spare me the last: "You think your specialness makes you invulnerable. It doesn't."

With that Paul walks upstairs. His only goodbye is the door slamming shut.

18

DESPITE MY EXHAUSTION, I LIE AWAKE FOR WHAT SEEMS TO be a long time.

Paul thinks I'm pathetic. Ridiculous. Naive, and proud, and a hundred other things I never wanted to be.

Maybe that seems like a stupid thing to worry about, compared to the fact that I'm being held captive by armed mobsters. But I was relying on my knowledge of Paul to protect me here, and now it feels like that shield is gone.

He saw more in me after *one day* than I saw in him after months of his practically living at our house. Of course I already knew Paul was perceptive. One of the reasons I fell for my Paul was because he saw through all my defenses. Somehow he saw the real me, and he loved what he saw.

This Paul looks at me and sees weakness. Immaturity. Even danger.

Okay, I did set out to kill you once, but I had a good reason.

Doubt he wants to hear that.

Whatever he's seen, he doesn't like it.

Maybe it was that splinter of my Paul inside him that knew so much. But that would be even worse. Does my Paul think all those things too? He can't. Otherwise he couldn't love me.

I imagine his soul within this Paul's. If they influence each other, it won't only be my Paul affecting him. Maybe this Paul's contempt will carry over. Maybe my Paul will begin to think of me as insecure and arrogant. Maybe he'll never see me the same way.

Even if I can put the three parts of Paul's soul together again, he might never be the same.

Then I hear something from above—a low, heavy thud. Another. Like thunder, but not—

I jump as I hear loud popping, over and over, super fast. My first thought is of one of those little bundles of fireworks—but I know better. It's gunfire.

Oh God, oh god ohgodohgod. What's happening?

Forget what Paul said about the cot. I kick at one of the legs, and it collapses. If I can pry one of the poles free, that would at least be a weapon. Even with my hands tied, I can probably manage that.

The door swings open. The sound of gunfire goes from loud to deafening. I push myself into the corner, like that's going to do any good. Paul comes downstairs toward me.

"Come on!" he shouts, grabbing my wrist. His grip is too tight, and the raw stripes on my skin beneath the zip tie sting. It doesn't matter. I follow him, stumbling up the stairs.

I scream over the sound, "What's happening?"

"You shouldn't be here!"

Not an answer. But I agree with him.

None of the shooters are visible in the dark concrete corridor, but distant sparks suggest ricochets. The gunfire echoes so that the sound doubles on itself, disorienting me.

Paul pulls me forward, and we turn a corner—another—and now the fight seems farther away. The roar of guns has muted, only slightly, but enough that my ears stop ringing. Paul opens a door to reveal a large closet. "Get in."

"What?"

"Get in!" he shouts. "You're safer here."

"How?"

Paul's hand fists in my sweater. "My father would kill you rather than let you be taken. Do you understand?"

I wish I didn't.

Terrified as I am, I try to use this moment. "Please. You have to untie my hands. What if someone else comes for me?" I hold up my bound wrists. "*Please.*"

He makes his decision in an instant; the butterfly knife seems to appear in his hand by magic. I jump a little, but then hold still so he can cut through the plastic. He does this deftly, in one smooth practiced motion.

All I have to do is grab him, grab the Firebird, and I can get the next sliver of Paul's soul back again—

But immediately Paul shoves me into the closet so hard I hit the back wall. It's not cruelty; this is his idea of keeping me safe. "Don't move until I come back for you. Do you understand? You must not move." Then he slams the door shut and turns the lock, sealing me in total darkness.

I miss my cell already.

Paul will come back for me. I'll have another chance. I take deep breaths and try to tell myself things are looking up, between bursts of distant gunfire.

At least Paul brought me to a safer place. Protected me. The man I love is in there after all, just buried deep.

My father would kill you rather than let you be taken, he said. Taken by who? A rival gang? The police?

Impossible to guess what's going on. I have no way to know until Paul comes back for me. And what if it's not Paul who opens the door?

I don't want to be here. Maybe I don't have to be here.

Even now, I don't want to escape this place before I've had a chance to rescue that splinter of my Paul's soul. Still, I could contact him again and ask to meet like actual normal human beings—hire a detective to locate him—

I can find another way.

Paul, I love you, but I'm getting myself out of this.

Lying down, back on the floor, I kick up at the doorknob with both feet, hard. The wood starts to splinter; this closet wasn't meant for anything but brooms. Two more kicks, and the door wobbles open.

I jump to my feet and start running away from the noise. Hopefully the roar of the guns kept anyone from hearing me break out. Even though my knees buckle under me, and I'm breathing so hard the world goes dark and sparkly around the edges, I push myself forward; there are no second chances, not with this.

The corridors bend, bend again, like the walls of a maze. This place is huge, maybe many buildings' basements connected into one compound. But that's good. If so, there are many ways out, and I only have to find one.

By the time I almost can't hear the gun battle behind me, I take another turn and see the most beautiful sight: light filtering in from a grid above. The rusty metal ladder bolted to the wall suggests this is for utility service. Which means *that grid comes off.*

The ladder is so rusty that it crumbles slightly beneath my hands and feet. When I get to the top, I press both hands against the grid—and it doesn't move.

The metal presses into my palms, carving cross-hatches into my flesh, but I give it all my strength anyway. Still it won't budge.

Breathing hard, trembling, I try to think of what to do next. One, go down the ladder and find another exit. Two, go down the ladder, but to search for something to use to pry the grid open.

Just as I'm about to descend, though, a shadow falls over the grid. I look up to see a backlit figure—

—who then crouches down so I can see his face. I shout, "*Theo!*"

"Marguerite!" He drops to his knees. "Thank God. Are you okay?"

"I'm fine." I reach through the grid with my fingers, which he takes for just a moment. "What are you doing here?"

"Firebird locator function, remember? I tracked your signal all the way out here to Brighton Beach. Once I was sure you were here—I tried to get to you myself, but I couldn't—so I phoned in an anonymous tip to the cops about your location."

Of course! I ought to have thought of that. "You're incredible."

"That's what all the girls say." His smile has the weariness of relief. Along one cheekbone I see a deep bruise beneath scraped skin, no doubt from when he was thrown to the ground during my kidnapping. "Did they hurt you?"

"No. I'm okay. I just need some help with this grate."

"Hang on."

Theo vanishes for a moment, and I hear the sounds of someone rummaging through trash. This must be a back alley; it's dark outside, nighttime, so the light I see must come from a streetlamp. I take deep breaths, trying to calm myself. Almost home free, now.

Then all I have to do is figure out how to encounter the mobster Paul Markov again—not exactly easy—but no. That's not all I have to do in this dimension. "We still have to ruin the Firebird data."

"Done and done. Your parents were distracted, so I took my chance. Put the virus on all their computers already, made it look like Ukrainian hackers."

I'm sure he's telling the truth, but not the whole truth.

Theo betrayed my parents so I wouldn't have to; he spared me that pain, even though he loves them nearly as much. "Thank you," I say quietly.

"Just call me your sin-eater." Theo comes back with a hubcap or something else round and metal; whatever it is, he's able to wedge it beneath the metal edge of the grid. "Who were those guys?"

I don't know how to even begin telling Theo about Paul in this dimension. "You don't want to know."

"Hang on—" With a grunt, Theo shoves harder against the grid, and the corner pops up with a clang. I push it aside and climb up, into freedom, into Theo's arms.

He sighs heavily, and I lean against his chest. After this long, terrifying day, it feels so good to be held. I clutch his jacket, pulling him even closer. I only want to stay here, safe and sound, forever.

But I'm not safe yet. "Come on. Let's go."

Theo grabs my hand and pulls me to my feet. I tell myself, *Just a few minutes now. Get this Marguerite to safety and rest. Then you can figure out your next move.*

Just as we're about to dash toward the street, one of the doors to the alley swings open, hard, metal slamming against brick. We startle, and Theo gasps when he sees Paul running out.

Maybe it's because Paul has a gun in his hand.

Paul stops short, staring at us. "I told you to stay put," he says to me, before looking at Theo. "Where are you taking her?"

"Marguerite's okay. I've got her, she's all right." Theo's relieved. He assumes Paul could only be here to help, maybe even that he's with the police. Which is why he steps forward, one hand up. "It's all good."

"Why do you act like I know you?" Paul demands. Something wild lurks within his voice, his eyes; he's had to pretend to be brave here, to be tough, which means he has no way to deal with fear. His grip on his firearm is tight. "Why do both of you do that?"

Theo grins. "Can't help it, pal."

He steps away from us, lowering his weapon, no doubt about to run. Even in my terror, I know I will never see this Paul again.

If I think, I won't act. So I hurl myself at him. He's too surprised to raise the weapon right away, which gives me my chance to make contact.

Even as we slam into the brick wall, even as I look down at the gun in his hand, I manage to grab Paul's Firebird and press it against his chest—against the dove—and there it is, that tiny warm vibration that means I've rescued the next part of his soul.

Paul curses in pain and shoves me back so hard I fall to the ground. Theo runs toward us, yelling, "What are you—"

What happens next is so fast that everything blurs together.

The sounds all seem to roar at once: swearing, screaming, gunfire. The few concrete images I see have no order, no sense, not even motion, as if they were a series of photographs flung in front of me.

Paul, swinging his gun toward us.

Theo throwing his arms wide to try to defend me.

Flashes of fire at the muzzle of Paul's gun.

Blood and bone spraying outward.

Theo falling.

My own hands reaching for Theo as I sink down beside him.

And one terrible moment when my eyes meet Paul's, and I see no regret. No remorse.

Paul says, "You don't know me." And then he runs away, disappearing into the dark.

The first thing I think is stupid, the product of shock: *This is real. It's all real.*

Then I hear Theo groan, and I pull myself together.

"Are you okay?" I roll Theo over, knowing he's not. At first I'm relieved, because he's conscious and his shirt is only flecked with blood. Then I see his legs. "Oh, my God."

"Jesus." Theo can hardly get the word out; he's trying not to cry, or scream.

From the thighs down his legs look like something from a butcher shop: exposed, broken bone, and flesh torn into ribbons. Shards of white jutting from the gory mess must be what's left of his kneecaps.

There's *so much* blood. It oozes down the wall where it spattered; it drips from my hair, my ear. It pools on the asphalt beneath us, black rather than red in the twilight darkness, and shining as each puddle enlarges. Theo could hemorrhage to death within minutes.

"Hang on." I undo his belt and pull it free of the loops, so I can wrap it around one leg as a tourniquet. I need to do the other one too. As loud as I can, I scream, "Somebody help!"

"Phone." By now Theo's voice is hardly a whisper, but that's enough. I fumble in his back pocket and pull out his cell phone. Thank God it lets me call 911 without the security code.

The next few minutes aren't much clearer. Theo's able to give me the address of our location. Emergency crews were standing by during the police raid, so EMTs get to us within moments. By then Theo's skin has turned white and his breathing is shallow, but he can still talk. I can tell by the way the EMTs act that they expect him to live.

But they don't have to tell me that he might lose his legs.

Paul shot without hesitating. Without blinking. He savagely destroyed a stranger's legs for no reason, and ran away without even looking back.

All that time I was held captive, I thought he wouldn't hurt me, but I had no idea who I was really dealing with.

I want to think the splinter of my Paul's soul within him would have made a difference—but this Paul is still Paul. They are more alike than unalike.

If we all have one essential self that remains constant through all the worlds, then the evil in this man exists within my Paul, too. Even within the splinters of his soul I've already rescued.

The Firebirds feel heavy around my neck.

As soon as Theo is settled on a stretcher, the paramedics

hook him up to a saline IV. Numbly, I watch the needle enter his skin. While they tape the plastic tubing in place, I lean over Theo. He whispers, "Did you get the splinter?"

Even after this, Theo is still thinking about Paul's rescue. "Yeah. I got him." He nods, then grimaces in pain. I can't bear to watch him go through this anymore. "You need to go on ahead, okay? You'll have the coordinates. Now get out of here."

"What?" His voice sounds hoarse, drowsy. "I can't just—it's my fault this Theo's screwed up—I have to—"

"Listen to me." I'm not sure he's going to stay fully conscious much longer, especially if the medics have injected any morphine. My hands shake as I manipulate my Firebird to get the proof of his sabotage, unlock the next coordinates, and share that data with Theo's Firebird, giving him the info he needs to complete this mission. "What's done is done. I feel like shit about it too, okay? But we can't help him. You have to take care of yourself now. People in this dimension shouldn't perceive the Firebirds right away, but at the hospital, they might. Then they'll take them off you, and who knows when you'll get them back again—"

"I get it," he says. "Come on. Let's go."

"I can't," I whisper.

"Can't what? We've done it. Everything—everything Conley wanted. So we can—"

He can't finish the sentence, because he was going to say, *rescue the last splinter of Paul.*

But Theo doesn't need me for that.

If he goes to Conley now, reports what we've done (fudging what happened in the Warverse)—then Conley will give him the coordinates to reach the final dimension where Paul is hidden. Theo will receive the potential cure for Nightthief. Even if Conley is angry that Theo came along with me, he won't renege on the deal if he thinks I did my part. Everything will be taken care of.

"I can't look at Paul right now. I can't be near him. Not yet." What I need now is a chance to think about what I've learned, and what it means. "I'm going someplace Paul can't be, where he can never follow."

"Marguerite—" Theo breaks off, like he's on the verge of passing out. So I put his free hand on his Firebird for him.

"Go to Conley," I murmur, as the paramedics open the ambulance doors. I brush a lock of hair from his forehead, then take off Paul's Firebird and put it around Theo's neck. I whisper, "Take Paul with you. Don't worry about me. I'm traveling to a safe place. And I promise—I won't be that far behind."

I take my Firebird in my hands. I remember Russia, a thousand images all laced with whirling snow. And I fling myself out of this terrible world.

19

I OPEN MY EYES AND SEE AN ORNATELY DECORATED CEILing: cherubs and nymphs painted around embossed gilded medallions, all of it encircling a sumptuous chandelier. As I stir, I realize I'm lying in a bed—one as richly carved as the decorations above me, and topped with an embroidered silk coverlet. Once again, I am Margarita, Grand Duchess of all the Russias, supposedly the daughter of Tsar Alexander V.

I sit up, then grimace as I realize how exhausted I am; apparently this Marguerite hasn't slept well, if at all. But what strikes me most powerfully is that I don't know this room at all. It's not so surprising, perhaps—when I was in this universe before, the royal family never left the Winter Palace in St. Petersburg. The Romanovs have many other palaces, so perhaps this is one of those.

Still, it feels . . . off, somehow.

My eyes widen as I remember—in this world, the tsar

wanted to marry me off to the Prince of Wales, heir to the English throne. *Oh, shit, is this Buckingham Palace?* But there's no one in the bed with me, and when I look down at my left hand, there's no ring.

A memory of Lieutenant Markov comes to me so vividly that it's as if I'm back in the Winter Palace. He is my personal guard, standing at the door, and he is speaking about my anticipated betrothal to the heir to the English throne—and saying so much more than the mere words would suggest.

"Surely, my lady, the Prince of Wales will prove a devoted husband. I cannot imagine that any man would not—would not count himself fortunate to have such a wife. That he could fail to love you at first sight. Any man would, my lady."

In that moment I knew what he felt. He lived for such a short time after that, not even two whole days after the one and only night we spent together. I hope Lieutenant Markov was able to understand how much I cared. He deserved that—and even more than that, more than he ever got to have—

I loved him so much. I love him still; I will always love him, I think, to the end of my life. But I've spent most of the past three months convinced that my love for him meant that I loved every Paul, everywhere. Every person he could ever be.

Could I have loved the Paul I met in New York? The one who could savagely attack a stranger and maim him for life? Part of me wants to say no—but as strange as our connection was there, we did connect. I saw how damaged he was by the horrible life he'd been forced to lead. I also saw his brutality. His capacity for cruelty. When I think of the Paul in the Mafiaverse, I don't know whether I'm moved by the vulnerability I glimpsed in him, or whether I'll always be afraid of him.

Both, I think. Somehow that's the worst answer of all. The only thing I know is that I can't be near that Paul or any other, now. Not until I've figured out what this means. I need safety and solitude.

Lieutenant Markov died fighting for the tsar, fighting to protect me. I held his hand and watched him die. The horror and pain of that moment will never leave me. But right now, I am taking advantage of his death, which made this a dimension no other Paul Markov could ever enter.

His death is my shelter. I think, *Even now, you're still protecting me.* Tears well in my eyes, but I blink them back.

A soft rap at my bedroom door makes me sit upright. "Yes?" I call in English. Hopefully that's the language I'm supposed to be speaking here.

The reply comes in French. "Are you ready for your breakfast, Your Imperial Highness?"

"Bring it in, please," I answer in the same language. (I've become better at French through a few of my visits.)

One woman opens the door for another, who comes in bearing a silver tray. She walks to a small table in the corner and begins setting out a feast: teapot, cream, bread, butter, some kind of pastry.

And now I know I'm not in any of the tsar's palaces. If we took meals in our rooms, those meals were simple, by his order. Also none of the servants wore a uniform like the one this woman wears, a long black dress with white apron, and they spoke Russian or English, never French.

A sky-blue robe lies on the foot of the bed. I reach for it, but the maid hurries from my breakfast to hand the gown to me instead. It's velvet, thicker and softer than any other I've ever felt. As I wrap it around myself, the maid curtsies, then hurries away, leaving me to my meal.

I ought to begin exploring immediately to figure out exactly where the Grand Duchess Margarita is. But my stomach is too empty; I almost feel sick. So instead, I go to the table and start eating.

This turns out to be the best thing I could've done. Not only because this pastry is amazing, but also because my seat at the window reveals the scene outside.

I'm about three or four stories off the ground, looking out at a plaza—one surrounded by elegant buildings, with an Egyptian obelisk in the very center. Despite the early hour, and the cloudy sky overhead turned milky by the morning light, many people hurry by outside, all of them dressed in clothes that look more like they belong in the 1910s: women in long dresses wearing big hats; men in three-piece suits and bowlers, all of them sporting mustaches.

I recognize this plaza. My family traveled to this city a few times when I was young to visit my Kovalenko grand-parents before they died. I'm pretty sure that in our universe, something besides an obelisk stands in the center, but I know the locale all the same.

The grand duchess has gone to Paris.

After I've stuffed myself with *pain au chocolat*, I feel steadier and begin to explore in earnest. At first I wonder whether the grand duchess is staying in some other royal residence. For all I know, the French Revolution never happened here. I might be the guest of Marie Antoinette's great-great-great granddaughter.

But I don't remember a surviving French monarchy in this universe, and besides, this building stands in the Place Vendôme. My mother explained to me once, when we were visiting almost a decade ago, that this was where the finest hotels in the world were located. I asked why we weren't staying there, then, which led to my dad giving me a really long lecture about how capitalism works, and how professors usually aren't the people it works best for.

On the hotel napkin, embroidered in white on white is a small crest and the cursive letter R. I remember Theo looking at the hotel in the Warverse and saying it wasn't the Ritz. This *is* the Ritz.

This has to be the nicest hotel suite that exists in the world. In all the worlds. Three bedrooms, enormous sitting rooms, a small kitchen, all of them decorated as richly as the room I woke up in. I think the ceilings must be twenty feet high, and—how many chandeliers can you fit in a hotel suite? Whatever the number is, this place maxes it out.

I must have come to Paris on my own. If the tsar were here, military guards would be all around; if my siblings had come along, they'd be in the other bedrooms. Yet it seems unlike Tsar Alexander V to let me romp to Paris alone.

The wardrobes are filled with elegant clothing, though much of it appears new and more modern—more flowing silhouettes, a dropped waist or none at all, and deeper colors than the pale shades I usually wore in St. Petersburg. Less lace, more beading. Apparently the grand duchess has done some hard-core shopping while in Paris. Who wouldn't?

She would be mourning for her Paul as deeply as I mourn him, probably even more. So she's consoling herself with this holiday, all the pleasures France has to offer. And the grand duchess has even gained a little weight. I cast a glance at the enormous breakfast behind me, or what remains of it.

I find a sketch pad sitting next to a box of pastels. At first I reach for it, but then I remember when I got those pastels. Lieutenant Markov gave them to me for Christmas. We stood just outside my bedroom door, the threshold all that lay between us, looking at each other almost dizzy with wanting—

She will have sketched him. I can't look at that now. Maybe not ever.

Instead, I turn my attention to a small leather book that seems like—yes. It's for appointments.

Her handwriting is so much better than mine, elegant and flowing, like a professional calligrapher's; ironically, that makes it harder to read. But I can make out two appointments for today: *11 a.m., Dr. N.* Then, *9 p.m., dinner Maxim's.*

When a maid comes to help me dress, a few careful questions reveal that I'm not heading out to a physician's office. Dr. N, whoever that is, will be coming to me. The perks of royalty, I guess.

Is she—am I—sick? Is that the reason for this trip to Paris? Surely if that were true, though, I'd be in a hospital rather than the Ritz. Also, I doubt my family would have let me travel alone; the tsar would of course never leave Russia on my account, but surely Vladimir at least would have come along.

The maid gets me dressed quickly—the Paris fashions are easier to wear than the long lace gowns from St. Petersburg. Also, *thank God* someone has invented the bra. It's kind of weird—triangles of satin, really, without any kind of structure—but even with the extra weight, my breasts have only grown to be "small" instead of "practically nonexistent." At any rate, I won't miss the corsets. My drop-waisted gown is the color of roses, and the hem stops well before my ankles. Shocking.

I wonder why I'm getting all fixed up for a doctor who's coming to me. So I have no idea what to expect at 11:00 a.m., but whatever it was, it's not what I get.

"Dr. N" turns out to stand for Dr. Nilsson, and Dr. Nilsson turns out to be female, which has to be unusual for this era. Her thick black hair is swept back into a tight bun, but her heart-shaped face keeps her from looking severe. She's not mean; she's not motherly; she is calm personified. Her clothes look like any other woman's from the street below, though they're a quiet gray. Instead of the black bag doctors used to carry in the old days, she has only a notebook and pen. And instead of asking how I feel, she takes a seat in one of the chairs nearest the long velvet sofa, takes out her notebook and says, "What shall we talk about today, Your Imperial Highness?"

At first I'm just glad she said it in English. Then it hits me—she's not a medical doctor. Dr. Nilsson is a psychiatrist.

The grand duchess came to Paris for therapy.

Seems extreme to me, but then again, if social history is evolving more slowly here too, psychology would be very new to this world. There might not even be an analyst in Russia yet. Or maybe the tsar didn't want anyone knowing his daughter is seeing a shrink.

Slowly I stretch out onto the sofa, again like in movies.

Dr. Nilsson says only, "Your Imperial Highness?"

I venture, "I guess—I guess I'm feeling, uh, conflicted about my father."

"Which one?"

"Which what?"

"Which father?" Dr. Nilsson keeps taking notes without ever looking up from her pad. Thank God she's not looking at my face. Instead, she continues, "Or have you given up your fantasy that your tutor is actually your father?"

It hits me so hard I can hardly breathe. *She remembered.*

The selves we enter during our cross-dimensional travels aren't supposed to remember anything we do while we're in charge of their bodies. I've seen other versions of Paul and Theo who had absolutely no clue about anything that happened while my Paul and Theo were within them.

But I'm a "perfect traveler." These voyages are different for me than they are for anyone else. Every single Marguerite I've ever visited must have remembered everything I did and said in her life.

Grand Duchess Margarita tried to talk about what she'd experienced, which is why she wound up in therapy. Nobody believed she'd actually been taken over by a visitor from another dimension; they think she's *cracking up*.

"Your Imperial Highness," Dr. Nilsson says. "Do you wish to answer the question?"

"The tsar is my father," I say in a rush. "But I'm angry with him sometimes, and it's easy to pretend that somebody else is my father. Someone kind like Professor Caine."

Did this Marguerite tell the tsar the truth? If so, she might have doomed my father to death by firing squad.

I don't feel as if I can breathe until Dr. Nilsson says, "So it's not a secret you were keeping. Only a secret fantasy."

Dad's safe. I breathe out in relief. "Yes."

"Good. You're better able to face reality now. That's progress." Dr. Nilsson keeps taking notes. "Do you miss your father on any level?"

"I miss my brothers and sister more." That much is the absolute truth. If I could see little Peter and Katya again—

talk with Vladimir one more time—that would be a gift.

"And Lieutenant Markov?"

At first I think I must trust Dr. Nilsson a lot—but then I realize, after the scene I made at the army camp after Lieutenant Markov's death, everyone must have known about us. About them. "He's dead."

"You no longer believe he still exists in some . . . shadow world alongside our own?"

I close my eyes. The grand duchess remembered *everything.* "It doesn't matter if he is. I can't reach him there. He's—he's very far away from me now." My voice starts to shake. "The other Paul might not be my Paul. He might not be as loving, or as strong. As good."

She tilts her head. It's easy to imagine what she's writing. *Subject retains irrational belief in "shadow worlds" but has begun to say these worlds are cut off from her. She expresses no more desire to visit them. This is a transitional step toward accepting the reality of her lover's death.* "Do you still feel that one of your shadow selves took over your body nearly the entire month of December? That your actions were actually her responsibility?"

"It—it seems like that's what happened," I venture. "But she didn't do anything I hadn't wanted to do."

"Do you think she might have come to see you on purpose?" Dr. Nilsson is humoring me now. "To take the actions you were afraid of? To do things otherwise forbidden?"

"I need to think about that some more."

That wins me a very slight smile. She definitely believes

we're making progress. "Have you had any dreams lately, Your Imperial Highness?"

How would I know? But the words well up anyway, spilling out to the only person I have to tell. "I dreamed that I was captured by armed men." What's the closest equivalent to the Russian mob in this dimension? "By soldiers loyal to the Grand Duke Sergei, the ones who rose up against us."

"What happened during your captivity, in this dream? Were you sexually violated?"

"No." Um, *rude*. Then again, I remember studying that the early Freudians believed absolutely everything came back to sex in the end. Dr. Nilsson's overly personal questions are going to keep coming. "But one of the soldiers turned out to be Paul Markov."

"What role did Markov play in your dream?"

"I thought he was there to protect me. To rescue me, no matter what." I swallow hard. "Instead, he turned out to be just like all the rest. Someone else came to save me, and Paul—Paul shot him. The man who tried to save me didn't die, but there was so much blood, and I thought he might lose his legs."

Dr. Nilsson nods. "How did this make you feel?"

"Guilty. Sad. Scared. Doctor, what do you think my dream means?"

"Only you can answer that, Your Imperial Highness."

"I know, but—I just wondered what it looked like to you. Please tell me."

She puts the notepad in her lap and folds her hands on

top of it. Instead of answering right away, she thinks for a moment—trying to give me an honest answer.

Finally she nods, as if agreeing with her own inner assessment. "Someone whom you have always regarded as a loving, protective figure instead, in your mind, became someone who could hurt you. In your dream, you only saw him attack another; this may have been your subconscious softening the blow."

"But Lieutenant Markov never would have hurt me. I know that. I know it."

"The dream of him can," Dr. Nilsson said. "So can the illusion that you might find him again."

My belief that Paul and I are destined to be together no matter what—that's the illusion. It shattered along with Theo's bones in that rain of bullets. And it feels like I've been destroyed along with it.

After Dr. Nilsson leaves, I sink back onto the sofa. This enormous room's grandeur seems to taunt me, because as beautiful as it is it's empty. I'm alone in ways I thought I never would be again, because I always thought that even when Paul wasn't with me, he was a part of me.

Before long I have to move on. No matter how unsure I am about Paul at this moment, I will never, ever abandon him to Conley. Yes, Theo has gone to the home office in the Triadverse; by now, Conley should have given him the coordinates for the dimension where the fourth and final splinter of Paul's soul is hidden. I've done Conley's dirty work. But Conley will never let it go at that. He'd endanger Paul again, if that was what it took to get me out of this universe and back under his thumb. So I can't remain in Paris for much longer.

What I need to do now is figure out what comes after.

My reverie is interrupted when the maid brings in my luncheon tray. She smiles as she delivers it to the dining area—which has a table and chairs so ornate they seem less like something you'd eat at, more like where you'd sit while writing the Constitution. I take a seat, primly as I did back in the Winter Palace, so the illusion of royalty is complete until she lifts the silver cover from the tray.

What awaits me isn't anything out of the ordinary—some kind of fish soup, I think, plus vegetables—but for some reason, the fishy odor hits me like a blow. Never have I smelled anything so disgusting; the scent seems to seep into my nose and lungs and gut like poison. Everything inside me turns over, tightens.

My stomach wrenches as the nausea turns from figurative to literal.

"I'm going to throw up," I say. The maid skitters back as I push away from the table and make a run for the nearest bathroom. I make it just in time to barf into the sink.

The smell of my own vomit almost makes me sick again. And in the bathroom there's the scent of cleanser, and perfumed soap that for some reason now seems repulsive—I can't stand it. Weakly I stumble out of there, and the maid gets me back to my bedroom. "I'll leave your luncheon under the tray. If you want another later, ring," she says as she backs out and closes the door behind her.

I flop onto my bed, now too queasy to be miserable about anything else.

It would serve me right, if after everything else I put the grand duchess through, I had to endure her bout of the flu. Groaning, I roll onto my stomach—but my breasts are tender, and I wince.

My eyes open wide.

The grand duchess has gained weight. Mom and I have the same problem: we almost *can't* gain weight. Don't even give me that crap about *boo hoo hoo that's not a real problem eat a sandwich.* Easy to say when you're not slightly wired all the time by your crazy metabolism. My body simply burns too many calories, too fast.

But here I am in a body that's heavier. Some of that weight is in my breasts, which must be a cup size larger. My sense of smell has turned sharp, and I'm vomiting for no reason at all.

Three months after Lieutenant Markov and I slept together.

Oh God. I'm pregnant.

20

I CAN'T BE HAVING A BABY. I *CAN'T.*

I sit on my bed, hands on either side of my head, trying to talk myself out of it. *Maybe you're premenstrual. That would explain the boobs, plus my belly could be water weight.* But my body never reacted like that to PMS before. Mostly I just break out, and start crying at the least little thing. *You could have the stomach flu. That would explain why you're throwing up.* People don't usually gain weight when they have stomach flu, do they?

All my denials fail. The truth is unmistakable on some level that goes beyond logic or even emotion; my body is telling me something that outweighs anything my brain could say. I'm pregnant, for real.

Slowly I reach down to splay my hand across my belly. No, it doesn't yet look like I have a "baby bump," but the weight I've gained there has a certain . . . solidity. A firmness that fat doesn't have. I don't feel the baby moving, but maybe I wouldn't yet.

Does anyone know I'm having a baby? No—they can't. Dr. Nilsson would have asked me how I felt about it. The tsar? I shudder at the thought. He probably would've locked me in a convent, if not a prison cell.

I'm horrified because *this isn't my body.* I did this to the Grand Duchess Margarita. I made the decision, I slept with Paul, and now—

How smug I was, telling Theo how hard we tried to do right by the other selves we visit. I'm so full of it. I took more than this Marguerite's only night with the man she loved; I took away her choices.

As bad as it would be for me to be pregnant at eighteen, for the grand duchess it's about ten thousand times worse. This society believes in virginity until marriage—for women, anyway, because they've got all the nineteenth-century hypocrisy to go with the nineteenth-century tech. And the tsar wanted to marry me off to the Prince of Wales! I'm pretty sure showing up with an illegitimate child wasn't part of that deal.

I have already endangered you, Lieutenant Markov whispered to me that night as we lay together in bed. He understood this society; he knew the risks. And he had the sense to fear the consequences.

No, I was the careless one. And these are the consequences.

I flop back onto the bed, and close my eyes tightly as if I'm holding back tears. But the remorse goes too deep for me to cry about it. There's nothing I can do to help her. *Nothing.* I have to assume she doesn't want to terminate the pregnancy, because surely she'd have done it by now if she could.

This must be why the grand duchess came to Paris. She knew she was in trouble, so she ran all the way across Europe. Obviously she needed to get out of Russia before her pregnancy began to show, before the tsar or any of the court nobles could guess the truth. Once the king of England learned that the grand duchess was not exactly sane—the engagement would be called off long before the truth could be revealed, and that would buy her more time.

The grand duchess might be smarter than I am.

I put my hand back over my belly, still trying to convince myself that there's an actual baby in there. *Paul*'s baby. Paul's and mine, together.

On the night my parents were such bad role models about Paul and me getting together, my mother wound up saying to me that the real reason he and I shouldn't have a baby together yet didn't have anything to do with our education or our careers, as important as those things are. She said, *When you have a child with someone, you're bound to them forever. That can be beautiful and miraculous, and yet a burden, too—the knowledge that your life is intertwined with another's, for all time. It transforms your relationship in ways I can't begin to describe.*

Before you take that step with someone, you must be ready to accept the destruction of the life you had together beforehand—and have faith that what you two create afterward can be even greater.

There is no "afterward" for the grand duchess and Lieutenant Markov. That night in the dacha was all they ever had.

I remember the way he held me, and whispered against my temple, calling me his little dove. Even though that Paul is dead, something of him lives on. He'll have a son or a daughter, someone who might have his gray eyes and his good mind. When I imagine holding that baby in my arms, I know—beyond any doubt—that the grand duchess wants this child.

But I now know something she doesn't: Paul Markov is more than the shy, devoted lieutenant I fell in love with in St. Petersburg. He can be cold, cruel. He could be a murderer.

On the train to Moscow, when the uprising began, Lieutenant Markov shot a guard who would have killed me and Katya. Since then I've remembered that moment as proof of how protective he is, how he would do anything to keep me safe. Now I remember how he never even looked down at the man he'd shot, bleeding to death at his feet.

The afternoon passes in a kind of daze. It feels like hours before I even move from my bed, and I do that only when I realize I'll be more nauseated if I don't eat than if I do. Every action I could possibly take—even something as inconsequential as sitting at the window to look out at the Place Vendôme—seems as if it could backfire disastrously. This is ridiculous, of course; watching the Paris scene is a lot less risky than having unprotected sex. But after screwing up this badly, I don't trust myself right now. Guilt paralyzes me.

As the pale sunlight begins to dim at dusk, the maid arrives to prepare me "for dinner." I remember the line in my planner—tonight I'm dining at the home of someone called Maxim. I wish I could tell the maid to go away, burrow back under the silk coverlet, and try to shut out the reality I'm in, the one I created for the grand duchess.

But I've screwed up her plans enough for one lifetime. The least I can do is keep her appointments.

I submit to the maid's ministrations. While she's not the equal of the attendants I had in St. Petersburg, she shares their knack for making the most out of my few good features. My curly hair is tamed into a soft cloud by ornate gold combs, enameled with cobalt-blue lotuses that seem vaguely Egyptian. The dress she gives me is a darker shade of blue, beaded with jet, and while it fits snugly around my newly acquired bustline, it flows down beneath that in loose folds. Even the closest observer wouldn't be able to spot the slight thickness at my middle.

I watch the maid carefully, wondering if her eyes will linger at my waist. Whether she knows. If so, she's too smart to give any sign.

She's not one of the women who attended me in St. Petersburg, I remind myself. I don't know how long I've been in Paris, but I almost certainly wouldn't have left until after I was sure of my pregnancy, so no more than a month to six weeks. *The maid doesn't realize my body doesn't always look like this.*

That buys me time, but how much? Another month, at most—

For jewelry, the maid chooses heavy, screw-on earrings of black pearls and a ruby ring so enormous it dwarfs my skinny fingers. (The Firebird remains around my neck, all but hidden under the dark gauze at the dress's neckline, unnoticed by the maid.) Then dark slippers are slid onto my feet, an elaborately beaded bag is put in my hands, and a heavy wrap of burgundy velvet and black fur is draped around my shoulders.

Turns out I'm staying in the "Suite Imperial," but the rest of the Ritz is nearly as swanky as my rooms. Red carpet, gilded ceilings—the splendor doesn't *quite* reach the levels of the Winter Palace, but it comes pretty close.

The doors that separate my area of the hotel from the rest swing open to reveal two large, stern men dressed in black. Instantly I realize they're my personal guard. I remember Lieutenant Markov, always standing at my door, always protecting me, his gray eyes searching mine every time we dared look at each other.

"Your Imperial Highness?" says one of the guards. "Are you unwell?"

I've stopped in my tracks, one hand over my heart. Through the beaded gauze of my dress I can feel my Firebird. "I'm very well, thank you. We can leave now."

They shepherd me through a corridor that offers only a glance of the opulent lobby, but I glimpse women in dresses as elaborate as mine, men in tuxedos and the occasional top hat. A rush of whispers trails behind me like smoke. If this dimension's technology had developed as quickly as our own, paparazzi camera flashes would light up around me. I have to maintain a neutral, pleasant expression even though on the inside I feel like crying.

The car is a low-to-the-ground roadster with running boards and a canvas top, the kind of thing they'd drive on *Downton Abbey*. Numbly I lean back in my seat and take in the view of this wholly different Paris. A few horse-drawn carts still travel on the streets, most of them apparently bringing in agricultural products from the countryside. I see one stacked with old-fashioned metal milk jars, another laden with enormous wheels of cheese. Stores and shops are smaller and darker, and each one looks individual, with hand-painted signs advertising their wares.

Most people I see on the street aren't dressed as elegantly as those of us staying in the Ritz, but compared to the fashions I'm used to back home, everyone looks more formal. Every man has a jacket and a necktie, even the ones walking into pubs with their friends. Every woman wears a long skirt, most of them with elaborate hats to match. Nobody eats or sips coffee while they walk; instead of cell phones or plastic shopping bags, they hold walking sticks, or fans.

I expect the car to pull up in front of some mansion or stately apartment building, wherever the mysterious Maxim lives. Instead, we stop at an enormous gaudy neon sign over what looks like the biggest, most bustling restaurant in the city: Maxim's.

"Your Imperial Highness! Welcome back." This man in the tuxedo must be the maître'd, or the owner. Whoever he is, he's really glad to see me. No wonder—having a Russian princess as a regular customer must be great advertising. "Your private room awaits you."

"Thank you," I say evenly, trying to disguise my relief. Whoever I'm meeting here, I won't be able to miss them, and any little mistakes I make won't be noticed by as many people in a private area. Either way, the delicious smells of beef and bread and cheese make my mouth water; my earlier nausea has given way to intense hunger.

Maxim's turns out to be almost as lush as the Ritz. Sinuously carved frames surround long oval mirrors that hang throughout the hall. The wood that panels the walls ripples in gold and brown as if it were tortoiseshell. Light shines from flower-shaped lamps held by bronze angels or through the enormous stained glass mural overhead. The other patrons are a blur of fur, satin, jewels, and candlelight.

The doors open to reveal an intimate dining room, complete with bookshelves and a chaise longue. At one end of the small table, rising to greet me, is the last person I expected.

"Your Imperial Highness," says Theo. "How enchanting to see you again."

The next brief flurry of activity—accepting menus and the fawning team of waiters—gives me a second to take this in. After leaving Theo in New York, where he was bruised and bloody, just the sight of him alive and well buoys me. And yet he's not precisely the Theo I know.

His suit is black, cut closer to the body than most men's seem to be—an avant-garde style, I'd guess. He has facial hair, which I find sort of hilarious even though the mustache and Vandyke beard look good on him. He's combed his hair back with that oil or pomade or whatever men used for gel back in the day. He speaks French to the waiters but English to me—with a slight Dutch accent. I've heard my own voice change accents before, but hearing someone else's change is even weirder.

Yet the way he smiles, the flourish when he hands the wine list back to the waiter, even the slightly rakish tilt of the deep red scarf knotted around his neck: All of that is very familiar.

I knew Theo lived in Paris; I hadn't forgotten the letters he sent me while I was in St. Petersburg, talking about the Moulin Rouge. But it hadn't occurred to me to look Theo up, mostly because I can't figure out how they would know each other. It's not like our Russiaverse selves have anything in common. Theo is a leading student of chemistry; I'm a member of royalty from the other side of the continent.

Together we fight crime, I think, and my own stupid joke makes me silly. I muffle my laugh with my lace handkerchief, trying to make it sound like a cough.

"Your Imperial Highness?" Theo asks as the waiters step out of the room, closing the doors behind them. Though my security detail waits just outside, for now Theo and I are alone. "Are you well?"

"Very well, thank you." How do I put this? "I'm just—I've been absentminded lately, and I completely forgot what you and I had intended to talk about—"

His eyes widen. "The amnesia has affected you again?"

"Amnesia?"

Theo nods, like he knows he needs to take this slowly. His voice is patient as he says, "The malady overtook me in December. It was during this time I wrote to you, forging our acquaintance. You contacted me in January with your intriguing ideas about our other selves who knew one another, the shadow worlds—"

She remembered *everything.* "Shadow worlds," I repeat.

"If your theory is correct," Theo says, "it was my shadow-self who inhabited my body last December, acting in my stead. Do you remember none of this?"

Then he sits up straighter, his smile fading. He's guessed the truth, now; the only way to keep his trust is to admit it.

"As a matter of fact, I'm from one of the—shadow worlds," I say. "I don't mean any harm, to the grand duchess or you or anyone."

Besides Wyatt Conley. But he doesn't count.

Theo doesn't know what to make of that, and no wonder. After a moment he says, "Can you explain the scientific principles at work?"

As in my universe, he's a hipster on the outside, pure science geek on the inside. "Not very well. But I'll try." I don't know what else to say. "Why did the grand duchess contact you?"

"To see if my impressions of December's events matched her own. She did not share my total amnesia, but as outlandish as her explanation was, I came to believe it."

In other words, she had to check to make sure she was sane. The letters I exchanged with Theo last December were the only proof she had that the shadow worlds were more than a delusion.

Amazement has animated Theo, turned him into a guy closer to one I know. "Do you perhaps have one of those miraculous devices?"

"A Firebird." I snag my finger under the chain. It takes him a moment to focus on material from another dimension, but his expression lights up when he does. I add, "If you ever need to check whether someone is native to this dimension, you can look for a Firebird. They'll almost certainly have it on."

I tug at his collar, as an example of how to check, but to my shock, I see another Firebird chain.

"Your Imperial Highness?" Theo says, still unaware anything is hanging around his neck.

I snatch up his Firebird, hit the reminder sequence, and—

"Owwww!" Theo pushes back, grabs his chest, and then looks around at our opulent surroundings. "Whoa. Okay, I don't know where we are, but I like it."

"What are you doing here?" I demand. "Did you already talk to Conley?"

"Hello to you, too." When I give him a look, he sighs.

"No, I didn't go to the coordinates you gave me. Instead, I followed you."

"We were supposed to go to him after we were done!"

"Which we will. He never said we couldn't take a short detour first."

Frustration tightens my fist around the lace handkerchief I'm still clutching. "What if Conley thinks we're skipping out on him? He could splinter Paul into another four pieces—" Or four dozen. Or four million, so I'd never get him back again.

"Hey," Theo says sharply. "You're the one Conley's after. This train doesn't move forward unless you're aboard. Besides, as far as Conley knows, we've been good little soldiers so far. He's not going to break the deal yet."

He doesn't know that any more than I do. Still, I sense he's right—for now. Conley won't put up with a delay for long. "You understand why I came to this dimension, right?"

Theo nods, but his smile fades. "Yeah, I know. You needed to get your head together. What happened in New York—that was intense."

"More for you than for me," I say.

"We can save the Most Traumatized competition for later, all right? Okay, you wanted to rest someplace—luxurious, I guess, someplace where you knew you'd be safe."

"You think I came here because it was 'luxurious'?"

Theo holds out his hands in a way that takes in the crystal chandelier above us, the painted murals on the walls, all of it, like, *Am I wrong?* But he adds, "And you needed to be safe.

Right? Otherwise it has to be sad for you, remembering—you know. The other Paul."

He honestly doesn't get it. "Theo, I came to this dimension because it's the only one where I knew I wouldn't see Paul. I couldn't even *look* at him, not after what he did to you."

Theo winces; he covers one knee with his hand. "That sucked beyond the telling of it. But it's not like *our* Paul shot me."

"The different versions—they're more alike than unalike. Don't you see that?"

"What, so, if one Paul did something crappy to me, I should hate every version of Paul from then on?"

"That's not what I meant."

The flickering gas lamps on the walls no longer seem to shed enough light. Instead of appearing luxurious, the heavy wood carving and enormous overhead chandelier begin to make me feel claustrophobic. A gilded cage is still a cage.

Slowly I say, "Theo, the first time I came to this world—this is where I began to believe that no matter how different we are in each dimension, something within us is always the same. Call it an eternal soul, or a spirit, but whatever it is, it's the most important thing about us, and that's the constant. That's the part that never changes, no matter what."

"The soul," Theo says, in a tone of voice I've heard my whole life from my parents and every single one of their grad students; it means, *This is not science.*

Sometimes they think nothing but hard, empirical fact matters.

Which is total crap.

"Yes," I shoot back. "The soul. And I thought I knew Paul's soul even better than I knew my own. But when he shot you, I realized there were ways I don't know him at all. I've seen darkness inside him. True darkness. And I still love him, which is scarier than anything else. But I don't know what to think or what to do—"

My throat closes up, and I blink back tears. *Pregnancy hormones*, I think.

Theo doesn't even know about the baby yet.

I look up at him for comfort, then pull back, because at this moment Theo is *furious*.

"One eternal soul," he whispers. The very quietness of his voice cuts me, as it's meant to. "Only one self, across the countless dimensions of the multiverse, and we all have to answer for each other's sins. Which means, to you, I'm still the Theo who helped kidnap your dad, and framed Paul for murder. The one who betrayed you. When you look at me, that's all you see."

I want to say, *No, that's not true.* But I can't. Still, when I look at Theo, I feel a flicker of doubt.

Only now do I realize that I'm the one who betrayed Theo. By refusing to see him for himself, to respect the choices he's made and the loyalty he's shown, I'm betraying him this very second.

"That Paul isn't our Paul," Theo says. By now he's so mad he seems to be staring through me, like I'm beneath even being noticed. "Just like I'm not that Theo. He didn't blame me for something an entirely different Theo did, and I won't blame him for what happened in New York. Dammit, Marguerite, I'm the one who got shot! If I can let it go, why can't you?"

He rises to his feet and shoves his chair to the table. Apparently the grand duchess will dine alone tonight.

Theo continues, "Believe what you want to believe. Doubt me, doubt Paul, hide in fin de siècle Paris if it makes you feel better. But if you won't save Paul, I will."

With that, he stalks out of the private dining room.

Now it's just me and the flickering gaslight. I lost Paul three times over—when Lieutenant Markov died in this dimension, when Wyatt Conley splintered his soul, and when I saw Paul shoot Theo. Now I've lost Theo, too.

Never, in any world, have I been so alone.

21

WHEN DAWN BREAKS THE NEXT DAY, I HAVEN'T SLEPT MORE than a few hours. Exhaustion weighs down my body and paints dark circles beneath my eyes.

Partly this is because of my pregnancy. At least I assume that's why I have to get up to pee about every two hours.

I thought babies only kept you awake after *they were born*.

Mostly, though, my insomnia comes from guilt. The many reasons boil inside my mind, hot and agitated, and as soon as I've set one aside, another bubbles up to take its place.

I got the grand duchess pregnant. The worst thing I've ever done. Hopefully the worst thing I'll ever do. How much worse than that could I even get?

Theo thinks I've spent the last three months hating him. I could never hate Theo. Not even after what the other one put me through, with his careful lies, the way he set up my entire family and Paul too, or how he cozied up to me by flirting and leaning close and calling me "Meg." (Even the thought of that nickname makes my skin crawl.) After the past few days, I know more than ever how much Theo's done for me, how much more he would give. How could I ever have doubted him because of something that happened to him? He was the main victim of the Triadverse's Theo—not me, not my mom, not even my kidnapped father.

Theo and I didn't move on to the home office. Conley probably thinks we've abandoned Paul. I haven't—I never would. Even if I'm not sure how to be with him again, there's no way I'm not going to bring him home.

I'm letting the actions of another Paul affect my emotions about my Paul, the one I love. After Theo's blistering lecture last night, I realize how cruel and unjust that is. Yet my heart remembers the homicidal dullness in Paul's eyes as he shot Theo over and over again.

After what feels like an endless weak sunrise, I finally accept sleep isn't going to happen. I wrap myself in the velvet robe and wander through the palatial Suite Imperial, wishing for some way to kill time. Sure, there are books on the shelves—histories and encyclopedias of this alternate timeline that would probably fascinate my parents. The kind of thing I ought to take notes on, but I can't, not with my mind racing like this.

No TV or computer, obviously. Life before Wi-Fi was a barren time.

Finally, I look at the grand duchess's sketchbook and pastels. I've avoided opening the sketchbook, because I'm completely certain Paul's portrait is on those pages. I'm not ready to see his face looking up at me, not yet. But I remember Lieutenant Markov giving me the box of pastels—the light in his eyes as he realized how much I loved his Christmas gift. Surely I could draw one picture with them, just one.

I pick up the sketchbook, determined to flip through quickly to a blank page so I won't see anything drawn within. But as soon as I take it from the desk, folded papers fall out onto the floor. As I squint down at them, I see how many of them are letters.

Am I violating the grand duchess's privacy if I read them? Compared to the fact that I'm walking around in her body, which I also *got pregnant*, going over the mail doesn't seem like a big deal. Besides, maybe the letters will tell me what she's planning—what's going to become of her.

The first one I open, written in badly blotted ink, is from Katya, the bratty little sister who might have saved my life during the rebellion by tackling an enemy soldier twice her size:

> *I told you to be quiet about that "shadow world" stuff, but you never listen to me. Simply tell them it's all a story you made up, so you can come home. Papa says it's not proper for me to attend balls while you're seeing your French doctor, and I'm tired of sitting around every night. Will you at least*

be home by the time we go to Tsarskoye Selo for the summer? You always enjoy that.

I smile softly; Katya misses me, though she won't admit it. I've missed her too.

But—summertime. I do what the other Marguerite must have done the first time realization set in, counting off weeks and months to late September. How can I possibly hide this pregnancy for so long?

If I could solve these problems for her, I would—but I can't. I'm not sure anybody can.

The next letter turns out to be more comforting; it's from my little brother, Peter.

Margarita, I wish you were here. I'm studying hard and Professor Caine is helping me draw a map of Africa. Papa has a lion skin from the time he went shooting in Africa when he was young, but I think it was mean to kill the lion just to take its skin. If I ever go to Africa, I'll take photographs of the animals, because that way the animals will be happy and I can still look at them forever. Also the lion skin smells nasty now. Please come home from France soon. I love you.

A laugh bubbles up in my chest as I envision Peter's sweet little face while he labored to write each word. He's so tiny for his age, or he was; maybe he's grown since.

I pick up the next letter, relieved and grateful to recognize my father's handwriting. Though, of course, this letter is signed from my "tutor," Henry Caine.

Your Imperial Highness,

I'm glad to hear that your time in Paris has proved beneficial, as we discussed. Although the tsar has expressed impatience, I've endeavored to convince him that psychotherapy has genuine medical value, and that your convalescence should not be rushed.

As we speculated, the king of England appears to have turned his attentions toward the Rumanian princess for his son's bride. The tsar feels this keenly, but your health outweighs all other considerations. Besides, now that Vladimir is courting that Polish princess, I suspect Tsar Alexander has matchmaking enough for now.

I admit, I can't help sympathizing with his eagerness to have a grandchild.

By all means, rest and take care of your health. Let me know how you're feeling, and whether I can send you anything you might need.

This letter says far more than it first appears to.

If this world's Marguerite remembers her night with Paul, that means she also remembers the truth about her parentage, which was the result of a brief, clandestine affair between the late tsaritsa, my mother, and the royal tutor, Henry Caine. She's kept the secret, and she and

Dad have built a relationship.

The Grand Duchess Margarita finally has a dad who loves her. I cling to this, the one thing I've given her after taking so much else away.

Dad clearly knows about the pregnancy, too. *A grandchild*, he wrote. Probably he helped devise this plan to get the grand duchess out of the tsar's sight for a long while.

But if my father has any ideas about what happens next, they're not in this letter.

Hearing from Katya and Peter warms me more than I could have anticipated. I've missed them ever since I left the Russiaverse, which was one thing none of the others ever fully understood. *You only knew them for a month*, Josie said once, irritated. *They weren't your siblings like I am. Come on!*

They weren't, and they were. There's a kind of magic to seeing yourself reflected in this entirely new person. When you're related to someone, you wind up sometimes connecting in ways that go beyond logic. I didn't just fall in love with Paul in Russia; in some ways, I fell in love with my other family, too. All of them.

I go through all the fallen letters time and time again, searching for one from my older brother, Vladimir, heir to the throne. It breaks my heart when I don't find one.

He'd write. He *would*. Vladimir's kindness was nearly the first thing I noticed about him. Whenever I wished I had a protective, loving big brother instead of the big sister who wouldn't let me use her skateboard, I envisioned someone exactly like Vladimir. And this Marguerite is close to her brother—that was obvious from the beginning.

They're close enough that she would have told him about the pregnancy.

And he's said . . . nothing.

Vladimir hardly seems like the *Scarlet Letter* type, but I have to remember what a different world this is. Their morality resembles that of a century back, when people thought racism was A-OK but freaked out about premarital sex. Would he hate her for that? Even if he didn't, Vladimir might feel that he had to cut her off, possibly forever.

Did I cost this Marguerite her brother, too?

Throughout the day, I keep expecting Theo to call—not literally, as the Suite Imperial doesn't have a phone, but by sending a message via the hotel. I check the appointment book, hoping to see more restaurant bookings, but there's only one note, and that's for tomorrow: *Word from Cousin Karin.* Though I search my memories, I can't recall writing a note to any "Karin" when I was in this dimension in December; then again, I'm supposedly related to half the royal families in Europe, so that could be anyone.

Not one line tells me when—or if—I'll see Theo again.

Could I ask one of the security guards to track down the chemist Theo Beck? Maybe. But I'm not sure how much they know about the grand duchess's friendship with this world's Theo, or how much they'll report back to the tsar. I need to be discreet if at all possible. If only I had some idea where Theo might be, or when—

—but then I realize, I do know. Really, I should've been able to guess on my own, but Theo himself told me in one of his letters in December.

So when night falls, I eat an early supper in my room and have my maid fix me up to go out (this time a dress in dark red velvet, with kimono-style sleeves, subtle gold embroidery on the chest, and black fur trim at the hem). Then I call for my car.

"Where to, Your Imperial Highness?" the chauffeur asks.

It's kind of a thrill to reply, "The Moulin Rouge."

When we drive up, I hardly know what to look at first: the red windmill sign, the mix of hoi polloi and bohemians streaming through the doors, or—holy cow, a ginormous statue of an elephant with a pagoda on its back. I thought that was something made up for the movie. Guess not.

As I walk inside, I spot clues that I haven't merely stepped back in time. I see several people of color—black, East Asian, Indian—and while a few are obviously entertainers, others are well-heeled guests. I bet that wasn't as common back home; points go to this universe for not being as racist. Plus there's a vivid poster on the wall in a kind of Art Nouveau style, featuring a beautiful woman with dark skin wearing a golden dress that glitters with a thousand lights; her hair curls around her in sinuous curves that remind me of Medusa's snakes. The name written at the top, in flowing elaborate type, is *Beyoncé.* At the bottom of the poster are the dates of her next performance.

Mostly, though, the scene is pure bacchanal. The club is

enormous—and hundreds of people dance on the wooden floors or cheer from the balconies. A full orchestra crashes its way through a number that it takes me a moment to recognize as a Taylor Swift song, which in this universe she apparently wrote for the cancan.

My guards don't look thrilled to have escorted me anyplace so bawdy, but at least one of them has fetched a person in charge. I nod politely as he welcomes me, then say, "Can you show me where Mr. Theo Beck is? The chemist? I know he comes here often. Is he in tonight?"

"But of course! Let me show you to the *Jardin de Paris*."

This turns out to be the back patio of the Moulin Rouge. The elephant towers over the scene while frilly-skirted dancers cavort on an outdoor stage, brightly colored feathers in their hair. Everyone around us is eating, drinking, laughing, smoking cigarettes, smoking stuff that might not be cigarettes . . .

Sitting at the end of the farthest table with nothing but bottles and a glass for company, is Theo. His ascot is askew; his hat is missing. I'd guess he's already sampled the bottles.

I motion for my guards to step back. They're not thrilled, but they obey. Alone, I go to Theo's table and take the seat closest to him.

He doesn't look at me as I approach, but he must have recognized me just from the corner of his eye. "Interesting place," he says. "Paris."

"If you know where to go," I reply.

Theo points at the elephant. "For the price of one

franc—just one franc!—I can go inside the elephant. It has stairs in one of its legs, you see. If you climb up there, you're entertained by belly dancers who'll give you all the opium you want."

"You've gone up already?" The last thing I need is Theo getting high while we need to concentrate.

But he shakes his head. "Just what I've been told." Then he pulls himself together, or tries to. "Can I fix you a drink?"

Instinctively, my hand covers my stomach. "No, thanks."

"C'mon. You'll never have another chance to drink absinthe like this. Yeah, you can get it back home, but they don't brew it the old way, with the wormwood. So you don't get the hallucinogenic quality." As if he hadn't heard my refusal, Theo slides his empty glass between us, then pours in what I assume is absinthe—a pale green liquor the exact same shade as peridot. Then he puts a strange, perforated piece of silver atop the rim, and sets a single sugar cube atop that.

"Next comes the ice water," Theo says as he lifts a bottle, frosted by its inner chill. "You have to go slowly if you want to do it right. Drop by drop, until the sugar cube dissolves."

"How long have you been practicing this?" I demand.

"Most of the night," Theo admits. Though he never takes his eyes off the water dripping onto the sugar cube, he adds, more quietly, "Listen—some of the stuff I said yesterday—I was out of line."

"No, you weren't." After I finally admitted it to myself, admitting it to Theo is easy. "I've been unfair to you. I let the things that other Theo did keep me from seeing you.

The real you, I mean. This whole trip, you've proved that you're one of the most courageous, loyal, *good* people I've ever met."

Theo's never been shy; he loves being praised. That's what makes it so astonishing when he actually blushes. "Thanks. You're not so bad yourself."

"*Please.* I've been such an idiot."

"Hey. None of that." His laugh is sloppy from the absinthe, but the sincerity comes through. "Seeing you in action like this—Marguerite, it's been incredible. The way you jumped in after the bomb during that air raid; you were bandaging wounds while I was still pissing myself with terror."

I can't help laughing. "Not literally."

"Close. You don't want to know how close." By now Theo has begun to smile, a lopsided, absinthe-tilted grin. "You size up these dimensions so fast. You hit the ground running. Hell, you got kidnapped by the freakin' Russian mafia and you escaped on your own!"

"You pried off the metal grid."

"Okay, you only did ninety-nine percent of it." He takes a deep breath. "Yeah, you drive me crazy sometimes. But you're amazing. I think you're the most incredible person I've ever known."

This conversation feels like it's going in a direction it maybe shouldn't go in. So I say, "You're right. We should go on to the home office, so we can reach the last dimension with Paul."

"Always Paul. You keep finding him in dimension after

dimension. That's got to be destiny, right?"

"Maybe," I say, though it's hard for me to believe in destiny right now.

Theo's eyes meet mine. "But it seems like you find me almost as often."

"Yeah. I guess I do."

Suddenly I want to tell Theo about the pregnancy. Talking it over with someone would help, and he'd understand more of why I've been feeling so confused. As I open my mouth, though, Theo puts down the water bottle—sugar cube only halfway dissolved—and takes one of my hands in both of his. "Listen," he says. "I'm just drunk enough to say this, so I'm going to say it, and then we can move on. Okay?"

Oh no. But I can only answer, "Okay."

"I love Paul as much as if he'd been born my brother. And—and I think you know by now that I love you too. Not exactly like a sister."

"Theo—"

He holds up one hand, determined to finish. "Hopefully we're always going to be a part of each other's lives. You, me, and Paul, all three. If you and Paul work this out, if you end up together, then I'm happy for you. And I'll be your good buddy Theo forever and ever, et cetera." Theo takes a deep breath, as if trying to clear his thoughts from the fog of absinthe. Nearby, accordions play and people dance, the hubbub swirling around me and Theo without ever touching us. "But maybe—maybe you and Paul don't end up together."

Even two weeks ago, I would have laughed at the idea of Paul and me drifting apart. We were destined, I thought. Fated. Eternal. Now the future stretches before me, blank and unknowable.

Theo speeds up as he gets the final words out. "I'm not the kind of guy who'd try to break up someone else's relationship, even if the 'other man' wasn't my best friend. And I am one hundred percent positive that you shouldn't split up with Paul because of what some other guy with his face did in another dimension. But—if that's not all there is to it, if your relationship with Paul isn't what you thought it was and you walk away—well. After the so-called 'decent interval,' if you think you might be interested . . ." Our eyes meet again, and he smiles, and then his voice breaks. "I know I would be."

People talk about their heart being torn in two, but I always thought it was a metaphor, no more. But it really feels like that, like something precious at the core of me is being ripped into halves, neither of them complete.

He lifts my hand to his mouth. The brush of his lips against my fingers is featherlight—the ghost of a kiss, over in an instant, and then he lets go.

"That's enough serious talk for tonight," Theo says, suddenly glib again. He laughs—too loud and hard to sound real—as he resumes pouring the water over the sugar cube. "See how the absinthe is turning that milky color? Like an opal. That's how you know it's ready to drink. Can't wait to give you your first glass of this stuff."

"I'm not drinking," I say.

"Hey, no legal drinking age here. Or if there is one, we're both over it."

I just blurt out the words: "I'm pregnant."

Theo laughs again—but then his face falls as he realizes I'm serious. His jaw drops, and he whispers, "Oh, my God."

The music and laughter around us seem to taunt me, and all I know is that I want out of here. I push back my chair and return to my guards. "Take me back to the Ritz immediately."

They begin shepherding me out under the watchful eyes of the elephant. Only once do I glance over my shoulder at Theo, just in time to watch him down the glass of absinthe in one gulp.

22

THE ENTIRE DRIVE HOME, I TALK TO MYSELF. *IT'S NOT LIKE you didn't know Theo had feelings for you. He'd said so before.*

I also argue with myself. *Not like that! Theo never laid it out there like that, not even once.*

Theo's confession moved me, but it changes nothing. I hurt for him without longing for him; I love him without wanting to be with him romantically. Even when I reached out for him in London that one night, I just wanted comfort and closeness, and in my drunken grief, sex was the only way I knew to ask for that. His feelings tear me apart inside because they force me to hurt someone I care about so much.

But that's not the only reason I was so shaken tonight. Not the reason I reacted so strongly to the relationship between the Marguerite and Theo of the Warverse. It's not that I want to choose Theo instead of Paul—it's that I've seen another choice is possible.

Do Paul and I truly share a destiny in every world, every life? Or is he just one of a thousand potential paths for my life? Theo Beck may be another path, another choice made by Marguerites in other worlds; I understand that now, but my heart still tries to deny it. Paul believes in destiny. I want to believe too.

Even after the blood and the betrayal, the emptiness inside me yearns for Paul. Only Paul.

And the way I told Theo about the pregnancy—could that have been any clumsier? I don't think so. Not without my actually vomiting or something. At the time I felt like I had to say something, anything, to change the subject from Theo's confession. Well, it worked.

Maybe it's just as well that I got it over with quickly and left Theo to deal with it on his own. By the time we discuss my pregnancy again, Theo will have had time to come up with some jokes and some theories and all the other things he uses to shield himself. He's more vulnerable than he lets on.

What will Paul say when I break the news? Although I know him more intimately—more than Theo, more than anyone else—I can't imagine his reaction. But of course I have to tell him. My Paul was within Lieutenant Markov, a part of him, when this child was conceived.

"Your Imperial Highness?" my driver says. "Are you well?"

Only then do I realize I've started crying into my handkerchief. I just shake my head. Let the chauffeur make what he can out of that.

Walking back into the Suite Imperial at the Ritz feels like stepping within the walls of a gilded fortress. In some ways, I'm locked in, but at least the rest of the world is locked out tonight . . . or so I think, before I see the potted orchids on the desk next to a small yellow envelope. A card on the flowers says: *With regards.*

I rip open the envelope. When I pull out the thin yellow paper inside, I realize it's a telegram, the first real one I've ever seen. Each word is written in flat block capitals. Yet before I read anything else, I see the name of the sender: WYATT CONLEY, NEW YORK CITY.

He's a millionaire inventor in this dimension, someone this world's Marguerite has never had the slightest contact with. So I know the sender isn't this universe's Conley, and the message isn't meant for the grand duchess. It's for me.

YOU FOUND A LOOPHOLE IN MY RULES -(STOP)- VERY CLEVER -(STOP)- DON'T TRY MY PATIENCE -(STOP)- COME TO MEETING AT THE HOME OFFICE WITHIN 48 HOURS AND THE FINAL SPLINTER WILL BE RESTORED TO YOU -(STOP)- DELAY ANY FURTHER AND WE WILL RENEGOTIATE TERMS LESS IN YOUR FAVOR -(STOP)- BETTER TO WORK FOR ME THAN AGAINST ME MARGUERITE REMEMBER THAT -(STOP)- GOOD WORK SO FAR -(STOP)-

The last sentence sickens me—or maybe that's pregnancy nausea again. I don't know. Maybe both.

It doesn't matter whether I feel ready. I have to save Paul, and that means I leave tomorrow.

I'd go this moment, if I didn't feel like I should speak to Theo one more time before we face Conley again. We need to present a united front—and right this second, if I leaped out of this dimension I'm not sure Theo would follow.

No, of course he would. He'd do it for Paul.

After I climb into bed, and only the one glass-shaded lamp beside my bed is lit, I take a deep breath. Finally I pick up the grand duchess's sketch pad and open it. Drawn on the top page is the portrait I couldn't look at before: Lieutenant Markov. Paul. The man who made me fall in love.

She's etched him in the softest, most precise lines. Only hinted at color. Yet she has captured something in him that blazes with life.

I know the expression on his face; I even know where he's standing, from the quality of the light. She drew this thinking of Paul leading her to the Easter Room where she could admire the Fabergé eggs. The portrait of my mother hung in the heart of a wine-colored egg he placed gently into my hands; I remember looking up from the intricate gold mechanism inside to see his face—strong, yet uncertain. Just like this. Like my Paul, too.

The next page is Lieutenant Markov again, this time standing at attention beside my door, the military uniform he wears outlining his broad shoulders and narrow waist, the scale revealing how tall and powerfully built he is.

Was.

One evening last month, when Paul and I were alone at the house, I asked him to sit for me. Since I'd ripped up the first portrait I'd painted of him, I needed to paint another one—a better one, that would capture the man I now knew so much better than before.

Unsurprisingly, Paul wasn't a natural model. "I feel strange," he said, sitting stiffly on the chair.

"Just relax." I made sure the drop cloth covered my bedroom floor, then took up my pencil to start sketching. "It's only me. Right?"

"Right." But he stared forward as if he were facing a firing squad.

Laughing, I said, "It could be worse, you know."

"How?"

"In my Life Drawing class last year, we had nude models."

I expected him to be relieved that I was sketching him with his clothes on. Instead, Paul's eyes met mine, and—very slowly—he reached for the hem of his T-shirt.

"Paul—" But my voice died in my throat as he pulled his shirt off and tossed it to the floor where it fell almost at my feet.

We'd taken things so slowly after the Russiaverse, and Paul had let me take the lead every step of the way. Or he had until this moment, when he began stripping down in front of me. I'd never imagined that shy, reticent Paul would take a step so bold—or that I'd find it so incredibly exciting when he did.

"You've already seen me naked," he said with a shrug that

wasn't as nonchalant as it was meant to be.

"No, I haven't." There's been a lot of touching since we got together in January. A *lot*. But relatively little looking.

"You've seen another me, then. And we're the same, aren't we?"

I started to argue with him, then wondered why I would do something so stupid. *Besides*, I told myself—*I'm just drawing him. That's all.*

He continued, "You're only painting me from the chest up, like most of your portraits, right?"

That had been the original plan. But as I tucked a curl behind my ear and tried to act casual, I said, "In Life Drawing, we usually tried to, uh, capture the entire figure. The whole body." Then, more boldly, I added, "If you dare."

Paul raised one eyebrow, rose from the chair, and unbuttoned his jeans; I stood there, pencil in hand, my cheeks flushed with heat. He let his jeans drop, but kept his boxers on—at least, for the moment.

Before this moment, I'd been smiling. No longer. Difficult to smile with your mouth hanging open. *Don't drool,* I told myself. *Keep it together.*

But Paul's body—he's a big guy, and well proportioned, but it was the rock climbing that did it. All those hours scrambling up cliffs had carved muscles into his back, his abdomen, his thighs. Not in a creepy bodybuilder way—in an *ohmigod freakin' hot* way. Even if he'd been some anonymous model from class, I would've been speechless at the sight of him all but naked, submitting to my gaze.

In Life Drawing, we sometimes asked the models for specific poses. At first it was awkward, but everybody got over the weirdness after a little while. Facing Paul that day, however, I wasn't as cool. "Um, could you—if—um, could you sit on the corner of the chair, your back toward me?"

"You get to look at me, but I don't get to look at you?" Paul said, even as he did what I asked.

"You get to look at me. Just—over your shoulder." Slowly he glanced back toward me, gray eyes intense. When his face was at the ideal angle, I said, "There. Right there."

For several long, silent minutes, Paul remained as still as any of the professional models. I sketched his perfect body with loving attention to every single detail: his broad shoulders, long-fingered hands, tapered waist. With my index finger, I smudged the lines slightly to create shadows and dimension; it was so easy to imagine really touching him.

Just put everything down, take five steps, and then you can put your hands on him, ask him to put his hands on you—

As I looked into Paul's eyes, I could see the answering echo of my own desire. He was breathing faster, unsure but willing. I hadn't known I could want someone so much it made me dizzy.

But as I took that first step forward, I heard the front door—and Dad's voice. "Marguerite? Are you home?"

Shit. I threw Paul's T-shirt at him; he was already leaping into his jeans in a quick change worthy of Clark Kent. Through some miracle, he was fully dressed again by the time my father got around to checking my bedroom. Luckily Dad couldn't see the sketch on my easel; I made sure to hide it afterward, too.

The grand duchess must hide her drawings of Lieutenant Markov. Even now, when her secret love for him has already been exposed, the tsar would be furious if he had to confront the evidence.

It's brave of her to draw these, I think, flipping through a few rougher studies of Paul's hands, his profile. *Brave of her to keep them.*

Then I come to a drawing in an entirely different style from all the rest—far softer, the lines less certain, as if the grand duchess were trying to paint an image within a cloud. Paul again, but lying naked in bed, the sheet tossed aside, his arm outstretched toward the artist. Toward her; toward me. The memory comes back to life so vividly that I can almost feel the heat of the wood stove, hear the wind whipping outside the dacha, and taste Paul's mouth against mine.

Wiping at my eyes, I set the sketch pad aside. As I do so, one more letter falls out from between the pages. When I look at the envelope, it proves to be unimportant—a staggering bill from a couturier for the gowns I've purchased here in Paris. Yet seeing this makes me realize this universe's Marguerite has never received a letter from the person she needs to hear from the most.

I find the fountain pen and a blank sheet of paper, and begin:

To the Grand Duchess Margarita,

How do I begin to tell you how sorry I am for what I've done to you? I never meant to stay so long in Russia the first time, and I promise not to stay more than another day here.

I should not have spent the night with Lieutenant Markov. As much as we loved each other, his love was more for you than for me, and I never should have stolen your only chance to be together. Most of all, I should have been more careful. Causing your pregnancy is the single worst thing I've ever done in my life, and there's no way for me to begin making it up to you.

Maybe you don't care how awful I feel about it. I wouldn't blame you. But what I can promise is that, after this, I'll never return to this dimension again. ("Dimensions" are what you seem to have called "shadow worlds.") From now on, I swear: Your life is your own. Your body is your own.

I'm glad that at least you've gotten to know Dad. Hopefully that helps, having someone who's always on your side. Because he is, in my world just as much as in yours.

Back home, Mom is alive and well. She's a groundbreaking scientist, happy with Dad and with her life. I don't have your siblings—who I miss so much—but I do have an older sister. Her name is Josephine, and I'm not sure what you'd make of her. She's another scientist, and so tough and strong she could probably outfight most of the cavalry officers. But I bet the two of you would hit it off.

And Paul—

I hesitate, pen in hand. What can I possibly say?

And Paul is alive too. He studies physics with Mom and Dad, which is how I met him. Although he and I were already close before I came to your dimension, this is where I realized how much I love him.

Writing down the words reminds me of a hundred beautiful moments: Paul and me standing beneath the redwoods, staring up at the canopy of green leaves so impossibly far overhead. Making out in his dorm room, hearing his breath quicken as he pulls me closer. His giving me a bouquet of pink roses on Valentine's Day, which I should've thought was cheesy but instead reduced me to a giddy puddle. Sketching him that evening, totally overcome by his physical presence.

Making lasagna together the night before Thanksgiving.

Talking about my paintings, and how he thought they always told the truth.

Learning that he'd risked everything to protect me and rescue my father.

Here, now, this moment, recognizing how much of what we are is truly between him and me alone.

As much as I loved Lieutenant Markov—what I feel for Paul is even more powerful. The love for him I'd tried to bury lives again inside me.

Shakily, I write the final paragraphs of my letter to the Grand Duchess Margarita:

You've given me so much—more, even, than I took from you. I don't only need to atone for what I've done to your life; I also need to thank you for some of the most beautiful days I've ever known.

For the greatest love I've ever felt, and even for giving that love back to me.

I fold the letter and slip it into her sketch pad. She'll find it when the time is right. My apologies have to be meaningless for her, but surely she'll take some comfort from finding out she's not one bit crazy. The shadow worlds, everything she went through in December: All of it was real. I hope knowing that helps. It's the best I can do.

I curl up in bed and turn out the light. Even with all the emotions churning within me, I'm tired enough to pass out within moments.

But then I feel something weird in my stomach. It comes and goes in an instant, the kind of thing that's easy to forget.

I feel it again, though, and this time the sensation is weirder. Honestly, it's as though a goldfish is swimming deep inside me—

—which is when I realize the truth, and my eyes open wide.

The next morning, once I'm done getting sick, I send a note down to the management, telling them to send a summons to Theodore Willem Beck. No, it won't be easy for them to find him—but dammit, in this dimension I'm a grand duchess of all the Russias. What's the point of being royalty if you can't make impossible demands once in a while?

Maybe not so impossible. Either the hotel had Theo's information on file after all or the Ritz Paris is extremely dedicated to customer service, because they soon reply that they'll have him here by noon.

That's still a few hours away. Maybe I have time to create a portrait of my family back home, using the grand duchess's pastels and sketchbook. She'd probably like to see what Mom would look like if she were still alive in this dimension. The pose for the family group requires some care; if anyone else ever sees this, it's probably best if the late tsaritsa and the royal tutor aren't in each other's arms. So I put us on the sofa—Mom and Dad on the ends, me next to Mom, Josie by Dad.

Just as I'm shading in Josie's chin, there's a rap on the door. That must be Theo, though I'm slightly surprised the hotel simply sent him up to the Suite Imperial. "Come in!" I call, just as I remember the notation in the appointment book, something about news from a Cousin Karin—

But my visitor is someone else entirely.

Dizziness washes over me again, but this time it's only from astonishment, and maybe joy. "Vladimir?"

"Marguerite!" He crosses the room and scoops me into his arms; his camel-colored overcoat is still cool from the outside air. "Oh, look at you. Are you well?"

"I'm better. I'm so much better, I promise." Why did I ever think Vladimir would have abandoned his sister? Instead, he crossed most of Europe to visit me. I pull back from his embrace enough to look at him again. In some ways it's still strange, seeing a guy's face that reminds me so much of my mother's, and my own. But this is Vladimir—same curly hair, same mustache, same open grin. I missed him even more than I knew.

"Better?" he says, then lowers his voice. "But you are—you remain—"

His eyes flicker down toward my belly.

Vladimir knows. He's known all along. Of course he still loved her; of course he's still on her side. Why did I ever doubt him? Relief washes through me again, even more powerfully. "Yes."

"Then we stick with the plan." Vladimir brushes my hair back from my forehead. "I've spoken to Karin. She will be discreet—you needn't doubt her, she's kept many secrets in her sixty years. Her house is in the Danish countryside, and she has only a handful of servants, all loyal to her. I'll explain to Father that you're still unwell, but tell him he was right about therapy being useless. When I explain that you need several months to recuperate in the country air, with family, he'll accept it."

Several months. Through late September. "And after? What about after?"

Maybe the other Marguerite already understands this. I have no rational reason to ask. But I have to know what will become of this child I helped create.

"Karin will prove her generosity and adopt an orphan

child. A new little cousin of ours, whom of course you will come to cherish during your time in Denmark. Naturally you'll want the child to visit often. Perhaps to live with the family in Russia in a few years, when Karin becomes old enough to wish to return to Copenhagen."

A cousin. A visitor. Already I feel myself rejecting this, thinking, *It's not enough.* This Marguerite has to have felt the same way; if she didn't want this baby, desperately, she wouldn't have asked Vladimir to find a solution.

But this is probably the best answer available in her world. The royal family pride will be preserved. The tsar will never learn of the pregnancy. And the child will live with this other me soon. The grand duchess will help to raise her, or him. They'll love each other, and someday . . . someday maybe she can tell the truth about how the baby came into this world.

To the small person-to-be inside, I think, *Your mother is going to tell you all about your dad. She's going to tell you he was the best man we've ever known.*

Vladimir cuddles me protectively. "You look so pale. Have you packed your things? Do you need someone to help you?"

"I haven't packed." Because I had no idea I was leaving. "And there's someone I should say goodbye to before we go. He should be here before noon."

"Very well. I'll settle your bills. Of course you had to shop to convince the tsar you were doing well in Paris, but I must say, you made a thorough job of it." He cups my chin in his hand, the way he must have done when I was a little girl. "Before I forget to say it, I've missed you terribly."

"I've missed you too."

By 11:00 a.m., Vladimir has helped me pack almost everything. I make sure my note to the grand duchess is folded in the back of the sketchpad, next to the portrait of my own family, before I tuck that into her trunk. Vladimir, meanwhile, is shaking his head at my new collection of broad-brimmed hats. "Honestly, Margarita. How can you need so many?"

"They're the only clothes that will still fit me in a few months' time," I say, which makes him laugh.

Then the concierge rings to tell me my guest is waiting for me in the garden. Vladimir gives me a look. "Your mysterious farewell?"

"Yes. I'll be right back, all right?"

Naturally the Ritz has made sure its gardens are as elegant as the rest of the hotel. Even though spring is only now settling upon Paris, the wide lawn already shines a light, vivid green. White marble neoclassical statues stand on pedestals throughout the long, narrow length of the garden, and the branches of the trees around the edges are already heavy with buds that will soon become flowers. Only a few flowers have appeared so far—tulips, mostly.

Theo waits for me in a corner of the garden, gray overcoat buckled rakishly tight at the waist, hat at a jaunty angle. Once he sees me, he immediately hurries to my side. "Oh, my God. Sit. You have to sit. How do you feel?"

"Still capable of walking. But thanks." Despite everything, I have to laugh.

He guides me to the nearest bench, his hands gentle on my shoulders as if I were made of spun glass. Once we're seated, he looks into my eyes and whispers, "Holy *shit.*"

"I know. I know!"

"I can't get over it."

"*You* can't get over it?" I'm the one who's had morning sickness.

"It's just—there's a little Paul in there. Or a little Marguerite." He stares at my belly like it's a viewscreen directly into my uterus, then shakes his head, visibly pulling himself back together. "This makes me Uncle Theo. The responsibility takes some getting used to."

He's overdoing his reaction—trying to cheer me up, because he realizes how overwhelming this must be. And maybe he's trying a little too hard to be happy about something that might be hard for him to hear. But I can tell his emotions are genuine, and it touches me in a way I wouldn't have expected.

I've never understood how anybody could be in love with two people at the same time. Your heart can only sing one song at a time.

What I've learned, though, is that being in love doesn't make everybody else in the world invisible. Someone you found attractive before? Yeah, they don't magically turn hideous when you fall in love with another person. You don't stop thinking their jokes are funny; you don't stop being interested in what they have to say. You don't stop caring about a human being just because he's not the one you care most about in the world.

It's not the same as being in love, of course. If anything, I'm more aware than ever before of the wide gulf between mere chemistry and actually loving someone. Even when I have these moments of profound connection with Theo, he stands on the other side of a line I have no desire to cross.

And finally Theo has accepted that line.

"I'm going to buy you your first beer," he whispers as he leans forward, addressing my belly. "Way before you're legal. Don't tell your parents."

"You're in the wrong universe for that. Here, I think you're off the hook."

"You never know."

"Theo, it's been so strange, the past couple of days. Every time I remembered Paul shooting you, I didn't know what to think. But now—*this*—" I pat the slight swell of my stomach. "Late last night I was thinking about Paul, and the baby moved, and everything I ever felt for Paul came rushing back."

"That's *Paul's baby*," Theo says in wonder. He's talking to himself, not to me. "Man, I wish I could see this kid."

"Me too." It feels so strange, knowing I'll never once look at this child, or hold it in my arms.

Theo's smile is sincere, but somewhat twisted. "I was glad to get the call from the hotel this morning. After last night, I wasn't sure you'd still be talking to me."

"Why wouldn't I be talking to you?" How stupid. We both know why.

He says only, "Might've crossed a certain line there. Definitely, I have some apologies to make to Paul."

"Well, you don't have to apologize to me. You spoke from the heart, and you have the right to tell the truth about what you feel." Here in the gardens, beneath the bower of the trees, we are in the heart of Paris and yet somehow all alone, too. I'm grateful for the privacy. "Listen, I need to be completely clear."

"It's still Paul," Theo says. "For you, he's the one. I know that."

I try to find the right words. "Last night, it was like it hit me all over again, how much I wanted to be with him. I need to work this out, but *with Paul.*"

Theo smiles at me, cocksure as ever. Nobody would ever guess that he'd just confessed his love, then unflinchingly put it aside.

"I'm not only in love with Paul because of Lieutenant Markov. That's not even how it began, really. Just what made me admit it. What I saw in New York scared me, and I still don't understand it, but it's like you said. I can't blame him for something another Paul did, just like I don't blame you anymore for everything we went through with the other Theo."

His lips press together tightly before he says, "You've promised that before."

"No, I mean it," I say, and even though it might be the wrong moment for this, I take his hand. "I doubted you because of things the other Theo did, and *I was wrong.*"

"The price of forgiveness is steep," Theo says. "Because when you forgave me—you forgave Paul."

It wasn't quite that simple, but it's close enough. "In some ways, I feel closer to Paul now than ever." My hand steals over my belly again.

"I should *hope* so."

Quietly I say, "You didn't have to ask whose baby it was, when I told you."

"Remember how I told you Paul and I had a sex talk?"

Yes, I do. And I *so* do not want to know any more about that.

My expression must look sour, because Theo misinterprets it. "Listen, if you're not ready, I could do what you told me to do in the first place. If I head on to the home office with our information, then we've fulfilled the terms of Conley's agreement. He'd have to tell me where Paul is, hand over my potential cure, all of it."

"Conley wants me there." I take a deep breath. "I'm ready to move on."

Theo reaches under the collar of his shirt and withdraws the chain of the spare Firebird, which has been around his neck since New York. I duck my head, and he places it around my neck—a silent, almost solemn transfer of responsibility.

I whisper, "Theo—thanks."

"For what? Following you around the multiverse? Just part of the service."

It feels like I have so many things to thank Theo for; I could start listing them and never stop. So I stick to the most important one: "For believing in Paul."

"Hey, this works for me too, you know. Like I said, if you forgave him for blowing my legs away, you've forgiven me for attacking you in a submarine that time."

Which is true. Finally I can let it all go.

"Happy endings almost all the way around," Theo says. One of his hands lets go of mine, to reach for his Firebird. "Are we out of here?"

"You go on ahead. I want to see Vladimir one last time."

Theo shakes his head, probably at my fondness for a brother I didn't know about before December. "Okay. Just catch up with me PDQ, okay?" He smiles—slow and almost sneaky. "So, we're headed back to the home office, the Triadverse, the same dimension that sent that other Theo here to spy on you guys."

"Yeah."

"He stole my body for months, and now I get the chance to steal his. If I have the chance, that son of a bitch is going to get the ugliest haircut of his life." I burst out laughing. Theo grins wickedly as he continues, "I'm serious. If anyone in the entire multiverse deserves a reverse Mohawk, he does."

"Do your worst."

As I rise to my feet, he takes my hand. For one moment, I remember everything he told me last night, and how much we are to each other in so many worlds I don't yet know.

"Do you really think this Theo might find this Marguerite again?"

"Maybe."

I find myself hoping he will.

Within half an hour, I'm in the car with Vladimir, leaning my head against his shoulder as we head to the train station. I need to go—I'm ready to go—but it's hard leaving my brother for good.

"Do you blame me?" I murmur. "For loving Lieutenant Markov?"

"Sometimes our hearts are wilder than we know."

"But you fell in love with the ideal girl. A Polish princess, no less."

Vladimir's grin can be nearly as rakish as Theo's, sometimes. "I'd love Natalia if she were a chambermaid. When you meet her, you'll see."

"Can't wait. Thanks, by the way. For everything."

"That's what family is for."

Goodbye, Vladimir, I think. In my mind I imagine them all: Peter, Katya, this world's version of my father. And the baby, too, whose face I'll never see. *Goodbye.*

Time to stop looking back. Time to leap forward. Time to rescue Paul.

23

MY HAND CLOSES AROUND THE FIREBIRD, PRESET TO THE coordinates Wyatt Conley gave us for the home office, and—

—I slam into myself, rocking backward into a broad, thinly padded chair. After the initial dizzy rush of traveling through dimensions, I immediately realize three things. One, the way I'm sitting in this chair, arms and legs braced.

My other self was prepared for this. Waiting.

Two, Theo is nowhere to be seen.

Three, I'm in some kind of office or lobby in what must be the top floors of the tallest skyscraper in the world. No, taller than anything in my world—or the Triadverse.

I thought Conley was bringing us back to the home office. Instead, he's thrown us into a dimension I've never seen before.

Where the hell am I?

The room I sit in could be found in any corporate

headquarters, if that corporation wanted to come across as chilly and forbidding. Brushed metal tiles shine dully on the walls; the large black chair I'm in, like the rest of the furniture around me, forms sharp dark angles and sits a bit too close to the floor.

But the city stretching out before me looks nothing like any city I've ever seen. Nothing like any city in the world I know. This has to be the hundredth story of this building, at least—but outside are dozens of buildings nearly as tall. When I went to the Londonverse, I saw strange, futuristic skyscrapers with spires and angles in every direction. At the time I found it intimidating. Now I look out at structures that all form the same darkly mirrored rectangles across the sky, the small windows giving off only the tiniest pinpricks of light. The buildings are so tall, so tightly pressed together, that I can't see the ground at all. Brilliantly colored company logos stretch down most of the buildings in letters that must be fifteen stories tall, and yet the black hulks of the high-rises themselves dominate the view. The sliver of sky above it all glows a pale, febrile red—cinnabar, I think, or rose madder. That must be dawn.

My body is once again its usual bony self, my belly no longer curved. The watery sensation in my abdomen I'd begun to recognize as pregnancy has vanished. It's not like I didn't expect it to happen, but for a moment I can only feel that sudden absence.

"I see our visitor has arrived," says a cool female voice. As soon as I register the English accent, I recognize who it is.

"Romola." I turn to see her standing near my chair, wearing clothes that look subtly, imperceptibly off—the long-sleeved shirt and pants are made of a fabric that seems stiff, even though the cut is formfitting, and everything from her collar to her shoes is the exact same shade of midnight blue. Belatedly I realize I'm wearing something very similar, but all in black.

"You recognize me?" She smiles with what appears to be real pleasure. "I'm not placed well in most of the important dimensions. I so rarely get the chance to travel."

"Where am I?"

"Precisely where you ought to be. Do you need some coffee? Our Marguerite didn't sleep a wink."

I do feel tired, actually. But I don't want anything she's offering me, coffee or food or anything else. It feels like a fairy tale, one of the old scary ones: If you drink or eat in the mysterious realm, you never get to go home. "I don't understand. Conley promised me that if I did what he wanted, he'd show me to the final dimension where Paul is hidden."

Or—is this the place? Instinct tells me it isn't.

"Naturally Mr. Conley intends to fulfill his bargain. After your meeting, of course."

"The meeting was supposed to be in the home office."

Romola laughs. "Where do you think you are?"

At that moment, I see the faint green glow reflecting on the skyscraper nearest us, and I recognize it as Triad's trademark emerald.

I thought the Conley I'd been dealing with—the Theo

that screwed us all over so badly—I thought their universe, the Triadverse, was the home office. But the core of the evil, the plot to dominate the multiverse: It all began *here*.

Then I realize how stupid we've been not to guess that another dimension was in on it, running the whole thing. We should have known that from the beginning. Because Triad means *three*.

Romola turns brisk. "We should get started. Sure you won't take a coffee? No? Then I'll take you to the conference room now."

"Wait. Where's Theo?" Did Conley even give us the same coordinates? Maybe Theo's already rescuing Paul. Or maybe Conley sent him off in another direction entirely, or into oblivion.

She reacts to Theo's name in a way I wouldn't have expected. Her lips press together in disapproval. "You needn't trouble yourself on Theo Beck's account."

"I'll make that decision on my own, thanks. Where is he? Did Conley kidnap him?" Dread swirls inside me. Does Conley intend to give me back Paul only after he's abducted and splintered Theo in turn? Will I spend the rest of my life working for Triad to protect the people I love?

But Romola shakes her head. "Mr. Beck is entirely beyond our control."

I'm not sure what that means, but I like the sound of it. I imagine him down in the stark metal city, looking up at this green-tinted building and flipping it off.

As for me, I appeared within a Marguerite who seemed

to be prepared. She was waiting—willing—to let me enter her body and take her over, right here in the heart of Triad headquarters. Slowly, I say, "In this dimension, I know about all this, don't I? About Triad's plans."

Romola smiles at me, fond and yet condescending, like someone talking to a very small child. "You've worked here for a while now."

Somehow, Conley is able to force me to do his bidding in this world, too.

I've spent all this time wondering whether the constants in the multiverse are destinies, or souls, or love. Now I realize the one constant in my infinite lives might be Conley's inescapable control.

Paul and I talked about this once—the constants in the universe. The things that change, and the things that don't.

Back in early February, we drove to Muir Woods to see the redwoods. The drive to Muir Woods always terrifies me; the only way up there is a narrow, winding road that seems to be barely hanging on to the hillside. Paul kept both hands on the wheel of my parents' new car, eyes locked on the road while I gripped the sides of the seat like that would help. At one point I laughed shakily. "This probably isn't as scary for you. I mean, you go rock climbing. You're used to heights."

"Yes, but when I'm climbing, I'm in considerably closer contact with the terrain and can judge my safety accordingly. Here, we have to trust a car with which I'm relatively unfamiliar." His eyes narrowed as we neared another curve.

"Our levels of fear are probably identical."

"You really didn't have to tell me that."

He was silent, trying once again to figure out the rules of human conversation. "I meant—we'll be okay."

I nodded, and tried to believe him.

Of course, we *were* okay. We got to the top in time for lunch, ate cold sesame noodles we'd brought along, and then went wandering through the forest hand in hand. (The way his large hand almost covered mine—it made me feel safer than anything else I could imagine. More than that—*treasured*. Like Paul held on because he never wanted me to drift away.)

Standing among the redwoods does strange and beautiful things to your brain. You're reminded of your own insignificance in the vast universe by these mammoth trees towering overhead, their leaves so far up that they seem to form a second sky. These trees live hundreds upon hundreds of years; some of the ones growing in Muir Woods today sprouted back in the Middle Ages. They'll still be there long after the entire civilization I know has changed into something I wouldn't recognize. Yet you don't feel meaningless. Instead, you remember that you're part of these trees' history—part of the whole story of this world—connected in ways you can't even guess.

"Is that what you see?" Paul said to me after I explained this. We walked up to one of the tallest trees; I let go of his hand to press my palms against the reddish bark. "The trees as a . . . bridge to infinity?"

"Yeah." I ducked my head. "Maybe it's the artist in me."

"You see more than I do. It's your gift."

I smiled at him as I kept walking around the enormous circumference of the tree. "What about you? When you look at the redwoods, what do they make you think about?"

"The fundamental symmetry and asymmetry of the universe."

When I hear something like this, from Paul or my parents or anyone else, I know not to ask any more questions unless I'm absolutely positive I want to hear the crazy-complicated answer. With Paul, I usually do. "What do you mean?"

He lifted his hand, two fingers mirroring the lines of two redwoods in the near distance. "Every one of these trees has a unique genetic code. They differ from each other in countless ways—the number of branches, the pattern in the bark, their root systems, so on. Yet they mirror each other. Parallel each other. The commonality overcomes the differences."

"And that's how the universe works?" I thought of all the different selves I've met, all the different paths that have led me to Paul. "We mirror each other over and over again?"

He nodded. "Down to the subatomic level. Quarks come in pairs—always—and if you try to destroy one, another will instantly appear to take its place and maintain balance."

Quarks are smaller than atoms. Smaller than electrons. I swear, that is all you ever have to know about quarks. But when Paul said it like that, the subject caught my interest. "Like, the universe *knows* the mirrored pairs have to exist?"

"Yes, exactly."

One thing I've learned from my parents is that the physical universe seems to understand a lot, in ways you'd think would require consciousness. Information between particles appears to travel faster than light. I knew better than to ask Paul about it, though, because that's a mystery not even he can solve. I like that it's a mystery—that the universe always knows something we won't.

"So symmetry is one of the fundamental forces of the universe." I kept pacing around the tree. Paul, standing in place, vanished behind the trunk as I wound my way to the other side. "Unbreakable."

"No. Not unbreakable."

"But you just said—"

"Physics sometimes violates its own rules." From the pitch of Paul's voice, I could tell he was looking upward at the branches swaying in the wind. "Luckily for us. Or else the world wouldn't be here."

"Okay, you have to explain that one."

"One of the symmetries in the universe should be between matter and antimatter," he says. "But you know what happens when they meet."

This much I understand. "They annihilate each other."

"So if the universe contained exactly equal amounts of matter and antimatter, it would self-destruct. Actually, it would have self-destructed almost immediately after forming. At some point at the very beginning of creation, the symmetry broke. Nobody knows how or why. That break allowed our universe to come into being."

I came around the curve of the tree and peeked over to see Paul. His hands were jammed in the pockets of his waterproof jacket; his thrift-store jeans showed wear that had nothing to do with being "distressed." The vivid dark greens of the forest outlined his strong profile, and his gray eyes remained focused—not on the leaves, I realized, but the one patch of blue he could see through them.

I don't know why that moment was so special, but it was. That image is one of the first I remember every time I think of how I feel about him. It was like I loved him *so much* in that instant, like he was part of my blood and my bones.

"So that's why the whole world is here. Asymmetry saved us," I said as I walked back toward him. "But symmetry keeps the universe moving forward."

"More or less." Paul turned toward me and smiled, holding out one hand.

Instead of taking it, I pulled his arm around me so I could snuggle against his side. "So it's symmetry that keeps bringing the same people together in world after world? That makes sure you and I always find each other?

"Maybe," he said. His expression clouded over. At the time I thought he was lost in thought about subatomic particles or the seconds following the Big Bang. Now I wonder whether he was thinking about the fact that the universe always seems to make sure we run into Conley, too.

Romola and I ride downward in an oddly cube-shaped elevator. Long narrow screens halve each wall, and each one flashes the exact same Triad Corporation motto I know from two other worlds: *Everyplace. Everytime. Everyone.*

At home, the motto is in an attractive serif font that's supposed to look quirky and creative. Here, it's in block letters you'd see on signs in a prison. In this dimension—the Home Office—nobody's even pretending this is about reaching out and providing fun new products for people to love. The motto's real meaning shows through. It's about control.

"Why isn't Conley's office on the top floor?" Most CEOs get the prime real estate for themselves—at least, in my extensive experience of watching TV shows where corporate titans always seem to have a spectacular view.

Romola gives me a look. "Not very secure, is it? The principals of Triad Corporation work from the very center of the building, of course."

"What do you mean, secure?"

"Market-share rivals could launch an assault at any time. Of course we *use* the upper rooms—the better to keep an eye on the competition—but that's no place for vital officers of the company."

Other companies might *attack*? "If—if some other company tried that—I mean, they'd go to jail, right?"

"I forget." Romola makes a *tsk-tsk* sound. "Your dimension still maintains the illusion of nation-states as the prime political and economic entities. In this world, we've outgrown such notions. Corporate allegiance is a very serious matter for consumers, who should not switch sides lightly."

I can't even wrap my head around that. Hopefully I won't be here long enough to have to worry about it.

When the doors slide open, Romola leads me down a long corridor and through a series of reception rooms—all deserted, at this early hour of the day. (I left Paris around lunchtime; if it's sunrise here, then this must be the East Coast of the United States.) Each room looks sleeker and more forbidding than the last. These are the barriers visitors have to cross if they want to see the big man himself.

"You must have been looking forward to this," Romola says. "Finally getting to the root of it all."

I laugh once, a bitter sound. "Before five minutes ago, I had no idea this dimension was even involved. I should've known, though. Triad means three. Three dimensions are in on it." We all thought Triad was just a name, any other cool-sounding noun chosen at random by a bunch of twenty-something tech entrepreneurs. Why didn't we ever question whether it meant something more?

Romola gives me an odd look. "The name of the company has nothing to do with the dimensions. How could it? This branch of Triad has existed for years longer than any of the others."

"Then the name actually doesn't mean anything?"

"It does. Triad stands for the three founders of the company. The geniuses behind it all."

With that, she presses a panel and the final doors slide open, revealing a spacious but windowless office. Behind the long, narrow desk is Wyatt Conley, his hair longer and tied back in a sort of tail; he nods by way of greeting. Sitting on either side of him are the two other founders of Triad—the two other masterminds of this conspiracy.

My parents.

24

"HELLO, MARGUERITE," MY MOTHER SAYS. "YOU MUST HAVE many questions."

Thousands. But I can't ask them. I have no voice. My body reels, and I need to sit down before I fall. The room contains only three chairs, however, and all three are occupied.

"Sweetheart?" My father gets to his feet—concerned and gentle and so like Dad that it makes everything even worse. "You don't look well. I told your other self to take it easy earlier; we didn't know when you'd get here. Of course she stayed awake the entire time, didn't she, Miss Harrington?"

"She did." Romola smiles at me like I'm something cute and helpless. A kitten, maybe. "As if anyone could stop Marguerite from doing what she's set her mind to."

"Stop talking about *her*." Those are the first words I can force out. "You're dealing with me now. Talk to *me*."

"She's right," Dad says, stepping aside to make room

for me. He's wearing the same sort of stiff-yet-formfitting clothes as Romola and I are, but in a deep oaky brown. "Come on, sit down."

Numbly I walk toward his chair. As I sink into the seat, Conley motions to Romola. "Get Marguerite some water. Maybe a cup of tea. I think she could use it."

If Wyatt Conley thinks I'm going to thank him for that, he's living in a dream world. I look past him, directly at my mother, who sits calmly with her hands folded across the desk. To her I say, "Romola told me you were the founders of Triad Corporation. All three of you, together."

Mom smiles. "Yes, that's true."

"That's *impossible*." My voice breaks, so I make fists beneath the table, digging my nails into the heels of my hands until it hurts. I'd rather claw myself bloody than let Conley see me cry. "You wouldn't. You and Dad would never—you wouldn't want to make a ton of money or rule over the multiverse. That's not who you are." They wear the same sweaters until the wool unravels; Mom wouldn't know "this year's handbag" if someone hit her with it. It's not that they're stingy, and we're not poor—my parents just don't care about *things* very much.

They all exchange glances, before Mom replies, "Money matters more here, I'm afraid. In your world, and so many others—they pretend other elements of existence are more important. Here, we're more honest. Everyone needs to prove their value to their sponsor or employer. Unwillingness to maximize profit is often considered a moral failing."

"Not by us," Dad chimes in. "We recognize the shades of gray involved. But Triad employs tens of thousands of people. Their welfare is in our hands. Their futures, too. We wouldn't want to let these people down."

My initial reaction is to snap at them: *Oh, so you'll betray me, not to mention* yourselves, *just so Triad's office workers get a slightly higher Christmas bonus. I guess that makes it okay to ruin people's lives.* However, Romola's words of warning echo inside my mind—there's no such thing as a nation here. Only corporations. Your fate rises or falls with your employer.

It's an incredibly messed-up way to live, but at least I see how my parents could've gotten involved.

Dad pats my shoulder. "Triad isn't only about profit. That's simply the only part you've had a chance to see. I *told* you we should have called her here before."

That was directed at Conley, who nods. His clothes are all in a dark emerald color, the shade associated with Triad and its logo. "I understand why you're upset with me, Marguerite. My other selves can be . . ." He searches for the right words, then finishes, "total assholes."

I can't help it; I laugh.

Conley smiles, overly encouraged. "I apologize for the way they've been acting. Their worlds don't even have the same demands for money. For them, it's nothing more than a power trip. And I'll be the first to admit their methods leave much to be desired. We began this collaboration assuming that we would all benefit, but I'm the first to admit that it's turned—exploitive."

"Why do you work with them, if you think they're so awful? Why did you even start this—this conspiracy?" *Collaboration*, my ass. I push my chair back from the table, farther from Conley, and look past him to my mother. "Why didn't you stop when the other Conleys started *kidnapping* people?"

"Oh, darling." Mom's eyes fill with tears. "You have to understand. Your father and I—all three of us—by now we're doing this for the same reason."

Dad quietly adds, "We're doing this because this is the only way we'll ever get Josie back."

The curving, blank walls of this room turn out to double as enormous viewscreens. On each one, a different video of Josie plays.

On the left: A family video from when Josie and I were younger, one with all of us sightseeing in some kind of glass-domed hovership. Dad's holding the camera. He goes back and forth from focusing on the seashore below to pointing the lens at each of us in turn. Everyone dresses in monochrome, all pink or all yellow. I'm wearing my hair back in a ponytail—as unflattering here as it is at home—and wearing gray. Onscreen I try to ignore Dad's filming while I take my own pictures, maybe to use as sources for artwork later. Mom keeps talking about how coastal irregularities always mirror fractal patterns. Josie just turns her face toward the sunshine, soaking it in.

On the right, Josie and Conley are at some kind of fancy

party. To me his clothes don't look that different from what he's wearing now, but Josie's wearing a long, melon-colored sheath dress, which wouldn't look out of place back in my own world; the fact that she's not wearing jeans would be enough to prove this is a very special occasion. Candlelight flickers from tapers mounted on the wall. Josie's chestnut hair is pulled back on one side with some sort of tropical flower pinned at her temple; it ought to look ridiculous, but it doesn't. Instead, she reminds me of some 1940s movie goddess—sultry and luminous. Conley's arm is linked with hers, and he gazes at her like she's the brightest light in the room.

The broadest screen, the one behind us, plays a video with the Triad Corporation watermark on the lower right-hand side. The brilliant aquamarine color of Josie's formfitting outfit reminds me of one of the wetsuits she wears to go surfing. Around her neck hangs a slightly different version of the Firebird. She's sitting at a desk, talking with her hands; I realize this is a post-mission debriefing. Josie sounds efficient, but enthusiastic. "Apparently Greco-Roman paganism had survived in dimension 101347. Temples to Zeus, Apollo, Athena, and Aphrodite were located on most major streets, but I also saw worship of other cultures' deities, such as Odin and Isis. Various forms of paganism must have coalesced over time as . . ."

I can't take it all in. Overshadowing all these videos, all this information, is the cold truth my parents have told me: in this dimension, my sister is dead.

"She volunteered," Dad says, in a way that makes me think he must repeat this to himself very often. "Josie *wanted* to travel through the dimensions. Her sense of adventure . . . nothing was ever entirely enough. Always, she wanted more."

Conley keeps staring at Josie's face on the screen. "So when she offered to be our first traveler—to be this dimension's perfect traveler—it seemed so natural to say yes. Who could do it better? Who would love it more?"

Nobody, I realize. Josie has always looked a little wistful when we talked about our travels in different worlds. At home, though, she's on her own scientific adventure, immersed in oceanography—pun intended, since it makes her and Dad laugh every time. She never volunteered to be a part of our parents' work. In this world, however, she followed in their footsteps.

Until—

"If it had happened in one of the more dangerous dimensions, I think we might have been better prepared for negative outcomes." My mother's voice sounds thin. Strained. "But Josie was in a world similar to yours. Technology was more primitive, but she enjoyed the easier pace of life. The access to forests, and the sea. So she kept returning—supposedly to test the effects of repeated reentries into a dimension. Really she went just because she liked it."

Conley closes his eyes. "I let her. I encouraged her. It seemed harmless. She did so much work for us. Why not let her have her fun? I—I never could deny her anything she really wanted."

Nobody offers the next part, so I have to ask. "What happened to Josie?"

None of them wants to be the one to say it. Dad breaks down first. "A random accident turned—horrific."

When it seems like Dad can't go on, my mother speaks up. "No doubt you've wondered what happens if a traveler is within another self at the time of that self's death."

I've definitely had reason to worry. The thought of Josie dying like that—it's terrible, but I've faced dimensions without her. Dimensions where either or both of my parents are dead; dimensions where all of them died while I was still a child. It never stops hurting, but I've learned how to endure that. I think of my own family back home and remind myself, *I'll be with them soon.*

For these versions of Mom and Dad—and Wyatt Conley, weird as that is—there's no such comfort. "That's how Josie died?" I speak as gently as possible. "An accident where she didn't have time to leap out again?"

My mother shakes her head. "In some ways, yes. But the truth was so much worse."

Realization strikes. "She splintered, didn't she?"

Conley answers me. "Josie attempted to leap out at the very moment of death. She didn't quite make it. Pieces of her mind traveled to at least a hundred dimensions she'd visited earlier, as if . . ." He struggles for the right words. "As if the Firebird was trying to find a safe place for her but couldn't. She probably made an error with the controls—she had no time, and she would have been so afraid—"

By now Dad is sitting, his head in his hands. Conley breathes shallow and fast through his nose, the way guys do when they're trying not to cry.

This seems like a problem with an obvious solution. "Can't you just put her back together again, using the Firebirds? The way I'm putting together my Paul?"

"No," Mom says. "We tried. We knew the splinters were too small—that we'd never find them all, and they'd be too difficult to extract from the other Josephines—but we tried anyway."

My parents have always dreamed big. But they don't attempt the impossible; instead, they stretch the limits of the possible. For them to keep trying when they had no chance of success? That was desperation. Or maybe it was the insanity that sometimes follows deep grief, the same madness that made me chase Paul across the dimensions when I thought he was to blame for my father's death. Thinking of how I felt then—how shaken, how *raw*—cracks open something inside me.

These sad, deluded people are what's left of my parents in this dimension. As angry as I am about everything Triad has done, I can't help feeling sorry for them, even for this version of Conley, a little.

I remember what it's like to hurt that much. I also remember that it fades. Grief never dies—I still have nightmares about the night a cop came to our house and told us Dad had been killed, even though he turned out to be fine. But grief changes. It softens, adapts its shape to become a part of you.

That kind of sorrow never gets any lighter, but you grow accustomed to the weight as you carry it on.

In time, maybe, this world's Mom, Dad, and Wyatt Conley might snap out of it. They could realize how crazy this has become.

"I'm sorry," I say. For some reason, that seems to hurt Dad even more; he actually flinches. "I know it's hard. I do. When I thought my dad was dead, seeing him in other dimensions . . . it helped me, for a while. If you need to keep visiting Josie—different versions of her—that's okay. But that doesn't mean you let the other two Conleys do whatever they want. I mean, they splintered Paul on purpose! Think about what they're doing, would you? Splintering Paul and holding each piece of his soul hostage, letting Theo get sick from the Nightthief—even kidnapping another version of you, Dad—that's so far over the line that nothing could ever make it right."

They all exchange glances, and Conley sighs heavily. "Things are at the point where we intend to step in. Within a few weeks, the other two of me shouldn't be a problem for you anymore."

That ought to be a huge relief. Why does it make me tense instead?

Maybe it's because they've done a lot of explaining, without giving me the answers I need most. Time to make my demands. "I want what I was promised. I want the coordinates to find Paul, and I want the cure for Nightthief."

I expect evasion, or some kind of further bargain. Instead,

Conley smiles as if in pride, and my mom and dad give each other the look that means they forgot something again. (The phrase "absentminded professor" exists for a reason.) Conley's hand moves across the tabletop—which I realize now is also a sort of touchscreen—and after a moment, both of the Firebirds against my chest buzz slightly, receiving new data.

"There you go," my father says. "You're programmed with your next coordinates, plus we sent you a data file with information about the Nightthief treatment. The minute you move on, you can collect Paul, head on to your home dimension, and see if you can't put Theo right. It *is* Theo who's suffering the adverse effects, isn't it?"

He acts so kind yet is so totally oblivious to the consequences of his actions. "Yes. It's Theo."

"The formula for the solution you've been given isn't a cure," Mom explains. It takes me a second to realize she means *solution* in the chemistry sense. "However, it greatly diminishes the toxicity within the body, and gives the patient's immune system a chance to heal itself."

"Yes," I say dully. "I know." All this, and the best I can give Theo is a chance. I think of his face at the Moulin Rouge, the naked vulnerability I saw there, and my throat tightens.

My mother comes to me and puts her arms around my shoulders. "You're tired. Come home with us for a while. Rest. Learn a little more about our world."

The tightness around my chest loosens slightly. Something about this still feels wrong to me, but I know I'd rather deal with my parents than any version of Wyatt Conley, anywhere. "Okay. That sounds good." I toss off the next in an effort to sound casual. "Just us?"

Conley laughs. "Don't worry; I'm not coming with you. I don't blame you for mistrusting me, Marguerite. In fact, I'd say it's proof of your intelligence."

I get to my feet, and my parents begin leading me out. Dad's hand touches my shoulder, maybe seeking comfort from the one daughter he has left. But I can't bring myself to walk away from this room just yet.

To Conley I say, "You're in love with Josie in New York too. The New York I just visited. If the other Conley had that kind of access, why didn't he go to that dimension and sabotage the Firebird project himself?"

"I told him not to." His voice is sharp. "Any dimension where Josie and I have a chance at a happy life—they're not allowed to interfere with that. Not ever. And I've already warned them away from Josie in either of the other two dimensions of Triad." His eyes search mine, and for once I see no hint of his usual arrogance. In this moment, he aches for Josie as much as I do. "Neither of them deserve her, do they?"

For once, Wyatt Conley and I agree.

My parents and I travel to their home via monorail. The monorails I'm used to, though, are slow-moving, sedate things meant to shuttle people between airport terminals or around a theme park. This one is sleek, and it moves at terrifying speed.

As I peer out the window, I see a tangle of buildings below us—skyscrapers on skyscrapers—but not one patch of ground. "Do I want to know how high up we are?"

"Probably not," Dad says, smiling, with only a shadow of his usual good cheer.

Dawn came less than an hour ago, which means only a few other passengers board the monorail car. They, too, stick to monochrome outfits, though now I begin to notice small details of cut and shading—which seem to correspond to the brand names stitched into the collars or cuffs, in thread almost the same shade as the clothes themselves. And the interior of the monorail car is all in tan, without even a single poster trying to sell soda or shoes or anything else.

"Where are all the ads?" I ask.

One of the other riders shoots me a look like I just said something obscene. Mom whispers, "Public transit was declared neutral territory in the last treaty."

Okay, then.

As the monorail snakes higher and the daylight brightens, the forbidding shadows of this world fade, revealing the sparkle of metal and glass. The tall buildings and skybridges now reflect silver or bronze, and I can see how this place might almost be pretty, if you lived and worked up this high.

Lower down, closer to the ground? I wonder if those people ever even glimpse the sun.

The relatively still skies around us suddenly burst into life; a thousand small silvery flying vehicles take to the sky, almost simultaneously. I think of blowing away a dandelion's fuzz with one hard puff. Dad notices my reaction. "Individual transport is restricted to certain times of day."

Does that mean Theo might now be on the move?

Once again, I take my Firebird in hand to search for Theo. This time, I get a more conclusive answer; he's not far from here, just a whole lot farther down. No doubt he's getting a very different perspective on this dimension. We ought to compare notes.

"Can we go get Theo?" I ask. When my parents stare at me blankly, I wonder whether they've met him in this universe, though they should be aware of him from everything else that's already happened. I'm pretty sure he asked about Theo. Even Romola knew him, after all. Just in case, I specify: "Theo Beck? The one traveling with me? And—I don't know if you guys work with Paul here or not—"

"We don't," Dad says. That would be a relief, if not for the short, clipped way he says it.

My father only talks like that when he's angry.

Mom leans closer to me and says slowly and firmly, "Paul Markov and Theo Beck have no role in the current Firebird project. You can coordinate with them as you move forward through the dimensions. It's unnecessary here. Do you understand?"

"Yes."

I understand more than they meant for me to.

My parents wouldn't act that way if they simply didn't know Paul and Theo in this world. Mom wouldn't specify the *current* Firebird project. All of them worked together here, until Paul and Theo turned against them. Exactly why or how, I don't know. If this world's versions of Theo and Paul are as screwed-up as my parents, they could have left Triad for the wrong reasons. *Very* wrong reasons.

Already I know I have to find Paul and Theo, no matter what my mother and father say. But when I do—will I be able to trust them?

In this dimension, I might be on my own.

25

THE MONORAIL RISES HIGHER AND HIGHER. I'VE NEVER been overly phobic about heights, but when we begin zooming over the tops of skyscrapers, my gut starts to churn with dread.

Then again, that might not have anything to do with heights.

My parents sit on either side of me, both of them comfortable and seemingly content. I don't doubt their love—both for their daughter from this dimension and even for me. Yet with every passing second, their cold words about Paul and Theo echo louder in my memory.

Paul and I aren't the only ones destined to meet; the countless symmetries of the multiverse touch everyone, in different ways. I seem to find Theo nearly as often as I find Paul. Josie and Wyatt Conley often come together too—even though I wish they didn't.

And the mysterious currents of fate and mathematics bring Paul and Theo to my parents.

They invent together. Create together. The technologies they develop shape the multiverse itself. I've seen it in countless dimensions. Even in the Warverse, where my parents were awkward with Paul because of me, they still worked with him and understood the brilliance of his mind.

In this universe, Mom and Dad claim Paul and Theo don't matter.

Why are they lying to me?

I steal a glance at my father, who smiles at me with his usual gentleness. They don't intend to hurt me; I feel sure of that. But they also didn't mean to hurt me when they founded Triad, when they collaborated with the Wyatt Conleys, when they allowed Paul to be kidnapped and Theo to be poisoned. Their intentions may be good, but their judgment isn't.

Against my chest, the weight of the Firebird reminds me that I have the information I came for. I want to learn more about this universe, and what the founders of Triad intend to do next; for once, I'd like our dimension not to be the one kept in the dark. Hearing someone else's perspective would be good.

And if that perspective came from Paul, or Theo, I have a feeling I'd learn a whole lot more.

The monorail slips into misty shadow, reminding me of morning fog on San Francisco Bay. Only then do I realize we've glided into a cloud. We are *too far up*. When we begin to slow down, for a moment I think the driver agrees with me—but then we arrive at another station. My parents stand; this must be our stop.

"We live this high off the ground?" I'm grateful for the cloud, because at least I can no longer see exactly how far we'd have to fall.

Mom shakes her head, which is a relief until she says, "We take the lift up from here."

I hope our house doesn't have windows.

By now, only a handful of people remain on the monorail, and most of those disembark at our station. The majority of the crowd heads right, while we go left. I glance at my father, confused, and he explains, "Most people take the lift down. They like to get off at the highest station they can still reach their homes from. It's the only way people can broadcast their status, in public transit space."

"I thought it was safer in the middle of the buildings," I say, recalling Romola's shock at the idea of an executive office on the top floor.

"For corporate headquarters, of course," Mom says. She sounds incredulous, as if she were having to explain why ovens aren't installed in bedrooms. "But the Intercorporate Conventions provide for severe sanctions if employees are targeted at home."

This dimension puts the whole Coke-versus-Pepsi thing into perspective.

Here, the station gleams an almost pearly white; someone must polish this floor pretty much every hour. But the relative swank factor of subway stations isn't important. What hits me now is that if I want to see the part of this dimension Triad will never show me—to find Paul and Theo—this is my last chance to vanish into the crowd.

To our far right, I glimpse two signs that read TOILETS—one in blue, one in pink. This is as good a chance as I'll get. "Hey, I should—"

My mother waves me off as my father smiles. They're so unsuspecting that I feel a little guilty. But as I walk toward the pink sign, I hear Mom call, "Marguerite? Where are you going?"

Oh, crap. I half turned and tried to smile. "The little girls' room?"

She points toward the blue sign. "Isn't blue for girls in your world?"

Here, pink is for boys. It's the little things that get you. "Oh, okay. Thanks."

I walk away from them, not too fast. My path intersects with the crowd headed toward the down elevators, and I have to angle my shoulders, step carefully, to keep from bumping into anyone. That gives me a perfectly natural reason to glance backward, and I see my parents talking intently to each other.

I shift direction to merge into the crowd. I walk as quickly as I can without drawing attention to myself, because I won't be in the clear until I get on one of those elevators. Will I be safe even then? Can my parents track the Firebirds around my neck? Probably, but I have to chance it.

Once I think I'm out of sight, I push forward, earning myself a few glares. But nobody says anything as I edge into an overstuffed elevator just in time for the doors to slide shut only two inches in front of my face.

My heart pounds. My ears tighten and pop with the pressure of descent. At any moment I expect the lights to turn red—or maybe Triad green—and start broadcasting some kind of futuristic APB. But it doesn't happen. Stop after stop, we keep going down. I decide to get off at the very last stop, wherever that might be. The farther I get away from Triad's space, the better.

Finally, when I'm one of only three people left inside, the elevator settles with a thump that I know means the end. I walk through the doors, out of the smaller, danker station—and into chaos.

Electronic billboards and signs cover every single surface, all of them shining in colors so strident it almost hurts to look at them. They clash with each other, as do the tinny recordings playing from speakers as ubiquitous as they are invisible:

Apollo Greek Yogurt! Up to 50 percent real dairy!

Explore Your World: Viking Supersonic Air Cruises.

Sentinel upgrades 10 percent off this week only!

Isn't your family's safety worth it?

Revlon EverLash—Wear Him Out!

Overwhelmed, I tilt my head down, but that doesn't help; the floor is thickly papered with adhesive posters for shoes, flying cars, movies. (Leonardo DiCaprio again.) Above is no better—it's the same posters, just less dingy from footprints.

At first I can't decide whether this is a mall or a street, but then I realize that, in this world, there seems to be no difference. Some stretches are open to the outside, but the stores and the pathways seem to meld into each other. Walking more than five steps without seeing a new product display is impossible.

I think of the trip our family took to Las Vegas for Josie's high school graduation; it was supposed to be kitschy and hilarious, but instead, we all hated it. I'd envisioned a casino as . . . well, a casino. A distinct building, a place you would enter. Instead, the minute we got off the airplane—still in the airport terminal!—we were bombarded with slot machines. You couldn't check into the hotel without being surrounded by gift shops and restaurants. Couldn't get to the elevator after check-in without walking past roulette tables. Vegas was just one big outstretched hand, waiting for your money. That's what this entire dimension has become.

When I've got my bearings, I tuck myself into a corner between two rotating cases of refrigerated, brand-name sandwiches. Then I take up the Firebird and check again for Theo.

The signal suggests he's right where I am—almost exactly—and I feel a burst of hope before I realize he's lower than me.

Lots lower.

With a sigh, I fight my way back through the crowd to the next series of down elevators—and the layer under that—and the layer under that. Each time I switch, the ads become more garish; the products they advertise seem cheaper. And the light through the mesh screens dims further at every stop.

When I finally go to what must be the final elevator, someone says, "Young lady." I turn to see a guy in a vivid pink uniform, which I guess looks super-butch here. "Are you sure you want to do that?"

What, get on the elevator? "Uh, yeah."

"Below is no place for anyone your age." The way he says it, I know Below is their name for whatever awaits.

"I'll be okay," I say, and I get on the elevator alone. Through the narrowing gap of the closing doors, I see him frown and shake his head.

When the elevator doors open again, only a handful of electronic billboards are here, and they glow dimly, as their images play without sound. The floor is just a floor, and the platforms are open to the air.

Outside, it's as dark as night.

I walk to the railing and look down; by now, I'm only twenty-five or thirty feet from the ground. Cracked asphalt—more like rubble—is all that remains of what were once sidewalks, or streets. Nobody walks down there. A few people hurry along these almost-deserted walkways beside me, but none of them appear happy to be there. They give me appraising glances; clearly my black clothing sets me apart from the shabbier taupe-and-tan material I see down here. I wonder if I'm about to get mugged. My hand closes around my Firebirds, protectively.

Then I hear the thumping of footsteps—many of them—and hear someone say: "If I'm reading this correctly, she's just around the corner."

It's Theo. I begin to smile as I walk forward to meet them. "Thank God you're—"

My words trail off. Just from the way he looks at me, hard and flat—I can tell this isn't my Theo. The one who came here with me is asleep within this world's version, who doesn't seem to know me at all. Is this Theo simply tracking an intruder from another dimension?

His whole group goes still. So do I. Because Theo just pulled something black and angular that I'm pretty damn sure is a weapon.

And he's pointing it at me.

Theo grins. "Not as much fun this time, is it?"

Not one person intercedes on my behalf. The few others walking along this stretch of road determinedly look away, not wanting to get involved. There are no pink-suited cops anywhere near.

I should probably be even more scared than I am, but my brain keeps repeating one phrase over and over.

This time?

"We've got her!" Theo calls. He wears his hair longer here, but it sticks up and out rather than growing down; he looks a little like a punk Beethoven. His clothes are baggier and more layered than the stuff worn above, but again it's all the same color—in this case, a dark burnt orange. "Come on, man, you have to see this!"

Even before the figure far behind him steps into the light, I know it's Paul.

He wears a gray so pale it almost seems white. Unlike most of the men in this dimension, Paul keeps his hair short—even shorter than at home. His long coat hangs past his knees; his boots are the first shoes I've seen in this dimension that look like they've touched the ground.

Paul gives Theo a look. "Is the gun really necessary?"

"How can you even ask that?" But when Paul gestures, Theo *hmmphs* and puts the weapon away.

"Thank you," I say.

Paul acknowledges this with only a nod. "We need to talk. Obviously you understand that, or you would never have come Below."

"Yeah, we do." I glance upward, imagining I'd be able to glimpse some pale sliver of the sky—but nothing. Down here the world is black on black. "Can my parents trace me through the Firebird? Could Conley?"

"It would take awhile for them to manage it, this far down," Paul says, with approval for my caution. "Come on. We'll talk."

Theo looks at the two of us, almost comically angry, but he makes no move to stop us, or oppose Paul. The other members of their gang—four women, three men—don't seem much happier than Theo, but none of them protest.

They lead me down the final set of steps. When I first set foot on the ground, it feels momentous. Forbidden. Maybe it is. But Paul's gang is used to it, quickly taking me along the crumbling, uneven path to the base of one of the huge monolithic skyscrapers. Apparently whatever corporation is housed there doesn't use their lower floors—and hasn't for years. I see squatters' laundry hanging on lines, smoke coming from windows, perhaps the product of makeshift stoves.

We walk into the low-ceilinged, dark rooms, which are lit only by a handful of small lanterns. The air smells familiar and almost comforting: dirt, leather, old books. Theo leans against the wall, folding his arms across his chest in exaggerated satisfaction, "Now what?"

"Now," says Paul, "we talk."

He steps closer to me, lantern light slowly illuminating his features. This is the first time I've been able to really look at Paul's face, and I draw in a deep breath. A pale, jagged scar runs along one side of his jawline, but otherwise, he reminds me so much of every other Paul I've known.

And yet this moment I don't see the Paul of the Mafiaverse, who shot Theo's knees. I don't see Lieutenant Markov. I don't see the besotted soldier I betrayed in a San Francisco under siege; I don't even see my own Paul.

I see one man—one unique person, a stranger to me. This is the person I need to understand.

Because we have an opportunity, one none of us should waste.

"You know I'm not the Marguerite from this world," I

say. They couldn't have found me without Theo's Firebird, otherwise; they wouldn't have known what to look for.

Paul nods. "You are, nonetheless, Marguerite Caine, the daughter of Doctors Henry Caine and Sophia Kovalenka, and a traveler through the dimensions."

"Just like you're Paul Markov, my parents' protégé and Triad's enemy." I nod toward Theo. "When do I get my version of him back?"

Slowly, Paul smiles—a genuine smile. "Not long now. You like your version better?"

"He never had a gang, or let anyone hold a gun on me."

This world's Theo has begun to scowl. "What are you doing with all the chitchat? We need answers from her, little brother."

Again, they're that close. I might not like this armed-and-dangerous Theo, but at least there's something within him I would recognize.

Paul says, "Be patient, Theo."

"What answers do you want?" I offer. "If you guys are anti-Triad, and I'm guessing you are, then we're on the same side."

Theo, Paul, and the others all exchange glances. It's Paul who says, "They're your parents. Conley was your sister's fiancé."

"My parents are grieving, and misguided. Wyatt Conley can't be trusted, no matter what his motives are. And Triad—they're trying to yoke together three dimensions so they can dominate all the rest. That's *not* going to happen.

Not if we help each other."

Theo shifts on his feet, restless. "She's just saying what you want to hear."

"Doesn't mean she's not telling the truth." Paul gestures toward a battered metal chair.

I don't sit until he does, too. His chair is farther away than I'd like for a conversation—it makes this too much like an interrogation. But I can work with it. This room obviously has no designated purpose; the furnishings in here run from office desks to these metal folding chairs to an honest-to-God wooden four-poster bed in the far corner. These guys are winging it too, which gives me more confidence when I ask, "What do you want to know?"

"Your story, as you'd tell it."

So I hit the basics: My parents being opposed to Conley, in this world and the other tied to Triad. The kidnappings. The hijacking of Theo's body, and the subsequent Nightthief poisoning. Paul's deliberate splintering. Conley's demands that I work for him, and his ultimate plan. Deciding to finish with a flourish, I say, "In my universe, you and I are in love."

"In love." Paul shakes his head. I can't tell whether he doesn't believe me, or he simply can't picture it.

"Madly. Deeply. But somehow, this is the second time in a few days that guys working for you have held me at gunpoint," I add. "Which I'm sick of."

"You came looking for your Theo," Paul says. "You'll have to excuse ours for being so cautious."

Apparently Theo doesn't like being spoken about in the third person any more than I do. "We still don't understand what she wants."

Paul nods as he gives me an appraising look. "If you're so in love with this other version of me, why haven't you run to rescue him yet? Obviously your Theo doesn't need saving. We wouldn't keep him here even if we wanted to."

"Which we *don't*," Theo adds. He gestures at the Firebird around his neck with disgust. "Knowing that guy's all zoned out inside me? Creepy as hell."

"I didn't come here to save Theo. Just to talk with him, and—" How do I put this to make them comprehend? "This is the Home Office. The universe where Triad started. That means the whole conspiracy started here. My parents and Conley have told me what they want—and I believe they told me the truth—but not the whole truth. There's more to this, isn't there? And this dimension is the only place I'll ever get the answers. You guys are the best source I'll ever have."

To my satisfaction, that catches Theo short. But then he switches tactics. "We could use more Firebirds, and she's wearing an extra."

I put one hand over my chest; the Firebirds press against my palm. "The second one isn't *extra*. It's for putting my Paul back together, and bringing him home."

"On behalf of my other self, I appreciate your commitment." Paul leans forward, studying my face by lamplight.

Hope flickers inside me. "Wait. Do you think—could you

be the one with the last splinter of Paul inside?"

"I doubt it," he says evenly. "Your Conley gave you a final set of coordinates. He's trying to win your trust, so I doubt he'd falsify that information."

Probably so. I slump back in my chair, disappointed.

Paul remains focused. "You sabotaged the Firebird technology in one world, but made sure it survived in another."

I nod. "It's not much. Still, we have to start somewhere. You guys are closer to the source. Maybe you know how we could get at Triad? Really take them down?"

Paul and Theo exchange another glance. Theo says, "She could be spying on us for Conley."

"Or she could be telling the truth." Paul's eyes meet mine, searching.

He wants to believe in me. I wonder if that's strategy or desperation.

When Paul speaks again, he asks me the last question I would've expected: "Which version of me did you trust the most? And the least?"

I don't even have to think it over. "The Paul from my own universe."

He cocks his head. "For which?"

"For both." My first leap into a new dimension comes back to me, as vividly as if I were still standing in London, rain spattering my face and hair, scrawling my mission on a poster: KILL PAUL MARKOV. "I trusted him the least, because it took me too long to understand him. When Triad framed him for my father's death, I believed it."

Paul forgave me for that—no. To forgive me, he would have had to hold it against me in the first place. He never did. I would have walked away from a love like that.

"But he's also the one you trust the most?" Theo sits in a chair of his own, arms slung slightly backward, legs stretched before him.

I nod. "Once I understood my Paul, I knew he would never knowingly hurt me, or anyone, except in defense. He's always going to do what he thinks is the right thing—and yeah, sometimes we don't agree on what that thing is, but his intentions are always good. He'd been lonely so long, before he found us. Every time I think about how lonely he was, it kills me a little inside." Why couldn't I have said all this to my Paul? I will, the first chance I get. The next universe over. My vision blurs as I blink back tears, refusing to cry as every other Paul I've known flickers through my mind, from a mobster's son to my cherished Lieutenant Markov. He'll have a place in my heart forever, and there are others I could have cared for, but . . . "I could go to a million universes and never find someone else who could make me feel this way. Only my Paul. Only him."

Theo makes a sound, totally familiar from my own Theo, like *Spare me the sap.* But Paul gives him a look that silences him instantly.

To me Paul says, "One thing's certain—you're not this world's Marguerite Caine. Even if you're not telling me everything, I can tell you hate Triad as much as we do."

"Great, here we go," Theo groans. There's no fire in his

voice, though; he might gripe as he follows Paul's lead, but he'll follow.

Paul rises to his feet. "Yes, we're working with her, and with the other you. So brace yourself for a reminder." Theo swears under his breath.

I stand up too, happy to no longer be a captive. Paul's understanding makes me suspect: "Did you travel between dimensions, when you were still with Triad?"

"Once or twice."

"So which one of *me* did you trust the most, or the least?"

It's supposed to be a lighthearted question, to break the tension. But Paul's expression hardens, like the mobster's did right before he fired. "I'd have to say you're the version I trust the most."

Me? He hardly knows me.

"Tell her the least," Theo demands as he sits down, preparing himself for the painful jolt of a reminder. Paul says nothing. Theo laughs. "Fine, I'll tell her."

"Tell me what?"

Theo smirks up at me and says, "The version of you we trust the least is *this one.* Our own Marguerite Caine, the most loyal follower Wyatt Conley ever had—and the coldest bitch in the entire multiverse."

26

I KEEP WAITING FOR PAUL TO TELL ME THEO IS JOKING, OR for Theo's expression to finally shift into his usual cocky grin as he tells me the look on my face is priceless. They don't.

Already I knew I was working for Wyatt Conley. But willingly? Why would I do that? As soon as I ask myself the question, though, I realize the answer. "It's because of Josie," I say. "My sister. I don't know if you knew her—"

"We did." Paul speaks quietly, but whatever's lurking behind his words, it isn't sympathy.

"My parents aren't like this. Not in most dimensions. You must have seen that for yourself, right?" When Paul nods, and Theo's smirk vanishes, I know I'm on the right track. "Here, they've lost one of their children, and they've fallen apart."

Theo folds his arms across his chest. "That's no excuse."

"No, it's not. Still, we just have to bring them around. All they want to do is see Josie again."

Theo snorts. "I'll say."

This version of Theo is kind of a snot. "What's that supposed to mean?"

It's Paul who replies, not with an answer but with another question. "You really don't know, do you?"

"Mom and Dad explained."

"Not everything. Not if you're still defending them." Paul looks at me as if—as if he feels sorry for me.

In the first moment I realized my parents were cofounders of Triad, shock and horror almost overwhelmed me. Those emotions well inside me again, deeper than before. "Tell me," I whisper.

Paul shakes his head. "If it comes from me, you won't believe it. You'll have to hear it from them yourself."

"It's not all about Josie," Theo shoots back. "For you, I mean. The Marguerite Caine in this universe *loves* screwing with all your minds. The power she has over her other selves—she gets off on it. *Lives* for it."

"How would you know?" I shoot back.

Paul steps between us, maybe fearing what would happen if we really got into it. "I'm sorry, Marguerite, but it's true. You say so yourself. You manipulate the lives of your other selves, just because you can. I've seen you quit schools, ruin paintings, wreck cars, pick fights." After a long moment, he adds, more quietly, "Sleep with other guys. Other girls, once in a while. Whoever. It doesn't matter to you, as long as it hurts someone."

He won't meet my eyes. He's felt the emotions of another Paul who went through that.

I keep my head high. "That doesn't sound like me."

Again with the snort from Theo. Paul at least has the decency to look sorry about what he has to say. "It sounds like the Marguerite Caine we know. *She* always says playing with other selves—seeing just how much she can change or destroy—she calls it an art form. Says it's sculpting, but instead of clay, she uses lives."

A hollow feeling opens up in my belly, but I don't let myself believe it. "Whatever. I'm not her, so deal with me. What do you want?"

"To keep Triad from expanding their power and taking over every world we could possibly reach." Paul walks slowly around me, assessing me. Judging. "We know they brought you here deliberately."

"They're trying to recruit me. They're going to fail." I step forward, breaking his orbit; he's not the only one who decides whether we go forward here.

"But you did their dirty work," Theo says. "Apparently the other version of me told everyone that, before he went under."

"Then he also told you why. I did what I had to do to save you both. And at least once I was able to figure out how to turn Conley's plan against him."

Paul gives Theo a look, like, *You should've remembered that.* "You're right. If we're going to defeat Triad, we'll have to work together. As a perfect traveler, you should be able to fight off our Marguerite, if she ever came to your world—"

"Which she won't, because it wouldn't be any fun for her, entering a body she couldn't steal," Theo says. For once I don't mind the smug tone of his voice; I'm too relieved to hear that the wicked Marguerite won't be knocking around in my head.

"We work together," Paul says, a little louder, an obvious hint to Theo that he shouldn't interrupt again. "That may mean you come here to interfere with our Marguerite's plans—even though they'll be on the lookout for you."

"Fine. But how am I going to know when we should meet? Or where?" Our secret rendezvous could take place anywhere in the entire multiverse.

After a moment, Paul says, "How do you think your Paul Markov would react to my entering your dimension for brief periods of time, only to communicate our plans?"

Let my Paul be taken over by this one? I have no right to make that kind of deal. But if this is truly the only way . . . "I'm giving you permission to come once. When you do, I'll let you know whether Paul has consented."

Paul's expression shifts slightly, into something that might even be respect. "Agreed."

We can do this. Finally, we're one step ahead of the Home Office—

Realization sweeps through me, wrenching and terrible. The other Marguerites I leap into remember everything that happened while I'm within them. Right now, I'm inside a Marguerite who's on Triad's side.

When I tell Paul this, however, he's unfazed. "It doesn't matter. You had no other way of reaching out to us, and Conley would've suspected we'd try something like this anyway. We'll change locations immediately after you leave."

"That's enough to protect you?" I ask.

"We're as safe as we were before. Which is to say—not much, but enough." Paul shakes his head, perhaps in wonder. "You actually care."

"I always care about you." Lieutenant Markov's words flicker in my memory—and despite everything I've seen on this journey, I can say them back to Paul now and mean them. "I would love you in any shape, in any world, with any past."

He doesn't reply right away. Anyone who didn't know him as well as I do would think he's unmoved. Instead, he's both touched and doubtful. "You don't love me in this one."

Not yet? Not ever? I say the only thing I absolutely believe to be true. "I could love you, then."

Paul breathes out heavily, as though he were weary. He doesn't contradict me, though, and I know he recognizes the same thing I do—the potential. The eternal possibility. The kindling only awaiting a spark to burst into flame.

Hope brightens inside me. Three dimensions, three versions of Wyatt Conley are conspiring against me and my family. Now, finally, we have a conspiracy of our own. We have sources in the Home Office, and maybe beyond. The Conleys won't always be one step ahead of us anymore.

Whatever else he's planning—we'll get a chance to stop him.

"You can ask my version for permission to visit his dimension right now, I guess." Theo steadies himself as he holds up the Firebird. "Go on. Do it."

He's speaking to Paul, but I'm closer. So I duck down, take the Firebird from Theo's hands, and hit the reminder sequence before he can protest. Although I manage to drop the Firebird just in time, some of the jolt burns my fingers. Theo winces and pushes back, his chair scraping on the floor—but when he looks up at me, he's my Theo once more.

"Whoa." He leans forward, elbows on his knees, to let the rush pass through him. "If I remember the last few minutes correctly—first, I was being a jackass. Sorry about that."

I attempt a smile. "Apparently neither of us is much fun to hang out with in this dimension."

Paul's tone changes when he's speaking to my Theo; it's more polite, yet more distant. "Do you recall our proposed plan?"

"I think so. Work together. Two dimensions united against Triad. Which means letting this world's Theo periodically take over my body." Theo looks sheepish. "Seeing as how I'm in his body at the moment, I have to admit it's a fair trade."

Why only two dimensions? The Warverse might help, if we asked . . .

But I abandon this idea. How could we possibly get every world to cooperate? We'd have to visit back and forth so much that we'd hardly ever know who we were speaking to, and it would be easy for our ranks to be infiltrated by still other versions of ourselves.

Conspiracies make my head hurt.

I focus instead on the best part of this. Between our two worlds, we might have the information and access needed to take Triad down, once and for all. It would be a relief, if it weren't for Paul's dark hint about my parents' true agenda.

Turning to Theo, I say, "Do you remember what this world's Theo knows about my parents? What they're up to?"

He shakes his head. "What they say and do is a lot more memorable than what they think. You get—emotional impressions, more than a recording of what's going on in the cranium."

So much for that plan. "Then we have to go to them and make them tell us."

"No," Paul says sharply. "Not Theo. If your version leaps out and strands our version there—where he can be tracked—Triad will have him in jail within the half hour."

"I'll go on my own, then. Though I actually don't know where I live in this dimension."

"I can give you the address," Paul says. "We have that information."

Theo gets up from the chair; even the way he stands is different. He's steadier, more confident, but not as wary. "I don't like this. You're sending her alone, so her parents can tell her something you know but oh-so-conveniently won't share."

"I'll tell you now," Paul says. "But as I said before, neither of you will believe me. Marguerite won't rest until she hears it from them."

I step closer to him. "Try me."

He pauses, and I wonder if we've caught this Paul Markov in a lie. Then I realize he's hesitating before the words because he thinks they'll hurt me. "Your parents—" Paul takes a deep breath, then finishes. "They don't just want to visit Josie in other dimensions. They want her back in our world, for good."

I would've known that even if Mom and Dad hadn't already told me. "Wouldn't you want your child back? But it's impossible. Josie splintered into too many pieces. My parents know there's no way they can ever re-create her again."

"There's one way," Paul says. "One thing they can do to every dimension Josie ever visited, to make sure each splinter of her consciousness returns home."

Theo and I glance at each other; he's as bewildered as I am. This outstrips any of our research at home. I ask Paul, "What do they have to do to all those dimensions?"

Paul speaks gently, as if he could soften what he says next. "Destroy them."

Twenty minutes later, I'm standing face-to-face with versions of my parents gone pale as ash.

Paul gave me the directions to find them. This apartment must be what counts as luxury in this dimension, but to me it looks bare and soulless: no houseplants, no chalkboard wall scribbled with equations, no piles of books. I could almost believe my parents had chosen to live in a hotel room instead of a family home—it's that impersonal and cold.

"You tried to find your version of Theodore Beck, didn't you?" Mom is doing that thing where she's really mad but is trying to hold it back for a Reasonable Discussion. "Below is dangerous, sweetheart. You shouldn't have—"

I don't need to hear it. "I found Theo. And Paul."

My parents exchange a glance. Dad says, "I suppose you're not going to tell us where they are."

"No, I'm not. *You're* going to tell *me* what . . . what you're going to do about Josie."

I don't repeat what Paul told me out loud because I still don't believe it. I can't.

My father looks like he doesn't know what to say, or that he's too ashamed to say it. Mom, however, has regained her poise. The only sign of her discomfort is the way she hugs herself, as if she were trying to keep back the nonexistent cold. "Journeys through the dimensions are dangerous, even for a perfect traveler. Of course we don't have to tell you that; you've faced considerable dangers yourself. Surely, at some point, you've asked yourself whether these journeys shouldn't be abandoned completely."

I have, but the doubts have never been more than a whisper in the back of my mind. The amazing things I've been able to see—the different selves I've been, and gotten to know in other worlds—for me, that outweighs the scary parts. So far.

"After Josie's death, we first thought we should abandon the project altogether," Mom continues. "The risks were too high to justify mere curiosity, or even technological advancement. But then your father and I spoke with Wyatt Conley, and we realized we had a new goal. One worth any cost. Worth every sacrifice."

"You want Josie back," I say. "But what are you going to do to make that happen?"

I want them to contradict me, to repeat that re-creating Josie after her splintering is an impossibility. Or if it isn't, to tell me the solution is something justifiable.

But from the way my parents go still, I know Paul told me the truth. Triad may be motivated by sincere love for my sister—but their plans are more horrible than anything my Wyatt Conley ever dreamed of.

My mother walks closer, standing directly in front of me. "Marguerite, the splinters of Josie's soul are scattered too widely for us to collect. But if that dimension could no longer contain her—"

"Because it ceased to exist?" I ask.

After a moment, my dad nods. "Nothing less would work."

I'm unnerved in a way that feels like physical disorientation, like the entire planet began spinning on a completely new axis. My whole life, I've joked about "Mom's crazy theories," though I always knew they weren't crazy, just *way out there*. But what I see in my mother's face now—and in my father's, too—it's insanity.

Not the metaphorical kind. Real, true madness has claimed them both.

"You can't destroy an entire dimension." I explain this slowly, like somehow that will help them understand. "Even if it weren't completely evil—I mean, how? There's no bomb big enough to take out a *universe,* much less several of them."

"Marguerite, think." Mom goes into professor mode, startlingly familiar in this bizarre moment. "Resonances between the dimensions are remarkably sensitive, as you should know. Remember, they can only be altered to create a perfect traveler once in each dimension."

I've never understood the scientific explanation behind "resonances," but the implications are clear. "Sensitive means—fragile. Breakable."

Dad smiles, encouraging despite his strain, the way he acted when I kept having trouble learning to ride a bike. "And each universe strains to achieve perfect balance. All we have to do is return it to its fundamental symmetry."

The memory of my walk in Muir Woods with Paul comes back so vividly I can smell the forest air. He stood in one small patch of light as he told me about the way that fundamental symmetry broke at the very dawn of creation. If it hadn't—if matter and antimatter were equal, gravity and antigravity too—then the universe would destroy itself in an instant. We wouldn't even know the disaster was happening—had happened—because time would collapse too.

"How do you do that? How is it even possible?" I whisper.

"The device is surprisingly simple," my father says. "Bit of a surprise nobody thought of it before. Then again, if anyone did think of it, they had the sense not to build it."

I grab at the only hope I see. "But you can't bring a device to another universe! Only consciousness can travel between dimensions. Not matter."

"Not *most* matter." My mother points to the Firebird hanging around my neck. "We've been experimenting with various alloys and compounds. It won't be long before we're able to construct a device that can travel as easily as the Firebird. Though, of course, not just anyone can activate it. Most people would be erased in the universe's collapse, without being able to escape."

"Only a perfect traveler," I say.

Finally it all makes sense. I knew Conley was too fixated on me, that there were too many other ways for him to get his dirty work done for him. What I didn't know was just how dirty the work would be.

"Wait, wait, wait." I form the time-out sign with my hands. "You mean, you want *me* to destroy entire universes?"

"Josie shattered into many pieces, too fragmentary to collect. But it wouldn't be impossible to travel to each of those worlds. After all, you needn't stay long." Mom puts a hand on my shoulder, a touch meant to soothe that instead makes my skin crawl. "You won't be killing anyone, Marguerite. The entire dimension will simply be erased from the multiverse. No one will feel any pain. No one will even know."

When a dimension died, it would take its entire history with it. The people within it wouldn't die; they would never have been born.

I think of the Warverse, of Josie as a fighter pilot. Or

my parents as military researchers trying their hardest to keep their country's hopes alive. Of Theo as the soldier who sneaked into my room at night and searched for moments of romance in that gray, scary time.

Of that world's Lieutenant Markov, who loved me so deeply, even when he knew I'd played him for a fool.

I don't dare return to that dimension, which means I'll never see any of those people again. But they deserve to lead their own lives and find their own fates. To have their chance to win the war, and survive.

And as much as it would hurt to learn that any of those people in the Warverse were dead, it would be infinitely worse to know that they had never been.

"You don't even understand what you're asking me to do." My voice shakes. "Destroying a dimension—that would be *worse than genocide*." They want me to destroy entire species, planets, stars, countless galaxies.

"Perhaps *destroy* is the wrong word," Dad says, like a change in vocabulary would fix this. "Think of it as 'unmaking' the dimensions, and that's really much closer to the mark."

They're so far gone they can't even see it. I strike out with the first thing that comes to mind. "Josie would never accept this. Even if you succeeded, and you put her back together again, she would hate you for what you'd done."

"I feel sure Josephine will see reason," my father says, with the same tone of voice he used when he and Mom didn't let Josie get her ears pierced a third time.

My mother adds, "Keep in mind that Josephine traveled

far longer than you have. She's seen how many versions there are of us, in all the worlds. One version more or less in the multiverse makes very little difference, mathematically speaking."

"This is bigger than math! You can't just swap one of us out for another!"

Mom seems almost irritated by my lack of comprehension. "All versions of us are the same person, on a very important level. Haven't you seen that yet? Your Paul Markov—isn't he the same one you love in every world, everywhere?"

Once I would have said yes. Now I know the truth is more complicated. As much as each version has in common with all the others, we're still unique. Every single one of us, everywhere, is irreplaceable.

"Your universe is safe," Mom says. That shouldn't make me feel better on any level, but it does. I'm coward enough to be glad we're not first on the chopping block. "Perfect travelers are a scarce resource. We can't go unmaking them right and left."

"You can see now why we need to keep the technology under wraps," Dad chimes in. "If every dimension had this power, can you imagine the warfare that would result?"

I shake my head. "But if you're the only dimension with this power, it's not a war. It's just a slaughter."

"You make it sound so *diabolical*," Dad says, as if it isn't.

"Please, sweetheart, think this over after you've had a chance to calm down." My mother is openly pleading with me, in a way she never has before. Despite everything, she's enough like my real mom that seeing her this way makes my heart hurt. "We want to work with you. We want to make this the best it can be for everyone involved. And we can give you so much."

"Like what?" The technology to turn our dimension into a hideous collage of Goya and Warhol, like theirs? *That's* supposed to make up for turning me into a mass murderer?

She pauses; her eyes meet my dad's. So Mom isn't looking directly at me when she says, "We want to protect you, Marguerite. You're our daughter too. But—if it came to it—Conley could travel to a new dimension and create another perfect traveler there."

I know what she means the instant she says it. But it's like my brain refuses that knowledge. Instead, I flush hot all over, and my stomach cramps, as if I drank poison that has to get out of me *now*, because if it stays inside it will destroy me.

My parents would kill my universe. They would kill *me*. All because one version is as good as another, because they think we're all fungible, replaceable, *disposable*—

"You know that wouldn't be easy for us," Dad says, straightening. "We didn't bring you to this dimension on a whim. You needed to learn the truth, though we'd hoped to break it to you more gently than this."

I spit my reply back at him. "There's no 'gentle' way to tell me to kill billions of people."

He continues as if I hadn't spoken. "Take your time. Think things over. Discuss it with us back at home! When you fully comprehend the difference between death and nonexistence—that none of those people would suffer the way Josephine suffered—"

Dad's voice chokes on a sob. My mother grabs his hand as he closes his eyes tightly. Somehow this is the worst of all—seeing that they're still my parents, still capable of love and compassion, and yet willing to order the death of worlds.

"I'm leaving," I say, backing toward the door. "Don't come after me."

By this I mean, don't follow me to the hallway, and definitely don't follow me to my own world. But they don't chase me. Mom and Dad simply stand there, looking sadder than I've ever seen them look in their lives.

They're not only feeling sorry for themselves, though, or for the daughter who died. Mostly they feel sorry for me.

I could jump out of this universe where I stand; instead, I go out the door. That way I can slam it behind me and create the illusion that they can't chase me, that I can leave everything I've learned here behind.

But they can follow me anywhere, and they will, until they get what they want. Or else they'll destroy my entire world.

27

WITH SHAKING HANDS, I SET THE COORDINATES MY PARents gave me—the ones that are supposed to lead to the final splinter of my Paul's soul. I close my eyes, press down—

—and slam into myself just in time to wobble out of control.

I'm riding a bike, I think, in the split second before I crash into a ditch.

Groaning, I scoot out from under my bicycle to see my knee red and raw, tiny droplets of blood beginning to bead up. Someone walking nearby says, in an English accent, "You all right, love?"

Honestly, at the moment, it's almost a relief to have my biggest problem be a skinned knee. "I'm fine, thank you."

That came out with an English accent too. Do I live in London in this world as well? Seems really green for that . . .

I look up and recognize where I am right away. Most

people wouldn't, but most people didn't grow up surrounded by graduate students, who often carried brochures from the best physics departments in the world while they tried to figure out where to do their postdoc work.

When I see the Bridge of Sighs, I know I'm in Cambridge.

This makes sense. Both my mother and my father could easily have wound up teaching here; in this world, they did. Now I have to figure out what else has changed.

My first task on leaping into a new dimension is always to understand the essentials as best I can: where I am, *who* I am. In this case, I desperately want to find Paul right away. I need him more than I ever have before. But for a moment I can only sit there in the grass, shaking, thinking of the lunatic versions of my parents I just left behind and what they want from me.

Green trees. The beautiful old university. Faraway sounds of traffic. Students laughing as they run across the grass. Triad might destroy this universe too.

Focus, I tell myself. *Freak out later. Find Paul now. Start by learning about this world.*

First I take a look at what I'm wearing: denim skirt, knee socks, Mary Janes, and a scratchy gray woolen sweater (should I say jumper)? Ordinary enough, if a little plainer than what I'd usually pick on my own. I like the floral scarf around my neck, though. The bicycle looks like one I'd pick in my world too—old-fashioned with fat tires, painted a happy shade of turquoise.

My purse is a cross-body bag in black leather; I open it up

to see what I find. My hand and arm hurt as I riffle through things; maybe I banged myself up worse in the crash than I thought. This Marguerite must be more practical than I am, and thank goodness, because one of the first things I pull out is a Band-Aid. I put it over the skinned place on my knee, then go back to searching. Lipstick: some brand I don't know called Sisley, but about the same color I'd wear at home. Sunglasses, cheap drugstore version, which is what I always buy because I never go more than two months without losing a pair. An e-reader—not a model I'm familiar with, but I can figure out how it works later. My phone, rock on. When I check to see whether it's a tPhone, however, I'm momentarily confused; in this world, I seem to own something called an iPhone. I wonder who makes this one.

And, yes, a wallet. I open it up to find a driver's license, complete with address. Plenty of British money, the queen staring serenely at me from bills in different sizes and colors.

A red mark mars the skin of my right wrist. When I push up the sleeve of my sweater, I reveal a long, livid scar. It's not grotesque or anything, but the sight still makes me wince in sympathetic pain. From the look of it, this happened sometime in the past several months; maybe the scar will fade over time.

But when I close my fist, I feel the ache quivering up my arm and realize how serious the injury was. More than the skin was broken. This tore through muscle and bone.

Still, it's obviously healing, and for now I can manage. I start spelunking through the phone, which turns out to have as intuitive an OS as my own tPhone back home. The camera shows plenty of pictures of my family—Josie too, I'm relieved to see—and various friends I haven't made in my own dimension.

But a quick search shows no pictures of Paul, and none of Theo.

Time to search contacts. Nope, neither of them is listed.

Josie is, though—and after learning what happened to her in the Home Office, I need to talk to her. So I go ahead and hit dial. After a few rings she answers, out of breath. "Marge?"

Marge? Thank God my Josie never thought of that nickname. "Hey. How are you?"

"Well, I'm fine." She sounds *so weird* with an English accent. "Is something wrong at home?"

"No, no!" Hopefully that's true. "I just—I don't know—I wanted to talk to you."

Her voice gentles. "Is everything okay?"

"Yeah. Sure. But I was wondering how things were with you."

"I'm having the greatest time." It's as if I can see Josie's grin. "The River Findhorn is seriously underrated for its whitewater rafting—it's *brilliant*, Marge. Absolutely brilliant!"

Doesn't matter how different the accent is. This is definitely the Josie I know. "Glad you're having fun."

"You'll have to come up with me next time. I know you're not sporty, but I promise, you'd adore it. And—I really do think you could manage. Despite everything."

Once again I glance at the nasty scar on my wrist. "Next time's a promise." What the hell. I bet this Marguerite would enjoy rafting too. And surely whatever's wrong with my arm will improve sooner or later.

"You're sure everything's all right?" Josie obviously finds it weird that I called her in the middle of her big adventure for no reason.

I try to cover. "Really, it is. But—um—last night I had this weird dream where you were gone, and I guess it made me miss you."

After a long moment, Josie laughs. "You'd *never* admit that to my face."

"Nope. So enjoy it now."

A little more chitchat—mostly about the smoking-hot Scotsman leading the rafting party—and then Josie hangs up. Simply hearing her voice for a few minutes was enough to make me feel better; it's like I have her back again.

For now, I think, remembering what the Home Office wants. What they might do to this dimension, or another like it.

A shiver passes through me. I stand up, righting my bike, because it makes me feel a bit stronger—but I don't ride off yet. First I open a web browser and search for Paul Markov, physicist. The results light up immediately, and I smile. He's here, at Cambridge.

He's *here.* I'll be with him before the day is out, maybe even as soon as I get home. I don't understand why I don't have any pictures of him yet—but maybe he didn't begin grad school quite as young in this universe. Paul might be new here.

I'm going to make everything right, I think. *If you ever thought I didn't love you for yourself, Paul, you're wrong. And you can help me figure out how to stop Triad.*

Then I search for *Theo Beck, physicist,* because Theo should have jumped into this dimension right after I did. While I trust that Paul's mercenary group in the Home Office meant what they said, I'll still feel better after I've spoken to him. When the results come up, though, I frown.

Theo's in *Japan*?

I email him, trusting that his leap into his other self will have woken him up. Sure enough, my phone rings only a few moments later.

"The hell?" Theo says, instead of *Hi there.* "I'm sleeping on the floor in some kind of group lodge. There aren't even any beds—"

"That doesn't sound like any Japanese dorm I ever heard of." Not that I'm steeped in the legends and lore of Japanese dormitory life, but if their students all lived communally without beds, I think I'd have heard about it.

"Hang on. I don't want to wake anyone up. Let me get out of here." I hear some shuffling, and the sliding of screens. Finally, Theo speaks again. "Okay. I'm on a porch. Proverbial dead of night, and—hang on, there's some kind of brochure or something out here in a few languages—holy *crap.*"

He sounds freaked out. My hand tightens around the handlebars of my bike, until my wrist aches and I have to relax. "What? What is it?"

"I'm on Mount Fuji."

"How are you—" Giggles bubble up inside me. Some of the terrible tension drains away. "What are you doing climbing a mountain?"

"I do *not* know. But for some reason, I decided to do it today." Theo sighs. "In related news, I'm not going to be able to reach you anytime soon. From your accent, I'm guessing you're back in London?"

"Cambridge."

"Got it. Is Paul there?"

The faint strain in his voice would be inaudible to most people. "Yeah. I mean, he's not here right this second, but he's at Cambridge too. I should be able to get to him today."

"Good. That's good." There's a long pause before Theo says, "Did you get any clarification on the collapsing-dimensions thing?"

Tension returns, a dull weight on my chest. "It's true. In the Home Office, my parents think—you know, what's a few universes more or less?"

"That is as effed-up as it gets. How close are they to being able to do it? They'd need a device that could move through dimensions like the Firebird, one that could affect fundamental resonance—"

He's already theorized that far ahead. It gives me hope that we might be able to outfox the Home Office yet. "They don't have the device, but they're heading into tests. So not long."

"Damn. Maybe I ought to head back home. The sooner I get there, the sooner I can tell Henry and Sophia what's happening."

"They need to know." But it feels weird to say, *Sure, fine, go on without me.*

Theo's been by my side this entire trip. More than that: I've realized how much more we can be to each other. Paul is the only one I love, but I've connected with Theo on an entirely new level. The friend I cared for so much before the Triadverse and the Home Office started screwing with our lives—I have that Theo back. And I'm so glad.

I can't talk about any of that here and now. Theo wouldn't want to hear it, not this way, not yet. So I say only, "If I don't get home within twenty-four hours, come back and get me, okay?"

"Always," Theo says.

The tone in his voice is supposed to sound casual. It doesn't. Just beneath the surface lurks a kind of longing I still don't know how to deal with—but I don't have to. Theo hangs up without even waiting for my goodbye.

For a moment I stand there, staring down at my phone screen. I wish I could call him back; I almost wish I could say what he really wants to hear. But I shouldn't, and I can't.

Instead, I find the Maps app and plug in the address on my driver's license. It's time to go home.

My trip takes me along the side of the River Cam almost the whole way, so I'm able to enjoy the scenery and the new warmth of a spring day. Gripping the handlebars makes my right arm ache beneath the red scar, but I can deal with it. In this dimension, it seems we live in a Victorian town house not very far from the university and city center—not far over the river at all. Parked in front is an absurdly small car in brilliant apple green. At first the grand yellowstone edifice of the town house looks so much like someone else's home that I'm reluctant to walk inside.

Then I see tangerine orange sparkle in one window: a suncatcher, dangling mid-pane just like it does at home. Reassured, I cycle up the driveway, lock my bike, and head inside.

The moment I open the door, I hear this strange jangling sound—and then a black pug runs into the hallway to greet me, all scrunchy nose and dangling tongue. Laughing, I duck down to pet him.

At last a dimension where my parents let us own a dog! I'll have to figure out how this Marguerite and Josie managed it.

"Who is it, Ringo, buddy?" My father's voice comes closer with every word. "Has Xiaoting come to see us—oh! What are you doing home already, sweetheart? Did the first showing sell out?"

He looks so like my dad back home, with his fusty cardigan and permanently mussed hair, that I want to melt. No more strange, crazy Dad manipulating and threatening the dimensions—just one like the Dad I know and love. "Yeah," I say, having no idea what movie I was going to see. "I got there too late."

"All right, then." He gestures for me to come farther into the house, as Ringo the pug runs to his side, panting happily. "At least you're here in time to tell Susannah goodbye."

Sure enough, as I walk into the small but bright kitchen, I see my aunt Susannah, wearing a leopard-print wrap dress and her trademark fuchsia lipstick. My mother—looking entirely like herself—is nodding in genial incomprehension as Aunt Susannah says, "And if you're not flying business class, I say, it's hardly even worth it. Because in coach, you might as well be *cattle*, you know— Oh, Marguerite, darling? Back so soon?"

"The movie was sold out." I stick to the excuse Dad supplied; no point in overthinking anything. Besides, I'm truly glad to see her. At home, it's been years since we visited—but Aunt Susannah was my guardian and caretaker in the very first new dimension I visited, and after hearing about her death in the Warverse, it's good to see her standing here, alive, well, and flamboyant as ever. "When do you leave?"

"Your dad's driving me to the train station at quarter past. So I get to tell you goodbye twice!"

She holds out her arms. Normally I'd try to dodge this, but now I walk into her embrace and hug her tightly. Her overripe perfume has never smelled better.

Aunt Susannah laughs, surprised but pleased. "Aren't you a dear? Henry, Sophia, you must send her to London with me this summer. We can go shopping for all the latest fashions, so you knock 'em dead at Oxford come fall."

Oxford? I applied to the Ruskin School of Fine Art and

got in? Pride and hope swells within me. If this Marguerite could get in, maybe I could too. I don't know if they take students starting in January—but I could go to their next SoCal portfolio review and find out.

"I think a London trip could be arranged," Dad says. "But if we're going to make the six-forty-five train, you and I had better hoof it."

"Right-o." After a couple of pats on my shoulder, Aunt Susannah lets go. I'm surprised to feel a lump in my throat as she waves. "We're off, then. See you soon, my dears."

"Goodbye, Susannah." My mother always has this look on her face when she's around my dad's sister—slightly overwhelmed, slightly confused—but in this dimension, there's also a deep fondness.

Once Dad and Aunt Susannah go, it's just me, Mom, and Ringo the pug. While my mother is busy putting together dinner—a Bolognese sauce by the smell of it, *yum*—I do some quick reconnaissance of the house. This looks like a place we'd live: books, plants. And my room is filled with oil portraits in a style very like my own back home. Josie, Mom, and Dad form a triptych on the wall, each vibrant in their own way. Yet I recognize the brushstrokes, the blended colors, the light. I could have painted any one of these myself.

Paul wasn't just being encouraging that night we talked in his dorm room; he was telling me the truth. Have I really been selling myself short this whole time?

If I could get into Ruskin, Paul could do his postdoc

either there or here at Cambridge. It doesn't take very long to get to Oxford from Cambridge, or vice versa. We'd be able to see each other every weekend at least. It can all work out, if we only try.

So I don't let it bother me that Paul's portrait isn't hanging on the wall.

What's weirder is that my easel isn't out. I don't see a box of paints; when I look in the hamper, it contains exactly zero paint-stained smocks. (I'm supposed to wash them separately, but sometimes I forget, with disastrous results for the rest of the laundry.) I'm supposed to be starting at Ruskin soon. Shouldn't I be practicing?

I head back to the living room, which is smaller than the one we have at home, but equally comfy. Plopping down on the overstuffed red sofa, I'm immediately joined by Ringo, who wants a belly rub. As I oblige him, Mom walks in from the kitchen, drying her hands on a tea towel. "There," she says as she sits near me. "We'll put the pasta on when your father gets back."

"Sounds good." If Paul's a physics student at Cambridge, even if I haven't met him yet, my parents must have. "Have you seen Paul Markov lately?"

My mother sits up straighter. "Have *you* seen him around?"

"I—uh, no. I haven't."

"Oh, sweetheart." She scoots closer to put her hands on my shoulders. "Are you still upset? I don't blame you."

Upset? "I'm fine. Really."

"You wouldn't be asking after Paul, if you really were."

Mom sighs. "Your father and I begged for more stringent measures, but the university code is as clear as it is lenient. Technically, he'd broken no university rules. So we couldn't expel him from the program. I almost wish we hadn't already canceled the Firebird project, so we could've had the satisfaction of tossing him out of that, at least. But other professors are supposed to be working with Paul from now on! They should have kept him out of your way—"

"I didn't see him! Okay? It's all right." It's beyond weird to see my mother talking about Paul without a trace of affection, or even grudging respect.

What I see in her eyes is pure loathing.

She rubs my shoulder gently. "I promise you, Marguerite—I *absolutely* promise—Paul will never come near you again. Never."

Just when I think I'm home safe, the whole world turns upside down again.

28

THIS TIME I GO THROUGH THE BEDROOM LIKE A FORENSICS team scouring a crime scene. Her closet is emptied out across the bed, every pocket in every coat or pair of jeans searched through. Each and every drawer gets inspected. The spines of each book on this Marguerite's shelf, and the titles of all the ones in her e-reader, are reviewed. I learn a few things about her—she's confident wearing heels, she shares my mother's passion for yoga, she's a bigger fan of the surrealists than I am. But I don't find the stuff that would tell me what I want to know.

What happened with Paul?

No blog. No journal. I don't keep those at home either, but why couldn't this have been another way she's different from me? The various apps on her phone show me the photos she's shared, her latest updates; all of it looks much the way it does on my own phone at home, except that, of course, she has lots of dog photos.

When I scroll all the way back to January, I finally see a picture of Paul. In it, he's sitting on our red sofa, Ringo happily in his lap. Paul looks completely at ease. At home. And now my parents don't even want to see his face.

Slightly heated by the exertion of ripping up this Marguerite's bedroom, I push up the sleeves of my sweater. When I do, beneath my thumb I feel the crooked ridge of the scar on my right arm. The scar seems darker now, which I know is my mind playing tricks on me because the ache has returned.

Well, if I can't find out anything else about this world's Paul, I can at least learn how to contact him.

A little time on her tablet turns up Paul's contact information without too much trouble. The university lists his housing and his email address, at least his school account. With a flick of my fingers, I open a window to write to him, then hesitate.

Mom wanted Paul *thrown out* of Cambridge—the same guy they practically adopted in at least a dozen dimensions. Anytime my parents and Paul have wound up at odds, Paul was the one who drew the line between them.

The fourth and final splinter of my Paul is here, sheathed within the body of this other Paul Markov. No matter what he's done, or what he's capable of, I have to face him. We have to be alone.

Until then, I refuse to worry. During my time traveling through the dimensions, I've been kidnapped, held at gunpoint, bombed from the air, nearly crushed in a submarine, exposed to the Russian winter until I nearly died of hypothermia, and chased by a torch-bearing mob intent on burning me for witchcraft. Every time, I've kept myself together. Every time, I survived.

Whatever happens next, I have to believe I can handle it. For Paul, I will.

The email I send to Paul is simple and direct.

> You and I should talk, soon. Are you free tonight? If so, let me know what time, and I'll drop by your flat.

(At the last minute, I remembered to use "flat" instead of "apartment.")

It would be easy to spend the next however-long staring at my in-box, hoping every second to see his reply. But that would only drive me crazy, and besides, Mom made spaghetti.

"Susannah keeps insisting we should visit her in London this summer," Dad says as he covers his plate with more Parmesan than most people could eat in a month.

Mom looks nonplussed. "But we go every summer, at least for one or two of the plays. I think I read that they're putting on *Julius Caesar* at the Globe in June."

My father shakes his head. "Oh, no, she's having none of our weekend jaunts. Susannah wants us for a fortnight at least."

More than a weekend sounds like a very long time to stay with Aunt Susannah, let alone two weeks or however long a fortnight is. To judge by the sound my mother makes, she agrees. It's kind of sweet that my aunt wants us there, though. At home, our relationship is so much more distant, because my dad and his sister are practically scientific proof of just how different two offspring of the same parents can be. I like that we all found a way to get along here.

As I eat, it's tough to keep my aching fingers tightened around anything as slender as a fork. My mother is watching me, her face falling as she sees me struggle with my utensils. Quickly I change the subject. "I had the strangest dream last night."

"Oh, really?" Dad raises an eyebrow in mild curiosity. At his feet, Ringo sits, panting, alight with hope that one of us will drop food.

I try to sound casual. "Yeah. In my dream, we all lived in San Francisco, and we looked and acted like ourselves but had these different lives—and then I realized, this wasn't my dimension. I'd traveled to another dimension with the Firebird, to see how we lived there. It was *so weird* how I knew the Mom and Dad and Josie I saw there weren't you guys, but at the same time they kind of were. I felt like I remembered the whole house, the whole neighborhood, everything."

Mom and Dad give each other a wistful look. "I suppose it might have been like that," she says, idly twirling her fork in her pasta. "Sometimes I still daydream about it—truly standing within another dimension."

"It could still happen," I venture. "Couldn't it?"

Dad sighs. "No point in going back to it now. The Firebird

project might have been our greatest glory, but it could also have been our greatest folly. Better to turn our energies to more productive ends."

Oh, come on. No way Mom and Dad would give up on their dream just because they thought it was impractical.

At least now I understand why Conley sent the final splinter of Paul here. Since the Firebird technology had been scrapped, there was no chance my parents would figure out what was going on—and no chance they could have used devices of their own to get him back home.

Then my mother says, "Sending information will be so much more useful than sending consciousness."

I pause, spaghetti slithering off my fork as I hold it above my plate. "How, exactly?"

She looks dubious, and I wonder if I've exposed myself; this world's Marguerite would surely know more about her parents' current research. Instead, Mom says, "You're right to insist that I keep explaining myself. If we don't revisit our first principles, we run the risk of losing our way."

Dad goes into professor mode. "Now, Marguerite, what do you know about information? What is the most peculiar thing about it?"

Maybe that sounds like a really broad question, but I understand what he's driving at. "Information is the only thing we know of capable of moving faster than the speed of light. The universe knows things it shouldn't know, before it should be able to know them. Like—like when a quark is destroyed, and another is created instantly to take its place."

Paul told me this, too, as we stood in the redwood forest, looking up into infinity.

"Exactly," my mom says. "Transferring consciousness—as exciting as it would be, and as revolutionary as it would be even to identify and isolate consciousness—it's not the best way of learning more about the other dimensions of the multiverse. We can structure 'messages' in the form of asymmetrical subatomic sequences and see how other quantum realities respond."

"If we figure out how best to handle this, we might even be able to speak directly to other versions of ourselves—or, at least, to the other scientists doing our kind of work," my father adds. "Much better than popping into someone else's body unannounced."

I think of the Grand Duchess Margarita, even now hiding out in a Danish country house until she gives birth to a baby—one I conceived for her. Of a Theo in New York City who's still in the hospital, wondering if he'll ever be able to walk again. Of Lieutenant Markov dead in my arms. I admit, "The ethics are a lot better."

Mom nods, but I can tell to her this is only a theoretical consideration, one she's never had to truly face. "We'll have far better reach, as well. Instead of only visiting universes where we ourselves exist, we should be able to learn something about virtually any dimension in the multiverse— *Henry*. Stop giving noodles to the dog."

"He *likes* noodles," Dad says, as Ringo slobbers down his one strand of spaghetti.

My parents the illustrious scientists begin debating whether or not pasta gives the dog gas. It offers me a moment to consider what I've just learned, the possibilities expanding in my mind every moment.

The Home Office and the Triadverse must have dismissed this dimension as a threat because Mom and Dad abandoned the Firebird project. What Conley never realized was that they would instead turn their attention to another way of contacting other universes. If we got that power—my world, and the Warverse, and even the Paul and Theo from the Home Office—and we could communicate with each other constantly, without the risks of jumping dimensions . . . we could form an alliance much larger than Triad's conspiracy. Much more powerful. We could prepare ourselves against any attack the Home Office could make.

This could be how we take them down.

As precious as the treatment for Theo is, as eager as I am to rescue my own Paul, I now know I'm bringing home a third treasure—or, at least, a chance. The coordinates to this dimension could save us all.

"How long?" I ask.

Mom huffs, "Until the dog begins stinking up every room he's in? Two hours at most."

"No. I mean—how long until you can communicate with other dimensions?"

"Sweetheart, you know we can't pinpoint these things," my father says, but with a smile. "Of course, if next month's test goes as well as we hope . . . wait and see."

It's all I can do not to laugh out loud.

As I walk back to my room, I'm already strategizing. I'm not going to "de-cloak" yet; first I should talk with my parents back home about everything we've learned. But as soon as I do that, we can start planning my return to this dimension. Then we can tell the truth, the whole honest truth, and get these versions of ourselves to join forces with us. Exhilaration bubbles inside me until I want to spin around and do some stupid victory dance. Once I'm alone in my room, I might.

However, when I look at my email, every other thought fades, replaced only by the sight of Paul's name in my inbox.

When I open his reply, it says only 8:30 p.m.

He's not exactly Mr. Talkative in my dimension either. This is all the information I asked for, the only thing I need.

Still, when I remember Mom's distrust of Paul, her fear for me, Paul's terseness becomes . . . unnerving.

But it won't stop me from going to him, and bringing my own Paul home.

Cambridge must be a relatively safe place, because when I tell them I want to go to the theoretical late show of whatever movie it was this world's Marguerite wanted to see on campus, Mom doesn't even look up from her reading as she nods. Dad says only, "Wouldn't you rather take the car?"

Of *course* he lets me drive only in a universe where I'd have to stay on the left side of the road. "I'm good."

"I'm glad you're exploring your interest in film," he says. "Definitely something to pursue."

Mom chimes in, suddenly much more interested. "So many people talented in one art form prove to be talented in another."

Maybe this world's Marguerite is thinking of becoming a movie director. I can't quite imagine it, but that's kind of cool.

As I cycle through the streets of Cambridge, my phone chirpily tells me where to turn and how far to go. Not all of the city is as picturesque as the university; I cross a few busy roads lined with buildings more blandly modern. The chain store signs lit for nighttime bear unfamiliar names: BOOTS, COSTA, PIZZA EXPRESS. But my directions keep me near the university and finally steer me toward a group of small, basic apartments immediately recognizable as the kind of place where students live.

I lock my bike, walk straight to Paul's door, and ring without hesitating.

Before my hand is back at my side, Paul opens the door.

He looks thinner in this dimension, and not in a good way; his clothes are the same shabby stuff he wears at home, but they hang on his frame, like he doesn't even care enough to get stuff that fits. Still, he's neat, and from the faint smell of shaving foam, I can tell Paul cleaned up for me. He's trying.

"Hi," he says. "Thanks for reaching out. It—it means a lot."

"Can I come in?"

Paul seems astonished. Did he really think I'd stand here and question him from the doorstep?

But he stands back for me to walk into his apartment. It's as small and plain as I would have thought, with worn, mismatched furniture bought at the Salvation Army or whatever the British equivalent is. Tidy, though—especially for a male college student. My Paul keeps things neater than virtually any other guy I've ever known; I wonder if the white-glove cleanliness of this room is something this world's Paul shares with mine, or whether it's the subconscious influence of my own Paul peeking through.

I ought to just press the Firebird against him now, get my Paul back, and get out of here. But something about this Paul's quiet misery touches me. He's hurting—terribly—and he seems to think talking with me would help.

I can give him that. His body has kept the last part of Paul's soul safe; we owe him.

Instead of *hi* or *how have you been*, Paul says, "Will you let me explain?" When I blink, surprised, he continues, "I guess that's why you're here. If it's not—"

"It's complicated." *About a thousand times more complicated than you could possibly guess.* Still, I ought to hear this. "Yeah, go ahead. Explain."

Paul stands there, looking lost in the way that always makes me want to shelter him. "It was *an accident.* Even your parents must know it was only an accident. I hate myself for it more than they ever could. Even more than you."

His eyes don't meet mine; instead, he's looking down at my forearm, at the ragged red welt I noticed earlier today. The ache has sunk down to the bone. I glance down at the scar, then back up at him.

"I was upset. We both were. So I shouldn't have been driving. You're not wrong to blame me for that." By now Paul is pleading. "But your dad seems to think I did it on purpose. Marguerite, I would never, ever have wanted you to get hurt."

We were in a car accident while Paul was driving. It screwed up my hand. But why do my parents hate him? A car accident could happen to anybody. Why have I refused to even see him?

Then I remember what Paul said first. I venture, "We . . . were upset."

"It all seems so stupid now," he says. "I wasn't going to come around the house anymore, and you said I should get over it. Deal with my disappointment, forgive your parents. God, I wish I had. Then you'd be fine, and we'd be happy, and you could still—"

Paul chokes on his own words, then sits down heavily, too upset to notice my confusion.

Slowly I say, "If you could do it over—without yelling this time—if we were back in that car, what would you tell me?"

He wasn't expecting that. But he tries to work with it. "I would say that just because I disagreed with Sophia and Henry about the Firebird technology didn't mean I felt any differently about you. When I avoided the house, I wasn't avoiding you. Only them. I felt like the greatest work of my life had been taken away from me."

Of course. Paul would have hated their decision to abandon the Firebird project. Once he tackles a question, he doesn't want to rest until he has the answer.

Paul continues, "I shouldn't have said angry things about your parents—at all, but especially not in front of you. It put you in a terrible position. And I guess it made it easier for them to hate me afterward."

If I'd had time to calm down after this awful argument in the car, honestly, I probably would have understood. As much as I love my parents, they still drive me crazy sometimes. And I would have realized what a crushing blow this was to his research and his hopes. So I still don't get why he's so freaked out about the accident.

Until he says, very quietly, "Are you any better? I mean—have you been able to paint?"

It all comes together, then: Paul's crushing guilt, my parents' anger. The lack of any art supplies or new paintings in my room. Spaghetti falling off a fork that hurts to hold—a fork that's still wider than most paintbrushes. My parents encouraging my new "interest in film," because they're afraid I'll never be able to paint again.

This tragedy belongs to the other Marguerite, not me. When I go home, my arm will be fine—unmarked—and I can paint as much as I need. But still, I feel the pain of this Marguerite's loss. Art is the only thing I've ever wanted to do. It's my vocation, my passion. And dammit, I'm good!

Not many teenagers get their own gallery showings. Not many have the skills that could get them into RISD, much less Ruskin. As hard as it is to make a living as a professional artist, I honestly believe I have a chance.

In this world, Marguerite's chance has been taken away.

Maybe my hand will get better, I think. But already I know this Marguerite's doctors don't hold out much hope. If there were hope, Paul wouldn't be sitting here in misery. My parents wouldn't hate him.

And this Marguerite wouldn't either.

I say the only thing I can think of. "It didn't help that we were arguing when it happened. That I was already mad at you."

He shakes his head. "No, it didn't. But you're not wrong to blame me. I drove the car. It was my responsibility to pull over if I was—distracted. I didn't, and I hurt you, and I swear to you, if I could go back in time and change things—even if I had to get between you and the other car, take the hit myself—I'd do it. I would." Paul makes a small sound, something that might have been a laugh but didn't quite make it. "Too bad we never tackled time travel."

"Mom and Dad shouldn't have tried to throw you out of the department. Not for that."

"Sophia and Henry felt guilty for not protecting you. For bringing me into your life." Paul meets my eyes only for a moment. "No, they weren't—reasonable. But there are worse things parents can do than loving their child so much that it made them unreasonable."

Worse things, such as being mixed up in organized crime, and being more loyal to the mob than to your own son. His betrayal by his parents makes him willing to forgive mine for turning on him.

I remember the way my mother talked to me after I first told her Paul and I were together. She said that as much as they cared about Paul, they'd always be on my side—even if I was wrong. I guess she was telling the truth. And now, after the Home Office, I've seen how my parents react to grief. It twists them up. Makes them lash out.

Paul dismisses the near-ruin of his academic career with a shrug. "I'm going to ETH Zurich for my postdoc. I'll move away as soon as I possibly can. You don't have to worry about me anymore, or ever again. I promise you."

"I believe you," I say. He breathes out, like he'd been holding his breath for a very long time. Paul doesn't ask for or expect forgiveness or redemption. He only wants me to feel safe.

What will happen to this world's Paul? Will he find other people to love him in Zurich? Mentors who become adoptive parents, like mine, can't come along that often.

Paul studies my face; I wonder what he sees there. Finally he says, "Is that all?"

"Not quite. Do me one favor?"

"Anything."

I get to my feet and take the spare Firebird from around my neck. He looks at it, uncomprehending; apparently the project didn't progress far enough in this dimension for him to recognize it on sight. So I simply say, "Hold still."

Paul nods, and remains rigid in his chair, not even looking directly at me as I drape the chain around his neck. Once all four splinters of my Paul's soul are reunited, he should awaken within this body.

Please let it work. Please let Conley not have lied to me. Please, please, let me have him back again.

I take a deep breath, hit the final sequence and drop the Firebird.

He jolts, grabs the arms of his chair, and opens his eyes wide. When he looks up at me, he whispers, "Marguerite?"

My Paul, at last.

We reach for each other at the same instant, and somehow I wind up in his lap, and we're embracing each other so tightly we can scarcely breathe. Everything I've had to do, everything I've gone through—it was all worth it for this. For him.

29

WE HANG ON TO EACH OTHER SO TIGHTLY THAT NOTHING could tear us apart. Paul's broad hands span my back as he rocks me; I kiss his mouth, his cheeks, his eyelids, his chest. Even our breaths rise and fall in the same rhythm, as if we'd merged together. As if I'd leaped not into another version of myself, but into him.

"I was so scared," I manage to choke out. "You were torn apart. Conley *tore you apart*—"

"You mean—my consciousness—"

"Splintered. Conley splintered you into four pieces."

He swears in Russian. "I only remember this world at all. None of the others."

"Well, trust me, you were all over the place. Italy and New York and even a terrible world war. You really don't remember that?"

"I only remember being here. We'll deal with the theory

later. I'm all right now." Paul kisses my neck, then frames my face in his hands. "I didn't find the cure for Theo before they caught me."

"It's okay! I got it for him. We—well, we had to do some dirty work for Triad, but it's all right, because I think I know how to turn it against them."

He frowns, no doubt wondering just how dirty the work was. But then I see his expression begin to cloud over. "A few minutes ago—the things I said—"

"Forget it. That's between another Paul and another Marguerite. It doesn't have anything to do with us." Knowing that makes me feel so impossibly, perfectly free. Like I could soar on wings, carrying Paul upward with me.

"But I hurt you." Paul looks down at my scarred wrist.

"Not on purpose. And it wasn't you, just like it wasn't me. Okay?" Explaining this to Paul will take time, just like it took me a long while to believe it.

He doesn't look like he can fully accept that. "You—she can't be an artist anymore."

That hurts, even if it isn't me. But I say to him what I hope this Marguerite will someday understand—something I might need to consider myself, really. "There are other careers. Other ways to be creative and lead a good life. She'll figure it out."

Paul isn't comforted. "Theo's safe?"

"Yeah. He even came on the trip with me, because he said if you'd do it to rescue him, he'd do it to rescue you."

"That idiot," Paul says, in a tone of voice that makes it the most affectionate thing he could possibly say. "Where is he now?"

"Japan. I mean, in this universe Theo Beck is getting his doctorate in Japan, but our very own Theo has already leaped home. He'll be waiting there for us."

Paul looks around at this apartment. "This Paul—" He laughs slightly, but without humor. I can tell he's embarrassed by how far this version has sunk. "He needs to get a life."

"Yeah, probably. Look at it this way; at least you're not stuck in an apocalyptic war. Is that coming back to you at all?"

If it is, he might remember me making out with another Paul. Uh-oh.

Instead, he shakes his head. "This world is the only one I have any memory of. I think there was . . . more of me here than anywhere else."

"Well, you didn't miss out on much in the Warverse."

I throw it out merely to distract him, but Paul latches on to the new information. "Conley hasn't forced you into working with him, has he?"

"Not any more than this," I promise.

"What aren't you telling me?"

There's so much, and the threat of the Home Office is almost too terrifying to speak out loud. Right now I only want to go home with Paul.

But Theo's back where he belongs, safe and sound. He's telling my parents the risks even now. Paul and I are together in each other's arms. There's no reason not to talk, if that's what he needs.

So I begin in Italy, with Conley's announcement of what he'd done, and say it *all*. If I hold anything back, it will only make it more awkward to talk about later. So I tell him about appearing in the bed beside Theo, in a world where I chose differently. I explain how I flattered him to try and get secrets, and that we kissed—that I hurt that world's Paul, and he lashed back. But I emphasize the deal we cut above everything else. "They'll be okay, so I didn't do any harm. I didn't have to play Conley's game. See?"

Paul nods. He looks like he's in shock. "And then what?"

"Then I went to a New York where—where you went into business with your dad."

His entire body tenses. I realize he wants me out of his lap, so I stand; Paul begins pacing the length of the room. "I couldn't have. I would never."

"Not often," I say as gently as I can. "But in at least one universe."

"How did you know? How did you find out?"

"I might have reached out to you in a way that freaked out your, um, colleagues and—well, they kidnapped me."

He blanches. "Oh God. My father didn't—"

"I wasn't hurt. Paul—you know you could have talked to me about your dad. I wouldn't have judged you for the things he's done."

"Things I would do." His voice has gone dull. "In the right circumstances."

"Don't obsess over—"

"How did you escape? I know you wouldn't have left the other Marguerite there."

"Theo led the cops to my location. I was able to get out."

Paul steps closer to me. "You're keeping something back."

"While Theo and I were trying to get away, you found us. When I retrieved that splinter—I think it made you angry."

"And?"

Deep breath. "And you shot Theo in the kneecaps. Both of them."

Paul groans and turns away. He slumps against the wall, facing it, both hands above his head like someone being put under arrest. "Did he die?"

"No! No, the paramedics were sure he'd make it."

"So he'll just lose one or both of his legs, then," he says flatly. "Our Theo had to feel it too."

"Theo specifically told me not to blame you for that! You're not the same man as the one who decided to work with your dad. I mean, how could you be?"

"Theo's a better person than I am," Paul says. His mood is darkening; looking at him now is like watching storm clouds roll in to blot out the blue sky. "What then?"

This is even worse—but here, I'm the one to blame, not him. "I went back to the Russiaverse. I wanted to be in a world where you weren't."

"I don't blame you."

"It was just so I could think things through, someplace where I thought I'd be safe."

Sensing my hesitation, Paul says, "What is it? Is the grand duchess all right? If her father found out about us—"

"She's kept the main secret." I force myself to meet his eyes. "Paul, she's pregnant."

He whirls toward me then, almost angry. In one of those flashes of understanding that's almost like telepathy, I know exactly why: His disbelief is so strong that he wants to think I'm joking, and he wants to hate me for making a joke that personal, that hurtful. Worse is seeing the truth sink in.

"She's having a baby?" Paul can hardly do more than whisper. "Because of me?"

"Because of me. I'm the one who chose, remember? You were just—a shadow in Lieutenant Markov's mind."

"But what if I made the difference? If I pushed him over the brink of what he dreamed about, and what he would actually do?"

I don't have any comfort for him, not about this. The most terrible mistake I ever made was in someone else's body, someone else's life, and I can never, ever put it right. "We both know I'm the one to blame."

"Is she going to be all right?" Paul's voice shakes, and I remember that he lived within Lieutenant Markov for nearly a month, loving the grand duchess as much as he loved me. It doesn't make me jealous, exactly—only reminds me that I'm not the only Marguerite he'd sacrifice for. "She can't hide that forever."

I walk to him and put my hands against his chest. He doesn't respond, even as I say, "She *wants* the baby. Vladimir knows, and he's taking care of everything."

"That's our child," Paul says. "Yours and mine."

I remember that faint goldfish-tickle, and the shivers that went through me as I felt Paul's baby inside. "Yeah. It is." I try to smile. "We managed to get pregnant before we slept together. That takes talent."

He doesn't laugh. He shouldn't. Even having cracked that weak joke makes me feel cheap.

So I try to bring us back to the here and now. "Listen to me. We have to deal with the consequences of our actions, absolutely. I'm not even sure we can justify doing this."

"Doing what, exactly?" Paul says.

I hadn't known I would say this until the moment it comes from my mouth. "Traveling through dimensions at all."

His eyes meet mine, and as surprised as he is, I think he might agree.

"We shouldn't stand around tearing ourselves up about it," I say. "There are things we need to do as soon as we can. I want to take this treatment to Theo, to see if we can get him back in shape. And we need to talk with Mom and Dad about everything—what the Home Office is, how we might be able to communicate—"

And about the Home Office's plan to collapse as many universes as necessary until they get their Josie back. I need to tell Paul that, too. But not this moment. He looks weary and battered by what I've said so far. Wounded. The rest can wait until we get home. When we're all together, able to make plans for defending ourselves, then he can bear it. Not yet.

I reach up to put my arms around his neck, but Paul pushes me away, gently but firmly. "Marguerite—I'm sorry."

"For what?"

He stands there a long moment, the harsh light from his one cheap lamp painting his profile in stark lines and elongating his shadow on the wall. This place smells musty—unclean and sad. The pretty green campus and cozy town house seem to belong to another world altogether.

"You've talked a lot about how the dimensions bring us together, time after time. You were the one who made me believe we belonged with each other in any world we could ever find." Paul takes a deep breath. "I believed in destiny even before I fell for you. I saw it written in the equations. Woven into the fabric of the universe itself. But you helped me understand that we were part of destiny, you and me."

"That doesn't mean we're the same in every single world," I say. "Yes, there's something powerful that we share—and maybe that's a soul. But we're separate people, every time."

This isn't the game-changing revelation for him that it is for me. "I know. When I traveled, and got lost within the other Paul Markovs—I always sensed the differences. The ways they thought and spoke and dreamed that I never would, or could."

He had told me this much before, but I didn't truly understand until now.

By this point Paul looks wretched, like he'd rather be anywhere in the multiverse than here. Yet he still gazes at me with a love so strong I can almost physically feel it. "Don't you see? We find ourselves in worlds so altered we can hardly understand them. When we're people so different we can't comprehend how we could ever be made of the same DNA. But so many times—so many—I only wind up hurting everyone around me. And more than anyone else, I hurt *you*. What if that's our shared destiny? What if it's not love but pain?"

That's not the journey I've taken. Not the Paul I've seen. But I look at it through the lens of what I've just told him—imagining Theo bleeding in a New York alleyway, and the Grand Duchess Margarita pregnant and in hiding—

"Hey." I embrace him around his waist. His hands come to rest on my shoulders, though I can't tell whether it's a caress or a prelude to pushing me away again. "You don't only hurt me. You help me, and you love me. You *save* me. Don't forget that, because I never will."

"Look at the scar on your arm."

"That was just a stupid accident!"

"Yes and no." His expression clouds over. "I remember the things Paul said to you during that last fight, because he keeps thinking about it, over and over, replaying it like a loop inside his head. That day, it was like—like my father had taken over my body. Like his words were coming out of my mouth. All that anger he threw at me, I kept inside to throw at you. So yes, I'm to blame for what happened to you, and it could easily have been worse."

"Not you. Another Paul Markov did that, and I'm not worried about him."

Paul isn't convinced. I can tell by the sadness in his eyes. But when he brushes his fingers through my hair, I take hope from his touch. He says, "You never know when to quit, do you?"

"I'll know when the time comes, but it hasn't yet." How can he be saying any of these things? After everything we've seen and done, how can he believe that he's only destined to hurt me?

But then I remember—Paul has spent the past couple of weeks within this world's version, who is mired in depression and guilt. That sadness lingers inside him; it's not the kind of thing you can shake off easily. I never should have told him about the shooting or the grand duchess when he was in this state, because now he's looking at me like it's the last time.

"Listen to me," I say. "The multiverse is infinite. So, yeah, we go through some terrible things together, and I've seen versions of you who are darker, and damaged, and I don't care. I want you even when you're broken. I want you no matter what. Your darkness, your anger, whatever it is you fear inside yourself—it doesn't matter. I love you completely, don't you see? I even want the worst of you because it's *still a part of you.*" I press one hand against his chest, as if I could send everything I feel straight into his heart. "I want you when it's crazy, when it's frightening, when it's impossible, because there's nothing within you that could hurt me half as much as not having you."

Paul struggles for composure; he won't look me in the

eyes. "Nothing could hurt me as much as hurting you, and that's exactly what I've done. I've broken your body, attacked your friends, left you pregnant and alone. Don't you see the pattern? Destiny is real, Marguerite. I have the equations to prove it, and now we've both *lived* it."

"Paul, no—"

"I loved you enough to give you up," he says. "When I used the Firebird for the first time, I knew I might not make it back. It didn't matter to me; nothing mattered to me as long as you were safe. You could lead your life without me. If I have to give you up again, I will. It feels like—like cutting off your own arm—" His voice chokes off as he glances down at my exposed arm and the dark scar there.

Only then do I realize—Paul may not consciously remember the other versions of himself or the universes they inhabit. His subconscious, however, has been profoundly affected. He can't see it yet, but I can. This fatalism—Paul's belief that he could only hurt me—has been built like a wall between us, stone by stone.

Father Paul in medieval Italy thought both God and the church would part us forever. Meanwhile, Lieutenant Markov of the Warverse had already pursued me in vain; he'd resigned himself to watching me love another. The Paul who wound up in the Russian mob? He's bitter at twenty, surrounded by violence, nearly as much a prisoner as I was, tied up in that cellar. He only knew me as a victim—*his* victim. And now Paul dwells within the body of a version who lost everything that mattered to him: first the Firebird project, then his close relationship with my parents, then me.

Did Conley do this on purpose? Or was it merely terrible luck? Either way, all the disappointment, anger, and misery of those four lifetimes has taken root within my Paul. He no longer believes in our destiny or in himself.

The past several days have taught me so much about the impact my actions have on the dimensions—and Marguerites—I visit. Now, in Paul's sorrowful eyes, I see that they have an impact on us too. Maybe I've been protected as a "perfect traveler," but Paul hasn't. His splintering has exacted a terrible price.

I've spent this entire journey trying to bring Paul back from these other universes. But as he stands here in front of me in this Cambridge flat, he feels farther from me than he has ever been.

Talking Paul down from this bleak place will take time—not minutes, not hours, but days or weeks—and that's time I don't want to spend in this dimension. When we're home, he'll come back to himself. He has to. "Let's go home, okay? Let's just focus on Triad and go over this together. We only have so much time to work against Conley. That's what matters most."

Paul nods. Having a concrete goal helps him steady himself. "Yeah. Let's. But—you should head home first. If the other Paul and Marguerite woke up with you in his apartment—"

"That would be bad. All right." I can't yet bring myself to step away, though. "You *will* follow me. You promise."

"Yes. I promise."

Then he pulls me close for a kiss.

When our lips meet, Paul clutches me to him—like he never wants to let go. I open my mouth for him, lean into him. The night we planned to spend together, during my parents' trip: I want Paul to understand that we'll still have that, and so much else besides. When this is over, we'll still have each other.

I can tell he's kissing me this desperately because he thinks it might be the last time. The way I'm kissing him should tell him it's not. Not even close.

Ten thousand skies, and a million worlds, and it still wouldn't be enough for me to share with you. Nothing less than forever will do.

By the time we pull apart, I'm shaky. Paul looks heartsick. He puts one hand over the Firebird on his chest. "I'll see you soon."

"Okay," I say as I head for the door.

I refuse to say goodbye.

As I cycle back toward my family's Cambridge home, I concentrate on the thoughts I need this Marguerite to remember best. She'll be my messenger to this world, the world we need on our side most of all. *We need to know how to communicate throughout the multiverse. That's the only way we'll ever be able to defeat Triad. And since Conley spied on this dimension once, he could come back eventually. If he does, and he sees you have this technology, you'll be in even more trouble than we are. But don't be scared. I swear, if we work together, we have a chance to win. To be safe from Triad forever.*

I know she'll believe me; she won't be able to help sensing that I'm telling her the truth. But what will these versions of Mom and Dad do? Will they stand with us, or tell us to stay the hell out?

As my bicycle glides into the driveway of our home, I bring it to a gentle stop. I already scraped one of her knees leaping into her dimension at the wrong moment; the least I can do is avoid scraping the other. I settle the kickstand, brace myself, and prepare to leap.

On impulse, I reach into my bag and pull out a compact. When I flip it open, I peer into the mirror—as close as I can ever come to looking this Marguerite in the face—and I say just one word, "*Please.*"

After that, I snap the compact shut, drop it into my bag. Across town, even now, Paul is preparing to leap through the dimensions with me. It won't be our last journey together. I have to believe that.

I take the Firebird in hand and watch this world vanish, like watercolors rinsing away.

Returning to my own body is always so much easier than any of the other jumps. Everywhere else the collision of selves jolts me in a way my parents haven't been able to scientifically explain. But coming home? That's as easy and effortless as slipping into a warm bath.

I open my eyes to see Theo standing above me. Though his face is too pale, his eyes shadowed, he smiles as he says,

"About time you got here."

"Good, you made it. How do you feel?"

He makes a face as he scratches the back of his head. "I've been better. But, hey, you got the juice, right? The data for the juice, I mean."

"Right. You'll be feeling better in no time." I rise from my bed and walk into the main area of the house in search of my parents. Theo must be as ready as I am to put them to work re-creating this solution. "Where are Mom and Dad?"

"They were out when I got here. Probably at the university labs, trying to figure some other way out of this, or building another Firebird."

No doubt. Well, they'll be back by dinnertime, because they never eat on campus if they can help it. From the slant of the sunshine through the glass door to our deck, I can tell it's midafternoon. "Have you checked to see if Paul has come back yet?"

"You found him, huh?" Theo doesn't high-five me, or celebrate in any obvious way. This is kind of odd—I've seen him do a victory dance just because he managed to flick a paper clip into his hat from across the room—but then I remember how weak he is. He's back in this battered body, the one on the verge of failure. We don't have any time to lose.

A wave of powerful vertigo sweeps over me, making my stomach flip-flop as the whole world goes sparkly and dark. "Whoa," I say, putting one hand to the side of my head. "What was that?"

Theo puts one hand on my shoulder, only a touch. "You've been through a lot. No wonder you're tired."

Tired is not what I just felt. The Firebird has to have operated correctly; if it hadn't, I wouldn't be home now. Whatever this sensation is, it hasn't left me. At least it's not so strong that I can't shake it off.

"So Paul was going to come back at the exact same time as you?" Theo asks.

"That's what he said." I know Paul wouldn't break that promise, and yet I won't feel totally reassured until I've spoken to him or seen him, here in our own world. Slowly I get to my feet, slightly dizzy but determined to keep going. "Where did I leave my phone? I want to call him."

"Don't worry," Theo says. He's already looking on the rainbow table, which isn't where I usually put my phone, but I guess it's a place to start. "Take it easy. You'll find him, Meg."

Meg.

Only one person has ever called me that—Theo.

But not my Theo.

I turn to him, horrorstruck. From the way his smile hardens, I can tell he knows that I know who he really is. The Triadverse's Theo has returned.

"Was it the nickname?" he says. "I bet it was the nickname."

"Why are you here?" I demand. "Why did the Triadverse send you? Theo can't take much more."

"He'll have to," Theo says, maddeningly calm. "Just like you."

Then he steps closer to me, and I see what he has in his hands: a syringe filled with emerald-green liquid. Nightthief.

I jerk away from him, but he tackles me, slamming into my back so hard it hurts. Landing on the wooden floor knocks the wind out of me, and for a moment all I can do is try to breathe.

"Sorry about that, Meg," Theo says as he kneels over me, pinning me down. "But, you know. The ends justify the means."

I feel the needle sink into my arm.

You idiot, I want to say. *Nightthief helps travelers take over their hosts. What is this supposed to do to me while I'm in my own body?*

Maybe he's just poisoning me with the stuff—

Then a shudder ripples through me. Overwhelming—paralyzing. I try to move my hand, but I can't.

I hear my voice come out of my mouth, speaking words that don't belong to me. "About time," I say.

Theo's smile has become more genuine. "Always a pleasure to meet anyone from the Home Office."

No. But I know it's true. The Marguerite who believes in Triad—who's willing to kidnap, blackmail, or kill in order to make our dimension obey her own—she's leaped into my world. Into my body. And because of the Nightthief, she's in charge.

She has turned my skin and bones into my prison.

"So," Theo says. "What's our first assignment?"

"Figure out what they're up to." There is nothing more

horrible than the feeling of glee within my captor. This Marguerite hasn't just captured me; she's *enjoying* it. "My parents aren't the kind of people to surrender even if it's the smart thing to do, in any universe. But once the versions here have been outsmarted a few times, sabotaged a few times more . . . well, we might be able to bring them in line yet."

Theo nods as he reaches down to help me—her—to her feet. "And if we don't get them to work for our cause?"

She laughs. "Then it's time for this dimension to die."

READ ON FOR A
SNEAK PREVIEW OF

1

I CAN'T BREATHE. I CAN'T THINK. ALL I CAN DO IS HANG ON to this cable and stare down at the river at least four hundred feet below me. Nothing stands between me and death but a few nylon ropes, clutched in hands that are already slick with sweat.

Traveling to other dimensions can be scary—but I've never been thrown into anything as terrifying as this.

Panic clouds my thoughts and turns everything surreal. My brain refuses to accept that this is actually happening—even as the truth stretches my arms and pulls my muscles. Every pound of my body weight cramps my fingers and tells me how immediate my situation is. The city lights from the ground below seem so distant they might as well be stars. But still my mind cries, *This is just a nightmare. You're seeing things. This can't be real—*

But the Firebird locket hanging around my neck still

radiates heat from my journey into another world. What I'm seeing—the mortal danger I'm in—is definitely real.

Then I realize that I'm dangling from a hovership, one projecting holographic advertisements upward into the dusky sky. My eyes finally focus on one detail from the metropolis beneath me long enough to recognize St. Paul's Cathedral—and, beyond it, a futuristic skyscraper that has never existed in my version of London.

The Londonverse. I'm back in the Londonverse, the first alternate dimension I ever traveled to.

Apparently it's also going to be the dimension I die in.

"Marguerite!" I turn my head to see my Aunt Susannah, who's hanging out of one of the hovership's passenger windows. Her dyed-blond hair whips around her face, blown by the same strong gusts that tear at my gray dress, exposing me to the world below. Not that I care who sees my butt while I'm on the verge of death. Aunt Susannah's eyes are wide, and dark lines of mascara streak down her cheeks with tears. Other passengers crowd around her, pressing their faces to the hovership windows, eyes wide as they stare at the girl who's about to die.

Okay, I think, trying to slow my breaths. *All I have to do is climb back in. It's not that far. Up four feet, over twenty?*

But it's not that easy. I don't have the upper body strength to climb the rope on its own, and the nearest metal strut is out of reach. How did I even get here? This universe's Marguerite must have tumbled from one of the hovership windows and grabbed a rope to save herself, which is why

I'm now dangling hundreds of feet above the city of London. . . .

Panic seizes me again. Every inch between me and the river seems to elongate. Dizziness courses through me. My muscles go weak. And my grip on the ropes trembles, bringing me closer to death.

Oh, God, no no no. I have to pull this together. If I don't save her, we're both doomed.

Because if you're in another dimension when your host dies, then, at the exact same instant, you die.

I could just get the hell out of this universe. My parents' invention, the Firebird, gives me the ability to travel to a new dimension at any moment. Now seems like a really good time to check out some other reality—any other reality. But to use the Firebird, I'd have to hit the controls and leap out. Both of my hands are currently busy gripping this rope to keep me from plunging to my death. Kind of a catch-22 here. The hovership flies so far up that by the time I fell all the way down, my body would be traveling at a velocity that would make hitting the water as instantly fatal as smashing onto concrete.

"Marguerite!" another voice calls out. In astonishment I look over and see Paul.

What is he doing on this hovership? We didn't even know each other in this universe!

I don't care why he's here. I only care that he is. My love for Paul Markov is one of the few constants in the multiverse. He would do anything, even risk his own life, if it meant he could keep me safe. If anyone can get me out of this, he can.

Normally I get myself out of my own perilous situations, but this, today? This is bad.

"Paul!" I shout back. "Please, help me!"

"They're landing as fast as they can," he calls to me. The wind ruffles his dark hair, and he edges out onto the metal frames for the hovership's projectors with total assurance; he must go rock-climbing in this universe too, because the height doesn't faze him. "Just hang on."

Sure enough, I can hear the changing key of the engines. The propellers send new winds to buffet me. London below comes slightly closer, though it's still mostly a blur of lights and murky twilight colors—dark blues and grays and blacks. My adrenaline-flooded brain refuses to make sense of the shapes below me any longer; I might as well be staring down at artwork by Jackson Pollock with its squiggles and blots and spills.

I imagine a Pollock painting with a huge red splotch in the center. Blood red. Nothing else will remain of me if I let go of this cable.

My fingers hurt so much. My shoulders. My back. No matter how badly I want to hold on, I won't be able to manage much longer. Within minutes, I will fall to my death.

Sweat beads along my face despite the chilly winds blowing around me. I can taste the salt as it trickles into my open, panting mouth. As I try to readjust my grip, people on the hovership scream. One of my black shoes slips from my foot and tumbles out of sight.

"Marguerite, no!" Aunt Susannah sounds like she's been screaming. "You don't have to do this, sweetheart. Don't let go! We'll make it right, whatever's bothering you, I swear it. Just hold on!"

I want to shriek back, *Does it look like I need any more encouragement to hold on?* But then I realize what my aunt just said. *You don't have to do this.*

She thinks I'm attempting suicide. And since I can't figure out any other way this world's Marguerite could've wound up in this situation, I think—I think Aunt Susannah is right.

But it wasn't this world's Marguerite who tried to kill herself. It was the other one. The wicked version of me who's working on behalf of Triad, even now. She attacked me at home and escaped into this dimension, but only in this instant—as I gulp in desperate breaths and hang on with the last of my strength—do I realize what her plan really is.

She's trying to kill me.

She's trying to kill every me, in every world, everywhere.

A THOUSAND PIECES OF YOU
NEW YORK TIMES BESTSELLING AUTHOR
CLAUDIA GRAY
TEN THOUSAND SKIES ABOVE YOU
NEW YORK TIMES BESTSELLING AUTHOR
CLAUDIA GRAY
A MILLION WORLDS WITH YOU
NEW YORK TIMES BESTSELLING AUTHOR
CLAUDIA GRAY

HARPER TEEN
An Imprint of HarperCollinsPublishers

by Claudia Gray

Bianca and Lucas will do anything to be together.